Psyche

Forrest Gladstone

Bosque Publishing

Cover Art: Charlie Wall

Cover Design: Lilian Gladstone

Proofread: Sarah Boyd

ISBN: 979-8-9986046-1-4

❀ Formatted with Vellum

For my sisters; I'm so grateful for every bit of time we get.

And for all the girls, but especially Brittney and Ambra, who didn't get anywhere near enough.

THE GODS

GOD	FUNCTION
Jupiter (Zeus)	King of the Gods
Juno (Hera)	Queen of the Gods
Neptune (Poseidon)	God of the Ocean Realm
Pluto (Hades)	God of the Underworld
Minerva (Athena)	Goddess of Wisdom
Apollo (Apollo)	God of Wisdom
Diana (Artemis)	Goddess of the Hunt
Venus (Aphrodite)	Goddess of Love
Ceres (Demeter)	Goddess of the Harvest
Vulcan (Hephaestus)	God of the Forge
Mars (Ares)	God of War
Mercury (Hermes)	Messenger of the Gods
Proserpina (Persephone)	Goddess of Spring
Cupid (Eros)	God of Erotic Love

QUICK REFERENCE: SIBLINGS

Cronos + Rhea*	Jupiter + Juno	Jupiter's Bastards
Jupiter	Mars	Athena
Juno	Vulcan	Apollo & Diana (twins)
Neptune		Mercury
Pluto		Proserpina (w/Ceres)
Ceres		

Note: Roman god names are used in this telling, as in the first known source of the myth of Cupid and Psyche; Greek names are listed in parentheses for reference

*Titans; the ruling gods before they were overthrown by their children

CONTENT WARNING

Psyche pulls directly from the Roman source Metamorphoses by Apuleius and explores themes of systemic violence, silencing, and power dynamics.

Specific triggers include sexual assault, rape, domestic abuse, forced pregnancy, miscarriage. Please read with care.

People say that memory shapes truth.
But the gods know that memories are just stories.

PART ONE

CHAPTER 1

Centuries before Psyche

D espite his parentage, Cupid was born of Venus in the same way millions of babies had been born before him, red and squalling as he emerged from her body and dragging behind him the bloody afterbirth. He nursed at her breast in the same way millions of babies had nursed at the breast before him, and if Venus's milk was shot with ambrosia, well, it was nonetheless the food of her body, that flowed forth to sustain her child.

Which is all to say that, as a god, Cupid's entrance to the world was as human an experience as he would ever endure, his understanding of the pain and beauty of mortality limited to subconscious impressions of violence and fear followed by sudden light and warmth.

Venus had not expected to love her child; she had not enjoyed carrying him in the least. Once the novelty of her changing form had grown stale, the whole ordeal had been cumbersome and inconvenient, even for a goddess. There were those of her lovers who delighted in the swelling of her body, but she found their sources of pleasure were not at all aligned with her own, and that left her peevish.

"It's no more than you earned," said Vulcan, to whom she was married, one day toward the end of the pregnancy. "You lay with a trickster and now complain to me that you've been tricked." Vulcan's hammer came down heavy on the axe he was forging, sweat dripping from the heat and exertion. Venus had a fleeting thought that he had been in such a state when she'd first felt the stirrings of attraction to him so many centuries ago.

"And you wed the goddess of love yet now whine that she loves too freely," Venus replied, adjusting herself on the chaise she had ordered brought into his workshop. "What I am saying, husband, is that the very least Mercury could do is drop by occasionally in my convalescence." Her fingers danced over her belly. "He's the one that wanted this thing in the first place."

Vulcan's eyes darkened across the forge. "I wanted one," he muttered, then raised his voice over the clangs, "but you told me it was impossible, that you would never submit your body to such use, that any child we might conceive would be as twisted as our affections." His hand rubbed hard into the muscles of one of his weak legs, the bitterness in his voice both a lament and an accusation. Venus seized on it.

"Yes, Vulcan, please, regale me with your woes while my stomach swells grotesquely, my breasts leak, and I can't even put on my own sandals. Tell me more about your hardships." She sniffed. "Of course I never wanted a child with you, when I come to you for comfort and all you can offer me is resentment. Besides, I'd long assumed my body ill-suited. Apparently, Mercury brings something to the table that you lack."

Vulcan let the clangs of his work echo in response.

WHEN MERCURY at last deigned to fly in for a visit to his pregnant lover, he found her bent over and using the wall for support, groaning in the early stages of labor.

"What excellent timing!" He landed light on her balcony, wings fluttering at his heels, and crossed to rub an enthusiastic hand in circles on her lower back. "Here, how does this feel?"

Venus shot him a venomous look through her hair, teeth clenched in pain. Mercury danced a few steps back.

"Ah, yes, I see. I shall give you some space, then." He collapsed in a nearby chair and watched her for several moments as a new contraction rolled over her. "Does it help at all to know I find you inordinately appealing in this moment? You really are fearsomely beautiful to behold."

"Get out!" Venus roared, briefly finding her voice before it gave way to a cry of pain, and with a rare frown of indecision, Mercury nonetheless complied. In a moment of inspired mischief, however, he flew directly to Mars, Venus's most frequent lover, and alerted him to the situation.

"And why do I care about the birth of your spawn, Mercury?" Mars asked as he polished his leather armor to a bold shine.

Mercury shrugged. "Well, mostly I would imagine you'd be eager to have Venus returned to herself—and, consequently, to yourself—but I did also think that perhaps you would want to be present, considering the circumstances."

Mars frowned. "Elaborate."

"Well..." Mercury examined his nails. "Are we sure it's my spawn? I was not, I think, the only god with whom Venus lay the night this impending blessing was conceived."

Mars stared at Mercury like he had grown a second head. Never, in all the months Venus had been growing this child, had there been a suggestion that the child was any but Mercury's. Venus herself claimed the messenger god as the father. But there Mercury was, beaming at Mars as though he had given him a gift.

"I'm only saying we don't know. And she's in pain right now, lots of it, and if you know anything, oh half brother of mine, it's pain."

There was a beat as Mercury's words sank in and then, with a curse, Mars stormed out, shouting instructions to his staff as he went.

When at last Cupid was born, Venus gripped Mars's hand hard enough to break bones as Mercury paced the balcony, waiting for that tell-tale infant wail. Juno herself pulled the child from Venus's body, snipped the cord, and wiped him clean. She laid him gently across Venus's breast and watched as the tiny mouth sought for food.

Venus gazed down at his face and burst into tears. Pulling her hand free of Mars's she wrapped her arms around her baby's warmth and held him close, marveling at his tiny little scrunched-up face with its squinty eyes and the dimple in its cheek and the way he looked at her with utter and complete adoration.

Venus did so love to be adored.

"Cupid," she whispered, "there you are."

CUPID'S CONCEPTION had occurred on an evening that Venus never intended to spend in bed sport. The Greek gods of Olympus had only recently undergone a Roman rebrand that, while successful, had necessitated long days collecting tribute and enough presence at their temples to keep such gifts coming. So, on the night in question, the night that would end up altering so many futures, Venus had returned home exhausted and ready for sleep.

Instead, she fell almost immediately into conflict with her husband, who had heard that she had paid a visit to his brother, Mars.

"You think that I don't know what goes on between the two of you?" The massive, hunched god of the forge stared at his clenched hands as if it was all he could do to keep them still.

Venus inhaled through her nose and held the breath for a moment before releasing it, attempting to exhale the irritation his words provoked. "What lies between the goddess of love and the god of war has been there since the beginning, since I first set foot on the beach and was called Aphrodite. We are not mortals to be bound so by an arbitrary code of morals; it need not diminish the union you and I have forged."

Vulcan barked a short laugh, flexing his fingers. "It seems I prepare my brother for his glory in every way, arming him for battle by day and keeping his mistress warm by night."

Venus felt a sharp pain settle between her eyes. "If this is the mood you are insisting upon tonight, then I will retire," she snapped, "and see you again when you've improved your perspective."

Vulcan stood, careful as he transferred his weight to his legs and moved toward her, the power in his body all the more thrilling for its limp. Her mind clouded with anger that he would attempt to so use her reaction to him against her. He crowded her against the wall, gaze level with hers.

"Have I improved my perspective, then?" His expression was harsh.

She met his eyes, her own flashing. "That depends; have you finished whining?"

He took hold of her jaw at that, forcing her chin higher. Venus twisted her head from his grip, snapping her teeth at his fingers.

There were no further words between them as they worked out their fury on one another in the language Venus knew best. When she did finally retire to her room, she was more than ready for a long soak and a massage. Upon reaching her quarters, however, she discovered she was not alone. Sitting cross-legged upon her bed, as though they'd had an appointment and she was late, was Mercury.

He grinned at her. "Sounded like Vulcan was having fun."

"Deliver your message and depart, Mercury; I've no patience for games tonight."

Mercury wagged a finger. "Then you're playing all the wrong ones."

Venus crossed to her mirror, where she began unpinning her hair. "The message?" she prompted.

"Hmm." Mercury uncrossed his legs, bounding up from her bed to come stand behind her, their eyes meeting in the mirror. "As I said, it sounded like Vulcan enjoyed whatever the two of you just engaged in; did you?"

The dilemma was that Venus had enjoyed it, had felt filled by the way Vulcan poured his anger into her and forced her own into submission. That said, this night, he had also taken spiteful pleasure in leaving her wanting after satisfying his own needs, and Venus was not one to deny herself on another's behalf. Thus, she had plans for giving herself the satisfaction Vulcan kept from her, but those plans began with a bath and a massage and could not be realized until she rid herself of the meddling voyeur behind her. She turned, placing a single long finger at the center of Mercury's chest and pushing until he fell back a couple of paces.

"The. Message. Mercury."

The winged god's face split into a grin that, damn him, made it obvious how he so often managed to wiggle out of the consequences of his constant intrigues.

"I have a message of my own," he said, glancing down at the finger still on his chest, nail digging into his breastbone. "Would you care for company tonight?"

This was not the first time Mercury had propositioned her, but it was the first time he had done it in the form of a question about her own desires rather than as some bald and bawdy jest. Venus frowned, withdrawing her finger and brushing past him to check the temperature of the bath her attendant had finished pouring.

"You waste my time; begone, messenger boy." Ignoring him, Venus dropped her robe and climbed carefully into the hot water, hissing with the near-painful relief on her muscles.

Mercury was not, it seemed, ready to give up. He followed her, crouching by her bath with his arms folded along the edge of the tub. His eyes traced every inch of her exposed flesh as he tutted.

"Ah, come now, Venus, I'm no boy. And I'm not here to take from you as Vulcan did. I'm here to give. I offer my services—in demand, ask any nymph or muse—to give your body the tribute and release you deserve. A game where I'm on my knees before you? Surely that's one you wish to play."

Venus eyed him. This was all very earnest and out of character. It made her suspicious.

"I am perfectly capable of finding my own pleasure without the headache you bring."

Mercury raised his eyebrows, inclined his head. "Of course you are." He lowered his voice, leaning toward her as if in conspiracy. "But—between you and me—is not a tongue better than one's own hand?"

Later, when considering why she finally capitulated to Mercury's wheedling, Venus would reflect that she was tired and still wanting from her encounter with Vulcan, and really, Mercury did have a point about tongues, and beautiful as her new attendant was, the girl was unused to servicing women in that way. Venus was not, at that moment, in the mood to take on the role of teacher. And Mercury was not wrong; Venus loved to see men on their knees.

So she accepted what Mercury was offering, and as with all who fell in with the messenger god, the trick that came with it. For when he had her at the brink, when her consciousness teetered on the edge of oblivion, he removed his mouth and his fingers, and Venus found herself filled once again in a way that was outside the terms they had set.

"You winged—ahh—ass," Venus choked out, trying to pull away.

Mercury laughed, his mouth coming to her ear. "Ah, but this is so much better even than a tongue," he murmured, kissing down her neck to devote his attention to her breasts.

And while she was angry, Venus was at that point too close to her own pleasure to continue fighting about it. Mercury had a gift, it seemed, for the simultaneous orgasm.

Afterward, both sprawled on her bed, Mercury yawned, eyes closed.

"Oh, I did have a message to deliver, actually," he said, then fell silent for several long moments.

"Well?" Venus asked, crossing to her now-cool bath to rinse herself of the effects of their activity.

Mercury yawned again. "It's from the Fates."

A chill ran down Venus's spine. The Fates were not known for sending messages one wanted to hear. "And?"

Shifting with a groan to lie on his side, Mercury propped his head on his hand, eyes gleaming with something that made Venus's stomach twist in dread.

"From love, this night, shall the goddess of love conceive greater love," he recited, the anticipatory delight in his eyes dancing as he watched for her reaction.

Venus thought she had spent all her rage on Vulcan, but as it turned out, there was fury left in spades. She reached such volumes that the god of the forge burst in, just as Mercury was struggling to tie his sandals while dodging blows from anything Venus could find to hurl at him.

The disgust that twisted Vulcan's face as he took in the scene was

9

checked almost before it was fully formed by the warning look Venus flashed his way. Rolling his eyes, he scowled as he backed out of the room. Moments later, Mercury succeeded in securing his second sandal and alighted to the window, naked, the rest of his clothes still strewn across the floor.

"Farewell, my goddess," he called, both delighted and mocking. "What a miracle we have wrought this evening!"

And if hate could spark actual flame, Venus would have burned as bright as the stars into which Mercury disappeared.

Chapter 2

Psyche's birth was unremarkable. The third daughter of parents hoping for a son, she was welcomed and cuddled and promptly handed over to the wet nurse. Her family had ruled in Lyktos, a city-state on the northeast of the island Crete, for several generations, but the reach of their authority had been in decline since her father was young. Thus, her father was often absent, ever working to strengthen ties with neighboring city-states and curry what favor he could with the increasingly present foreign powers. Her mother, while she remained more at home, spent her days entertaining local aristocracy and presiding over small disputes and proposed municipal improvements, maintaining the family's relevancy to the local community.

Psyche's older sisters, however, doted upon her. Not mature enough at that time to understand the gentler consideration required for an infant, Psyche's cradle was forever adorned with flowers and woven chains of colorful thread and smooth rocks collected from the seashore. Though the nurses cleared the cradle each day, fearing Psyche might ingest and choke on such gifts, fresh ones always appeared, and despite their exasperation, the nurses were forced to admire the strength of the older girls' affection for their sibling.

And so Psyche, who in another family could have found herself neglected, grew with a grace and warmth and pleasing presence that was the gift of genetics and privilege and the security that comes with knowing that one is loved.

PSYCHE'S SISTERS were as similar as the sun and the moon and as central to her world. Aglaura was calm and steady, a warm place for Psyche to land. Devoted to her loom, she spent long hours showing Psyche the tricks of a smooth weave, stressing the importance of proper weight distribution. Though she did not display much natural aptitude for the task, Psyche nonetheless loved to sit and watch her eldest sister, guessing at the designs she intended as the pattern revealed itself, line by painstaking line.

Cidippe, second-born, seemed to change with the tides but brought a constant sense of wonder and discovery for all that. Cidippe taught Psyche to climb trees, to throw herself headfirst into the surf, to walk over rocks until her feet built up the callouses to run. It was with Cidippe that Psyche most often quarreled, and while it was to Aglaura's arms she ran for comfort, it was Cidippe's hand Psyche found extended when she fell.

Despite their differences, the two older girls continued to share a fierce devotion to their baby sister throughout her childhood that allowed Psyche uncommon space to explore. Their parents held the highest expectations for Aglaura, and as long as Cidippe behaved herself in their presence, she received their approval as well. They hardly seemed to notice Psyche, and Psyche herself didn't much mind; who needed parents with sisters such as hers? Besides, with parental absence came as much freedom as the girls could wheedle from their nurses, and the three were a unified and persuasive force in such matters.

"Please, Agatha, if we do any more weaving today, we will hardly have any left to do tomorrow," said Cidippe, struggling to keep taut the wool she was winding. "It is such a beautiful day; surely we could take a small break?"

Little Psyche bounded up from her position by the loom, where she had been watching Aglaura weave a simple striped pattern for a rug. "I want to swim!" she said, knocking Aglaura's elbow in the process. The older girl closed her eyes, taking deep breaths until her frustration calmed, then pulled the shuttle out from where it had thrust through the back warp threads with a careful hand.

Agatha, who had been with the children since Psyche's birth, eyed her charges.

It was a beautiful day, and they were ahead on their work. Further, keeping the girls indoors on such days almost always resulted in short tempers and discord. Agatha sighed.

"To the beach, then," she conceded. "But we must return in time to tidy up before the evening meal."

The younger girls whooped with delight, donning their sandals and racing ahead of the amused nurse. Aglaura hung up her shuttle, tidied her space, and followed.

On their way out the door, they encountered their mother, who raised her eyes at her daughters.

"Is this the speed at which ladies move?" Despite the mild reproach, her voice held amusement.

Aglaura stopped, eyes hopeful. "We're going to the beach, Mother; will you join us?"

Agatha had stepped back as her charges engaged with their mother, lowering her chin in respect. The lady of the house glanced back at her, then again at her children, sighing.

"Not today. I have several meetings scheduled, and your father is due home today, so there is much to be overseen around the house. Do be back in time for dinner," she said, the last bit directed to Agatha, who inclined her head in acknowledgment.

Disappointed but unsurprised, the girls bid their mother farewell and continued on their way a bit more slowly. When the small party reached the beach, a private area that was part of the larger complex in which the family lived, Psyche turned to Agatha.

"May we swim, may we swim?" she asked, even as Cidippe was already completely bare.

Agatha inclined her head, reaching down to gather the discarded clothes. "Just don't go too far out," she cautioned, "and stay together."

Agatha folded their clothes into two neat piles, then sat and watched as Cidippe and Psyche waded out into the surf, the elder keeping tight hold of her little sister's hand as Psyche tripped over herself trying to keep up. Aglaura walked the shoreline, collecting stones before settling by the water's edge, where she began to construct a little castle of pebbles. When they grew tired of the water, Cidippe and Psyche ran to join their sister, Cidippe hands on hips and head cocked as she critiqued Aglaura's progress, Psyche darting away to collect stones of her own.

After some time, the three abandoned their half-built fortress and trudged back up the beach to their nurse, stretching out alongside one another, soaking in the warmth of the sun.

"I heard Mother and Father talking about our marriages," Cidippe said, abrupt. Psyche looked up from the smooth, flat stone she was turning over in her hand, eyes round.

"We're getting married?" she squeaked.

Aglaura reached out an arm to pat Psyche's hand. "No, no, not yet," she assured her. "Cid just heard them talking about the future, right, Cid?"

Cidippe was lying on her belly, chin propped on her hand. "I don't know how far in the future; you've started your courses, haven't you, Ag?"

Aglaura glared at Cidippe, cutting her eyes at Psyche and then back in an effort to communicate without words. Cidippe huffed. "I'm just saying I heard them, is all. They were saying it was lucky we were all turning out pretty as they can get us better matches that way."

Agatha, who preferred to let the girls talk uninterrupted, could not contain a frustrated sigh at that.

Aglaura sat up, her focus on the older woman. "What is it, Agatha? Do you know something?"

The nurse waved a hand. "Oh no, no, don't mind me. But Psyche, I think Aglaura is right—whatever Cidippe heard is not something to be concerned about for several years yet."

Psyche settled back, satisfied, but Cidippe scowled.

"I didn't *say* it was happening *now*, only that I heard them talking about it!"

Agatha patted the girl's hand. "Shh, of course, I don't want you all worrying about things before you must."

"I'm not worried," Cidippe said, stubborn, flipping onto her back. "I think it's exciting, the idea of getting married and going somewhere new."

"I have dreamed of seeing Athens," Aglaura conceded.

Psyche's gaze was darting between her sisters with increasing alarm. She crawled into Agatha's lap as she said, "I don't want to go anywhere."

"Shh, and nor must you," soothed Agatha, hugging the child close. "Breathe in, breathe out," she whispered into Psyche's hair until the child's body calmed. She looked up at the older girls. "And I caution the two of you not to dream too much of a future over which you will have no control."

Aglaura tilted her head. "What do you mean?"

Agatha sighed. "Only that the three of you are used to an unusual amount of independence; womanhood and marriage will diminish that. Better to be content as you are, for as long as you can."

There was silence as the girls considered this, Cidippe's brow furrowed in thought. After a while, she spoke again. "How will becoming women diminish our independence, Agatha? Mother does whatever she wants."

"Your mother does what she can," Agatha corrected. "It may be that much of it is also what she wants, but they are not necessarily the same."

Aglaura's brow furrowed. "Like how I wanted to weave a blanket with all the colors of a sunrise, but we only had thread in brown and yellow, so I used those in my pattern instead?"

Agatha nodded. "Similar, yes."

In her nurse's lap, Psyche spoke up. "I will just marry a man who can give me all the colors."

The nurse laughed, but the sound was dark. "I hope you do, child, I hope you do."

Cidippe was studying Agatha. "Why does this make you upset?"

Agatha hesitated, arms tightening around Psyche before she began to speak. "I had a boy I dreamed of marrying once—have I told you? Leon. We grew up together and loved each other, but when he approached my family, my father said it was not a good enough match. I was angry," she whispered, "and unwilling to accept such a judgment. So we ran away together and had three perfect days." Agatha's eyes gazed past the sisters, out over the water, as though seeing into the past.

After several moments of silence, Cidippe nudged her with her foot. "So? What happened?"

Agatha started, gaze returning to the children, who were waiting, wide-eyed. "We were found by... unkind men," she said. "They killed Leon and, um, *hurt* me very badly. When I made it back to my father's house, I was met with pity and scorn. Months later, I learned I had been pregnant only when I lost the child."

The four of them listened to the water lapping against the rocks, to birds calling over the horizon. Less tuned to the nuance of the discussion but sensing its weight, Psyche played silently with the bracelet on Agatha's wrist.

"I'm so sorry, Agatha," Aglaura said, soft. "I didn't know any of this."

Agatha gave a small smile, arms tightening around Psyche. "Nor would you, but it was the milk from that doomed child that brought me to you when your mother's breasts were not filling. So there was a light, then, at the end." She dropped a kiss on Psyche's head as she looked back up at the older girls. "I'm just saying—the world is as kind to you now as it will ever be, and the three of you are more fortunate than most; do not be in a rush to depart."

Cidippe tossed a pebble into the surf. "I think you should have prayed to the gods, Agatha. Diana would have helped you," she said, confident.

Agatha laughed, but the sound held no joy. "Oh, we prayed, child. We left sacrifices at the altar of Apollo, for Leon was a musician, and prayed to Venus for protection of our love. But the gods abandoned us, if ever they were listening."

"Why did the gods abandon you?" Psyche's voice held the puzzled confusion of a child for whom the rules of the world were clear. "Were your offerings not good enough?"

Agatha shrugged. "Perhaps. Or perhaps they didn't care."

CHAPTER 3

Centuries Before Psyche

Becoming a mother was not something for which Venus had prepared. Truth be told, since her encounter with Mercury and the subsequent evidence that the Fates had spoken truly, Venus had focused on navigating the immediate reality of pregnancy and on mitigating the effect of that reality on her image as a goddess. One could not simply exist and expect mortals to worship you; a certain presence was required, a delicate balancing of awe and fear to ensure steady devotion and tribute. Venus had been aware as soon as she conceived that having a child would diminish her capacity for such direct involvement and thus had embarked on a goodwill campaign that had lasted right up to her first pangs of labor.

So now that the child was actually born, the goddess found herself seeking advice for the first time in her immortal life from the likes of Juno and Ceres, of all beings.

"How am I supposed to discern what he wants?" Venus asked Juno, a keening Cupid restless in her arms.

Over the great table in her receiving room, the queen of the gods looked up from the documents she was reviewing, propping her chin on a hand and fixing Venus with a sympathetic eye. "Truly, I just remember rotating through food, burping, sleep, and letting them roll around on the floor until something seemed to work."

Venus gritted her teeth. "Yes, well, I have been through those options and he is still unsatisfied," she said, pushing hair away from her face.

Juno shrugged, turning back to her reports. "By the time Bellona and Juventas came along I handed them over to Rumina and she handled it all. Shall I reach out to her for you?"

"No, he's my child." Venus's answer was immediate, the accompanying sigh evidence of the degree to which she wished she could be comfortable entrusting someone else with his care.

Juno was unimpressed. "Well, you could go ask Ceres. She was annoyingly responsive to Bacchus and Proserpina; she'd have better insight than I."

And with that, it was clear that the audience was over.

Venus exhaled her frustration as she left, bouncing and cooing to Cupid. What an absolute joke that Juno should oversee the sanctity of marriage and safety in childbirth and yet be so useless a resource in the actual practice of either. Venus did not want to visit Ceres. The goddess of harvest bored her and was so damned insipid—Venus would be shocked if the woman had ever had a proper orgasm. And what about the half of the year that Ceres spent depressed simply because her daughter, Proserpina, was living with her husband? It was the way of children, wasn't it, to grow and leave home? Venus was already fantasizing about it. But Ceres let herself be so affected by the absence of a child that the whole Earth suffered. Melodramatic and insipid.

Still, Cupid keened. And so the goddess of love boarded her chariot and ordered Palaemon, her elf-charioteer, to bear her to Ceres' farm. At least it was summer, and the woman should be in good spirits.

By the time they arrived, Cupid had fallen asleep in Venus's arms, a situation she was both gratified by and terrified of disrupting. Ceres, ever working outside in her fields and gardens, spotted the entourage and made her way over.

"Greetings, Venus, Palaemon," the older goddess called, wiping her hands on her apron. It bothered Venus that Palaemon received equal billing. Ceres came around the chariot, where Venus sat propped against the carriage wall in exhaustion, Cupid tucked into her arm. Mother and babe wore matching furrows in their brows.

Ceres crouched down. "Oh, he's beautiful, Venus," she said, offering a smile.

Venus frowned. "I've hardly a moment to appreciate that; the child never stops crying." Remembering she was addressing one of the few goddesses with seniority over her, Venus swallowed and started again. "I've come to beg your advice. He stops crying only when he sleeps, and he never sleeps for long. See, even in rest, he struggles." The two women observed the babe for a moment, Cupid's tiny body wriggling with apparent discomfort, even as his eyes stayed shut. Ceres reached out her arms, and after an extended pause, Venus relinquished Cupid to her.

Ceres stood, cradling the boy with an easy confidence that made Venus burn with envy even as she felt relief wash over her body at the reprieve. "Come in." Ceres inclined her head to her modest residence. "Let us sit, eat, and have a chat." She turned and made her way to the house, confident that Venus would follow. After reminding herself that she needed Ceres' help and should watch her mouth, Venus did.

Inside what struck Venus as a poor excuse for a home, even if one used human standards, the two goddesses settled at a low table across from one another. Venus tore into the fresh bread cooling there as soon as it was offered. Though the gods did not technically need to eat food, as it was ambrosia that sustained them, most chose to for the pleasure of it. Venus had found that since Cupid's birth, her appetite was voracious.

As Venus ate, Ceres asked questions.

"How is he nursing?"

Venus swallowed. "Oh, he's nursing well." She glanced down at her breasts, utilitarian for the first time in her existence. "He'll need to eat soon, or I'll start to leak." Leaking was one of her least favorite parts of this whole experience.

"What about his bowel movements?"

"He has them; they're not frequent, but he urinates plenty."

Ceres hummed. "Sometimes that can be a source of distress." The goddess turned to retrieve a thickly woven blanket with her free arm, then stood, arranging the blanket in a cradle shape on the table and laying Cupid within. She began dragging her hands with gentle but firm movements down his belly.

"What are you doing?" Venus stared.

"This can help move along his digestion if that is the source of his discomfort. Tell me, how are you finding motherhood?"

Venus glared at her, unable to censor her response to what felt like a direct hit at her most vulnerable area. "I hate it," she said. "My body is at the disposal of another at all times, and if it's not leaking, it's bleeding. I've no time for any of my lovers or to collect tribute from my shrines or even care for my beauty, and the last time I got a full night's sleep was before I knew I had conceived. Meanwhile, Mercury flits about as he always has, Vulcan ignores me, and Mars is busy claiming cities I don't want in my name." Venus had expected to shock Ceres, had been steeling herself to endure the rebuke she was sure would come. But Ceres just laughed, her eyes compassionate.

"Ah, I felt the same with Proserpina," she said. Without pausing her gentle massage of Cupid's belly, she indicated the fields beyond the window. "Sustaining life—it is the hardest thing we can do, I think. And too often, it rewards our efforts with failure. And yet"—she smiled down at the baby under her hands, who—to Venus's surprise—was beginning to visibly relax—"there is no more worthwhile pursuit in all of creation."

This went a bit far for Venus, who felt there were a significant number of other very worthwhile pursuits, but she took the point. Though she hated the experience, though she never wished to endure it again, she nonetheless adored her child. Her very presence in this hut was evidence of that.

The quiet of the room was interrupted by the sudden, noisy rip of Cupid emptying his bowels. The force of the expulsion startled the child awake, and his eyes went wide, hands flailing with panic. Venus was there before he could let out his first cry.

"Shhhh, it's alright, you're alright."

Ceres watched as mother scooped up child, holding him close as she murmured in his ear. Venus met her eyes over Cupid's shoulders. "Thank you," she said, the words stiff but sincere.

Ceres pressed her hands together. "Of course. Come again, anytime you need."

VENUS'S TREPIDATION at visiting Ceres and her surprise at the easy aid she received there was not unfounded. Venus herself had not been born of a woman, immortal or other, and between that and her position as the goddess of love and lust, she had always felt a gulf between herself and the other goddesses.

"Sprung from testicles—can you imagine?" she'd overheard Minerva, the goddess of wisdom, comment to Diana before one council meeting. "It is no wonder she emerged from the ocean as every god's wet dream, she's little more than fantasy become flesh." Diana had not agreed with this sentiment, but neither had she rejected it, responding instead with a noncommittal hum and a shrug. Minerva had then noticed Venus, her brows rising in challenge as she realized she'd been overheard. At that moment, however, Jupiter had entered, signaling the start of council, and—as required whenever the lightning god was present—all attention had shifted to him.

Venus never again overheard the gossip surrounding her, but she well imagined it: lusty, love-hungry, never satisfied, taking lovers as often as Jupiter himself. And, in truth, she did not see an issue with that. So she liked to feel good—was that so different from the satisfaction Juno drew from overseeing a successful birth, or that Diana pursued in her solitary, moonlit hunts? No, it wasn't that Venus minded what was said, but the result was that she never became close with any of her fellow goddesses, so when she found herself in a position to need their wisdom, she was not confident of the reaction she would receive. Even Juno's presence at the birth had come as a shock to Venus, her surprise sharpened when the queen of the gods visited the new mother again several weeks after the fruitless office visit.

"And how is your body adjusting?" Juno asked, settling herself upon a chair beside the cradle where a swaddled Cupid lay, resting peacefully now he was shitting regularly. Venus heard the question with suspicion. Was the interest sincere, or an effort to pry into the oft-speculated-upon reproductive details of her body? Through the window, the clangs from Vulcan's workshop rang sharp and heavy. Venus poured herself wine before responding, wordlessly offering Juno a glass as well, which the older goddess declined.

"It's doing well, thank you. I don't much enjoy leaking from every orifice, but the bleeding has stopped, at least, and Cupid's eating on a more reliable schedule now, so I'm not soaking the front of my gowns with such regularity." There. Let Juno know Venus's body was as capable of sustaining life as it was of giving and receiving pleasure.

The queen was not one to smile, but her eyes were approving. "Good, that is good to hear. And how has Vulcan been? It sounds like he's productive, at least." Her tone was light, but Venus's senses sharpened as the conversation moved into trickier ground. Vulcan was Juno's son, as was Mars.

"He has been well." Venus matched her tone to Juno's. "Busy supplying Mars, I think, in preparation for his next campaign. To be honest, we've seen little of each other since Cupid's birth."

Juno inclined her head in acknowledgment. "Yes, it is the only way they know to support one another, I'm afraid. My fault, perhaps." Venus took a sip of her wine, covering her surprise. Juno was not known for her confidences. The queen of the gods was gazing out the window as though listening for meaning in the steady ringing of metal on metal. She glanced back at Venus. "I certainly can't deny there have been plenty of times I've disapproved of the way you operate in this world, especially when it has caused pain to one or both of my boys." There was a pointed look at the cradle that made Venus want to spring up and grab Cupid in her arms, protecting him from the judgment in that gaze. Still, she remained where she was, and Juno continued. "But I also recognize that whatever Jupiter and I gave them has resulted in a great deal of suffering, which was never my intent. Perhaps, raising this one in love, you will achieve a different outcome." And so saying, Juno rose, stooping to place a gentle kiss on Cupid's forehead before bidding Venus a curt farewell and departing the way she came.

. . .

Since her marriage to Vulcan centuries before, Venus had resided in his home, albeit in her own private wing. However, once Cupid was born, she found that she desired more space. Her relationship with her husband, ever strained by her constant affairs, frayed almost to a breaking point after weeks of Cupid's cries echoing through the halls. If she hoped to again improve her relationship with Vulcan, Venus thought, she needed to remove the evidence of her extramarital activities out from under his nose.

And so, for the first time since she emerged from the sea, Venus established her own household. She arranged for the construction of a house on the island of Kythera, overlooking the very beach onto which she'd first stepped, where she could hear the water crash against the shore and smell the salt in the air. She cultivated cliff roses and orchids, her haphazard attention to gardening resulting in a chaotic riot of blooms that shone in bright contrast to the shining white marble of her home.

She found that without Vulcan's dour presence hovering at all times, she was much more comfortable with the idea of accepting help in caring for Cupid, and when selecting her household staff, she reached out to Juno about her offer to contact Rumina, goddess of nursing infants. The goddess was prompt in her response, one of Rumina's devotees arriving mere days after Venus had moved in, and the relief Venus found in sharing the weight of her child's needs was profound. She could tend to herself again, to her beauty and amusement. She began, in these small but crucial ways, to feel like herself once more.

One morning, while a toddling Cupid napped in his nurse's arms, Venus went for a walk along the beach, relishing the feel of wet pebbles beneath her feet and the way the wind blew ocean spray high enough to dot her bare legs. She was trying to determine the exact location of her original arrival when she became aware of a small white bird hopping alongside her, head cocked so that one black eye followed her every move. Venus stopped.

"Can I help you, tern?" Venus asked, addressing it by type instead of asking its name. There were too many birds in the world and they lived for too short a time to start learning individual names.

The tern hopped higher in excitement. "Oh, my lady, I find myself simply awed by your presence," the tern said. "My family has passed down tales of your emergence on our beach; indeed, it has been a point of pride and distinction for us, but never did I dream I'd have the honor to stand in your presence."

Venus sighed. She'd forgotten terns often built their nests along cliff faces. It wasn't that Venus disliked the birds but rather that their constant chatter made her head spin. Very little was less erotic than a colony of terns chattering away outside one's window. Venus eyed the tern.

"I appreciate the devotion of your family," she said, mind turning over a possibility. "It is such long memory and affection that made this beach the only one I would consider for my home." Many of the immortals had animals that did their bidding, birds in particular. Jupiter had his eagle, Minerva her owl; Diana had that cursed buzzard hawk she claimed, which mystified Venus no end. Venus herself had tried to claim, at different times, the swan and the turtle dove but found herself in competition with Apollo and Ceres, respectively, for their allegiance. Perhaps she could shift this tern situation to her advantage and earn herself some peace and quiet in the bargain.

"Tern," Venus began, slow, "I am so moved by the story you tell of your family that an idea forms."

The tern's eyes, already wide and round, became wider and rounder. "Tell me, my lady," the bird said.

"It is not an easy thing I— no, I cannot ask; it would be too much of an imposition." Venus waved her hand, seeming to dismiss the very thought.

The tern was vibrating now with excitement, wings outstretched for balance as it hopped from one foot to the other. "No, no, my lady, for you, nothing is an imposition, only an honor. Tell me, I beg you."

"Well," Venus said, with apparent reluctance, "delighted as I am with my home here, it is a bit more removed than I am accustomed to being—from the rest of Olympus, I mean. I intended to do a fair bit of traveling back and forth, to remain informed, but if I had an emissary, someone to bear messages and report to me with current happenings..."

"Oh, oh!" The tern was airborne now, zipping one way and then another, level with Venus's shoulder. "We can do that! We can be such emissaries for you! We have relatives all over, many with nests near Olympus. We can be your winged eyes and ears and carry your words as well when need be."

Venus beamed, offering a finger onto which the tern jumped with alacrity. "What a generous offer! I thank you from the bottom of my heart. The peace it brings me to know I shall not have to be separated from my son in order to remain informed—it is a priceless gift."

If birds could blush, the tern would have been bright red.

"Now," Venus said, "at your leisure—I would never wish to rush you—I greatly desire to know what is going on in my husband's home, as well as that of Mars."

The tern bobbed its head. "Just so, my lady, just so. I shall fetch my brother, and we shall depart at once!"

Venus drew a single gentle finger down the bird's head. "You are too good," she said and watched as the small tern soared away toward its nest in the cliff, apparently to round up the referenced brother. When she saw two light spots on the horizon flying away from her, Venus let out a satisfied breath.

"Yes," she said to herself, "I think this shall work fine."

CHAPTER 4

Agatha left Psyche's family a year later to work for another house, and the loss sharpened the sense that the sisters' support of one another was the most important thing they possessed. When, a few years later, the conversation Cidippe overheard came to fruition, the prospect of one of them leaving felt to Psyche like the impending loss of a limb.

"Scoot over, Psyche, I can't see," Cidippe whispered as the two girls pressed together at the edge of the doorway. Within the room beyond, Aglaura was sitting with their parents, receiving the news of her betrothal.

"Georgios is a good man, who runs one of the most profitable olive orchards in Gortyna," their father said, voice suggesting his daughter's agreement was a foregone conclusion. "This alliance will secure our city's supply for years to come, and you will be mistress of a fine and respected estate."

Aglaura's hands were folded in her lap, her expression cautious. "It does sound a good match, Father, but..." She hesitated, fingers white with the strength of her grip despite their delicate placement. "Is he not a bit...old?"

"So your father seemed to me when we first wed," their mother cut in, placing her own hand atop Aglaura's. "But you will find that as the years pass, age matters less than position and character; we have met Georgios many times, including with his late wife, and he will take good care of you. What more can we wish for you? You are fortunate."

Aglaura fixed her gaze on the tangle of fingers on her lap, considering. From the doorway, Cidippe and Psyche saw the moment she accepted her fate. Looking back up at her parents, Aglaura nodded.

"As you say, Mother. Fortunate."

At this moment, Psyche shifted, her foot landing on Cidippe's toe, causing the older girl to cry out, and the two of them rushed away before they could be caught.

Later, in the room they shared, the sisters considered the implications of the change ahead.

"But how often will you visit?" Psyche asked Aglaura. The sisters were sprawled across the great bed, each absorbed in their own tasks.

Aglaura did not look up from where she lay on her belly, using a linen cloth to polish her fingernails with vinegar and olive oil. "I really don't know, Psy," she replied. "I suppose that will be up to my husband. Ugh, what a strange thing to say—my *husband*."

"Gortyna is not so far; it's still in Crete, at least. I heard the nurses say that a woman who knows what she's at can make a man do her bidding with a single look," Cidippe said, peering over her scroll and nudging her older sister with her toes. "You'll need to learn fast so you can give Georgios the look that says, 'Take me home to my sisters immediately!'"

"Or—'Send for my sisters to keep me company!'" Psyche sat up in her excitement. "The three of us can explore your new home."

Aglaura finished polishing her final nail, and tossed the cloth to Psyche, who dutifully began attending to her own digits. "I don't know yet what I will be able to do, but he is old and, Father says, excited for a young bride, so I'd say our chances are good," Aglaura said. She stood and stretched, walking to the balcony and drawing open the curtain to gaze out over their family property for a long moment. "I will miss home," she said, prompting both younger girls to hop up and throw their arms about her.

When the time for the wedding came, the days passed in a blur of food, wine, and celebration, and when the dust had settled and the last guest departed, Cidippe and Psyche found themselves in that same spot before the balcony, the space Aglaura had occupied only weeks before seeming to vibrate with her absence. Cidippe broke the silence.

"Well, now we have known the worst; to lose one of us to the outside world. But we know the shape of it now, and everything before us can only be better."

CIDIPPE MARRIED NOT LONG AFTER, her bridegroom younger and more handsome than Aglaura's, always with a wide smile and a ready jest. Marinos was a Roman merchant recently moved to Crete but with a young and profitable fleet, and once more, the city of Lyktos saw immediate benefit from the match. The sisters saw each other rarely, and it wasn't until both of the older girls' bellies were swollen with child that they were able to convince their husbands to allow them to convalesce for a period at their childhood home. Psyche was incandescent with excitement and flooded their rooms—for, of course, they were to have their own rooms now—with sweet-smelling flowers and soft linens and every other indulgent comfort she could find. When at last Aglaura and Cidippe arrived, Psyche rushed to greet them, only to halt in confusion and concern when she beheld their appearances.

Aglaura was pale and exhausted, swollen and uncomfortable in pregnancy. She nonetheless smiled when she saw Psyche, holding out her arms into which her youngest sister flung herself without further hesitation. Cidippe, however, held herself apart. Though her body was clearly also growing life, she lacked Aglaura's soft abundance. The sharp lines of her collarbones, shoulders, and elbows stood in contrast to the distension of her belly, and her eyes were sunken and distant, barely acknowledging her sisters. Faded purple bruises peeked out from the neckline of her gown. Psyche pulled away from Aglaura and turned to Cidippe, holding out a tentative hand.

"Cid?" she said. Cidippe's eyes dropped to the proffered hand, a long moment passing before she brushed limp fingers to Psyche's palm. Psyche grabbed them, holding tight and blinking back tears. "Mother had a feast prepared," she whispered. "Let's go inside."

Cidippe allowed Aglaura to take her other hand and they walked together into the house.

Dinner passed as a tense, awkward affair. Psyche was never sure whether her parents truly did not notice the change in Cidippe or if they chalked it up to her pregnancy, but Psyche found her anger increasing with every mild, neutral word that passed her mother's lips and even more so by the distracted, oblivious presence of her father. She exchanged a glance with Aglaura, whose eyes warned her to say nothing. So Psyche settled for chewing her food with extra force and imagining all the ways she would restore her sister while she had her.

"WHAT HAS he done to her, Aglaura?" Psyche demanded, busying her hands with plucking the Laconian thyme from the bouquets in Aglaura's room, as her older sister had admitted the smell currently made her feel ill. She heard Aglaura sigh from where she lay propped on the bed.

"I don't know, she won't say, but I suspect those bruises on her wrists are not the only ones. I knew she was not happy, but I never imagined her in such a state." Aglaura chewed her lip. "I worry for the child."

Psyche spun around. "The child?! I worry for Cidippe! That child, the one *he* put in her, could kill her! From the looks of it, if it takes after its father in any way, it will want to." In her passion, Psyche had begun waving the bunches of thyme held in her fists, and Aglaura's hand flew up to cover her nose, a violent jerk of her head indicating for Psyche to cast the offending flowers off the balcony. Psyche did so, then sank next to her sister on the bed.

"What can we do?" she asked.

Aglaura's hand came up to play with Psyche's hair, but her eyes were far away. "Agatha warned us," she said. "She told us that day on the beach."

"What day?" Psyche asked.

Aglaura bit her lip. "You were still small; perhaps you do not remember. But she told us the world was not the adventure we dreamed it."

29

Psyche was beginning to get flashes of memory, of salty water, smooth pebbles, and uneasy shivers under a warm sun.

"She told us," Aglaura repeated, frustration creeping into her voice, "but in her story, she ran away, defied her parents. I thought we did everything right."

Psyche raised her hand to still Aglaura's, where it was toying with her hair with increasing agitation. "What do you mean, Ag? Of course we did everything right—what else could we have done?"

Her sister's shoulders drooped. "I don't know," she said. "Probably nothing." She stood, then, stretching as she continued to think aloud. "If we tell Father, he will get angry, but I'm not sure he'll act on it. He needs the connection to Marinos; that was plain in the hastiness of the wedding. And I fear for Cid, too, if Marinos gets wind of any interference. The best we can do may be to listen and love Cid as best we can before we are all separated again."

Psyche stared for several long moments at the curtains billowing gently from the outside breeze. Aglaura's fingers on her scalp had been warm and comforting—Psyche realized in that moment that affectionate touch had departed with her sisters.

After some time, the two girls settled beside one another on the bed.

"Is it so bad for you?" Psyche asked. "Being married?"

Aglaura sighed. "It's not so bad for me. Georgios is old and sick, but he is a decent man. Most of my time is spent as nursemaid rather than wife." Her hand went to her belly. "Even the conception of this child, though not pleasant work, was achieved relatively simply, and he is little interested in me in that way now. I do not love him, but he is kind, and he has given me a child. I am mistress of one of the finest homes in Gortyna; I am fortunate."

Psyche absorbed that. "How did things go so wrong for Cid?" she asked. "How will I know whether the man I marry is like Georgios or like Marinos?"

Aglaura reached over and seized her hand, squeezing. "I have to believe men like Marinos are few."

. . .

THE REMAINING time the sisters had together was spent doting on Cidippe, visiting her favorite spots, bringing in musicians to play her favorite music, and harassing the chefs to cater to her every craving. Psyche rarely let go of her middle sister's now-bony hand, trying to say with touch all the things it would be too hard to voice.

I see your pain. You don't deserve this. I love you.

For her part, Cidippe came gradually out of her shell over the few weeks, flashes of her once-animated countenance rising occasionally to the surface, albeit with a darker bent than she'd possessed before. She confessed to Aglaura and Psyche that she was excited for the child, but she stayed tight-lipped when it came to Marinos.

"I hope it is a girl," Cidippe admitted one day, the three of them lunching in the family lemon grove. Her body was soft with rare ease as Aglaura plaited her hair. Psyche lay on the blanket they had brought, her chin propped in one hand. Her face twisted in response.

"Why in Juno's name would you want a girl?" she asked, popping an olive into her mouth. "Boys are the ones permitted to shape the world. When I wed, I wish to have only boys."

Aglaura laughed. "A boy would be helpful to me around the orchard," she said, "though ultimately, I don't think I care which I have." She tied off the end of Cidippe's braid, and the two separated, moving to sit so the three formed a triangle.

Cidippe plucked at the grass. "Boys are one thing," she said. "Men are quite another. I don't want to be responsible for raising a man." Psyche's eyes darted to the now pale-yellow bruises, and she felt shame wash over her. Before she could say anything, Cidippe continued. "I am terrified of raising a man like Marinos when that is the model before the child, when that corruption is present in the seed. I pray to Diana daily for a girl."

Aglaura's response was hesitant. "Are you— I mean, is there any part of you worried he might—" She drew a deep breath, squaring her shoulders. "If this is how he treats you, what concern do you have for a daughter?" The question hung between them, an ugly thing no one wanted to touch.

Cidippe stared off into the horizon. "I don't think he will pay much attention to the child, girl or boy," she said, her voice tired. "But your point is taken."

Since her sisters had returned, Psyche had been turning over a question in her mind. Hearing an opening, she rushed out the words before she could lose her nerve. "Could you not get a divorce?"

Technically, divorce could be initiated by either party in a marriage, but a woman usually needed to prove her husband could not support her and required the backing of family for a successful outcome. There was a beat of silence between the sisters, Psyche having brought into the open the unsaid.

Cidippe swallowed. "I..." She stopped, started over. "It has occurred to me, but—"

"But what?" Psyche cut her off, springing to her feet and forgetting her intention to tread calm and careful around this matter. "He hurts you, Cid. We can see it; your bones enter a room before you do. What can there possibly be to consider here?" She was pacing, arms exploding in wild gesticulation as if movement would shake Cidippe from the dull trance she seemed to be in. "Divorce him, and be free from this! Come home, be with me; you and I will raise your child. We'll teach her to swim and build sandcastles and climb trees and everything else she needs to know, far away from that beast!" Her sisters watched, waiting for Psyche's energy to run its course.

Studying both their faces, Psyche suddenly felt very young. She slumped to the ground next to her sisters, and her voice when it came again, was small. "Why not, Cid?"

Cidippe closed her eyes. "He has not hurt me since I began to show; the marks you see are the result of pregnancy making my skin more prone to bruising. And he does not mean to hurt me; it simply explodes out of him sometimes, mostly when something has gone wrong with business and I ask silly questions. I'm getting better at not doing that. I don't expect you to understand, and he is not the man I would choose were I free to make a choice, but I cannot leave. Especially now I'm carrying his child—he would claim his paternal rights. Besides, Father is relying on the connection with Marinos; you know how fragile his position is. I can do it; it will be fine. I'm just tired is all." She gave a wan smile. "My body does not take to pregnancy as yours does, Aglaura."

The wind blew through the trees, and Psyche felt goosebumps rise on her bare shoulders. After a long moment during which none of them could meet the others' eyes, Aglaura broke the silence.

"It is, of course, your call to make, Cid," she said, voice gentle. "Know we are here, always on your side." Cidippe leaned into her older sister at these words, and Psyche raised her own eyes to take in the two of them.

"Always on your side," she echoed, her anger spent. In its place was a bleakness she'd not known before.

That evening, after she'd bid her sisters goodnight, Psyche lay on her bed, counting the stars she could see out her window. As a child, Aglaura had tried to teach Psyche to see the constellations held in the night sky, but despite Aglaura's patient attempts, Psyche's eyes—or perhaps her mind—could never quite see form in the stars. There were too many of them to consider any given star or group of stars in separation, to Psyche's way of thinking. Even in her counting, every time she got to around fifty, she'd lose her place and have to begin again. It was in her fourth attempt that she finally drifted into an uneasy sleep.

CHAPTER 5

Centuries Before Psyche

Venus commissioned Cupid's bow and arrows several months ahead of his fourth birthday. It was a joint project between Apollo and Vulcan, Apollo acquiring the wood, bone, and rare feathers while Vulcan crafted the arrowheads. Once these tasks were completed, however, they realized that they still needed to join all the various elements before any giftable product would emerge. For this, they went to Apollo's twin, Diana.

"This is for whom, again, exactly?" asked Diana, eyebrows hovering by her hairline as she stared down at the raw materials dumped at her feet.

"Cupid," Apollo supplied. "You know, Venus and Mercury's boy. Or maybe Mars's? Not totally clear, but Mercury is the one who claims him."

"I know who he is," said Diana, "but he's barely out of diapers. Why in Jupiter's name are you making him—excuse me, asking me to make him—a bow and arrows?"

Apollo stared at his sister for a long moment, then scratched his head. "Well, it's, I mean, because—"

"Because Venus asked it," Vulcan said. "And we all do what Venus asks, somehow. Even me."

Diana gave a short laugh. "Ah yes, even you, Vulcan. Titans, but am I grateful to be free of such desires. Well, I think it's stupid, but fine, I will take these materials—fit for Jupiter's own bow, I might add, you both have a keen eye, whatever else you lack—and form them into a tiny weapon for a tiny child."

Diana was as good as her word. The bow and arrows she crafted for Cupid were among the finest work she'd ever done, even Mars admitting to the quality of her craftsmanship. When Venus presented them to her curly-haired, dimpled toddler he beamed with such excitement that she thought her heart might explode.

"Now you and I can have our own little adventures, can't we, sweet one?" She ran her fingers through his hair, marveling at its shine and softness.

"What adventures, Mama?" Cupid asked, struggling to notch the arrow as he'd seen Apollo do. Venus smiled, wrapping her arms around his shoulders and hugging him tight.

"Any we wish, love."

At that moment, there was a commotion at the entrance of the house, and mother and son both turned. Through the doorway of the room burst Mercury, hair windswept and eyes twinkling as he fell to one knee before his son. Cupid edged closer to his mother, studying the god before him.

"Who are you?" Cupid asked, hugging his gifts to his chest. Mercury's eyebrows drew in, and he glanced up at Venus.

"Who am—Venus, have you not told him?"

Venus let out an irritated sigh. "Cupid, darling, this is Mercury. Son of Jupiter and Maia, errand boy of Olympus, and general nuisance."

"Ah ha, but you weren't calling me a nuisance when we were making this little one," Mercury chided, chucking Cupid under the chin, which caused the boy to turn his head away and close his eyes tight. Mercury stood, eyeing Venus.

"Why does he not know his father?"

"Why should he?" she returned, "I have not seen you outside council since his birth. You've certainly not bothered to visit."

"Have I not?" Mercury sounded surprised, then shook it off. "Well, now here I am. And I have a gift." From below, one of Cupid's eyes peeked open. Mercury saw, and his grin returned in full force. He crouched down again. "Would you like to see what I've brought you, son of mine?" Cupid's head swung to face the god of mischief as he nodded. Mercury gave a laugh. "Excellent! Wait here." And, rising to his toes, his winged sandals began to flutter until he was aloft, zipping out the side window.

"Exhibitionist," Venus muttered, turning in a swirl of diaphanous silk to recline on a nearby chaise. She had just arranged herself to her satisfaction when the buzzing sound of tiny wings announced Mercury's return.

In his arms, he bore a linen-wrapped parcel almost twice as large as the boy for whom the gift was intended. Venus narrowed her eyes as she watched.

Mercury landed, then strode forward and dropped to a seat on the ground next to Cupid, parcel across his lap. He patted the stone floor next to him.

"Have a seat, boy." Cupid obeyed, his eyes shining with curiosity but his body still leaning away from the older god.

When Mercury made no move to unwrap the parcel, Cupid said, "What is it?"

"Ah, what do you think it could be?"

Cupid's small shoulders bobbed in a shrug. "I was hoping it might be a dog, and it looks big enough to be a dog, but it's not moving, so I don't think it can be a dog—unless it's dead. Did you bring me a dead dog?" His voice pitched high in sudden alarm.

Mercury burst with laughter. "Oh, by Neptune's impotent trident, no, it is not a dead dog, but never have I wished more that something was." Mercury leaned forward, lowering his voice as if to make them coconspirators. "I don't think your mother would appreciate a dog, do you? Dead or otherwise." Cupid gave a slow shake of his head as Venus scoffed from the corner.

"Get on with your business, you winged ass."

36

"She's called me that before," Mercury confided, "under quite different circumstances."

"Mercury." Venus's voice was ice.

"Alright, alright, the gift, then. But first, a story. Do you like stories, Cupid?"

"I like gifts more than stories," the boy admitted. Mercury settled back, leaning on his hands.

"Oh, as do I, but alas, context is ever the thing. So settle in and listen. Jupiter, king of the gods, reluctant father to yours truly, and oblivious grandfather to you"—he touched Cupid's nose—"likes the female form. In fact, he likes it so much that he is often led to make decisions not by the great logic of his brain but by the lesser inclinations of his—"

Venus coughed.

"—body. Anyway, he had an affair with a nymph named Juturna. Do you know what an affair is, Cupid?"

The boy nodded. "Jupiter likes to play with women other than Juno, and that makes Juno angry. I know all that."

Mercury inclined his head, surprised. "Yes, indeed. Well then, the point is that this affair did not stay a secret because Jupiter is actually really bad at having affairs, and this time, Juno learned of Jupiter's, ah, playing, from another nymph named Lara." He turned to Venus.

"Do you remember Lara? Almo's daughter? She attended your wedding; what a joyous day to recall." Venus scowled at him. Mercury winked at her before continuing. "Anyway, Lara always was a big talker; I thought about playing with her myself at your wedding but found her incessant chatter was a bit much even for me—"

"Remarkable," Venus interjected, "how quick you are to bore without the sound of your own voice."

"—and one day, Lara chattered to Juno about Jupiter's little play-dates with Juturna."

Cupid yawned, tracing the elegant rose carved into his quiver of arrows with one small finger.

Mercury continued, undaunted. "When Jupiter learned of this, he ripped out Lara's tongue himself and summoned me to deliver her to the entrance to the Underworld—Avernus—before her father learned what had occurred. Now pay attention, Cupid, this is the important part."

The boy, who had perked up slightly at the mention of a ripped-out tongue, shoved his hands under his thighs and stared up at the man who still possessed across his lap what was promised to be a gift.

"The journey to Avernus is long and unpleasant, and I could see in Lara's eyes that she desired comfort."

"What, pray, tipped you off? The tears? Or the blood trailing her chin?" Venus's voice was honey sweet.

Mercury waved a hand. "No, no, there was no blood. I healed the stub as soon as I arrived. The least I could do. But back to the story: I provided Lara comfort—we played together, if you will—and I later learned that from our playing, she had conceived and borne twins." Here, he paused to take a breath. Cupid scratched his nose.

"Anyway," Mercury continued, "it was quickly clear that the twins could not remain in the Underworld as they somehow turned invisible, and Proserpina found their presence unpleasant. Invisible children are apparently quite troublesome."

"As are invisible fathers, Mercury; what can this possibly have to do with your gift for Cupid?" Venus exploded, her composure finally deserting her. "Will you please get to the damn point, or else leave the way you came."

Mercury beamed. "As it happens, I have arrived at the point. Cupid, I know that you do not know me, but I am your father, and as a father, I do not abandon my children." A high laugh from the corner. "I have claimed the twins and installed them as caretakers in an estate I've been building. They will maintain and live in comfort on the estate, but I would like to gift the estate itself to you, as the highest ranking of my children. Oh, you need not live there now"—he raised his voice over the sputtering sounds of outrage coming from Venus—"but I imagine one day you will want a place of your own, and the Lares—those are the twins—will make sure the home is waiting for you, in good condition." He concluded his story with the air of one well satisfied with himself. Cupid's face screwed up, confused.

"But I don't need a house. And that is not big enough to be a house." He pointed at the parcel in Mercury's lap. Mercury glanced down, starting in a way that suggested he had just recalled the gift.

"Observant of you; indeed, this is not a house. Here, come with me." Standing, Mercury carried the parcel to a table nearby, laying it down gently. Cupid trailed behind, watching as his father began to untie the silk cords binding the wrappings.

When all the cord had been removed and the linen unfurled, Cupid crept up, peeking over the edge of the table at the treasure revealed within.

It was a set of wings, smooth and shining, crafted from feathers of the most brilliant colors Cupid had ever seen. Though it was clear they would topple him over at this point, Cupid nonetheless had never wanted to don something more in his life. Mercury grinned at his excitement.

"Well, come here, then, let's see how they fit." He lifted the wings, holding them by the soft leather harness, and knelt down to help Cupid slide his dimpled arms through. Over his shoulder, he spoke to Venus. "You know, this is Daedalus's work; I tracked him down after his escape because I was so impressed with what he'd achieved. It took a bit of convincing, but I got him to expand his design and had Diana collect the feathers, and I must say, I'm incredibly pleased with the result."

Venus did not love hearing Diana had been instrumental in both of their gifts.

"Didn't Daedalus's son die from a flaw in the design of the wings?" Venus asked, watching Cupid bounce about the room wearing the wings, bow and one arrow still clasped tight in a hand. Mercury had a hand on the top of the harness to help bear the weight of the wings and had to lurch to keep up with the child. The messenger god shrugged acknowledgment of her words.

"Icarus the imbecile; yes, he did. But as I said, Daedalus improved on the design—there's no wax to be found on these wings. And besides, our son is immortal."

"Immortals can still be gruesomely maimed," Venus said.

"Sure, but Cupid isn't stupid, are you boy?"

Cupid laughed at the lyrical cadence of the question. "Nope, Cupid isn't stupid!" he sang back.

Venus pressed her fingers to her brow in a futile effort to ward off a headache. When Cupid grew tired, shrugging out of his wings to collapse onto the floor to study the feathered marvels more closely, Venus grabbed Mercury by the arm and drew him aside.

"You've got to stop suggesting to people that Mars is his father," she hissed. "The rumors are getting out of control, and the last thing I need is Mars taking it into his head that he's actually got progeny to raise in his image."

Mercury grinned. Mercury always grinned. It was infuriating.

"Well, for all I know, he could be."

"He could not."

"Ah, well, but then he certainly could be Vulcan's."

"A point I'll ask you to continue keeping to yourself," Venus snapped. Mercury gave a dismissive shake of his head.

"No worries on that front; Vulcan is far less fun than Mars."

"Regardless, you will cease speaking of either of them in connection with Cupid."

"Why?" The question was as close to sincere as Venus had ever heard the messenger god. She hesitated before answering.

"Because he's mine," she said, "and you don't require I share him."

When Mercury departed, Cupid's gaze followed his retreating form until he was nothing more than a speck against the blue sky. "When will he come back?" he asked, eyes still fixed. Venus huffed out a sigh.

"Whenever he feels like it," she said. "Now, let's go practice with your new bow."

THE OLDER CUPID GREW, the less constant care he required and the more Venus decided she enjoyed being a parent. Finally, there was someone who was hers—just hers—who understood and loved her just as she was.

It was in the city of Cyprus, during an annual festival thrown in her honor, that Venus first observed Cupid strike someone with one of his arrows and the fallout that could occur because of it.

As a city that claimed her as its primary deity, Cyprus was a frequent and favorite spot for Venus to stoke the flames of her own worship, and never more than on Cypriote, the celebration of love and the goddess of such. On that particular visit, Venus wandered the streets, loud and colorful with the devotional festivities, Cupid's hand tucked tight in her own despite the fact that it was large enough now not to need constant holding.

They were both dressed as mortals, Cupid having left behind the wings that were recently beginning to fit him, but the boy had, unbeknownst to his mother, smuggled his bow and a single arrow in the folds of his cloak. He had a theory about the effect of his arrows and, if he was correct, felt it both the perfect tribute to his mother as well as an entertaining diversion for himself.

Cupid saw his opportunity around midday, as he and Venus stood with the crowd, observing Cinyras and Cenchreis, the king and queen of Cyprus, overseeing the public sacrifices made in Venus's honor. Behind the monarchs stood their daughter, Myrrha, on the brink of womanhood. Her gaze was fastened on the young priest performing the ritual, and though he'd yet to feel it himself, Cupid had grown up in his mother's house and knew lust when he saw it. He grinned, one hand tightening on his bow as he reclaimed the other from his mother. What might this princess do with a little nudge?

It took mere seconds for Cupid to notch his arrow, aim, and let it fly. The people around him gave him confused looks at the sudden movement of his arms, but only his mother saw the bow or the arrow. The arrow sped through the air, past the ear of the priest, straight for Myrrha's shoulder, and Cupid tensed with anticipation of the magnitude by which her lust for the priest was about to grow.

Before the arrow found its home, however, King Cinyras spoke. And when King Cinyras spoke, his daughter's gaze flicked from the priest to her father. And just as Myrrha's gaze fixed on the back of her father's head, Cupid's arrow sank deep into her right shoulder.

The chaos that resulted from what appeared to be an attempted assassination ended the festivities for the day. Venus was furious with her son.

"What were you thinking?" she asked, red with anger. "This is my day, my one day, and you could not resist bringing your little play toy!"

Claiming Cypriote as her "one day" was a bit rich as far as Cupid was concerned, but he held his tongue on that. "It was for you," Cupid tried to explain. "My arrows do something, make people feel things. I wanted to provoke an uninhibited expression of love in your honor!"

Venus frowned. "What do you mean?"

Cupid explained the way animals he shot didn't die but rather began to hump whatever they'd been looking at when he shot them. "In some unpleasant situations, it's been my own leg," he said, "and they don't stop! I have to kill them to get my leg back. But it's like they cannot help it, like they are compelled by something greater than themselves. All fear, all rationality, all sense abandons in the face of a sudden affection and desire and need for release." He took a moment to breathe, to measure his mother's focus on him. Satisfied, Cupid lowered his voice as he continued.

"And what's more—I can provoke the opposite as well. I tried my hand at making my own arrows, but all I had for the heads was lead, and when I struck a sow with one of *those* arrows, well, she abandoned her own piglets, ignoring even their most desperate squeals." He paused again, seemingly back in the moment. "It was rather sad, really," Cupid mused.

Venus's mind raced. She'd never observed him hit something other than a target; she had left him to his own devices as soon as he was old enough to not accidentally shoot himself. In light of this new information, however, she agreed that they should observe the effects of the arrow on Myrrha.

The fate of the princess of Cyprus would become one of the most twisted tragedies in mythos. Cupid's arrow did, as intended, provoke an uninhibited expression of love, but the object of Myrrha's devotion was her own father. So obsessed did she become that she disguised herself one night, waiting in the dark for him to return to his bed, and before he realized her identity she had become pregnant. Fleeing

Cyprus to escape his wrath, the wretched Myrrha wandered, pregnant and alone, for thousands of miles until she finally collapsed in exhaustion, praying to the gods for mercy.

Having followed the girl's story with fascination for nearly a full human year by that point, Venus took pity on her and transformed her into a tree, henceforth known as the Myrrha. When she returned home, she sat her son down to discuss the powers he possessed.

"Love is not a thing with which to trifle," Venus said, stern, and while she was sincere in this conviction, the gleam in her eye nonetheless belied her words.

Cupid shrugged. "Okay. I won't trifle with it, then. I will treat love with the utmost respect."

"Yes, see that you do," Venus said, satisfied she had discharged her parental obligation.

And Cupid did try to keep his word; love just made for such entertaining spectacle in mortals and immortals alike. Despite being one of the youngest and least serious of the gods, even mighty Jupiter was vulnerable to Cupid's arrows, and the power of that was a heady thing.

As the centuries passed, the only incident for which Cupid felt true remorse was that of the mortal Adonis, whom he'd selected as a lover for Venus at a time when he really needed his mother's attention elsewhere. Adonis, Cupid was later amused to learn, was actually the very child Myrrha had conceived with her father, delivered of the tree by Juno and raised by nymphs. He'd grown into the loveliest mortal Cupid had ever beheld, and gifting the man to Venus by way of a well-aimed dart to his well-formed buttocks seemed both a thoughtful gesture on Cupid's part and an effective distraction from his own misadventures. However, upon witnessing his mother's devastation when Adonis was run through by a boar, Cupid felt the uncomfortable twinge of guilt.

No more, he decided. At least, not around his mother.

When Venus learned of his involvement, the full force of her wrath turned for the first time on her son.

"If this is the sort of thing that amuses you, then you are not worthy of the gift, and I shall take it back," she said, face blotchy and eyes still red from mourning her lover, her hands fisted tight around a bouquet of anemones she'd coaxed from the blood Adonis had spilled.

"I should like to see you try," Cupid responded, by this point a full head taller than her and much broader. The wings Mercury had given him, once longer than he was tall, appeared comic now, though they still supported him well.

"I grew you in my body and pushed you out into the world; do not question my ability to reclaim what I have given," Venus said.

"Moved now to threats on my life, then?" Cupid masked his discomfort with a lazy drawl designed to infuriate. "Really, Mother, he was a mortal. He would have died one day, anyway."

"Remove yourself from my sight," Venus choked, vibrating with fury and grief. "Return only when you are prepared to grovel at my feet for what you have done, for your thoughtlessness has robbed me of the greatest love I've known."

Cupid did remove himself then, but only far enough away to be out of sight. When he observed his mother departing, he followed her until he realized she was going to visit Vulcan. He had no interest in witnessing what was about to happen in the smith's forge but was satisfied that she would be cared for well enough and set off in search of his own distraction.

The relationship between mother and son was never quite the same after this incident, both too proud to apologize for anything they'd said or done, but neither prepared to abandon the other completely. And so they existed, in a state of uneasy truce, until the day another princess, this one of Crete, divided them once more.

CHAPTER 6

The visit with her sisters had left Psyche unsettled in a way she had never experienced before. Their leaving at the time of their marriages had been disruptive but expected; the natural order of things. But the pain she saw Cidippe navigating and the awareness that there was nothing she could do about it left Psyche's stomach twisted and sour.

This could not be the world, could it? And if it was, it did not have to be accepted—did it? Psyche thought about speaking to her parents but dismissed the idea, knowing that despite their nominal status as rulers of their small city-state, they were dependent on the terms of the wedding contracts. Psyche knew her own would be a strategic alliance as well.

She was not bothered by this, truly, but what she did want was some say in the process by which that alliance was selected. She would not marry a man who hurt her, not if she could help it. A few days after the first potential suitor had departed, Psyche saw her opportunity.

When Psyche's parents made it known that their youngest daughter was at last of marriageable age, they expected a quick engagement and marriage. The first man to visit was a winemaker from Athens, a successful and influential businessman with a poetic tongue and words so sweet they made Psyche feel a bit embarrassed. Nonetheless, he seemed kind enough, and from her father's expression after the two men emerged from discussions, a candidate under serious consideration.

It was Psyche's maid who first brought her the news three days later. The winemaker had visited a local tavern before he had departed, singing Psyche's praises with such passion and apparent eloquence that by the end of the evening, several songs had been composed in her honor, sung in rousing chorus by a full and well-soused audience. Psyche's name was on the lips of all those in the marketplace, her maid said, everyone wondering whether the little girl they remembered running after her sisters by the sea was now truly a beauty worthy of such composition.

Psyche did not hesitate, nor did she ask permission. She'd walked the markets during the courting periods for both her sisters; she knew the way the romantic unions of her family captured public imagination. She donned one of her finest gowns, had her maid dress her hair to its best advantage. The two women then set out for the market, baskets in hand, ready to be seen, to feed the curiosity of the rumor-mongers.

To the extent Psyche had thought through this impulse, her logic was that the more discussion her prospective marriage generated, the more invested the people of Lyktos would be in its outcome—after all, the alliances she and her sisters made were, ultimately, for the good of the city-state. The more invested her father's people were, the more he might have to consider their opinions. And if Psyche could influence those opinions, then maybe, just maybe, she could claim a bit of agency for herself.

Unfortunately for Psyche, however, the Fates had already turned their eye on her.

LYKTOS WAS KNOWN for its fair beaches, its port at Chersonesos, and its devotion to the lord Apollo. Psyche's own father had, in his youth, studied at a local temple of Apollo, and the sun god was a frequent visitor.

On one such visit, collecting tribute from his temples, Apollo was joined by Mercury, the two of them strolling through the marketplace, hoods up to protect their identities.

"Tribute would be a great deal more satisfying," Apollo groaned, rolling his shoulders, "if we didn't have to collect it ourselves."

Mercury laughed. "You sound like Neptune, complaining about the unfairness of Pluto's tribute being delivered to him."

Cutting his eyes at the messenger god as he sidestepped a youth barreling down the middle of the road, Apollo raised his eyebrows. "If anyone should be complaining about that, it's you. I've never understood how you manage to find time to do your own collection, especially with Mars ramping up by the day the number of souls in need of escort."

Mercury jiggled one winged heel at him. "Get yourself a pair of winged sandals, my friend."

Apollo's attention, though, had shifted. Coming toward them, about a hundred meters away, was a mortal woman of marked loveliness. "I think," said Apollo, "that perhaps I shall get myself one of those instead." He ran eager fingers through his hair. "I've not had a mortal in, oh, a decade?"

Mercury squinted at the figure in question, who had stopped to speak with a vendor selling flowers. He whistled. "I believe that's a princess of the island. The locals were singing of her beauty the other night; it was quite a riotous affair, actually."

The sun god was already nodding. "Yes, yes, such beauty in a human would be a princess." He clapped his hands together. "Well, Mercury, it appears I have one last appointment before I leave Crete, so I'll see you next at council."

Mercury put a hand out to stop him. "Wait—there, on the horizon?"

It was Apollo's turn to squint, and into focus came the form of an enormous eagle. The sun god groaned, throwing his head back in frustration. "Now? Truly?"

The eagle landed with smooth power on Apollo's shoulder, causing no shortage of cut eyes and outright stares from the surrounding crowd. Mercury muttered a few words of command into the air, and once again, eyes slid away from the small group, activity resuming around them. The eagle swiveled his head so one dark, severe eye fixed on the gods. "Greetings, Lord Mercury, Lord Apollo."

Inclining his head in return, the messenger god responded, "Aetos."

The great bird addressed Apollo. "Jupiter summons you, Lord Apollo, to Mount Olympus."

"Only me?" Apollo complained. "What about him?" He jerked a thumb at Mercury.

"The lord Mercury has other duties to complete."

Apollo rolled his eyes. "Well, tell my father I shall be there directly as soon as I've finished here." Aetos blinked at the sun god, the natural downward curve of his beak seeming to deepen. Apollo threw up his hands. "Fine, fine, I will come now, nevermind that I had *plans* and that it doesn't suit at *all*."

Mercury bid both the eagle and his half brother farewell, watching as Apollo strode out of town to where his chariot waited. Then he turned his attention back to the figure now departing the flower stall and coming his way again.

It amused him to consider that this girl would never know how close she had come to being taken by a god.

Without thinking too much about it, the god of mischief whispered a few more words into the air, then blew them toward the princess as she passed.

If the words reached her intact, and it was rare Mercury missed his mark, she would be rendered like a goddess for any mortal who gazed upon her, overwhelming and terrifying in her beauty.

In effect, she would be ruined for all but a god without ever even a threat to her virtue.

It was too delicious. Mercury took one last look at the girl. "Good luck, Your Highness," he said with a mock bow. Then he departed, leaving nothing but dusty footprints and a few fateful words in his wake.

· · ·

IF PSYCHE'S appearance in town had stoked the embers of interest the wine merchant had lit, the effect of Mercury's meddling was to set everything aflame.

As Psyche walked home from the market that day, she was startled at the way people gaped at her, averting their eyes as soon as she looked at them. A child pointed at her, saying, "Mommy, it's Venus!" and Psyche started to laugh at the silliness of that statement until she saw the mother's terrified expression, ushering her child back inside. She was feeling very strange by the time she arrived home and, in a rare occurrence, sought out her mother.

"Mother?" Psyche leaned into the room where her mother was sitting, speaking with one of the cooks. Both heads turned at the sound of her voice; both froze in uncommon stillness when their eyes fixed on her.

"You may depart, Apollonius," Psyche's mother said, gaze still on her daughter as though by force of will. The cook scrambled from the room, bowing low as he passed Psyche. "What have you done, child?" her mother asked, voice low and strained.

"I?" Psyche cried. "Nothing!"

Psyche's mother had always been, even in the bloom of her youth, considered more of a handsome woman than a beautiful one. Despite never speaking of it directly, all of her daughters had felt, at one point or another, their mother's relief at their own more conventionally attractive appearances.

Beauty, her mother had once been overheard to remark to a friend, was like money—best to have enough to comfortably secure options but not so much that one drew unwanted attention.

The expression Psyche witnessed now said that her youngest daughter had shifted, somehow, into the latter category.

Standing, her mother crossed to the doorway where Psyche stood, stopping a meter away. "You have prayed to Venus, is that it? She has granted you this?"

Psyche's head tilted, the panic she'd tamped down on her walk home rising. "I've prayed to no gods, just been to town. People gave me the strangest looks on my walk home, and now you shrink from me as if you fear me. What is going on?"

Her mother didn't respond, but turned and retrieved a hand mirror from a nearby table. Wordless, she held it up. In the glass, reflected back to her, Psyche saw her own face. Nothing more.

"Do you not see it?" her mother whispered when Psyche said nothing.

"No," Psyche whispered. "What should I see?" She watched the long column of her mother's neck move in a swallow.

"Gods help us."

GOSSIP TRAVELLED SWIFT AND FAR. By the time the next suitor arrived, he had heard whispers that the sweet Athenian wine merchant had been too awed by the princess Psyche's beauty to remain in her presence. When this new suitor at last beheld Psyche himself, he was overcome, falling to the ground at her feet.

"My lady," he said, breathless, eyes level with her toes. Above him, Psyche huffed.

"Stand, Phineas, we've known each other far too long for you to be behaving like this." She did not know him well, but Psyche could remember visits his family had made to stay with hers, days the children had spent playing on the beach.

Phineas did as instructed but kept his gaze averted. "You are far from the little girl I remember," he said, ears going pink.

"Well, I should hope so," said Psyche. "As you're here to discuss the possibility of marriage."

Shifting on his feet, Phineas went pale at her words. "Oh—no, that is, I would not presume, I am not—" He drew a deep breath, met her eyes for the barest of seconds. "I am not worthy, Lady Psyche."

And so saying, Phineas of Polyrrhenia fled the room.

WITH EVERY WEEK THAT PASSED, the rumors grew. Psyche was blessed by the gods, they said, raised above other mortal women by divine favor. Crowds gathered outside her home, first small, then larger and larger, all hoping to catch a glimpse of the famed princess. Trade through the port at Chersonesos slowed with the influx of visitors, inns becoming overcrowded, the markets low on food. More than blessed, many decided, Psyche must be the daughter of a god—Venus, perhaps—raised among mortals in secret.

The sturdy, political match her parents had hoped to find was impossible. Suitors showed up now for the spectacle, and none made serious offers. Psyche felt scared and angry and silly—had her impulsive trip to the market truly sparked all of this madness? She took to wearing a hood or face covering in public and withdrew more and more, spending most days in her rooms or private garden, and the sudden scarcity of her appearance drove the speculation to a fever pitch. There were those who began to call her the new Venus.

Altars sprung up outside her home; flowers, tokens, and other tribute were left by the door, more appearing almost before the previous could be cleared. Of even greater concern, ill-wishes began to appear, tucked among the offerings, tossed through windows, smuggled into the house in deliveries. They were herb-based charms, for the most part, but the intent behind them was nonetheless chilling. It was her cradle all over again, devotion that could kill her, only this time, her greatest protectors were gone.

CHAPTER 7

All of this might have remained a human hysteria had not Psyche been a princess of Crete. As an island, Crete was a frequent stop of the goddess Venus on days she traveled the seas. Though not the most devoted to the goddess of love, the island nonetheless was conveniently near her home on Kythera and a consistent source of prayer and tribute. Which was precisely what Venus was seeking on the fateful day that she learned of Psyche's existence.

"There is dust on the floor of this temple," Venus observed, withdrawing her bare foot from where it had been poised to step. Palaemon rushed ahead of her with a broom. "Stop!" Venus said. "It is beneath you. I shall chastise these priestesses for their indolence and visit instead the shrine on the east side."

But that shrine, too, was in clear neglect, with only paltry tribute to offer.

"What," Venus demanded of the priestess there, "is going on? Are the people of Crete so happy in love that they have forgotten whom to thank for the gift?" The priestess shook her head, an awkward endeavor from where she lay prostrate on the temple floor.

"No, my goddess," she said. "They have simply become distracted by the frenzy surrounding the princess Psyche. They shall return, I promise, once this fever dies down. I will continue to maintain your shrine so that it is shining for their return."

Venus studied the girl. "The princess Psyche?" she asked.

"Yes," came the priestess' quick reply. "Her beauty is apparently so great that no man can bear to wed her, and the people are saying she is blessed by you, and, well, others have mistakenly turned their devotion to her image, but they will soon see their error and return! I know they shall. The princess may be lovely, but she is just a human. She cannot compete with your magnificence." The girl snuck a peek at the goddess above her, then hastily returned her gaze to the floor at the fury she saw there. Counting the pieces of dust beneath her nose for what felt like years, when the priestess finally dared to glance up, Venus and her retinue had vanished.

VENUS STOOD at the entrance to Vulcan's workshop, wearing nothing more than a sheer wrap of white gauze. Vulcan's hammer did not freeze when he saw her, rather continued its work, falling still only when the blade was finished and ready for its final thrust into water. At this point, Vulcan lay his hammer carefully on his worktable, lifted his other arm to wipe sweat from his brow, and then finally, *finally*, turned to face his wife. His eyes consumed her lack of apparel, then rose to meet hers.

"What is this, then? Mars tired of your foot on his neck?"

Venus stepped forward, the gauze floating away. "I wouldn't know. He's been away, killing things. I'm here. Trying to make them grow." Her gaze flicked downward, and Vulcan snorted. At his laughter, Venus's face grew dark, and she stamped a foot. "I'm trying, Vulcan! You always complain that my attention is ever elsewhere, and now that I am trying you—"

"You're not trying," Vulcan said, stepping closer. "You're hurting. You only ever come to me when you're hurting. When you want to be hurt some more. Is that why you're here, oh Venus, wife of mine, for the hurt I can give you?"

Venus softened in an instant. "Yes," she breathed.

Vulcan considered her.

"Down," he ordered, and the goddess of love complied without protest, falling to her knees. Vulcan studied for a moment how the soot of the floor marred the clearness of her skin. Then he used a finger under her chin to lift her face so their eyes met. "If you truly want what I give you," he said, "I'll find you in this exact position when I return."

When he removed his hand, he saw he'd left a smudge of grease on her chin. Wiping his hands down the front of his apron, he left the workshop without a backward glance.

MUCH LATER, after Vulcan had indeed found Venus in the same position he had left her and after Venus had received that which she so desperately sought, Venus lay sprawled, sated, across the worktable as Vulcan began pulling on his clothes.

"The humans of Crete have begun worshipping one of their princesses as if she was a daughter of mine," Venus said to the ceiling. Vulcan was silent, then,

"That must be unpleasant for you."

Venus's leg shot out and kicked him in the stomach. "It's not only unpleasant for me, it's blasphemous," she snapped. "They're but a few generations into knowing me as Venus instead of Aphrodite, and now this. How would you like it if the mortals began seeking the work of some mortal smith over your own?"

"I wouldn't," Vulcan admitted, "but it has never come to that because I mind my position."

At this, Venus sat up. "Are you suggesting"—her chin rose as she spoke—"that I am in any way lax in my responsibilities?"

Vulcan regarded her. "I'm not suggesting, I'm stating. You visit the temples only when you are low on tribute, miss more council meetings than you attend, and flit from lover to lover like a bee collecting pollen. No, worse than that—more like a hunter collecting trophies."

"I am the goddess of *love!*" Venus's spine was straight and her voice high. "I believe that *lovemaking* falls within the job description."

Vulcan's laugh filled the room. "Do you call what we did here lovemaking?" His tone was mocking. "Regardless, I'm glad to know the source of your sudden ardor for me. I hope you got what you needed."

Venus's eyes filled with sudden tears, which she wiped away with an impatient hand. "I do," she whispered. And then louder, "I did." And then she slid off the worktable, swept up her now soot-stained gauze, and was out the door before Vulcan could so much as utter another word.

CUPID DESCENDED onto his mother's veranda with caution. The tern that had summoned him had been more agitated than usual, with feathers in disarray, and Cupid had more than enough experience to know what that meant.

"Cupid!" Venus's voice came from inside. "Come, join me!" Taking a steadying breath, Cupid swept aside the curtains and walked into the main room.

"Mother," he greeted her, pressing a kiss to her cheek. She leaned into him, one hand going up to cup his face before he pulled away.

"How are you?" Venus asked, standing back to admire her son with a sharp eye. "Your hair is lighter—you've been outdoors more." Cupid nodded, wandering across the room and snagging a peach leftover from his mother's midday meal.

"Mhmm," he hummed in agreement, biting into the peach. He used the back of his hand to wipe juice from his chin as he chewed and swallowed. "Had some business to clear up with Apollo; it took longer than anticipated."

Venus narrowed her eyes. "Cupid." She drew out his name in the way of one who suspects they will not like the answer to the question they are about to ask. "What have you done?"

Cupid's eyes went wide, his hands waving in protest of his innocence, sending drops of peach juice flying. "I did nothing, Mother, besides defend my name and"—his gestures of protest slowed, and a slight smile curved his mouth—"perhaps provide a bit of humility to the all-powerful, infallible Apollo." He finished his peach as Venus continued to consider him. Once done, he tossed the pit out the window before collapsing onto a couch in a heap of long limbs. Venus exhaled in irritation.

"Go pick that up, I do not need a peach tree growing in the middle of my lilies."

Cupid closed his eyes, head falling to rest on the back of the couch. "Not now, Mother. I'll get it before I depart, I promise."

Venus blew out a breath of irritation but let the subject drop. She sat in a chair across from her son. "Tell me about this endeavor to spark Apollo's humility."

Cupid did not open his eyes. "Do you really want to hear or are you just going to scold me?"

Venus arched a brow. "Both."

"Ah. Well." His posture changed in an instant, spine straightening and leaning forward to rest his elbows on his knees as he met her gaze with an eager pride. "Apollo has always been a prick; you've said so yourself." Venus inclined her head. "Listening to him go on about how fortunate he felt to keep his name while everyone else had to reshape their public identities was bad enough but after he turned that wretched Python at Delphi into a pincushion, he became insufferable. Spouting off about it to anyone who was around and hosting reenactments of his great feat and beginning construction at Delphi for a new temple in his own honor. Insufferable. But I paid it little mind until the day he found me preparing to go on a hunt of my own."

"A hunt for what?" Venus asked.

"Honestly? I hadn't yet decided. I was a bit bored and looking to try my hand at something new—perhaps it would be amusing to cause a stag to fall in love with a rabbit, I don't know. Anyway, Apollo sees me stringing my bow and starts in on me." Cupid squared his shoulders, puffing out his chest and tilting his chin up in a rather uncanny imitation of the oracular god. "'Boy, when are you going to trade a child's weapons for those of a man? If you've tired of playing your little games of love, I can teach you to hit wild beasts and wound your enemies with a single shot—you remember what I did to the Python at Delphi!—but you will need to let go of your mother's skirts and drop that baby bow first.'"

Venus began to laugh. "Oh dear," she said, rubbing a hand over her face.

Grinning to see his mother's amusement, Cupid leaned back, one foot coming up to rest on a knee and hands lacing behind his head. "Precisely. So I decided to show him just how powerful my 'little games of love' can be."

"Cupid, did you have anything to do with—"

"Daphne? Of course." He beamed.

Venus sighed. "Tell me the rest of it, then."

"A couple of months ago, when I was visiting Thessaly, Peneus complained to me of his daughter Daphne, who had gotten caught up in this cult of Diana's and was swearing she would remain a virgin forever and this was a problem for Peneus because he's a sentimental old bastard who wants grandchildren. So I offered my services in the matter, figuring it would curry favor with Peneus for the future."

Venus frowned. "I'm wary of the shape this story is taking, but continue."

"Well, when I finally found Daphne, Mother, she was beautiful. I mean, what a waste as a virgin. And I was halfway to convincing her of that and potentially making Peneus my own father-in-law when Diana showed up and stuck her own damn arrow in my ass and told me if I ever came near the nymph again, she'd set her hounds on me." Cupid's expression soured with the memory.

Venus sighed. "So you managed to offend both of the twins, then."

Cupid shrugged. "It was my business they interrupted, not the other way around. Regardless, a few weeks later, after Apollo interrupted my hunt, I saw my opportunity."

Venus held up a hand to halt him. "Wait, I suspect I will want something stronger than ambrosia for this part of the story." She stood and crossed to the table, granting herself a generous pour of wine before turning to face her son again, cup cradled between her palms. "Continue."

"Daphne visited Delphi."

Even as Venus's brows lowered in disapproval, the corner of her mouth twitched."Oh, no—no, Cupid, you didn't."

Cupid's grin reached his ears. "What? It was so easy. A golden arrow to Apollo to provoke love, a leaden one to Daphne to cement her disgust, and I sat back and watched them play the game. Well, I chased them together a *little*, but mostly I just watched."

"But Cupid"—Venus tried to be upset—"she was turned into a *tree* in her efforts to escape Apollo's affections. That alone is going to affect our relationship with Peneus for decades, possibly centuries!"

Cupid's brow furrowed. "What? No, Peneus is the one who effected the transformation."

Venus was startled. "He was?"

"I was as surprised as you; I'd thought to have a little fun, a little revenge—maybe even complete my service to Peneus in the process. But I guess old Peneus figured if he wasn't going to get grandchildren in nymph form, at least he could have them in flower form and keep his daughter from being raped in the process. Unexpected, these river gods."

"Just so," Venus murmured.

"And now"—Cupid started laughing—"*now*, Apollo's declared the winners of his idiotic Pythian Games will henceforth be crowned with *laurel leaves*, in Daphne's honor, and honestly, Mother, it's too good."

"Hmm." Mother and son sat in silence for a while, the former sipping her wine and considering Cupid over the rim of the glass while the latter remained sprawled across her couch, head resting on a pillow and eyes shut.

"What is it Mother?" Cupid asked without opening his eyes. "I can feel your gaze hot on my face, and your wretched tern was quite perturbed, so I know you have summoned me for more than an update on my escapades. What do you need?"

Venus's response was cool. "I? What could I possibly need beyond love and affection and the occasional unprompted visit from the very one I brought into this world?"

Sighing, Cupid cracked his neck. "Here we go," he muttered.

Venus's eyes flashed. "Watch your tone, child. Never forget how I allowed my body to swell and morph and rearrange its very organs to create space for you to grow. The least you can do is visit me, particularly when my soul is under attack."

58

"Your soul?" Cupid was skeptical. "Is that not a touch dramatic, Mother?"

"It is not," she snapped. "It is accurate. Do you know how little tribute I collected there? Hardly enough to be worthy of a demigod. The mortals on Crete are abandoning my temples en masse; who is to say their disrespect won't spread? Daily, your father works to tempt my followers to his own religion of commerce, dismissing love as a frivolous pursuit of the foolhardy. I cannot afford to have Crete's trend spread; already, I feel weaker."

"I don't know what's happening on Crete, but let's not pretend that Mercury's hobbies are of any threat to your standing. You and I both know that love is as vital to humans as the air they breathe. Dispense with the theatrics and speak plainly: what lesson would you have me hand down in Crete? Shall they all fuck themselves to death in an island-wide orgy?"

Venus sniffed loudly, then sighed. "It is not a hard thing I ask." A plaintive note crept into her voice. "You need not speak so crudely. I've half a mind to send you away, so hurt and insulted am I by your lack of care."

At this, Cupid scrubbed both hands over his face, then swung himself off the couch, falling to one knee before his mother and taking one of her hands in both of his. "I am sorry," he said. "Tell me what you need."

CHAPTER 8

Cupid landed outside Lyktos just as the rolling storm clouds he'd been racing caught up, a boom of thunder reverberating along his spine as the lightest raindrops began dotting his chiton. Cursing under his breath, he shrugged out of his wings, pulling from his satchel the treated leather covering he'd crafted to protect them and shoving in the wings with as much care as he could.

Water would not ruin them by any means, but they did take a bit of time to dry, and Cupid was not interested in being stuck waiting on Crete.

Once his wings were protected, Cupid slung them up to hang across his shoulder and made his way uphill in the increasing downpour toward the small temple dedicated to his mother that stood at the top of the hill. Reaching the building, he bounded up the stairs, sighing with relief once he was under cover. There was a flash of lightning and the side of Cupid's mouth pulled up.

"I wonder whether Jupiter and Juno are fighting or fucking?" he mused, then grinned to himself. "Maybe both?"

He swung his satchel and his covered wings down to rest against the base of a statue of Venus, moderate both in size and skill, rolling his shoulders and squeezing out his wet hair as he considered this likeness of his mother.

The statue looked nothing like her, of course, but it did possess a certain magnetic quality she had—it was hard to look away. Created decades before, the goddess of love was depicted nude, a red painted apple held in one hand, moments from a bite, a red gold robe falling from her waist as if it had only moments before slipped down from her shoulders. When Cupid looked closer, he saw there were even tiny holes in her ears where earrings would have once sat, though they were empty at the moment, doubtless robbed years before.

It was not a magnificent statue, but the love of the sculptor was clear, and it ignited in Cupid a resentment on his mother's behalf. How dare the humans of this island abandon her with such casual ease. He might find her trying at times, but that was a different thing, and besides, he was a god and her equal. The mortals needed a reminder of their place in things, of their responsibilities to the gods.

There was a sound from the rear of the temple, and out scurried a young priestess, who started upon seeing Cupid. It took her but a moment to register her situation, and she sank to the floor in homage.

"The temple is honored, my lord," she whispered, nose to the cold stone for the second time that week.

Cupid smiled, crouching beside her and running an appreciative hand down her shoulder.

"As you should be," he said, sitting on the floor and clasping his arms around his knees. "And I thank you for the respect; please, sit up and be comfortable. Mother directed me to you as a loyal servant of her temple; you have nothing to fear from me."

The girl hesitated for a moment, then pulled herself up to sit, kneeling across from the god.

"I am grateful to hear Venus recognizes our devotion," she murmured. "It has been hard of late—I imagine that is why you are here?" She dared a glance up at Cupid from under a sweep of hair that had loosened from her plait, then immediately returned her gaze to her lap. Cupid considered her, a small smile spreading as he studied her.

"Yes," he said, "it is. But we need not tend to business right away." He reached out a hand, drawing one finger gently down her cheek. "Mother appreciates your loyalty, as do I." The girl remained silent, and so Cupid was more direct. "Have you ever spent the night with a god?"

"I am a virgin, my lord." Her voice was faint. Cupid smiled.

"So many of you are." His thumb strayed to trace her neck from ear to shoulder and back again. "What a waste, don't you think? How can you ever properly serve the goddess of love if you've never known it yourself?"

"I have," she said. "I have known love; I serve the goddess in her memory."

"Ah"—Cupid's tone was warm—"one of the greatest tributes you could offer. What was her name?"

"Adamantia." She was barely audible, Cupid having to duck his head to catch the name.

"Adamantia," he repeated, shifting to his own knees and reaching for her hands. "Well, in Adamantia's memory, let me give you the pleasure she no longer can."

The priestess's eyes stayed fixed on her lap, where the god's large hands now covered her own. Cupid used a forefinger to tilt her chin up until their eyes met. Hers were wide.

"Say yes," he said, soft. Her chest rose and fell with her breaths, increasingly erratic. Cupid leaned in, brushing a featherlight kiss across her cheekbone. "Say yes." He repeated both the words and the kiss, moving to her other cheek, then to her forehead. "Say yes." Now he was at her ear, his mouth brushing just below, tongue glancing across her pulse and making her flinch. Her shoulders fell.

"Yes," she whispered.

LATER, when the storm had passed and Cupid had been sated, he lounged, half-dressed, in the priestess's narrow bed, watching as she pulled on her clothes and replaited her hair.

"I would hear your thoughts," he said, "on the best way to draw close to the princess Psyche, undetected. From Mother's report, she seems to have become a recluse."

The priestess nodded. "That is what I have heard," she said. "It is, in my observation, my lord, a hysteria created and driven by those caught up in the mythologizing that has taken place; the princess is innocent."

"Innocent?" Cupid laughed. "What does that matter?" The girl flushed, and the corner of Cupid's mouth raised in amused consideration. "Little priestess—what is your name, by the way?"

The priestess bit her lip, tying the end of her braid carefully. "Iolanthe."

"Violet flower, lovely. Well, Iolanthe, come back to bed and let me tell you a story." The girl sat on the edge of the bed, but Cupid pulled her down to lie beside him, resting her head on his shoulder. He played with her braid as he spoke.

"When I was a child, centuries ago now, I was often alone, with only a nurse or one of my mother's birds for company. Consequently, any time I was permitted my wings, I would use them to search out playmates, and though Mother always insisted one of the wretched terns accompany me, still those flights were bright spots for me, especially when I spotted children my age in play." He paused, lifting Iolanthe's hand to place it on his chest. "Gentle caresses with the tips of your fingers," he ordered. His own went behind his head, and he closed his eyes in memory.

"On one such day, I was playing with two boys, brothers, on the beach in front of their house. We had run and swum and built structures in the sand, but at some point, one of them laughed at my castle, boasting his own would stand far longer. Angry, I declared that, in fact, it would not stand a second more and I kicked down the little village he had been crafting. He shoved me, then, so that I fell, and his yells brought the attention of their mother, who, upon seeing me and spotting my wings against a nearby rock, turned pale with the knowledge of my identity and ushered them inside. I finished my castle, then returned home, mentioning only in an offhand way to my mother what had happened." Cupid's eyes opened, seeking those of the priestess.

"But the next morning, at the foot of my bed, lay two right arms, one shorter than the other, and a dead tern. When I ran to Mother about it, she said yes, the tern had confessed to the incident, and so she had sent her servant, Palaemon, to deal with the matter. When I sought Palaemon, I asked him why he had taken an arm from each boy—only one of them had presumed violence on me. Palaemon did not even look up at me, polishing Mother's chariot as he replied, 'I didn't know which one pushed you.'"

The priestess was silent, her fingers stilled on his chest. When Cupid spoke again, his voice had cooled. "So you see, violet flower, the princess Psyche's innocence is hardly the point."

Iolanthe sat up as his hold loosened on her, spine straight.

"My apologies, my lord, I overstepped. I offer you rumors that would-be lovers have found success sneaking into a garden adjacent to her rooms, but I cannot speak to the accuracy of this."

Cupid nodded. "Excellent. I shall rest in your room until daybreak; I now need my privacy." So saying, he flipped to his side, tucking a hand beneath his head and closing his eyes once more.

Iolanthe lowered her eyes as she retreated from her own room in a half bow. "Of course, my lord. Rest well, my lord."

CUPID REACHED PSYCHE'S PARENTS' estate by mid-morning, with only one additional stop for directions. Upon arriving, he quickly located the gardens that Iolanthe had referenced and stood, legs apart and hands on hips, considering the overlooking balconies.

"Which one, do we think?" he murmured. A frog croaked a response from somewhere among the flowers. Cupid's gaze sharpened. He crouched down, holding out a gentle hand and humming softly in the back of his throat. "Come here, little friend. Come, sit upon my hand."

After several long minutes, the frog emerged, tentative, from the bright peonies. The amphibian lowered its head as it eyed Cupid, still suspicious despite the lulling cadence of Cupid's words and humming. Eventually, however, the magnetism of the god could not be denied, and the tiny creature hopped closer and closer until it sat right in the center of Cupid's palm. Slowly, so as not to startle the frog, Cupid brought his hand close to his face, regarding the animal seriously.

"Thank you," he said. "Your sacrifice is appreciated." He gently closed his fingers around the frog and then slipped the squirming animal into a small satchel at his waist, pulling the drawstring tight to prevent escape.

The centerpiece of the garden was an ancient olive tree, thick as ten men standing together and so deeply gnarled that it was a favorite hiding place of all sorts of animals and insects. This also made it an excellent climbing tree, as Psyche and her sisters had discovered when they were children, and the dense foliage on top rendered the climber virtually invisible once they ascended into the upper branches. Into this tree, Cupid now hauled his body and his weapon, settling himself on a thick branch, back against the knobby trunk, to wait for the appearance of the princess Psyche. On his thigh, his satchel hopped and jerked about in indignation.

He was not waiting long. Days after a storm had long been Psyche's favorite in the garden, the wet smell of the soil and cheerful chirrups of insect life calming her in a way that little else did. A bit before noontime, she emerged—not onto one of the upper balconies as Cupid had expected, but instead from a door at ground level that opened directly into the garden itself.

Cupid shifted on his branch, straightening as he craned his neck to see through the leaves. What an unfortunate situation. His position was best suited for an arrow shot upwards, through the leaves and toward the balconies. He'd been counting on this. Was this really Psyche? Perhaps it was another woman of the house.

Cupid caught sight of the woman in the garden and let out a sigh. This had to be Psyche. She was the right age, quite lovely, and she looked sad. When he heard someone from inside the house call her name and her head turned in response, he was certain. Well, he'd done his work under less ideal circumstances; he'd just have to make do.

Psyche sat on a stone bench several meters away from the tree where Cupid sat concealed and closed her eyes as she tilted her face up to the sun. Cupid saw his chance. A quick arrow to her side, a deft transformation of the frog in his satchel, and the great myth of the beautiful Psyche of Crete would end in the horror of her love for a hideous, inhuman creature, her lust for such a being making mockery of the devotions so many on Crete had redirected from Venus to this girl. The trickiness of the shot notwithstanding, it was a simple plan—elegant, even—and as Cupid reached behind him for an arrow, he applauded his own cleverness.

What happened next was not clear, but all would later agree it was a mistake. One moment, Cupid was drawing out an arrow. The next, the frog on his thigh gave a great leap before soaking the small satchel —and Cupid's thigh—with its urine. And then, as Cupid fixed his eye on Psyche to line up his shot, something shifted.

Had he thought her lovely? What rubbish. With her face illuminated like that, she was as fair as a goddess—more fair than most. His eyes fixed on the shine of her hair, the slope of her breasts, the curve of her waist. His breath caught in his throat. He'd never been in the presence of more exquisite a creature.

The frog was getting frantic. Cupid returned the arrow to its quiver, his fingers finding the ties on the satchel and loosening until the terrified amphibian was able to lurch free, tumbling down the branches of the tree, all while Cupid's eyes never left Psyche. It was more than beauty; he could tell. She was kind. And generous. And loving. And she would be so soft to touch—oh, how he wanted to touch her! To tell her! To tell her what?

Cupid froze. He loved her. He knew it with a certainty deep in his being; she was the love of his life, and he was on the brink of hopping down from the tree to tell her that when another image flashed through his mind.

His mother, eyes glittering over a glass of wine, lips curled as she described the fate she wished Cupid to bring about for Psyche of Crete.

Cupid groaned, a soft sound swallowed by the rustling of the leaves in the breeze. He could not admit his love; it would be as a death sentence to Psyche, and more, he'd have to ride out the waves of his mother's wrath alone, bereft of his beloved.

No, he could not proclaim his love. Not now. Not like this. But surely there was a way for them to be together, surely, if he put his mind to it.

Cupid remained in the tree for the next hour, his eyes devouring

Psyche's every move, every exhalation, the quiet words she exchanged with a maid who came out to relay a message. When she finally returned inside, he climbed down, crossing to the bench where she'd sat for so long and resting his hand on the still warm stone.

"Soon, my love," he promised. "We shall be together again soon."

PART TWO

CHAPTER 9

Cupid paced in front of the entrance to Apollo's suite of rooms on Mount Olympus, nervous for perhaps the first time since he was a child. Just as he drew a deep breath and was about to enter, a voice came from within.

"I can hear you, Venus's spawn, either come in or depart immediately. And if you come in, I expect groveling."

All nerves fled in the face of the irritation this aroused, and Cupid marched into the room.

"You'll have none of it, sunspot, and do tell me—how are the laurel leaves working out?"

"They are perfection," Apollo snapped from where he sat at a window, plucking at a lyre, "as was their origin, whom you ruined with your inability to curb childish impulses."

Cupid's eyes widened. "*My* inability to curb impulses? Uncle, I do believe it was from your ardor Daphne sought protection. How many times must a woman say no before transforming into a tree becomes preferable to lying with you?"

Apollo's eyes shone with unshed tears, his fingers absently plucking low, mournful chords. "Ah, Cupid, we both know you soured her affections against me, and now, for the crime of challenging you to better yourself, I have forever lost the love of my life."

With a start, Cupid realized that while Apollo correctly identified the role Cupid's arrows had played in Daphne's feelings, the sun god seemed oblivious to the influence of those arrows on his own. He pressed his lips together and inclined his head in an effort to mask the triumphant delight threatening to burst forth from his expression.

"That is, indeed, a tragedy, and one for which I offer both my condolences and my, ah, apologies."

Apollo eyed him with suspicion, then sniffed. "Why is it you are here? You are not sorry for your actions, so you can dispense with that pretense."

Cupid shrugged, picking up a discus and tossing it into the air, then catching it when it came down. "Well, I am sorry, Uncle, insofar as I now need your help, and while I consider our disagreement a thing of the past, I recognize that your loss places me on the back foot. So I've come to ask what I can do, what service I can offer, that might induce you to aid me."

Apollo set aside the lyre. "Nothing springs to mind," he said, "but pray, continue with your request."

Cupid heaved a great sigh, the nerves returning so that when his admission emerged, it did so in a sudden, jumbled exhale.

"I've fallen in love."

Apollo gave a short laugh, which, upon observing that Cupid did not speak in jest, turned to a full-bodied guffaw.

"Oh, you are your father's son, to come to me now, in the time of my bereavement, asking for help in love. Titans, but one Mercury was enough. Go on then, tell me of this object of your love. Nymph? God? Demigod? Male in form or female? Does their nature seem more flower to you or fern? Trees are passé at this point, but I'm confident anyone worthy of your love would make a stunning fern." Apollo's voice was so acid that Cupid nearly turned and left. Only by fixing an image of his mother's reaction if she ever learned of his love did Cupid manage to stay in the room. When he found his voice again, it was firm.

"I will continue this conversation only in good faith, Apollo. I am sorry that Daphne ended up as she did, but that was ultimately out of my control. I do not expect any favors; I offer my services in exchange for your own. If such an agreement is of no interest to you or is currently beyond your emotional capacity, I'll depart. I shall not tell you the name of the one I love until I am secure you will not act against us."

The gods' eyes met, Apollo considering his nephew. "You really are bit by your own arrow, aren't you?" Apollo murmured, scratching his jaw as he thought. Cupid did not respond, merely held his gaze. At length, Apollo let out a lingering sigh.

"Alright then, let us come to an agreement. There is, as it happens, a youth whose affections I could use your help obtaining."

"Oh?" Cupid refrained from commenting on the speedy nature of Apollo's apparent recovery from the loss of Daphne. "Do elaborate." Apollo wagged a finger at him, crossing the room to retrieve a pomegranate. Pulling a knife from his belt, he sliced the top of the fruit enough that he could pry it open with his thumbs. Leaning against a marble column, he plucked a few seeds from the rind with delicate fingers, popping them into his mouth.

"Ah, no, Nephew, a name for a name. And considering the scales, you will go first." Cupid noticed Apollo's lips had darkened with the stain from the pomegranate juice.

"Well, there is one more promise I need before I tell you," Cupid admitted. Apollo continued to pick out pomegranate seeds. "My mother must not, under any circumstances, learn of my love or of our arrangement." Apollo started, spewing seeds.

"Oh ho, intrigue! Nephew, you have much to learn. If you had begun the conversation with this, we could have skipped the tiresome back and forth." He set down the remaining fruit, then sat on a couch, indicating for Cupid to sit next to him. "Come. Share. Tell me exactly what it is we must keep secret from the goddess of love and why you have come to me and not your father."

Relieved with the sudden shift in mood, Cupid sank down beside Apollo. "Well, I should think it obvious why I came to you; for all your faults, Uncle—and you have many—you are able to keep a confidence. Mercury is not."

Apollo nodded his agreement. "This is true."

"As for why it must be kept from my mother," Cupid continued, "I fear the strength of her displeasure should she learn the identity of the one to whom I've given my love."

Apollo studied him. "Venus's displeasure is indeed a thing to be feared, but I confess myself confused. She's only ever been delighted by your love affairs—bragged of them, even, and of the beauty and intelligence of your lovers. You are her creation, and so your loves bring honor to her own purpose, unless..." Understanding dawned. "Oh, Cupid—you didn't—don't tell me you were stupid enough to—" Cupid's unhappy face was more than sufficient a response. Apollo nodded slowly. "Well. I, too, would be scared; how on Gaia's green Earth did this happen?"

Cupid stood, pacing, anxious hands flexing by his sides. "It was not intentional, I swear it! And it was Mother's own fault, really. She asked me to hit Psyche with an arrow to make her love the lowliest, most horrifying creature I could find. She's angry, of course, that the humans in Crete are neglecting her temples for the cult of Psyche, and as well she should be. But none of that is Psyche's fault; she does not seek her beauty, it but radiates from her soul."

"I imagine that was not in your mind when you set out to do Venus's bidding." Apollo's voice was dry.

"Of course not," Cupid snapped, "I had not yet beheld her. I intended to do as Mother asked—I'd even found a creature suitable for the purpose—but Apollo, when I saw her face, her hair, the curves of her body..."

"Yes, yes," Apollo laughed, "I understand quite where your mind went. Though I'm still astounded it managed to rule over your loyalty to your mother. Is it possible you were, in fact, literally pricked by your own arrow?" Cupid froze, coming to an abrupt stop as his mind turned over this possibility, Apollo watching him with one eyebrow by his hairline. Cupid's response was slow.

"No," he finally said, "or possibly?"

Apollo shrugged, rolling his shoulders. "Well, I suppose it doesn't matter; what is done is done, and now you cannot rest until you've had this girl, but Venus can't know, or she'll have her killed, and Mercury can't know because it is far too delightful a piece of gossip to keep all to himself, even for his own son. Do I have the gist of it?"

74

Cupid nodded, miserable, collapsing once more beside his uncle. "And what of you?" he asked. "Can you keep it to yourself? Was I right to come here?"

"That all depends." A gleam in his eyes, Apollo shifted to face Cupid. "Are you prepared to hand over one of your arrows?"

"My arrows? Of course not, but I am at your disposal for their use. You mentioned a youth you want—yours, if you help me."

Apollo stood, retrieving his half-eaten pomegranate, hand waving a dismissal of Cupid's words. "No, no, that won't do at all. I will have Hyacinth, but I will not trust you to deliver his affections. I am prepared to let the issue of Daphne rest, but I would be a fool to forget your treatment of us. No, if you want my aid, that is my price: a single arrow given to my hand for my own use as I see fit. There is no negotiation." So saying, he raised the shell of fruit to his mouth, using his teeth to scrape down the remaining seeds, red juice flowing down his chin and neck and chest. He closed his eyes as he chewed and swallowed. "Perfectly ripe; sweet and tart in equal measure." Apollo lifted the neckline of his tunic, wiping away the mess as Cupid considered his words. Finally—

"Agreed."

Apollo clapped his hands. "Wonderful! Now, how can I help?"

CHAPTER 10

Psyche's parents journeyed to visit the acclaimed Pythia at Delphi less from religious conviction than a growing sense that the phenomenon surrounding their youngest daughter was reaching levels beyond human ability to navigate. Even with Psyche confined to the house, the flow of devotion had not slowed. There were even those who had been found sleeping along the outside walls of their home, waiting for hours on the off chance that they might catch a glimpse of the princess whispered to be a goddess.

"Crazy," Psyche had heard her father mutter one morning as he peered out a window to the packed street below. "They're all crazy."

"Not crazy," her mother had corrected. "They're devout, and therein lies the danger."

Something needed to be done, words passed down to all of those elevating Psyche to such a precarious pedestal, and those words needed to come from an authority higher than that of men.

Apollo's temple in Delphi, founded after his legendary defeat of a monstrous python plaguing the area, was the seat of his oracular practice. He was said to speak through a chosen priestess, who was given the title of Pythia, and the oracles issued were accepted as divine proclamation.

So it was to Delphi, with offerings of laurel branches and gold, that Psyche and her parents made their way.

The temple itself stood at the center of a great complex, surrounded by smaller temples and residences. The whole complex was built into the rocky side of a mountain, and grassy terraces softened the angle of the path to the main building.

As they climbed, Psyche watched the children playing on the grass from beneath her hood. The sun shone on their hair as they ran and laughed and screamed with delight. Psyche felt a pang; when had she last played? Could she join them rather than continue up these never-ending stairs? Temple children needed care like any others; perhaps the Oracle would demand her service—Psyche did not hate that thought.

When they finally reached the top and stood before Apollo's temple, Psyche's mother laid a hand on her daughter's shoulder as the three of them considered the statues before them: Apollo in the center, flanked on one side by his sister Diana, and on the other by Minerva, the goddess of wisdom. Psyche stiffened under her mother's touch; she was not used to such physical comfort from that quarter.

"We will find guidance here, Psyche, I can feel it," her mother said, not quite meeting her eyes. Her father grunted in agreement.

"If any god holds the answers, it's Apollo."

A priest emerged from the temple, his steps sure and unhurried, his gaze somehow both fixed on them and miles away.

"Welcome"—the priest opened his arms—"to Apollo's Temple and the Oracle at Delphi. Psyche of Crete, we have been expecting you."

Psyche blinked. They had not sent advance notice of their visit in an effort to avoid further feeding the rumors. Psyche's father, however, looked pleased at the greeting.

"Our thanks. We seek an audience with the Oracle and guidance for our daughter's future."

The priest nodded. "Your audience has already been secured; the Oracle will see you after the midday hour. Rest here or in the gymnasium just beyond—there you will find students engaged in sport and lessons; you are welcome to observe them while you are here."

Psyche's parents murmured their thanks, and the priest disappeared back into the temple. The three visitors made their way toward the building the priest had indicated. Psyche hurried her step to walk beside her father, head tilted in confusion.

"How did they anticipate our arrival?" Psyche asked. "Did you send a messenger after all?"

Her father glanced down at her as he led them into the gymnasium. "No, but I take this as a good omen. Surely, the gods themselves have seen our plight and prepared a solution."

Somehow, Psyche did not find this thought as reassuring as her father intended.

Inside, a great open space bustled with activity. In one corner, a group of young boys sat around a table, tablets in hand, as they listened to a lecture handed down by a priest who appeared little older than Psyche. In the center, on an open, grassy expanse, another group of boys, slightly older, practiced wrestling. Scattered about were small groups or lone students apparently working independently. The novelty distracted Psyche from her worry, and she absorbed it all with fascination. She'd never imagined such a place.

Her father was leaning forward, elbows on his knees as he also took in the activity. "Nothing like a temple school," he commented to Psyche, and she imagined one of his hands twitched as though in memory of his own days spent wrestling. "My days at the Temple of Apollo on Crete were wonderful. Best times of my life."

Psyche searched for something to say in response but came up with nothing. The family found a quiet bench along the wall to sit, resting their legs and observing the activity. After some time, another priest came to offer them some water and bread with olives, which they accepted with thanks. Unused to being in each other's presence, they exchanged very few words as they ate, and Psyche's attention wandered back to the boys at their studies. She wondered what their futures held, whether even they knew yet. Why did the possibility of their uncertain futures seem like a gift, while her own felt like a sword at her neck?

As the sun began to sink lower on the horizon, they were summoned.

"The Oracle will see you now."

Psyche started, tearing her focus from her attempt to make out the topic of study across the room. Before them stood the original priest, his expression solemn. Parents and daughter stood, brushing crumbs from their laps and following him toward the main temple.

A hand slipped into Psyche's, and she glanced over, noting the apprehension written on her mother's face. Surprised, Psyche offered a tight smile.

"It's going to be alright, Mother," she whispered. "You said yourself you knew we'd find guidance here." Both women eyed the wisps of smoke beginning to curl out from the temple, wrapping about the top of the columns.

"Yes," her mother whispered back, "but I have a sudden foreboding about what that guidance may be."

IT WOULD LATER OCCUR to Psyche that her mother's foreboding was well-placed.

"A snake-like monster." Psyche repeated the words the priest had translated for them from the incomprehensible mutterings of the Pythia. "This is a dream; it must be a dream."

The three of them sat outside the temple, on the grass, her father's hand on her mother's knee. All were miserable. Her father scraped a hand down his face.

"What do we do?" he muttered. "What kind of answer is this?"

Psyche held out some hope, on the journey home and for the days after they returned, that perhaps her parents would disregard the Oracle. Though they raised Psyche and her sisters to respect the gods and observe the proper devotions, they had never been as fanatical as Psyche knew some could be. Surely, they would find another way to pacify the gods; a donation to the temple school, perhaps, or a city-wide feast in Apollo's honor. The Pythia might be the most famed and feared oracle in all of Greece, but Psyche was their daughter, and that had to count for something.

"Adorn this girl, O king, for wedlock dread,
And set her on a lofty mountain-rock."

That was what the Oracle had decreed. That she be left on a

mountain rock to be fetched by her bridegroom, who was to be a "barbaric, snake-like monster." The absurdity of it strained credulity.

The day after they arrived back home, Psyche listened at her parents' door.

"We can go again to the Pythia," Psyche's father said, voice high with nerves. "Ask for a different prophecy. That priestess was hardly more than a child—perhaps they got it wrong."

Psyche felt her hopes rise at this. She heard her mother sigh, and the despair in it was less encouraging.

"What time do we have for such an effort, and to what end? The prophecy has been made; to question it now would be to challenge the voice of Apollo himself."

"Well"—her father was struggling, it seemed, to find words—"but who is to say it was Apollo? Could easily have been a human trick; surely Apollo wouldn't begrudge us a second opinion."

Psyche's mother barked out a laugh at that, the sound brittle. "I cannot believe I'm hearing this from one who attended school in one of Apollo's temples. Hear me, then, since you doubt the priestess: to be a woman is to be a tool that others wield, and the Fates are working through our daughter. We would be fools to deny them."

At another time, in another place, Psyche would have rolled her eyes at this. Never in her life had her mother professed blind faith, but the effect of the hysteria around Psyche on the quiet, comfortable routines of their home had been profound. The overcrowding and inflation of the markets showed no signs of slowing, and the people of Lyktos were turning on her parents, even as they worshiped their daughter. Though she'd always felt an afterthought to her mother and father, Psyche had nonetheless felt confident in the security of her position. Now, though, she realized that having failed to contain the madness on their own, her parents were desperate for a solution, and it was through desperate people that the gods did their best work.

Psyche felt tears sting her eyes and crept away to find wine and a private corner in which to fall to pieces.

. . .

PSYCHE SPENT the night staring at the stars, their form becoming fuzzier and fuzzier the more wine she consumed. Perhaps she should run. Yes, she could run, couldn't she? To Aglaura, or to Cidippe—they would want her to run, wouldn't they? They loved her.

Of course, her parents said they loved her, too.

What would her sisters have said about all of this? Psyche believed, or she liked to believe, that they would have rejected the prophecy whole cloth. That they would have stood between Psyche and her parents, protecting and caring for their little sister as they had done her whole life.

But her sisters had their own cares now, husbands and children and estates to be put at risk. Psyche didn't know the effect of such things on the limits of a person's compassion—how could she?—but she saw now in stark clarity the order of her parents' priorities.

Perhaps it was better she'd been unable to get word to her sisters in time; their abandonment would have killed her more surely than any monster that may appear with the dawn.

Psyche swallowed another sip of wine and wiped her mouth. "But where even could I go?" she whispered to the night, grateful for the numbing effect of the alcohol as the truth of that question sank in. She had nowhere to go, and even if she fled for parts unknown, her face had proven it would draw trouble as surely as a flame drew a moth.

Once, perhaps, she might have hidden away, unknown. Before that day in the market, before the madness. Once, she might have stood a chance.

"Or maybe I never did," she mumbled, fumbling her glass and watching with detached interest as it fell, shattering on the stone of the balcony. Eyeing the shards of glass, Psyche considered her current ability to navigate the mess without injury. Concluding she was safer where she was, the youngest princess of Crete curled up in the chair where she sat and fell asleep under stars that remained as silent as ever.

EARLY THE FOLLOWING MORNING, Psyche stood at the edge of a cliff in a ceremonial gown of sacrifice, the breeze lifting her hair and her arms wrapped about her body to ward off the chill. Her head ached with sharp pain, feeling as though it might split in two. She drew an unsteady breath, then looked over her shoulder at her parents, who stood, shoulders touching.

"What now?" Psyche asked, voice dull. "Shall I jump?"

"No!" Her father took a lurching step forward, arm outstretched. He caught himself, expression unsure. "No," he whispered. "Perhaps no beast will come."

"Hush," Psyche's mother said, and though there was pain in her voice, it was nonetheless firm. "Utter no doubt of the Oracle. Psyche's fate has been written; ours must be to stand witness."

Psyche's head pounded, and she stared out over the edge of the cliff to the rocks and river and green valley beyond. Beautiful—it was so beautiful. And yet it was, perhaps, to be the scene of her last moments on Earth. She closed her eyes. She wished her sisters were with her.

At that moment, a great gust of wind came, causing Psyche to lose her footing, staggering close to the edge of the cliff. She cried out, reaching toward her parents.

"Mother!" she called, but though tears shone in the corners of her mother's eyes, she stayed where she was. Just as Psyche thought she'd found stable ground from which to inch away from the edge, another gust came, toppling Psyche and sending her over before she even had a chance to cry out.

Her mother's scream echoed through the air, her father's hoarse shout coming after it. Psyche thought it strange she registered that—she had never considered the time it took to fall. Psyche closed her eyes, noting the cool air against her skin, the way her dress tangled around her body, bracing her mind for impact.

But the impact never came. After what felt to Psyche's mind far too long to be falling, she peeked open a single eye, fully expecting to see the ground rushing toward her. Instead, her distance from it seemed to hold steady. Confused, Psyche opened both eyes. She was not falling; rather, she seemed to be moving along with the wind, the breeze catching and holding her.

Psyche scraped hair from her face, then let out a shout as the movement caused her entire body to flip over. Still, the wind did not drop her. She held herself perfectly still.

"Where are you taking me?" she called, more nervous now than she'd been when she'd approached the cliff.

Hush... Psyche, Princess of Crete... The voice that responded was low and resonant, seeming to come from all around her. *I am Zephyr, the West Wind... I have been charged with your safe delivery... Remain still, and we shall arrive soon.*

Delivery, was Psyche's last conscious thought, *like a package.*

CHAPTER 11

When Psyche awoke, it was to the scratch of grass beneath her cheek and the slight chill of the air against her bare arms. She pulled her body in on itself, curling around her arms for warmth, keeping her eyes tightly shut. It occurred to her that she was reacting in the same way she had when she was a child and her sisters or one of their maids had come to wake her before she was ready. If only she kept her eyes closed and her body still, perhaps the demands of the present would remain a future problem.

Then, of course, she would be coaxed out of bed by tickling or being dragged, laughing, by her ankles or with promises of what the day would bring. Here, Psyche's rejection was met only with the soft play of the breeze and the quiet hum of frogs. Gradually, she noticed the burble of water over rock and the sharp, sweet smell of freesias. She was never sure how long she lay there or what it was that eventually led her to open her eyes, but when she did, her breath caught, and her mind stuttered in a halting exclamation.

She lay in a grassy expanse alongside the central path of a garden, meticulous in its planting and resplendent in its care. Purple, pink, and white anemone swayed in the wind, and the brightly painted nude statue of a beautiful man cradling a discus gazed down at her from the center of a fountain, cheerful carved fish surrounding his place of honor, water pouring from their pouting mouths. The path of the garden was laid in bright white stone, which Psyche followed with her eyes until she beheld the estate beyond.

The house was a wonder. Marble terraces with golden columns intricately carved and supporting lofty painted ceilings. Mosaic floors bursting with color and golden walls depicting various beasts in silver relief. As Psyche approached, she glanced up and beheld a ceiling paneled in citron wood and ivory. Psyche and her sisters had grown up in wealth, but this was a palace that could have been fashioned for Jupiter himself, and Psyche found she could not cross the threshold, so intimidated was she by the shining splendour. As she stood there, still in shock and not quite sure she wasn't dead after all, a voice came from within the house, carried as if on the wind.

"Welcome, Psyche, daughter of Crete. Come, enter and retire to your room, for you are weary with the ordeals of your day. All that you see is at your disposal, and once you are refreshed, a feast shall be laid to welcome you and revive your spirits." Without realizing she did so, Psyche took a single step inside, her eyes searching for the source of the voice.

"Hello?" she called. "I thank you for your kind invitation but ask that you show yourself. Who are you?" There was a tuttering on the wind, like several people clicking their tongues in response. The voice that responded, however, was the same that had spoken before.

"I am one of the Lares, and we will serve you with care and diligence. Alas, we cannot reveal ourselves further, for we have no corporeal form. Be assured, however, that we mean you no harm. We are here for your comfort."

Psyche absorbed that and its implications.

Very clearly, she was in the house of a god—or, at the very least, the house of one strongly favored by a god. A demigod, perhaps. She was not sure what to make of this. Until recently, the gods had never been present in her life outside of feast days and casual ritual. Now, within the turning of a moon, she found herself condemned by the Oracle of Apollo and rescued by an unknown entity with a home of such opulence that it could only have been built by a divine hand. It was the breeze that had borne her to this place; was she perhaps to be the bride of one of the winds? Psyche cleared her throat.

"Thank you again. Can you, at least, tell me whose home I will be entering? You say that everything I see is at my disposal, and yet I am still only a princess of Crete; such magnificence is beyond even our finest craftsmen. Whom do I thank for the hospitality I now enjoy?" More tuttering, and Psyche thought she heard the faintest edge of exasperation enter the voice of the one who responded.

"The lord of the house will reveal himself in his own time, but know that all you see is at your disposal. Now, please, enter and allow us to tend to your toilette."

There were no more protestations to be offered, and in truth, Psyche saw little point in revisiting those already put forth. Where could she go? She didn't even know where she was. Whenever this master appeared, she sensed things would go better for her if she had submitted to the ministrations of his staff. And she was tired. At least she wasn't currently being devoured by a beast.

And so Psyche stepped inside and let the gentle urging of unseen hands lead her to a steaming, fragrant bath, into which she sank, her muscles releasing for the first time in what felt like weeks. When the dirt and weariness had been soaked from her body, she rose and, wrapping herself in the soft linens provided, curled up on a great semicircular couch and fell fast asleep.

When Psyche awoke several hours later, the sky had darkened and candles were flickering to life on the property. A voice at her ear prompted her to follow the lights to the feast, and she obeyed, shuffling with the linen robe still wrapped tight around her. Upon reaching the table, a glass of sweet wine was pressed to her hand, and when she sat down, plates of food began to float to the table, the wind bearing them quickly but setting them before her with such gentleness that not a single drop of soup or sauce or oil escaped its vessel. As Psyche tore a piece of bread to drag through oil, the sounds of a lyre being tuned echoed softly through the room, and in short order, the unseen lyre player was joined by a beautiful voice, their music so reminiscent of that which she'd heard so many times before at family feasts that tears sprung to her eyes, and she had to sip her wine rapidly to keep them from spilling over.

She had hoped the lord of the home might reveal himself during dinner, but she was disappointed in this. When she made her way to her rooms, head light with wine, it was with no more awareness of her situation than when she left them.

PSYCHE WAS WOKEN by the sensation of the mattress dipping under the weight of another. Though her heart began to race, she held still, cursing her cowardice even as she clung to the hope that if she just didn't move, didn't even breathe, then maybe she had imagined it. Maybe it had been part of a dream that roused her rather than evidence of an unknown presence, and with time and a little patience, the dream would claim her once again.

A soft touch on her shoulder shattered that delusion.

"Psyche." The voice that came was warm, melodic. The hand on her shoulder swept down her arm, lacing fingers through her own still ones. "My love, wake." A kiss was pressed to the hollow between ear and eye. The lips, like the hand, were smooth. Psyche gave an involuntary flinch at the contact, and the game was up. Even as she resumed breathing, Psyche kept her eyes shut, one final, stubborn defiance of fate. She felt two hands cup her face.

"Ah, no, Psyche, look at me. You have nothing to fear from me. Look at me, love, and see how long I've waited to be with you."

Psyche opened her eyes. Above her hovered the shape of a man, but more than that, she could not make out. The room was dark, lit only by the gleam of stars through the sheer curtains of the balcony. Psyche swallowed.

"Might we light a candle, my lord, so I can see you?" The shape above her shook his head, a hint of regret to the movement.

"Alas. Would that were possible, but the shadows have their gifts as well, those of awareness, of heightened sensation. You will not miss the light if I love you as you deserve."

Psyche seized firm hold of her panic, pushing herself to a seated position. In response, he moved to recline on his side, the dark pools of his eyes steady on her, his fingers still linked through her own.

"You are so beautiful," he breathed, this man who had joined her in this great bed and who now raised their joined palms to press a kiss to the back of her hand. "I, of all beings, have seen great beauty and you, Psyche—all of it pales in your presence."

Psyche blinked several times, gathering her thoughts. Did he have the eyes of an owl to speak so of her beauty in such blackness? Or was he speaking from memory? Was this lord someone she had met before? He sounded young, perhaps her own age.

"Do I know you, my lord?" she asked. She felt like she should say something else as well, ask another question, but she found she was having trouble forming words. He lifted a hand and brushed the hair away from her forehead.

"In this lifetime? No. I could not court you openly, still cannot be with you in the light of the sun. But I know our souls must have known each other before they found their way to the bodies we now inhabit. I knew it from the moment I saw you, knew you were destined to be mine."

At his use of the possessive, Psyche shrank. "Who are you?" she whispered.

He sighed. "Who am I? What a question. I am not sure I can answer it." He flopped from his side onto his back, withdrawing his hand to lace his fingers behind his head. "I thought I knew who I was; I was very sure. If you had asked me this question a mere week ago, I would have been able to tell you with utmost confidence and certainty both my identity as well as my place in the world. But now I'm not so sure. Not since I saw your face." His head turned toward her, his hand coming up to stroke her cheek. She held herself still and waited, sensing he had more to say. His hand dropped as he let out a long exhale, staring at the ceiling. "It was a mistake, you know. That I saw you as I did. The stupidest mistake, and yet I cannot regret it, for I've never felt the way I do now. You, Psyche, you make me feel this way." There was both adoration and hunger in his voice; she wasn't sure which terrified her more. Silence stretched long before she realized he was waiting for her to speak.

"You... honor me, my lord."

He waved a hand. "Enough, I dislike being named lord by your lips," he said. "Call me... Love." He sounded amused at some private joke, but the command was clear.

Psyche hesitated. "Yes... Love."

The man groaned, a deep sound that set Psyche's hair on edge. He turned, propping himself on an elbow, head in one hand as the other reached over her, took confident hold of her breast, palming it. "I've waited so long to hear you call me that," he said, his face suddenly close to hers, so close. There was a pounding in Psyche's head and a ringing in her ears, but her body was frozen, somehow disconnected from the commands her brain was sending to run, run, run.

"By your own admission, you could not have been waiting more than a week," she whispered, the words leaving her mouth without any conscious decision to say them. He threw back his head and laughed.

"Clever, as well as beautiful! What a woman you are. After seeing you, of course, every day that followed without you in my arms felt like an eternity." He sat up, taking her hands to pull her closer to him. "Let me see you, Psyche, I've waited so long." His fingers went to the straps at her shoulders, started to push them down, but finally, Psyche's body listened to her brain, and her own hands came up to still his.

"Please, um, Love"—she cleared her throat, then continued carefully—"your words are kind, but I must ask about your intentions. Grateful though I am not to be in pieces upon the rocks"—this came out more bitter than she intended, and she drew a breath to steady herself—"I must know to what purpose you have brought me here." His voice, when he responded, was dismayed.

"To what purpose? Have I not been clear? To be mine, of course! I shall love you and provide for you and make you happier than you could have ever dreamed." His hands shook free of hers, continuing in their intent until her nightgown was pooled at her hips. He stared at her, hands on her waist; she heard the wet sound of his tongue sweeping over his lips. "You are..." he breathed, "perfect."

So that was it, then. Psyche could not pretend, even to herself, to be surprised. This was what men wanted women for, and well, wasn't it better than being dead? So she lay there as he continued his heated worship of her. Whether it was this night or the next or a turning of the moon from now, she had nowhere to go, and he had desires, and wouldn't it go better for her if those were satisfied? This man, whoever he was, clearly had the favor of the gods—the happier he was, the safer for her. So he did as he would, and she reminded herself throughout the act of all these things.

And when at last he lay, spent and snoring, his body flung in blissful disarray, Psyche curled on her side, hands tucked beneath her cheek, and told herself that, surely, she was lucky to have captured the interest of such a privileged, adoring young man. What was it her mother had said to Aglaura, so long ago? Fortunate.

She was fortunate.

WHEN PSYCHE WOKE the next morning, she was alone, light pouring in through the window and illuminating the rumpled sheets next to her. She stared at the empty space for a while, her mind coming to full consciousness in stages.

She was not at home; she was in this grand and mysterious estate.

She was alone now, but she had not been alone all night. A man had come; her husband? No vows had taken place, but he had acknowledged arranging her journey here for the purpose of being with him, so did that count as marriage?

He had lain with her. Her body was still sore with the evidence of it. She wasn't quite sure how she felt about it, but the experience itself had been less uncomfortable than she had feared. And while her journey here was different than expected, she had known that one day she would have to share her bed and her body with a man.

So, fortunate. That was where she'd landed last night.

Fortunate.

She was hungry. Her stomach gave a growl that pushed Psyche to roll out of bed with a groan. She had eaten little the night before, too distracted with the spectacle of the house, and now her hunger felt like a living thing within her, forcing her focus until it was sated.

At that moment, the door to her room opened, seemingly on its own, and in floated a tray of fruit, bread, and cheese alongside a folded pile of fresh linens.

"Good morning, Lady Psyche," came the voice from the day before, from somewhere around the tray as it was set on her table. "I trust you slept well." Psyche swallowed, forcing her body to move at a casual pace toward the food. Her hand claimed a hunk of cheese as soon as it was within reach and before she'd even registered reaching for it.

"Mmmm," she responded, mouth already full. She swallowed. "It was… fine. My lord joined me."

Over by her bed, sheets were lifting and flying to the ground as if on their own accord, a neat pile of laundry accumulating as fresh sheets were laid out. The voice hummed.

"Ah, good, then you can feel at ease, knowing now that you are in the home of a man, not a monster." Psyche frowned, chewing her bread more slowly now that the sharp edge of her hunger had been dulled. How much honesty could she allow herself?

"Indeed," she said, "but I'm afraid my silly mind has forgotten already the name he gave; I fear causing offense when I see him this morning." She winced at her own awkwardness. Psyche's hair was lifted, and a comb began to work through the tangles of the night.

"Rest easy on that account, my lady. He has departed for the day and shall not return until the sun has set. The day is yours to use at your pleasure." Though the comb was hitting many snags, the Lares was gentle and patient with their work. A suspicion rose in Psyche's mind.

"Oh, I see. But still, how shall I greet him when he does return? It would be a poor way to show gratitude, to greet him by the wrong name." There. That was as direct as she could be. She held her breath as she waited for a response.

"I apologize, Lady Psyche, but that is one service I cannot render. His lord will share his name with you in his own time, or he will not, but it is not my information to give. I do assure you that he will not hold you the least accountable for information that you have never received."

Psyche exhaled. There it was. The Lares was aware that the man who came to her in the night had not told her his name, and despite ostensibly being there to serve her, the greater loyalty was to this secretive lord. Psyche sighed. It had been too much and too early to hope for a friend, she supposed. The rest of her breakfast passed in silence, the Lares leaving with the pile of laundry in tow once Psyche's braided hair had been wound about her head.

Alone once more, Psyche looked around her room. It was beautiful. She could hear birds calling from outside the window, feel the warm morning breeze beckoning her outside. Her legs felt sticky; the Lares had left a bowl of fresh water and a cloth with which she could clean herself before dressing. There was a whole house and grounds to explore; she should ready herself for the day and then set out. Her eyes fell to her bed, made again, with a fresh gown laid out.

Psyche pushed the gown aside, crawled into the sheets, and went back to sleep.

CHAPTER 12

Psyche did not leave her room that day, and when the lord returned to her that night, she remained quiet again, too demoralized to push for answers. Again, his hands were sure and skilled on her body, at once worshipping and claiming, and again, Psyche fell asleep reminding herself she was fortunate. This sequence repeated itself for several weeks, the days blurring as she slept through them, the nights hazy as her mind drifted farther and farther from her body. It was the lord who noticed Psyche's detachment, after several nights during which he could rouse no response from her at all.

"You seem less happy than I would expect, lovely one," he said after taking his pleasure and sprawling, contented, beside her. "What troubles you?"

Psyche lay, still, staring at the ceiling. She tried to answer, she really did, even opened her mouth, but no words came out. She closed her eyes. *Breathe in, breathe out.*

Fingers laced with Psyche's as the lord drew closer, his breath on her shoulder. "Tell me," he said. "Whatever it is, I will fix."

Her chest rising and falling with her slow breaths, Psyche screamed in her mind. Why would he not go to sleep? Why would he not leave her alone? He'd had her body, she'd done her bit, now let her be. She adjusted her leg, which had started to go to sleep. She tried again to speak but found, once more, she had nothing to say.

The lord sighed, rolling away. "This is my fault," he said, half to himself. Psyche's heart leapt; her body stilled to hear his next words. "The Lares have reported to me how little you have been eating, but I chalked it up to a feminine appetite. Clearly, we have not provided food that suits you, and you are now diminishing with hunger. Tell me—what foods please you most? They will be on the table tomorrow."

Food? Why was he asking about food? There was plenty of food; she wasn't hungry. It did strike her, then, that this was out of the ordinary, for she had always maintained a healthy appetite—Aglaura was the one who ate like a bird and was most likely to demur when offered second portions. The thought of her sister stirred something in Psyche.

"Aglaura," she said, "and Cidippe."

"What's that?" His confusion was evident. "Are those dishes native to Crete—"

"My sisters," she said, "they're my sisters." A beat of silence.

"Oh," the lord said. "Well, you can't eat them."

Psyche heard the attempt at humor but would not be distracted. "Let me visit them, please. Let me see them. They must believe me dead, these long weeks."

The lord let out a noisy sigh, swinging his legs from the bed to retrieve a cup of water from across the room. "Anything, my love," he said, "except that."

Psyche felt her chest, which had been hollow before, start to burn with desperation. She kept her voice steady. "Then I beg you, Love, by the affection you bear me, bring my sisters here."

The dark was, as ever, blanketing, but Psyche thought she saw him shake his head. "It is impossible," he said, "and carries far more danger than you know. They believe you dead? All for the better; I know you miss them, but that will lessen with time, and believe me when I say that any contact you might have with them would only set in motion the wheels for utter destruction of what we have."

Psyche pushed herself up now, eyes searching for his in the darkness. "And if I promise not to speak of us? Could you then consider it? I feel myself only half whole; less than that, even, and with every day that passes, I feel further and further from myself. You see how even the thought of them has woken something within me; please, Love, please—imagine how restorative a visit would be."

The lord returned to sit heavy on the bed, one hand coming out to trace designs down Psyche's spine that made her shiver.

"I cannot refuse you," he said, soft but reluctant. "I do see how you have drifted away from me, and it breaks my heart. If this is the medicine you need—I can hardly believe it, but if you feel it so strongly, well. Perhaps I can arrange for them to visit you here."

Psyche vibrated with excitement, clapping her hands together in a way that made her feel suddenly very young again. "Thank you, thank you, thank you," she said. He wrapped his arms around her for a moment, then held her apart, the dark space of his eyes studying her.

"I do not offer this in good conscience; you must not forget what I have said. Do not speak of me or of us; should you do so, we shall be at risk for losing everything."

Psyche scarcely heard his words, buzzing as her mind was with the promise of being reunited with Aglaura and Cidippe. They would know; her big sisters would know what to do. They would come, and they would see her circumstance, and somehow, they would make everything right again. She just knew it.

THE LORD WAS true to his word, reporting several nights later that he had learned her sisters planned to journey together to the site of Psyche's disappearance.

"Once there," he said, still reluctant, "I've asked the West Wind to bear them as it bore you."

Psyche hesitated, then pulled him to her, trying to thank him in the way he seemed to best appreciate.

As the day of their visit drew near, Psyche returned more to herself. She began bathing again, instead of sitting, passive, as one of the Lares completed the task. She dressed, even ventured out of her room. Food became appealing once more, and Psyche summoned the Lares one morning to discuss the menu planned for her sisters' visit.

The lord did not comment on these changes in a direct way, but his relief at her renewed engagement with life was clear. Still, he remained apprehensive.

"What do you fear from them?" Psyche asked one night, curled on her side facing him. The lord scoffed at the suggestion.

"I do not fear them; I fear their influence on you."

"But, as you've seen, it is only positive!"

"Maybe," was all he said in response.

Aglaura and Cidippe trudged up the hillside, stepping with care along the rocky path to avoid a twisted ankle. Cidippe, especially, was slow-moving as she was in the early, sick days of carrying another child, a condition she had learned reliably caused her head to swim and her agility to suffer. Aglaura, strong and fit from running her husband's farm, kept her hand at her sister's elbow and her eyes ahead, scanning for danger.

"Father made it up this path?" Cidippe said. "I don't believe it."

"It does seem an odd location for a sacrifice." Aglaura bent down to toss a fallen branch from the path. "I'm still trying to figure out how it all happened—and so quickly."

Cidippe snorted. "You know how it happened. Men. Men and their damnable pride and condescension and disregard for anyone—"

"Shhh." Aglaura tightened her hold on Cidippe's elbow. "Careful. Getting worked up, even over things that may justify it, will only bring you distress."

Cidippe didn't respond, her lips pressed to a thin line. After a few minutes of strained silence, she said, "I'm not sure when, Aglaura, you think I'm not in distress."

At that moment, they crested the hill, eyes scouring the vast, rocky valley that spread abruptly before them.

"This is it, then," Aglaura whispered. "This is where Psyche last drew breath." Her voice caught, and Cidippe had to pull her arm away from her older sister's sudden vice-like grip. Cidippe rubbed her forearm as she gazed out, brows drawn and mouth still tight.

"This is where they left her, you mean," she corrected. "Where our parents—*our* parents, who may never have displayed much affection but whose love we never had reason to question—where they abandoned our baby sister on the whim of some self-important priestess who dreamed she spoke to a god."

Aglaura's brows drew together, but the admonishment caught in her throat as she surveyed the sharp, unforgiving edge of the cliff.

"Yes," she said finally, "I guess that is what I mean."

"Well, we've seen it. Now what?" Cidippe lowered herself carefully to the rough ground, massaging her aching calves. Aglaura watched her.

"I don't know," she admitted.

In that moment, a great gust of wind swept the cliff, causing Aglaura to stagger forward and Cidippe to throw her hands back to steady herself on the ground.

"What in Ceres' name—" Aglaura's words were lost in the howl of wind that swirled about them, wrapping their dresses tightly to their bodies and yanking hair loose from its careful confines.

"Aglaura!" Cidippe's hand came up, seeking and finding her sister's forearm, and just as Aglaura's own hand wrapped around Cidippe's, they both were lifted from the ground in a swirling tempest.

Be still! a voice echoed through the air. *You seek Psyche, and I have been instructed to deliver you to her, but if you struggle further, you risk falling from my grasp to the rocks below.* Both women froze and stared at one another in wide-eyed fear as the wind carried them over the cliff's edge and far, far down into the valley below.

PSYCHE WATCHED with eager impatience as Zephyr bore her sisters closer and closer. She had heard their voices on the wind that morning and thrown herself into a frenzy of cleaning and preparations. As her invisible staff kept the home immaculate, there had been very little to do, so at the height of her excitement, she found herself reorganizing for the third time the flowers she'd gathered knowing that the more she handled the fragile blooms, the less cheerful they became, but unable to still her anxious hands.

When, at last, the West Wind laid the paralyzed women at her feet, Psyche sank to her knees and threw her arms around them, bursting into tears. Still in shock, Aglaura and Cidippe stared, empty-eyed, for several moments at their little sister.

"Psyche?" Cidippe whispered, pushing up on an elbow. "How?"

Aglaura shook her head and, trembling with emotion, wrapped tight arms around Psyche, her own tears falling and soaking into her little sister's hair. "You're alive," she murmured, over and over, "you're alive, you're alive, you're alive."

It was several long minutes before the disbelief and tears and clutching holds gave way to joy and laughter and embrace. When it did, however, Psyche's heart sank to see how even her sisters' eyes could not meet hers for long. When daydreaming about their visit, she had imagined they would prove immune to whatever had begun in the market that day, but that had, it seemed, been too much to hope.

As they began to make their way toward Psyche's home, Aglaura and Cidippe walked together, a body length apart from Psyche. Both sisters gasped at the gleaming marble edifice before them.

"What immortal has brought you here, Psy?" Cidippe asked, eyes tracing the smooth curves and perfect scrollwork. "You cannot convince me it is a human who dwells here." Psyche was the one who avoided eye contact then, the warning from the night before ringing in her ears.

"My lord is certainly blessed," she said carefully, "as am I, by association."

Aglaura ran her fingers gently over the pictorial relief of the walls. "I've never seen such fine artisanship," she said. "Truly, this must be the work of the gods themselves."

Psyche stood apart, awkward, fingers playing with nervous agitation among the folds of her dress. Her promise to the lord pounded through her head, and her laugh was brittle to her own ears as she said, "Come! See what I've had prepared—all of our favorites!" When there was no response, she rushed on. "If none of it is to your taste, the kitchen can make whatever you like." Her sisters frowned but followed her inside to the table laid high with food. Aglaura's eyes went round.

"But Psyche, how do you have fresh apples? They will not be in season for another two turnings of the moon."

Psyche pretended not to hear, focusing instead on pouring and distributing wine. "I know the table is set, but the gardens here are truly magnificent; perhaps we could take some dishes outside and sit under a tree like we used to." Cidippe and Aglaura exchanged a look.

Cidippe, making a clear effort to hold Psyche's gaze, said, "Well, if we are going to do that, I will need a chair. My joints will not tolerate sitting on the ground these days." Though her sister's eyes dropped sooner than they would have before, Psyche was encouraged by this effort and exhaled in relief.

"Of course! I'll have them move chairs for us all now." And so saying, she disappeared into the interior, her sisters' eyes following her retreating form.

THE BREEZE PLAYED SOFTLY with the leaves shading the sisters, shadows dancing across their faces. They had eased into conversation with neutral topics, Psyche purposefully centering her sisters' lives. The longer they spoke, the more at ease Aglaura and Cidippe appeared with her, muscles relaxing and smiles coming quicker and with greater ease. They still could not look her full in the face for any length of time, but they were both clearly trying, and Psyche thought that was about as much as she could ask.

"Eleni is about to turn three and reminds me so much of you at that age, Psyche," Aglaura smiled. "Curious and bright and ever so content to be petted and cared for." Both Aglaura and Cidippe laughed while Psyche rolled her eyes, masking the sudden uneasiness this comment provoked in her.

"Was I ever content in that, or were you two determined to be second and third mothers to me?" she countered, popping a grape into her mouth. Cidippe gave an exhaled bark of disbelief.

"Oh, I'd say you were content, Psy." Her face arranged itself into an imitation of Psyche's, eyes peering up from under dark lashes and mouth pulled to the side in a half smile. "'Please lace my sandals, Cidi?' 'Cidi, my legs are so tired, and you're so strong when you carry me!' 'Cidi, will you braid my hair like yours?'" Psyche threw a grape at her, and there was a still, uncertain moment before Cidippe, mouth turning up, rustled in the grass until she found the grape and threw it right back at her little sister.

"Maybe both things can be true," Aglaura allowed. "At any rate, I certainly have the experience to now handle my daughter's attempts to wind me about her finger."

"Which is to say"—Cidippe pointed a finger at her older sister— "that you absolutely let her do it." Psyche saw irritation flit across Aglaura's face and so jumped in before she could respond.

"And what about your children, Cid? You have three now? Agneta and Aindreas have got to be, what, almost three as well?" Cidippe nodded confirmation.

"Yes, and Ianthe has just turned a year. This one"—her hand rested on her still soft belly—"will be born after the harvest if she makes it to term."

"You believe it's a girl?" Aglaura asked. Cidippe shrugged.

"I know it is."

Psyche was fascinated. "How can you tell?"

Cidippe didn't answer for a moment, gazing up through the branches of the tree to watch the clouds move across the sky. Finally, she spoke.

"I feel strong, healthy, all things considered. The ones that did not make it were both boys, and I could feel the wrongness long before the midwife pronounced their fate. I tried to tell Marinos, to prepare him, but he, ah, doesn't trust my word." The sisters were quiet for a moment.

"But you have Aindreas," Aglaura said, "and he is strong and healthy."

Cidippe shook her head. "But he has always had Agneta, even in the womb. I like to think she protected him." The words that came next were hesitant, halting as if escaping Cidippe's thoughts for the first time. "I think... I think my body rejects boys because of what their father is. I think it refuses to nurture any that could grow to be like him."

"No." Aglaura's voice was fierce and immediate. "No, Cid. Your body cares for each of your children as fully as it can; if there is indeed any truth to your theory, the defect comes from Marinos, not you." Their eyes met and held.

Psyche watched her older sisters, the unsaid words flowing between them with such strength Psyche felt she could almost see them in the air. She felt suddenly bereft, aware in an instant of how much they shared that she did not, how much she had missed. She cleared her throat.

"Well, that's certainly what I hope to believe whenever the time comes for me," she offered. Two sets of eyes swung to consider her before sliding away.

"Has that time come?" Cidippe asked. Psyche shook her head.

"Oh no, no, it hasn't, I just mean—of course, I've thought about it, and, well… I just hope Aglaura's right about our bodies not being the deciding factor." She raised her arms in a gesture of helplessness. Her sisters remained quiet, waiting for her to continue. "I guess I hope mine is as strong as yours are, stronger than I believe it to be," she whispered at last. Cidippe glanced at Aglaura, then back at Psyche.

"Psy," she said, "we'd heard stories of your changed appearance, but I hardly believed it until now. It is strange because your features are as familiar to me as ever, and yet to look at you too long is over-whelming to my senses; it feels a transgression." Aglaura nodded agreement as Cidippe continued, "And now we find you in a home fit for a god, but you've said little about the lord who brought you here."

Words piled up in Psyche's throat, threatening to spill out, even as tears pricked her eyes. Before either could fall, Aglaura laid a hand on her knee.

"We only want to know what happened, Psy," she said, lifting her arm to indicate their surroundings. "It's like something out of a story."

Psyche had been absently wrapping the tie of her dress around one of her fingers, but now she began twisting it, the fabric digging into her skin. "It is not a story I've written," she said, then panicked at the bitterness in her tone. She rushed to continue. "I am cared for," she said, "even as I'm often alone." She laughed, the sound too bright even to her own ears. "My lord is away during the day for work, so I see him only once he returns at night. He was so disappointed to miss your visit," she lied.

Cidippe frowned. "But how would he have known we were visiting? How did you know?"

"Oh." Psyche was flustered. "Oh, well, he had information that you were planning to visit the cliff, and well, yes, I asked that you be able to visit, and he said yes but that he was so sorry he'd miss it." Her sisters heard every one of the holes in this tale, and Psyche knew it. Aglaura scooted her chair closer, reaching out to take Psyche's restless hand in her own, unwrapping the binding tie with gentle fingers.

"Psyche, we love you. You can tell us anything—or don't tell us if you cannot. But we are here for you—we are yours. You can speak to us as though to yourself."

Tears welled in Psyche's eyes, threatening to spill over. "I cannot," she whispered. Aglaura nodded, slow.

"At least tell us if he hurts you," Cidippe demanded, voice low and heavy with old pain. "Does he hurt you?"

Psyche paused before answering. "No—no, he has not hurt me. He does not."

Cidippe let out a breath of relief. "Well, that's something, then," she said.

Aglaura studied Psyche's face for as long as she could, then dropped her gaze to her sister's tense shoulders. "Talk to us, Psy," she said, and then the words came tumbling from Psyche's lips.

She did not speak of the lord further, she had promised she would not, but she told them about visiting the market that day and the way everyone had responded to her after. Of the Oracle at Delphi and the prophecy and how their mother had seemed not to hesitate at all in her acceptance of it. She spoke of falling from the cliff, only to be caught and carried as they had been, waking to find herself alone. And she told them about the Lares, ever attentive but invisible and removed, never the company for which she was so desperate. She was alone, so alone, with nothing to do but eat and sleep and wash herself and stare at the perfectly maintained home, and she was about to go mad with it all.

Aglaura and Cidippe listened, letting their sister finish without interruption. When she was done, they all sat in the quiet her words had made, considering all that had been shared. Cidippe broke the silence, plucking at blades of grass with a focused fury.

"I don't know that I will ever be able to speak to our parents again for what they did."

Aglaura's spoke and her voice was tight. "Cid, we don't know the pressures on them, the fear of retribution they must have held. And Psyche is alive and mostly well. Your anger will only hurt you; let it go."

"Let it go, Aglaura? So tell me, if an oracle told you to abandon Eleni on a cliffside to become the bride of a monster, you'd just do it?"

Aglaura pressed her lips in a thin line. "I mean only to say that what is done is done, and we must endeavor to move forward in ways that preserve our own health and happiness. Psyche"—she turned then to her youngest sister—"I do feel for you in this aloneness; when I first wed Georgios, I knew no one but him, and the workers on the estate had been there for so long and were so established in their routines that there was no space that needed filling for me to occupy. For the first several weeks I existed as you have described, floating about, feeling increasingly like a ghost. What I learned I needed to do was be the one who reached out, who established my own routines. Once I did that, things became much more bearable."

"But she has no one here to reach to," Cidippe said. "That is part of the problem."

"But I could set myself more of a routine," Psyche broke in, eager to head off further arguments. "I could begin by establishing a plan for each day."

Aglaura nodded, approving. "That is all I was trying to say; it will not solve everything, but I do think it will help."

"You've not said more of this lord—your husband? Have you wed?" Cidippe asked.

"I don't know; I don't think so," Psyche said. "The prophecy said bride, but then the prophecy also said monster, and the lord is not that, I think. Or at least he has not behaved as I would expect a monster to behave. Regardless, there has been no ceremony, no exchange of vows."

Cidippe hummed. "He would have his pie even as he eats it, then," she said.

"Cid," said Aglaura, warning.

"What? Have I not seen enough of this behavior with Marinos to justify my observation? There are a few women with whom he maintains relations, and honestly, I prefer that because when he's not with them, he brings his volatility home to me. I simply am trying to clarify the position Psyche is in."

Psyche was stricken. "I had not thought of that," she said, "though I should have. He only ever comes at night."

Both her sisters started at that.

"What, he's not here during the day? Ever?" Aglaura asked.

Psyche felt panic rising in her throat. "No— I mean, he— I just— please, forget I said anything." Psyche stumbled through the words, her body flushing with anxiety. It was the one promise he'd asked of her; if she broke it, who knew if her sisters would ever be allowed to return.

Cidippe's hand came to cover Psyche's trembling ones. She shot a meaningful glance at Aglaura as she spoke. "It's okay, Psy," she said. "It's okay. We won't ask anything else. It's okay."

THE REST of the visit passed in food, reminiscences of their childhood, and more stories about Aglaura's and Cidippe's children. Psyche felt a pang of longing with every detail shared about her nieces and nephew; perhaps she could, after a bit more time, convince the lord to allow her to be the one to visit. When Zephyr whispered in their ears that it was time to depart, Psyche was lighter than she had been in a long time but still far from ready to say goodbye.

"Thank you, I love you," she said, into first one sister's neck, then the other's. Both Aglaura and Cidippe hugged her tightly, Cidippe to such an extent that Psyche felt the imprint of her fingers on her shoulders long after she let go.

Psyche watched as the wind carried them away, the exercise far more dignified than their arrival. She rolled her shoulders. Aglaura was right—it was time to reclaim control of her days, to make the best of where she was. How many were there in the world who desired even a fraction of the beauty and luxury with which she found herself surrounded? The time for mourning had passed; Psyche was determined to live again.

And if there was a part of her mind that protested this, that begged for validation of its pain, well, Psyche tucked it away. She was, after all, fortunate.

CHAPTER 13

Of course, what that meant—to live again—was harder to define. Psyche had never been one much for indoor hobbies. Where Aglaura weaved and Cidippe flitted from one hobby to the next, Psyche had always preferred to climb trees, to walk along the beach, observe the life she found there. And while she could and did pursue these pastimes, she nonetheless felt her spirits sink again every time she walked into the home with no one to whom she could recount her experiences.

The Lares were polite and attentive but expert at avoiding conversation that sought to go any further than the maintenance of the home or what was to be served for dinner. And so one night, soon after he arrived, Psyche asked the lord for a loom.

"A loom?" Doubt laced his voice. "Whatever do you need with a loom?"

"To weave," Psyche said and thought her own restraint in this response remarkable.

"What do you want to weave?" he asked. "You've never spoken of this before."

"I wish for something to fill my days," Psyche said, "to occupy my mind when you are away from me." Suggesting that their time apart was hard for her was always a good tactic. She felt him soften.

"Ah, of course. I shall tell the Lares; one shall be set up for you tomorrow, and I will bring back yarn in every color imaginable."

And he did. Within the week, Psyche found herself in possession of more colors than she'd known possible, as well as a sturdily constructed loom and set of weights that, she realized with belated frustration, she did not know how to warp herself. Aglaura had always done it for her.

After several failed attempts, and then several more that saw the warp threads correctly laid but unevenly weighted, Psyche managed to begin, choosing simple colors in the most basic design Aglaura had taught her. She did not think this piece would ever be one to brag about, but by the time she set down the shuttle several hours later, she was quite pleased with her progress.

Mornings became her time to weave, the hours passing in quiet contemplation and focus that Psyche came to crave. As a child, weaving had been a way to spend time with her sisters, particularly Aglaura. Now, though, the steady rhythm of the shuttle and the kanon served as a safe and welcoming place to lose herself.

HER TIME at the loom fast became Psyche's favorite time of the day, but she found it was hard on her body. Standing for so long demanded she then move in different ways, and so in the afternoons, Psyche began to seek out the most menial of tasks—jobs in her former life she had barely been aware needed doing—because they used different muscles, and in them, she found both a new sense of self-sufficiency and a consuming focus that kept her darker thoughts at bay.

She spent weeks polishing the walls carved in gold and silver relief, acquiring, and sometimes creating, increasingly task-specific tools to bring the animals depicted to their highest shine. She spent over a month scrubbing the mosaic floors, experimenting with different combinations of cleaning liquids in order to lift dirt not only from the tiles themselves but also from the grout between them. If the Lares felt any sort of way about the mistress of the house engaging in such work, they kept it to themselves. Psyche's body ached in places she had never realized it was possible to ache, and her hands grew raw and dry, but her mind felt sharper and better able to navigate the emotions swirling ever just below the surface.

Every night, the lord came, and while he was pleased with the apparent buoying of Psyche's mood, he commented often on the effects her days were having on her body.

"These fingers," he said, drawing one into his mouth as he smiled around it, "feel as rough as a fishwife's."

While it gnawed at Psyche that she had still never seen his face, moments like these made her grateful for the dark and the ability to conceal her own expression.

"A small price to pay, I think," she said, mild, "for the peace these fingers and their work bring my mind."

"Hm," he said, pressing a kiss to her palm. "Perhaps, but you are too beautiful for your hands to feel as they do. I shall bring you cream for them so you can find peace and remain soft."

He took her then, as he did every night, and Psyche flew away to the place she'd built in her mind that kept her whole and safe during such encounters, at times allowing her just enough presence to achieve the much-needed release of orgasm, which he never failed to try and coax from her. Nights when such release was impossible, she assured him it was her own fault, rather than his as a lover, which she found was the fastest route to him sighing with resigned contentment and drifting off to sleep.

The lord brought her a cream for her hands, as promised, and Psyche used it as directed, though it did seem an uphill battle. Her next project was gardening, and because it was ever warm and Psyche found that she liked the feel of dirt on her skin, her knees became stained dark with soil from hours of weeding, even as thorns and rocks and tiny barbs continued the ruining of her hands. But when she saw the blooms she'd coaxed from the earth, the sunlight reflect off the golden walls, or set a foot on one of the small rugs she'd woven, she felt a surge of pride in herself that overcame any last traces of vanity, and she thought that perhaps she was building herself stronger than before.

Several months passed thus, and then, as the summer blooms began to fade, Psyche found her body challenged with a new task.

THE SMOOTH PEBBLES of the beach rolled against the bottom of Psyche's feet, pushing into her soles with a solid resistance that felt therapeutic so long as her steps remained slow. She focused on the way they felt beneath her toes, cool, damp, both shifting and unyielding. Shining, glistening with water, then dulling under the sun until the next wave swept to shore. Psyche thought she could stay here forever, observing the play of the tides, the constant inconstancy.

It was how her body had felt of late—constant inconstancy. At first, she had thought she had caught a sickness, but her symptoms had not abated, and when she failed to bleed at her normal time, she knew in her bones what was happening. Life was growing within her, potential life at any rate, and she was as powerless to stop it as the stones were to protest the ocean.

Psyche didn't know how she felt about it. Mostly, she was tired. So tired. Standing to weave for more than an hour was, at this point, laughable, and by the midday meal, she was ready to sleep again. He came, still, every night when he was home, and despite his attention to the roughness of her hands, he had yet to notice any difference in her. She accommodated him as best she could, offered what feigned enthusiasm she could muster, but every evening, she seemed to find a bit less within her, and she found herself hoping that perhaps she could bore him away and win herself some peace to process what was happening.

She was not upset, she didn't think. This was the way of it, to marry and have children. But her situation was so outside the norm— was she even married?—and she had yet to see her lord outside the dim light of the bedroom. It was a confusing dynamic, and she was very unsure how she felt about bringing a child into it.

She suspected the man she called Love might be a demigod of some sort. That he had the gods' favor was without question; the home in which she now dwelled was evidence of that. But why he held such favor, much less whose—that mattered. The gods were always at odds with one another, alliances shifting as quickly as an offhand shrug or a disgruntled exhale. Another constant inconstancy. What future did her child have, outside this estate, if its father fell out of favor or, more likely, was targeted as a means of retaliation against his benefactor? How could she protect and prepare the tiny life she would birth if she didn't even know its father's name?

Psyche needed, she realized as she tossed a pebble out into the surf, to see her sisters again.

THE LORD WAS NOT PLEASED. He was confused; she had already seen them, they knew now she was alive—more than that, they'd seen for themselves the splendor in which she lived. They had their own lives and families; did she expect their childish connection would remain unchanged into adulthood? Did he not provide plenty to occupy her time? Was he not enough for her?

Of course he was generous beyond measure, Psyche assured him; she was grateful and counted herself the luckiest of women. But also —he had seen the darkness into which her mind could descend. The emptiness it could embrace. If a visit from her sisters helped her skirt that, where was the harm? It was not his deficiency but hers, and if he could only allow this one thing, she knew she would be able to maintain the peace she'd found.

One night, after he had his pleasure, the lord cleared his throat as he traced figure eights on her back, hesitant to say something. Psyche didn't open her eyes or move her cheek from where it rested on the pillow but said, "What is it?" He let out a sigh.

"It's your sisters," he said. "I've news that they've communicated a desire to one another to visit again the site of your disappearance in the hopes of achieving a second visit. I worry that hearing their voices on the wind, you will become distressed and push harder for me to bring them here."

Psyche sat up so quickly they almost bumped heads. "Of course I want you to bring them here; that's what I've been asking!" She tried to keep the accusation out of her voice and mostly succeeded. It was dark as always, but Psyche imagined his face adopted an expression of displeasure.

"As I have told you, time and again, they should not visit. It will bring us only pain." He remained silent for a long time, and Psyche swallowed her own words, waiting. Finally, he continued, "What can I deny you? Nothing. But I do fear their further influence upon you and how it will affect our relationship. We have come to such a perfect understanding; their counsel cannot possibly conceive of the unique perfection of our union."

Psyche bit her lip, holding in her response until she had folded away all the hate that had bubbled up at his characterization of their situation. "It would mean so much to me," she said, "to see and spend time again with the people I love most in the world—besides you, of course." Her hand rose to cup his cheek. "It would be so healthy for me." She let the emphasis fall on the promise of health, knowing his concern at how little she had been eating before, at his relief in her renewed vigor and spirits over the last several months. The lord heaved a great sigh.

"Yes, yes, of course I will say yes. I shall instruct Zephyr to carry them here when they visit the site."

Psyche's heart leapt in her chest.

"Thank you," she whispered. He reached out, gently scratching her back.

"What can I deny you? Nothing," he repeated. "But hear me"—he pulled his hand away, and while she could not see his eyes clearly, she had the sense they were fixed upon hers—"I do not lightly warn of their influence. They cannot understand what lies between us, much less the consequences of an attempt to force a human understanding on a pairing that has been destined by the Fates. If you speak of us, they will attempt to sway your mind from me, and should they succeed, it shall be our ruin."

THEY ARRIVED as they had before, in the invisible arms of the West Wind. They were set down gently, about a hundred meters from where Psyche stood, and the moment their feet touched down, the three women ran to close the gap.

"Thank you for coming," Psyche whispered into the press of bodies as the three of them embraced. Aglaura's hand stroked her hair.

"Of course. Of course we came."

Psyche was the first to pull away, dashing tears from her eyes and laughing. "It's so silly that I'm crying; I'm overjoyed to see you. I've such a day planned for us, I don't want to ruin it with weeping." Cidippe, who'd yet to speak, crossed her arms, eyeing her younger sister.

"You're not a crier," she said to Psyche. Then, indicating Aglaura with her chin, "That's usually her job." Psyche gave her a watery smile.

"Ah, well, there is a lot I need to tell you." Her hand strayed to her abdomen, and both the older girls' eyes widened.

"You're—" Aglaura whispered.

"I knew it." Cidippe gave a satisfied nod, her hand coming to rest on her own protruding belly.

Psyche shrugged. "I suppose it was only a matter of time, but I have so much to ask you both." The sun shone hot on her face, and while she ordinarily would have relished the late summer warmth, pregnancy had her body running hot, and she craved the coolness of shadow. "Let's get inside."

THE WOMEN SPRAWLED across the great bear rug in Psyche's room, picking at platters of food the Lares had provided and listening as Psyche detailed her situation. Aglaura and Cidippe seemed to have adjusted more quickly than before to whatever effect her appearance had on them, and this set Psyche more at ease. She did not hold back, this time, about the lord and the dynamic between them, about how confusing it was and how even with the work she'd thrown herself into, she could not find contentment. When she paused for a breath, Cidippe jumped in.

"I hear what you're saying, Psy, I do, but I can't help but think you're worrying a bit too much. Have I had my doubts about this man whose name and face you've never even seen? Of course. I still have those doubts. But your situation is in many ways enviable. He is clearly besotted with you. You live in godlike comfort. There is enough hardship in childbirth without inventing problems whole cloth."

Psyche stared at her sister, feeling like she'd been slapped. Outside, cicadas sang and a bird called. Psyche turned her head to the sounds, trying to focus her mind on them to keep the tears at bay. She had so many tears these days. Aglaura sat up, shooting a reproving look at Cidippe.

"How are you, physically?" she asked, attempting to shift the focus. "I don't see you eating much."

Psyche gave an absent shake of her head. "No," she said, "I'm not very hungry. I felt ferociously sick for the longest time, though nothing ever actually came up, but now I'm just tired and mildly nauseous."

"That's how I felt as well," Cidippe offered, pulling her own legs beneath her in a sitting position. "I did not know such fatigue was possible until I was pregnant." Psyche did not acknowledge her words, gaze fixed on the tray of food as she blinked away more tears.

There was an awkward silence, then Cidippe let out a deep breath.

"I'm sorry, Psy, I am. I just..." Her voice trailed off as her eyes found a spot on the floor and she wrung her hands. "I just got jealous since we last saw you, that's all," she whispered.

Psyche's head whirled around. "Jealous?" she repeated. "Why? I'm alone. I'm so desperately alone. And I don't even know the man who acts as my husband—really, I don't even know if I am married—or his place in the world or what tomorrow or the next day may bring, and while I am glad not to have been devoured by a snake monster, for the gods' sake, am I not permitted to wish for more?"

Cidippe stood, throwing her hands in the air. "Of course you are! But you have blessings, too. You may not know this man's name, but he is good to you. Gentle with you. He does not approve of our visits, and yet he brings us here on your behest. Some of us but dream of such basic kindness." She gestured to Aglaura. "Aglaura works her fingers raw day in and day out running that farm her husband is too feeble to manage—show her your hands, Ag! You are barely aware of a need before it is filled by these Lares creatures. I'm not—I don't mean to be—" She broke off, closed her eyes for a moment, then sat down, shoulder to shoulder with Psyche. Neither could look at the other as Cidippe pressed on. "I'm not angry with you Psyche, and I don't begrudge you these things. And I know it is not all roses." Her voice dropped to a whisper. "But I am jealous. I'm jealous because of all you have that I will never possess."

The three of them sat there, listening to one another breathe, as Cidippe's words sank in. Aglaura, as usual, was the one to break the tension.

"Your life is so different from ours, Psy," she said, tone apologetic. "It is hard, to ignore the comforts."

Psyche swallowed, a bitter taste in her mouth. She wanted to yell at them, to say that the beauty here came at too high a price, but then she glanced at Aglaura, soft skin hardened by days under the sun, and at Cidippe, pregnant again by a man who not only claimed her body but marked it with pain, and the words would not come.

"I'm sorry if I spoke thoughtlessly," Psyche said, quiet, eyes spilling over. "And I'm sorry I'm crying again! They just don't seem to stop."

Aglaura reached, brushing tears away with her thumb. "We're sorry, too, Psy." Cidippe nodded confirmation. "Tell us more about this lord; the fact that you don't know his identity seems the most concerning thing to me."

Psyche wiped her nose. "I can't help worrying that I'll have this child only for it to be revealed that I've lain with a monster and all that would mean. Even if my lord is simply a demigod of some description, why the secrecy? How can I plan a future for my child when I do not even know the shape of the world it is being born into?"

Aglaura nodded at this. "I think the solution is pretty straight-forward."

Cidippe hummed her agreement. "You've got to see him," she said.

Psyche felt cold to hear the words, even as she knew they were right. The lord had made it very clear that he had no wish for her to know his identity, and she was scared to go against his wishes; she said as much.

"What reason has he given you for the fear?" Cidippe asked.

"Mainly the strength of his determination to remain unknown," Psyche said. "He is generous and easy with most other things, and so to challenge him on this—well, it feels a bit like the one thing that would upset the apple cart, as it were."

"But you need to know," Aglaura stated. "You've said as much. What's more, I'd say you have a right to know."

Psyche stared down at her palms. "I just don't know how."

"Yes you do," Cidippe said, taking and holding Psyche's hands. "You hide a lamp and striking stone beneath your bed, and when he has fallen asleep, you light it and observe him. If you are careful and quiet and if he is in deep enough sleep, he need not ever know you saw him."

It did sound very simple when Cidippe put it like that.

Psyche agreed she would consider that plan, then changed the topic to that of her sisters and their families, catching up on all the joys and trials of their children and estates. She led them on a tour of her projects, swelling with pride when they admired a task well completed or when Aglaura ran an approving hand down the half-finished blanket Psyche had begun for the baby. When it came time for her sisters to depart once more, she held on to them until the very last moment so that Zephyr had to all but rip them from her grasp. As she watched them disappear into tiny dots on the horizon, Psyche drew a deep, shaky breath. She needed to find a lamp.

CHAPTER 14

Night came, and with it, Psyche's resolve. What had flustered her to consider in the daylight filled her increasingly with certainty as the sun dropped lower and lower on the horizon.

She must know the man whose child now grew within her. She must. There was no world in which she could make the safest choices for herself and for her child without that knowledge.

And so, pushing the lord's warnings deep into the recesses of her mind, Psyche prepared. As she had once prepared her sisters' rooms for a great homecoming, she now prepared her own bedroom for her lord's best comfort. She laid out refreshments, lit sweet-smelling candles, and filled vases with the most bright blooming flowers from the gardens. When she had completed these tasks, she bathed herself with fragrant oil and, once dried, curled up on the bed, a thin blanket all that shielded her from the night's chill. And then, she waited.

She was not ever sure how long it was that she waited, for she dozed off, her body exhausted both from the exertion of her preparations and the heavy internal work it was doing to support a growing life. She awoke to the shifting of the mattress beside her and opened her eyes to find a dimly backlit head of curls above hers.

"Hello, my sweet," he said, pressing a kiss to her forehead. "What occasion do we celebrate?" His hand swept to indicate the room, and

Psyche noticed several candles were no longer burning—whether from having burned down or been blown out, she could not tell. She sat up, sweeping her hair from her face.

"Good evening, Love," Psyche said. "How were your travels?"

"Ah"—he dismissed her question with a flick of his head—"tiresome, as ever. Pleasurable only in that they sharpened my longing for you." As he tilted her chin to kiss her mouth, Psyche found herself irritated with the evasion. Before, she had little interest in where he was or what he was doing when not at home. She'd simply been grateful for the reprieve. Now, however, with Aglaura's and Cidippe's words echoing in her head, she saw how neatly he sidestepped her questions.

Psyche pulled away, clearing her throat. "I am grateful you are home, Love, for I have news I hope will please you." Her voice sounded halting to her own ears, but the lord showed no indication of noticing. He was already running an impatient hand down the side of her body, tightening his hand to grip her hip.

"Hmm?" he inquired, his head bent to study the indent of his fingers into her skin.

Psyche took a deep breath, then gently removed his hand and laid back, drawing down the blanket and bringing her hand to rest on the soft curve of her belly. She met his eyes as best she could in the near dark. She felt, rather than saw, his squinting confusion, rapidly followed by agitated excitement.

"A child?" he asked, sliding down her body to lay his lips upon her stomach. "Truly?" Psyche nodded, then remembering the dark, found her voice.

"Yes, a child. My bleeding hasn't come for many weeks and I've been sick in all the ways my sisters spoke of feeling during their own pregnancies." She winced at the mention of her sisters, worried he would seize on it and launch again into his disapproval of their visits, but he did not seem to have listened to anything beyond the word "yes."

"What a miracle!" he exclaimed, pulling her into his arms and tucking her head beneath his chin. His fingers stroked through her hair. "I never dreamed there might be a child," he said, half to himself.

Psyche stiffened.

"You never dreamed this could happen? Were you unaware how babies are made?" Her words came out sharper than she intended. She felt the lord laugh and shake his head above hers.

"Of course I knew; it's just never happened for me before. Not in all the years I've lived and all the women I've loved."

Psyche saw her moment and seized it. "And how many years might that be?" she asked. He went immediately still, and a pulsing silence rose between them. Then,

"You've been speaking to your sisters," he said. "I warned you about allowing their ideas into our home." Psyche felt the familiar crawl of nerves up her spine but nonetheless pressed him further.

"I need to know who you are before I birth our child. How can I raise a child in ignorance of its parentage? Ignorant of what threats to its safety may exist? Children grow, and they leave, and I cannot prepare a child to enter the world if I don't know how that world will receive them." Her words were impassioned and sure, and the lord drew back, cupping her face in his hands and bringing his own close to hers until they were nearly nose to nose.

"What fire my child has lit in you!" he said, warmth creeping into his voice again. One hand slid from her cheek down to her breast, cupping it for a moment before pushing her onto the pillows and moving above her. Psyche held her breath. "Fear not, sweet one, our child shall want for nothing in the world. I shall provide for him the same way I provide for you, and when the time comes for him to take his place in the world, I shall use all the powers at my disposal to create a living to his liking." He pressed kisses down her throat, urgent hands running down her body. "Your concerns do you credit," he whispered in her ear, "and show me how exquisitely I have chosen, but they are unnecessary. I will care for you. I will always care for you."

Psyche let out her breath. She wanted to scream. She wanted to beat his chest and scratch his face, transfer all her internal pain to his external body. Instead, she poured the anger and impotence she felt into responding to his advances, and when he cried out in completion, her nails raked red streaks down his back. They lay there until his body softened and his weight grew heavy on hers and his snores tickled the fine hairs in her ear.

For a long while, Psyche remained still, feeling his warm breath against her face and his body curled, like a child's, into hers. When she was sure he had reached the deepest level of sleep, she slid out from his embrace and climbed from the bed as smooth and quiet as a shadow.

Now had come the moment Psyche had planned, and yet she paused, considering the implications of what she was about to do. She was safe. She lived in comfort beyond her wildest imaginings. Perhaps she was an ungrateful girl to desire this one thing that he was unwilling to give when he offered her the world in every other way.

And yet. This was the one thing he had asked of her, because everything else he wanted he took without hesitation. Her body he claimed the first night she arrived, as though it was his by right, and all subsequent nights had borne out the same message—he would attend to her pleasure as well as his own, but he would not be denied. He had spirited her away to this hidden home, separated her from not only her family but from the world and connection with anyone but him. She had no evidence for it, but she suspected his involvement in Delphi, in the prophecy that had brought her to that clifftop. Now, he asked her to trust him with the future of the child growing within her, and Psyche's spine stiffened with the realization that his considera-tion for this child would stem always, first and foremost, from what was best for him.

Psyche did not hesitate further. From beneath the bed she drew out the oil lamp she had hidden, tiptoeing across the room to the single candle that remained burning in the far corner and carefully using the small flame to light her wick. The moon shone brightly through the curtained balcony, and, cradling the lamp in her hands, Psyche looked up at it for a moment, closing her eyes as she whis-pered a prayer.

"Lend me strength, Diana."

She inched back across the room, hardly daring to breathe as she drew closer, the light of her lamp creeping slowly over the slumbering body on the bed. First revealed were his legs, long, well muscled, and unblemished, the skin of his feet soft and free of callouses. Psyche knew from his touch that his hands were the same; this was not a man of labor. Higher, higher the light drew until she beheld the lean expanse of his chest, as strong and beautiful as his legs had been, almost amusing in its perfection, for what human could ever hope to reach such an ideal? Psyche's hand trembled as she drew close enough to illuminate his face.

It was breathtaking, of course. His curls, into which she had sunk her fingers so many times before, framed a face gentle in repose, both clear featured and sharply drawn. A faint smile played at the corner of his soft mouth, amused even in his dreaming. Though she had known he was not physically a monster, she nonetheless found herself stupefied for a moment by his beauty. What god could this be? A son of Jupiter, perhaps? Of Neptune? She remembered the oracle that had sealed her fate and gasped—could this be Apollo himself? Tearing her gaze away, she swung the lamp around to search the room for clues.

His clothes lay in a haphazard heap on the floor, simple but finely woven linen lined in golden thread. Sandals of sturdy construction lay beneath a nearby bench, but when she crouched to examine them, they were wholly ordinary in design, no magical wings fluttering at the heels. Not Mercury, then.

Something gleamed at the corner of her eye, and Psyche turned. The curtain fluttered at the balcony, and the moon seemed to beckon her forth. Without thinking, she walked forward, drawing back the gauzy fabric and stepping out into the night.

There, leaning against the balcony railing and illuminated in the silver light of the moon, were the most beautifully wrought bow and quiver of arrows that Psyche had ever seen. Psyche crossed to them, crouching to better study the details. Significantly smaller than weapons she had observed used by her father's guards, the wood of both was polished to a brilliant shine, the bone accents gleaming. Carved into the side of the quiver, with inhuman skill, was the image of a blooming rose. Psyche nearly dropped her lamp.

Venus. That was the symbol of Venus. If this man in her bed bore the symbol of the goddess of love, then certainly he was here at her behest in some way. Psyche looked at the sleeping figure, then again at the bow and quiver. She reached out, intending to bring the quiver closer, to examine it further, but as she did, her hand bumped the bow. It clattered onto the floor, knocking the quiver with it, arrows sliding out in a haphazard pile on the floor.

Psyche froze for a moment, listening to hear if the noise had disturbed the sleeping lord. When she heard only the even rhythm of his breath, she swiftly began gathering up the arrows and thrusting them back into the quiver, anxious to arrange it just as she had found it.

In her haste, the soft pad of her palm grazed the edge of one of the arrows, slicing so cleanly that for a moment, she didn't feel the pain. Biting her lip to keep from crying out, she brought the wound to her mouth, sucking and applying pressure as she finished righting the quiver and bow with her uninjured hand. Something tugged at her mind, and once the weapons were as they had been, she gathered the curtain together, pulling it fully away from the wall and floor.

Psyche forced her breathing to calm as she beheld the truth. Laid gently along the balcony floor, upon a blanket for protection, were a pair of wings so brilliant in color that even in the dark, it seemed they shone against the white marble and the spotless curtain. With the fabric of the curtain fisted in her hand and her lamp lifted high, she could make out the gleaming feathers and delicately boned frame. They were not massive, but she imagined they would support a man. Her lord flew here, which explained the ease with which he came and went, as well as the improbable softness of his feet. He flew, and he bore a bow and quiver with Venus's mark, and finally, all of the pieces clicked into place.

Cupid. The lord was Cupid. The god of eroticism, son of Venus, and tormenter of romantic relationships. What game was he playing with her? She had never heard of Cupid taking human lovers, merely sowing havoc among them with the pricks of his arrows. Had he pricked her? She didn't think so; she didn't love him, but then, would she even be able to tell if he had? Psyche dropped the curtain and walked to the bed, staring down at the man who had told her to call him Love.

The moment her eyes fixed on him, Psyche realized her mistake, but by then, it was too late. The same face that she had, moments before, observed with objective detachment now lit an unfamiliar flame in her belly. She wanted to press her mouth to his neck, to taste his skin in a way that had never occurred to her in the dozens of times they had lain together. She wanted to run her hands down his body, to have him run his down hers. Psyche realized she was trembling, and she thought she might explode if she couldn't figure out a way to pour herself into him.

Even as part of her mind protested her body's sudden reversal, another part welcomed these new feelings with a sigh of relief. How much easier it would be with him to feel this way.

The need to touch him became too strong, and Psyche reached a hand out, brushing curls away from his eyes. In that moment, her hand slipped, and a few drops of oil fell from the lamp onto Cupid's shoulder. His eyes flew open and met hers, and for a beat, they stared at one another. He reached a hand to her cheek.

"Psyche..." Then full consciousness struck and Cupid's face contorted with pain and anger.

"Foolish, inconstant woman," he said, rising from the bed to stand before her. He was not tall, but he was taller than she was, and the force of his emotion made her stumble back a step. He was so, so beautiful. "Did I not warn you? Did I not tell you that your inability to trust would be our ruin?" His words were sharp with fury, his hands raking through his hair in agitation. Psyche felt her own come up, reaching for him.

"I needed..." she whispered.

"You needed what?" he said, voice like a lash. "What could you possibly need? I have provided every comfort, indulged every whim, I even allowed those snakes of sisters of yours to visit. And you repay me with betrayal?"

Psyche's mouth opened and shut, but no sound emerged. She felt as though she were outside her body, watching from above as Cupid snatched up and pulled on his clothes, then stalked to the balcony to retrieve his wings and weapon.

"Do you know I defied my mother for your sake? Oh, she ordered you wed to a beast, the meanest of creatures, where you would live out your days in humiliation and fear—if you were not eaten on sight —but when I saw you, I knew that I could not deliver you to such a fate. I loved you, foolishly, desperately; I still love you! And yet you regard me with so little concern that you would risk all we have for a glimpse of my beauty. Well, here it is, Psyche; was it worth the price?" He turned toward her, framed by the balcony and haloed by the moon, his arms out wide.

"That wasn't what it—"

"It doesn't matter," he sighed, as if she hadn't spoken. His arms fell to his sides. "It was but a dream all along. Now I wake and find myself injured and in need of my mother's care; what irony!" And, shrugging into his wings, he turned and alighted.

Something in Psyche came alive again, her body panicking at the thought of separating from him, her mind screaming indignation that he would flee, and she lurched forward, grabbing hold of his ankle as he rose into the air.

"Wait!" she cried, her own feet rising from the ground as he flew. Her other hand scrabbled to join the first until she was dangling from his leg, the strength of her arms the only thing keeping her from plummeting two stories to the courtyard below. Cupid looked down at her, anger and pain and lingering intimacy in his expression. He descended as best he could, shaking her off with an ungentle kick when they drew close enough to the ground. She collapsed in a heap, then scrambled to her feet. She pushed hair from her eyes and glared up at where he had perched himself in a tree. Her body might burn for him, but her mind could still hold fury.

"You would leave? Now? When I am pregnant with your child?"

Cupid shrugged, not meeting her eyes, a hand pressed hard against the burns on his shoulder. "Women have children every day, less commonly by gods, but that happens, too. Go to your sisters since you have chosen their wisdom over mine."

Psyche felt hot, whether from desire or rage, she couldn't tell. "My sisters have cared for me my entire life and treat me as their equal. My sisters do not conceal things and seek to placate me with baubles and attempt to turn me into their own pretty doll to play with at their whim. Yes, Cupid, *Love*, I trusted their wisdom, and I would again."

123

His eyes flashed to hers, and he opened his mouth to reply, then paused, jumping down from the tree and striding until he was right before her, studying her face. His hand came up, brushed her cheek.

"Now?" he said, mournful, "Now you look at me like this? Now you feel the love I've carried for you since the moment I saw you? Now that you have ruined it all?"

Psyche held his gaze, raised her palm so he could see. Blood dripped down her wrist. "It was an accident."

Cupid took her wrist, brushed the gentlest of fingers over her wound.

"Love cannot live without trust," he murmured.

Her eyes bored into his, pleading with him to understand. "I only wanted us to be on equal footing."

He released her hand, then. "More fool you, then, *love,*" he said, "for you see, we are not equals, and we never could be. I am a god, and you —" He hesitated, the barest hint of regret dancing across his features. "You are just a human, beautiful for now but doomed to time." And so saying, he rose into the air and disappeared into the night without a backward glance.

PART THREE

CHAPTER 15

Psyche's conviction departed with Cupid. Stumbling up to her room after watching his form grow smaller and smaller against the night sky until it disappeared altogether, Psyche fell upon her bed and sobbed until she lost herself in uneasy dreams.

The next morning, she was awakened by one of the Lares.

"Lady Psyche," the unseen voice said in gentle acknowledgment as a plate of food floated to her table and items strewn about the room began to tidy themselves. Psyche did not respond but stared at the ceiling, her fingers picking at the skin of her nail beds. "Are you well, Psyche?" the Lares asked, a formless and yet firm weight brushing Psyche's hand.

In all the time Psyche had spent at the estate, neither of the Lares had ever touched her. They had never strayed from their role as servants and keepers of the house, seeming at times to endeavor for as much invisibility in presence as they possessed in physicality. So a touch to her hand, slight a gesture as it was, registered as so great an expression of empathy that Psyche's eyes filled, and only rapid blinking kept the tears from spilling over.

"He's gone," she said, and what she was appalled to realize she meant was that it felt like half of herself was gone as well. The Lares made a noise of acknowledgment.

"Yes, we saw his departure last night."

"He says he will not return."

"If he's gone to his mother, we expect he shall not."

The tears fell then, Psyche cursing herself in her mind. What a presumptuous, grasping fool she'd been. For the sake of imagined future problems, she had created for herself a host of present ones, not least of which was the now ever-present need she had for Cupid's touch—the loss of it ached. She glanced over at the breakfast, her stomach turning over.

She was pregnant, and she was alone, and she was scared.

Once the Lares had departed, Psyche dragged herself up, not bothering to wash her face or change clothes as she picked at her food, attempting to take nibbles small enough to placate her rolling stomach but with enough sustenance to fuel her body. As she ate, she thought.

Her mind was at once familiar and foreign, the thoughts and feelings she had held prior to the arrow scratch still very much present alongside newer, complicating ones. The physical desire for Cupid was easy to diagnose as a result of the arrow, but the sympathy she now felt for him? The self-hatred that bloomed from the very idea that her actions had caused him pain? Were those hers, or were they planted? When she pictured his face right before he departed she saw not only the cowardice of a man running from challenge but also the bitter despair of betrayed devotion, and trying to hold both in her mind made her head spin. A small part of her wished that the arrow had done its work more completely, removing all traces of what had been before. She felt ashamed to think it, and yet how much simpler that would be.

As far as Psyche could see, she had two options. She could remain at the estate, with none but the Lares, and hope that her pregnancy continued smoothly and Cupid calmed down enough to return sooner rather than later and that the contradictions of her mind didn't drive her mad. Or she could try to depart, find her way to one of her sisters, and take shelter with them while she figured out how to find Cupid.

It was not an obvious choice; there were arguments to be made both ways, and Psyche made them. By late morning, however, she had decided: sitting and waiting would be worse than action. The last time she had contemplated this question she had drunk herself to sleep on a balcony; she would not make the same mistake twice.

Besides, despite its risks, action brought with it a sense of control and of companionship—both things Psyche had not felt for months. She would ask the Lares to pack her a bag or do it herself if they refused, and she would depart the following morning.

THE LARES, as it turned out, had no qualms about helping her pack. Though they said nothing that constituted outright support of her decision, she nonetheless felt a vague approval in the speed and efficiency with which they attended to her request.

"Did you know we were born voiceless?"

The even, mid-range voice startled Psyche from the stupor into which she'd sunk, staring at the oil staining her bedsheets. She looked up, quickly realizing that searching for the speaker was silly. It was one of the Lares who had spoken, of course, but something in their tone was different than she had heard before. More... real. More present.

"I did not know," she said, trying to balance the belatedness of her reply with curiosity. "There must be a story there."

Across the room, a plain linen dress was folding, as if on its own, and sliding into the gaping mouth of a tidy traveling bag.

"Oh yes," the Lares said, and again, Psyche had the sense that they were somehow more corporeal than they had ever been around her, despite their continued invisibility. "We were born as voiceless as our mother, who lost her tongue for the crime of speaking truth. But a child who cannot cry for food is, too often, never fed, and so we traded our bodies for the power to form words."

Psyche opened her mouth, then closed it again, processing this. She hesitated a moment before asking, "What form were the bodies you gave up?" In her bitterness, she could not help thinking that perhaps she, too, would have traded her female body if it meant gaining a voice. If it meant being heard.

It occurred to her too late that her question was, perhaps, impertinent. "I'm sorry to pry, I don't mean—"

The Lares cut her off. "A babe has no awareness of, nor purpose for, such distinctions; those details are lost to time. And what does it matter? The politics of bodies belong to those dwelling in them. They do not interest us." The bag they had been packing floated across the room, landing soft on the bed beside Psyche.

"Oh," she said. "I'm sorry."

For the second time in almost as many hours, Psyche felt a touch, this time to her hair. "We were lucky, to be born as a pair, to have our experience always validated by the other. And still, it was not a painless trade to make. Every choice comes at a cost with the gods. Remember that."

Swallowing, Psyche nodded, opting to keep her own words in, lest she stumble into greater offense. She sensed the Lares drift back toward the door.

"Sleep now," they said. "Bodies need rest."

And somehow, her mind turning over all the Lares had said, Psyche did.

LATE THE NEXT MORNING, after a fitful and too-short sleep, Psyche set out from the estate. Slung from her shoulder was a bag containing food, clothes, and coin, and a skin of water hung at her hip.

When she reached the grassy area where her sisters had been left, she called out.

"Zephyr!"

She set her jaw and called again,

"Zephyr!"

A breeze lifted the ends of her hair.

"Zephyr!" Psyche called for the third time, and this time, he came, swirling around her, lifting her from the ground.

Why do you summon me, Psyche of Crete?

"I need you to take me from here to—" A thought struck her. "Can you take me to Venus's home?"

There was a rumbling, a laugh like thunder. *What I can do and what I will do are very different things, little princess.*

Psyche disliked the address, but she needed his help. "Then will you take me to my sister's home in Chania?"

I will take you close enough.

Psyche nodded. "I am grateful; thank you, Zephyr." The speed of the wind about her picked up, her body starting to move through the air.

Oh no, thank you. I look forward to watching this play out.

BY THE TIME Zephyr set her down somewhere outside Chania, night was falling fast. Spotting a temple in the distance, Psyche set off toward it. She reached the steps of the building as stars were emerging against the dark sky, a full moon illuminating the stone edifice. Weary but flush with pride, Psyche climbed the steps, then sank down against one of the supporting columns.

Psyche's body, as though aware of the physicality she needed from it, had granted her relief from the symptoms that had been plaguing her since the onset of her pregnancy. She had noted with cautious hope that this might mean she was through them for good.

The moment she sat down, however, the realities came rushing in as though her child had withheld complaints for so long that now they must all be lodged at once. Her back felt on fire, her stomach roiled, and her chest burned. Groaning, Psyche shifted, using her bag as a pillow for her head as she propped herself on her side as best she could. The moment she was horizontal, fatigue settled on her like a blanket, and her last thought before drifting off was gratitude for the warmth of the night.

"WELL, well, well. It is you, after all." An amused, lyrical voice floated above Psyche, interrupting her already restless dreams. Disoriented and stiff, Psyche pushed herself up from the stone floor, hissing at the pain in her joints. Blinking, she located the source of the disruption.

Standing above her, taller than seemed possible, was a man, arms folded and expression fixed in what appeared to be extreme delight. Psyche's mouth was dry and words fled her brain. The man crouched down, reaching out to tuck her hair behind one ear, a gesture that made her flinch away.

"Oh no, Psyche, don't fret. You're not for me," the man said, smiling. "Not anymore, at least. I just wanted to see you for myself, and so when I realized you were sleeping in my temple, of all places, I could not resist paying a quick visit." His temple? Psyche registered, with a start, the implications of that statement and, with belated urgency, shuffled to her knees, bowing her head.

"Lord Apollo," she said, counting her breaths to calm her heartbeat. Apollo stood again, eyes still studying her.

"It is so fascinating to see you. You have no idea. Even more, now you've upset his little scheme. Delighted with you for that, by the way. Always fun to see the prick get a taste of his own medicine."

Despite his familiar language, she could not bring herself to respond, choosing instead to focus on her breath and the feel of the rock beneath her knees. Above her, Apollo frowned.

"You're very meek for a woman who defied the son of Venus. Do speak, before my trip begins to feel like a waste." Psyche breathed in, then out. Then—

"What would my Lord Apollo like me to say?" She hadn't intended it as a challenge, she'd meant to communicate her subservience to him, but the weariness of her body and the general outrageousness of her position got the best of her.

Apollo nodded, approving. "Yes, yes, here we go. Play with me, Psyche. Tell me why you've broken my poor nephew's heart and how it is that I can aid you to rip it further apart."

Psyche drew a steadying breath, let it out.

"Any pain I've caused Lord Cupid was unintended," she said, still to the floor. "I journey now hoping to reunite with him; I—" She stopped, not ready to say the word that had sprung first to her lips, and substituted instead, "I *want* him." The cut on her hand ached with sudden intensity.

Apollo groaned. "Oh, but that's boring, so does every being he encounters. That's exactly what I was hoping you wouldn't say."

A desire to ask the god what exactly he *did* want her to say crawled up Psyche's throat, but she tamped it down. Above her, Apollo had cocked his head, studying her.

"He got you with an arrow, didn't he? Got tired of your little depression and fixed you right up. I did think I'd goaded him out of that, but I admit my powers of persuasion seem to be lacking of late."

Psyche's mind stuttered at the implications of his words; Apollo was right—Cupid could have pricked her at any time to gain her devotion, and yet she now knew with certainty that he hadn't. Why?

"Lord Apollo," Psyche said, slow. "Might I beg a boon?"

Apollo shrugged. "You may beg, certainly."

"The lord Cupid and I had a disagreement; I planned to stay with my sister, to convalesce together in our pregnancies while I search for him, but now that you're here—"

Apollo's sputtering sound of surprise cut Psyche off and alerted her that she'd shared information he had not possessed. She cursed herself.

"Pregnant? You're carrying a little demigod Cupid in that mortal womb of yours?" Apollo began pacing, talking to himself, and Psyche snuck a glance upward, then dared shift her legs when she saw he was paying her no attention. Succumbing to the numbness, Psyche adjusted to sit with her legs crossed, a hiss of pain escaping as she made the change. The noise seemed to remind Apollo he was not alone; he looked over.

"You're in trouble," he said, and Psyche could not tell from his tone his feelings on the pronouncement. She pressed her lips together. *Breathe in, breathe out.*

"Yes, I am aware."

Apollo gave an emphatic shake of his head. "No, you're not. I'm not referring to whatever discomfort is involved in carrying a child or the inconvenient timing of your lovers' spat." Psyche opened her mouth to respond, but Apollo waved an imperious hand, continuing. "What I mean is that the life within you has raised the stakes in this story much higher than I—and I'm sure Cupid—ever anticipated. Venus never wanted to be a mother; how do you think she'll respond to learning she's to be a grandmother? What's more, she hates you."

"Me?" Psyche's eyes widened. Apollo gave her a glance of irritation.

"Yes, girl, you. Of course she hates you. All of Crete was worshipping your image in place of hers not ten moons ago; you're her enemy."

"But I didn't want any of that!" Psyche was too taken aback and terrified by this information to worry further about her tone. "Surely, she must know, I never meant for that to happen!"

Apollo threw up his hands. "What do your intentions have anything to do with anything? It is what happened; thus, she hates you. And now—now! You are going to give birth to her son's child. Oh no, no. This is more than I signed up for."

"Signed up for?" But Apollo was pacing and talking to himself again, distress raising his voice so Psyche caught snatches of his words.

"Titan's teeth, what an irresponsible—I mean, it's hilarious, but I don't—Venus can't know my part in this. She'll come after Hyacinth and I *can't* lose Hyacinth. What a mess. Cupid and his fucking messes." Coming to an abrupt stop, Apollo turned again to Psyche, resolute.

"I must depart. Tell no one of our meeting; I cannot be further associated with you."

"As you say—"

Apollo interrupted her. "You've not asked my advice, but I shall nonetheless offer it to you this once: go to your sister's home. Have the babe. Tell no one of its father. Live your human life, die, let Mercury guide you to the Underworld. Seek no more gods."

"I seek only one god," Psyche ground out. Apollo's face fell, and he heaved a massive sigh.

"You're not going to heed my advice. I can already tell. More fool you, then. I'm done with this drama." And so saying, he strode out of the temple, Psyche's baffled stare following his retreating form. She jumped to her feet, calling out before she lost her nerve.

"Lord Apollo! Might I beg you take a message to Lord Cupid for me? Or at least safe passage to my sister's home?"

Apollo didn't even glance back. "No."

Psyche stared until he disappeared from sight, and dawn began to peek over the horizon.

CHAPTER 16

When Cupid arrived at his mother's home, Venus was all solicitousness. He had been away for months without so much as an afternoon drop-by to regale her with his escapades, much less update her on the task she had set him. Even from her perspective as a goddess, with little regard to time measured by mortal standards, she had missed her boy and the way his affection made her feel.

"I must lie down; I'm exhausted from flying through the night, and my shoulder is grievously injured," Cupid said, shrugging out of his wings and collapsing on the first piece of furniture he encountered. Venus snagged a blanket from a nearby chair and spread it over him, humming with concern.

"Oh sweet boy, what has happened? Who hurt you so?" Her fingers fluttered to the dark spot on his shoulder, where already, the raw, blistered skin had begun to heal, a fading line of red slashing across his chest where the oil had run down.

Cupid shut his eyes. "It doesn't matter," he said. "Wine, bring me wine, Mother."

Venus pursed her lips, torn between her displeasure at the directive and her desire for him to share more and as quickly as possible. Ultimately, she fetched the wine, as well as a servant to tend to his burn.

"My angel," she said, taking his hand in hers and stroking it. "Tell me what happened, that I might avenge you."

Cupid swallowed a hearty gulp of wine, then leaned back, closing his eyes again. "No, Mother, let it be. I shall be well soon enough. Within the year, at least." And he drifted off into a fitful sleep, the summoned servant still dabbing at his wound.

"Wake him with your ministrations and you shall suffer the same injury," Venus warned the young man kneeling by her son, then stood a moment to admire her own taste as she watched the light play through the servant's sun-streaked hair. Venus only ever kept beautiful servants; perhaps when Cupid woke, she would offer to share this one as a means of renewing his spirits.

Now, however, she meant to discover what was afoot.

The terns in Venus's employ had proved eager gossips, and through all the generations that had served her, they had never brought Venus false intelligence.

Which was why when, nearly a quarter hour into their meeting, the tern had failed to provide her the information she sought, Venus's eye began to twitch.

"And Bacchus's parties are truly shaping up into a debacle, what with gods fucking humans and humans fucking animals and animals fucking gods; and to be sure, his cult is strong, but one can only imagine the offspring we will collectively be supporting months from now. Really, someone should rein him in. But"—the tern paused— "what I've heard is that a certain god has taken part in Bacchus's festivities of late and is protecting him as a means of protecting his own reputation as well."

Venus, who had been burying her foot in the sand where they sat at the surf's edge, perked up, cutting her gaze to where the tern had perched on her shoulder. "Oh? And who might this be?"

The tern gave an expressive flap of his wings, head cocked with one sharp eye twinkling at Venus. "Now that I do not know mistress."

Venus let out an irritated breath. "Well, for Jupiter's sake, what do you know, then? Unless this mysterious, debauchery-seeking god you speak of is my son—into whom I inquired when you arrived and whom you have yet to mention—I hear nothing but an utter waste of my time." She stood in a fluid motion, brushing sand off as she did and startling the tern so that it had to make an awkward lurching adjustment to remain on its perch.

"No, my lady, no!" the tern called out. "I do have information on your son, only…" He tilted his head and fixed Venus with one beady black eye. "I do not think you will like what I have to say."

Venus raised her chin. "Say it, then."

"Well…" The tern shifted weight from foot to foot, distressed. "They say, my lady—and I cannot stress enough that this is gossip several degrees from the source—that your son has been jilted by a human lover."

Venus's eyes sparked. "A human lover? Absurd! His last lover was a muse, the one before that a nymph. Had he descended so low as to bed a human—had there been a human worthy of such attention—I would know of it…" Her last words trailed off as her mind spun. There had, actually, been a human many thought worthy…

"They say it was Psyche, my lady, of Crete."

Venus heard the words as if in echo, as though she had heard them before and the tern was simply repeating himself. Psyche. Of course. How obvious. How had she not seen it herself? Psyche had disappeared, and the people of Crete had returned to Venus's temples with their tribute, and so the goddess of love had assumed her son had completed the task she had set him, albeit not in the way she had asked. But Cupid had disappeared, too, long enough that she had noticed. Had missed him.

Venus's face grew hot as she thought of the way the other immortals must be whispering about this betrayal.

"My lady?" The tern's head twisted back and forth, each eye trying to catch a better image than the other. "It is mere hearsay."

"Get out of my sight," Venus hissed, "and see that you spread such lies no further."

A sudden breeze bore the sputtering tern away as Venus spun on her heel. She needed to talk to her son.

. . .

138

WHEN VENUS RETURNED to her home, she found Cupid where she had left him, alert now, picking at a bowl of fruit as the servant Venus had charged with his care ran a comb with oil through the god's curls. Cupid glanced up as she entered, watching as her eyes cut down to the burns across his shoulder and chest. He cleared his throat.

"I suppose you are curious how I came by these."

Venus's jaw was tight. Her son was angled just enough that she caught sight of several long, fading scratches down his back. At her silence, Cupid's gaze met hers. His voice was light.

"It's a tale I know will entertain you, but first, I really must consume something other than fruit." Pulling his head out from the servant's reach, Cupid swung his feet to the floor and made to stand, only to be met with a single long finger, pressed with threatening care into the very center of his wound. Hissing in pain, Cupid sat back, his eyes flying up to hold his mother's.

"Sweet boy"—the ice in her tone belied the gentle words—"do not rush your recovery. In my home, of all places, you need not fetch things for yourself. You"—keeping her one finger where it was, she raised her free hand and snapped at the now-idle servant—"go fetch a goblet of ambrosia for the lord Cupid, to speed his healing." The comb clattered onto the table as the boy hastened to obey. Mother and son watched him go, neither moving.

"He is truly very beautiful, Mother," Cupid said, grasping at flattery. "I've always admired how you find such singular beauty with which to surround yourself."

Venus's mouth twisted. "Like attracts like, and I have an image to uphold." The mention of her reputation caused Cupid to wince, a subtle tightening of his features that was not lost on Venus. She removed her finger from his shoulder, watching as the skin flooded once more with color. She crouched down, tracing the lines of the wound with one gentle nail; Cupid sucked in his breath. "My poor, beautiful son. Who has marked you so violently? Tell me. Let me seek vengeance on your behalf; let me bring you the hand that did this so that never again may it cause such harm."

Cupid paled, clearing his throat. "Ah, no, I mean, thank you, Mother." He swallowed, pulling away ever so slightly from her touch and pushing himself up to a less vulnerable seat, wincing as his back scraped against fabric. "I've dealt with the offender already as I see fit; truly, I seek only your love and care and refuge for a time."

Venus stood, staring down at the face she loved more fiercely than any other, and she saw his gaze shutter under her own. Her heart felt as though it was no longer in her chest but there, on the couch, bleeding out more rapidly with every evasion Cupid uttered.

Cupid, of all the gods, knew how hard she had to fight for legitimacy, to be considered with the same reverence and gravity as the older goddesses. He had seen from infancy the way they slighted her, diminished her abilities, reduced her to her body. And now, for him to not only consort with but protect one of the acutest threats to her name—well, it made her a joke. Anger burned hot and blinding through Venus; she clenched her fist to keep from slapping her son across the face.

"My love is always yours," she said, her throat burning on the words. "And refuge I insist on providing until you are well enough to return to the world. But I fear you've arrived at an unfortunate time for my care; there are matters of council that demand my presence and attention, so I must leave you in the hands of my servants. Take your rest, heal your body, and I shall return as soon as I can." Leaning over, she pressed a hard kiss to his forehead, then spun to leave. By the door she paused, observing Cupid's wings where the servant had placed them against the wall, packed neatly into their protective leather case. Reaching down, Venus picked up the case by its strap and swung it over her shoulder. She looked at her son.

"As you shall not be needing these anytime soon, I'll take them to your father for some cleaning and care. Rest well, my love."

On her way out of the house, Venus seized her head guard by the arm, not bothering to lower her voice as she spoke. "Lord Cupid is not to depart this house; keep him within by whatever means necessary. Should you fail, know I will have your head as payment." And so decreeing, the goddess of love called for Palaemon, boarded her chariot, and was gone.

· · ·

140

Cupid had suspected he was under house arrest the moment his mother had picked up his wings; overhearing the order to her guard only confirmed it. He groaned, pressing the heels of his hands into his eyes. What wreckage this was. And the worst of it was that despite the burning pain across his chest and the hot shame that flooded him over betraying his mother—despite all, the largest part of him yearned to be with Psyche. To fold her into his arms, tell her he forgave her offenses, and make love to her soft, accepting body until his own was spent and he drifted off into contented sleep. He wanted it so badly that even when his mother's servant returned bearing the requested plate of food, Cupid could not find it within himself to satisfy his desires with him. None would do but Psyche. She had ruined him, and now his world would burn for it. Miserable, self-pitying, and increasingly bored, Cupid collapsed onto the couch and stared at the ceiling until his thoughts finally gave way to oblivion.

Chapter 17

The priestesses of the Temple of Apollo were kind when they discovered Psyche later that morning, bringing her to eat with them and listening as she relayed her need to obtain travel to Chania. As it happened, one of the priestesses had family nearby who did regular business in town, and she offered to walk with Psyche that day to the family home. This Psyche accepted with gratitude, and by midday, the two were walking in companionable silence along a dirt road. It was the priestess who broke the silence.

"Forgive my curiosity, but why do you not remove your hood?"

Psyche thought about how best to answer. "I... my face is not like others," she said. "It is easier to keep it covered."

The priestess accepted this with a nod, and they finished the walk in separate contemplation.

When they reached the priestess's family home, Psyche was greeted with distracted warmth, as though a last-minute traveler accompanying them on their trade route was a commonplace thing. The priestess's mother pursed her lips when Psyche declined to remove her cloak but nonetheless offered her a pallet on the floor beside her children, which Psyche accepted with grace if not enthusiasm.

That evening, as she ate her portion of soup, Psyche asked what it was the family traded.

"Honey!" said one of the children, soup dribbling out the corner of his mouth as he spoke. "Father has bees, and I help him with them."

"Father says honey is good for sickness," added one of the little girls, "and I've felt very sick today." She shot a hopeful look at her father, who laughed and shook his head as he reached out to tousle the girl's hair. Psyche swallowed her own laugh at the way the child's shoulders slumped in resignation, even as she pushed down a bitter ache at the easy display of parental affection.

They set off the next morning, Psyche seated in the back of the cart with the children and the honey. There were four children, the eldest about twelve and the youngest around four, and they found Psyche fascinating.

"Why are you by yourself?" the older boy, Alexios, asked, leaning so far over in his effort to better see under her hood that he nearly toppled over. "Mother says women should never be alone in the world."

"I can't say your mother is wrong," Psyche said, angling slightly away. "Which is why I'm grateful to your family—riding with you will allow me to reunite with my sister in Chania so that I am not alone any longer."

"Do you like your sister?" the littlest girl piped in. "I mostly like Chloe, but sometimes she tries to tell me what to do." The little girl leveled an expression at her elder sister that made Psyche laugh. Her sister, Chloe, rolled her eyes.

"If you did what you were supposed to, Dimitra, I'd have less to say."

"My sisters are both older than me, too," Psyche confided in Dimitra, "and often tried to tell me what to do as well." As she leaned forward in confidence, the hood of her cloak slipped further back on her head, exposing her face to partial sunlight. Even as Psyche scrambled to pull the fabric back in place, she was aware of Dimitra's eyes, wide and staring.

"Are you a goddess?" she whispered. Psyche shook her head in agitation, pressing a finger to her lips to quiet the child.

"Ermis!" Chloe's attention had shifted, and Psyche was relieved to see that her exclamation had diverted Dimitra as well. "Stay out of the honey!" The younger of her brothers withdrew a finger, sucking off the sticky sweetness without apology. Psyche saw Alexios and Dimitra watching their brother, new gleams in their eyes. Chloe saw it, too. Huffing, the girl shifted so that access to any of the pithoi containing the honey required reaching past her body. Her siblings slumped with visible disappointment. Psyche swallowed another smile, gazing out at the landscape.

The cut on her hand had scabbed over but now had a slight itch, which she covered with her other hand to keep from scratching. She found herself wondering what her child might look like now she had the face of its father to consider alongside her own. She was uncomfortable in the awareness that her feelings for their child had increased now she felt such a physical need for Cupid. Before, the fluttering movements within had been reminders of what she had endured; now, they were a precious connection to what she had lost. It was not a pleasant truth to acknowledge.

The journey was rough at times, some bumps jolting Psyche so much that she had to hold on to the edge of the cart. Dimitra said nothing more but kept sneaking glances at Psyche, and so Psyche kept her own attention fixed elsewhere. After watching hills and farms and pastures roll by for some time, Psyche found her stomach beginning to turn and closed her eyes against the nausea.

When, at last, their small party reached the city gates, Psyche thanked the couple, pressing into their palms generous payment that, though unsought, they made no pretense of refusing. The children shouted frantic goodbyes as the cart pulled away from the corner where Psyche stood, waving, until they disappeared from sight.

It took very little time to determine the location of Cidippe's home with Marinos. He was well known, as all prominent Romans were, and so after only a few inquiries, Psyche found herself at the gate of his property. She was gearing up to push open the gate and step inside when she heard a startled exclamation.

"Psyche?"

Psyche swung around. Behind her, apparently returning to her home from the market, based on the basket on her arm, stood Cidippe. Psyche felt the air rush out of her in relief, and she managed a wobbly smile.

"Hi, Cid."

CIDIPPE USHERED PSYCHE INSIDE, calling to her servants to take her parcels and visiting the nursery to drop kisses on the heads of her children before leading Psyche to a bedroom at the back of the house, where she confirmed their privacy before shutting the door.

The story came flooding out almost the second Psyche found herself alone with Cidippe. The realization of the lord's identity, his waking and anger, his abandonment. The priestess and her family and the journey that had brought her to her sister's doorstep.

She skipped the arrow scratch, not ready to face the ramifications of that.

Cidippe sat, listening, her face a careful mask, breaking only at the reveal of Cupid's identity.

"I knew it was an immortal of some kind, I knew it!" she said, pounding a fist on the bed in emphasis.

When Psyche was done, when she had spent herself of words, she collapsed onto the bed next to Cidippe.

"If I had not seen the home myself, if I had not ridden the wind to get there, I would hardly believe it," Cidippe said, and for once, her voice held no trace of irony or amusement. "Our little Psyche, consort of a god."

Psyche remembered the conversation she had with her sisters during their last visit, felt the shame of it again. "I'm sorry," she said. "I don't mean to bring you all of my problems when you have more than enough of your own, I just—"

Cidippe cut her off. "Don't apologize to me, Psy. I'll tell you if you become tiresome." She pulled a lock of Psyche's hair to punctuate the point and adjusted so that she could lower herself down beside Psyche. The two stared at the ceiling for several minutes. It was Cidippe who broke the silence.

"Will you go looking for him?"

"I do not have a choice," Psyche admitted, still not confessing to the brush with the arrow.

Cidippe's voice, when it next came, was careful. "In that, perhaps not. But your marriage could—"

"You forget, I'm not wed," Psyche reminded her.

Cidippe waved a hand. "Details, regardless, it does seem likely you could gain his favor again, yes?"

Psyche thought about Cupid, the broken look in his eyes when he left, and nodded. Whatever else he may feel, he still wanted her as much as she now wanted him.

Cidippe sat up, a frenetic excitement creeping over her. "You could do it, Psy," she whispered, "you could get us out of here."

"I could—?" Psyche stopped, realizing what Cidippe meant. "I could have him take you away from Marinos, you mean." She turned the thought over in her mind as Cidippe clasped Psyche's hand in her own, squeezing hard.

"And the children. We could live together, you and I, and you wouldn't be so alone."

"What about Father's reliance on the terms of your marriage?"

Cidippe waved a hand. "Cupid is a god; he can set whatever terms he wants. Whatever terms *you* ask of him." Her eyes were bright, fevered with hope, and Psyche bit her lip.

"Of course, I will do whatever I can for you, Cid, but I have no idea where he's gone or how he might greet me if I find him again. I can promise you nothing except that, if ever presented with the opportunity, I will try."

Cidippe's smile lit her face. "That's all I ask," she said, shifting down next to her younger sister. "Aren't we the pair?" Cidippe gestured to their protruding bellies, hers markedly more pronounced than Psyche's. "May I?" she asked, floating a hand over Psyche's stomach. Psyche nodded, reaching out her own hand to rest on Cidippe just as her sister's hand settled below Psyche's ribcage.

"Is the baby kicking yet?" Cidippe asked.

Psyche nodded. "Yes, though it is still hard to feel from the outside —oh!" She started as Cidippe's belly suddenly jumped beneath her hand, taut softness giving way to something hard and determined. Psyche laughed, "Obviously yours is."

The sisters lay like that for a long time.

"I'm glad you're here, Psyche," Cidippe said. "And not only for your own sake or for what I hope to gain from your situation, but selfishly because it means you'll be with me for this birth."

Psyche closed her eyes. "I'm glad to be here too, Cid."

PSYCHE HAD BEEN WORRIED about how Marinos would react to her presence, but Cidippe dismissed that concern the next morning. The women were on their way back from the altar of Diana where they'd left tribute for strength during the birth.

"When I'm pregnant, and especially when I'm so close to the birth, he doesn't care what I do or who I see, as long as the babe is kept safe." Cidippe stopped to examine some amulets, sorting through the stones available. She ignored the seller's attempts at assistance as she held them to the light, squinting. "Best times in my marriage, the end of pregnancies," she added, mouth twisting with the admission.

Cidippe turned to Psyche, holding out an aetites, an eagle stone, bound and strung with copper onto a leather thong. "Here," she said. "To protect you and the child through its birth." She paid the seller, then urged her sister on. "We should cover it with the skin of a sacrificed animal, but we can do that another day. It bothered me and Ag that you didn't have one when we learned you were pregnant."

Psyche turned the lumpy brown stone over in her hand as she walked, eyes stinging. Reaching up to fasten it around her neck, she became aware Cidippe was speaking to her again.

"Psy? I know you've been here only a night, but is there anything else you were hoping to do today, anything you need?"

Psyche couldn't help wondering at the subtext of that question, whether Cidippe was prompting her to begin her search for Cupid. She shook her head. "No, thank you, food and a bath and a clean bed were my greatest needs, and you've provided them all."

Cidippe nodded and, Psyche was relieved to see, expressed no disappointment with her answer. "Well, you know I want you here as long as you can stay. I will ask you help with the children," she said as they reached the gate to her home, "as I'm at the point where I physically cannot do many things. Besides, that should keep you pretty secluded, which will help with all *that*." She waved her hand in the general direction of Psyche's face, and Psyche nodded, even as her heart sank at the reminder.

Despite wearing her cloak, she had gotten several curious stares on their walk, and already, the servants who had caught sight of her face had started whispering.

"You seem less affected by it, though," she observed. Cidippe shrugged, leading them back inside.

"It's still strange, but I'm getting used to it."

PSYCHE'S BODY relaxed in degrees. She and Cidippe sent word to Aglaura to fill her in on the circumstances but did not expect a response for some time. So the days passed, as Psyche turned over and over in her mind what she should do, trying to ignore the way Cidippe's eyes found and followed her, weighted with expectation.

In some ways, the most tempting option was, of course, to do nothing. Before that infernal arrow scratch, it might not have occurred to her to do anything else. To stay with Cidippe, have her baby, and then just never leave, raising the child alongside Cid's brood. Aglaura would welcome her too, she was sure, but she had the sense that Cidippe might need her a bit more, that there might exist a more even exchange of support.

But there was now within her a physical need to return to the god of love. His arrows did their work well, and Psyche felt his absence like the loss of a limb, the site of the injury always a low-grade source of pain and her thoughts turning to him in every unoccupied moment. It was both a physical and emotional need to be with him, even as her mind listed for her on loop his numerous offenses. She didn't know what would happen if she was unable to reunite with him; it felt simultaneously like she might fade into nothingness and combust into a million pieces.

The other piece that refused to let Psyche's brain rest was Apollo's reaction to her pregnancy. True to her word, Psyche had excluded mention of the sun god when recounting her tale to Cidippe, but his surprise and immediate agitation were often on Psyche's mind.

He had said that Venus hated her, that she was her enemy. Psyche supposed this notion should terrify her, but instead, she found it allowed several pieces of her story to fall into place. Cupid's secrecy, for one, as well as the dramatic way in which he abducted her. Immortals tended toward the theatrical already, if the myths were to be believed, but a betrayal of his mother's trust cast Cupid's actions as self-preservation, as opposed to malignant manipulation. It should not endear him more to her, but Psyche was frustrated to find that it did, as did the realization that Cupid had not used his arrows on her. Venus, according to Apollo, was the one who should concern Psyche.

Venus. As she helped her niece and nephew dress their dolls in scraps Cidippe had fashioned into small clothes, Psyche turned over in her mind what she knew of the goddess. Venus was the goddess of love, of course, and of beauty—it was in this latter domain that Psyche must have come to the goddess's attention.

"Ke?" Aindreas pushed his doll at Psyche, demanding her attention.

"Hm?" Psyche glanced down at the wooden figure with moveable arms and legs; her nephew had shoved a leg through what was intended to be an armhole. She picked up the doll and began to adjust the clothing. The children had shrunk from her at first, hiding their faces in Cidippe's skirts, but extended exposure had acclimated them to her presence, even if they still could not look her full in the face.

"Look what I do!" Agneta held high her own half-clothed doll, beaming at her success. Aindreas frowned at her, reaching to reclaim his own toy from Psyche.

"I have, I have," he insisted, pulling at the doll's leg as Psyche scrambled to complete the tie at the neck before releasing the toy. In his possession once more, Aindreas dangled his doll in front of Agneta. "Me too, Aggy, me too!" The twins giggled and darted off to the corner of the nursery to tuck the dolls into the cradle that waited there for the new baby. Psyche watched them.

How had she landed in this mess? All she'd ever wanted was a home near her sisters, to raise children who would be as close as she and Aglaura and Cidippe had always been. Her pitiful efforts to influence that fate had snowballed into insanity and, she now had reason to believe, made her the enemy of a goddess. Which seemed to have, in its turn, made her the consort of a god and now the mother of—what? A god? A demigod?

Cidippe, despite her clear eagerness for Psyche to reunite with Cupid, was calmer and appeared more at peace than Psyche had seen her since before her marriage to Marinos. Psyche asked about her sister's newfound tranquility, but Cidippe waved a hand.

"Oh, it's like I said, the end of a pregnancy is actually the calm in the storm around here."

Psyche wasn't convinced that was all there was to it, but she didn't press, occupied as she was with her own worries.

CHAPTER 18

There had been no question where Venus was heading when she left her home, and it was not to find Mercury. Oh, she would track him down later and ask him to refresh the wings, for they were a bit worse for the wear, but she needed something Mercury couldn't give her. Something only one being had ever truly been able to give her.

"Mars!"

Venus entered the residence of the god of war, a cold and massive fortress of stone. He was not here often, preferring to sleep in tents alongside his men on campaigns, which meant the castle had a perpetual air of abandonment, fine layers of dust present on nearly every surface. It was the primary reason that she rarely visited him here, but today, her need was too great.

Loosening the straps of her dress as she walked, Venus began to climb the winding staircase to Mars's quarters. As the garment fell away, cool air brushed her body, welcoming her home. Her hips swayed, the soft skin of her breasts and belly and thighs moving as she did. She was beautiful; she was terrifying; she was a goddess, damn it.

Reaching the landing, Venus turned down a long, dim hallway, calling again.

"Mars!" This time, an answer:

"Venus?" The voice came from within the great war room. Of course it did. The door slammed against the wall as she opened it. She stood, framed in the doorway, considering the scene before her.

Mars was seated before a long table covered with maps and markers and notes detailing the names and situations of the current human rulers of every country before him. His shoulders squared under her gaze, broad like his brother Vulcan's, but without the hunch that came from working bent over the forge. His eyes were dark and hooded, his mouth set in a semi-permanent scowl. So, so like his brother. And yet not. Venus raised an eyebrow.

Mars waited a beat, then crossed to stand before her. Their eyes met; Venus's other brow shot up. Mars sank to his knees, eyes still locked with hers.

"Better," Venus said, lifting her chin. She reached out a hand, tracing the side of his face with her nail. "It's been so long since I've been here; however have you been keeping yourself?"

"Poorly, goddess," Mars said, his voice low and rough. "You know there is none but you who satisfies me."

"None but me?" Her tone was arch. "From what I hear, you've certainly been putting that notion to the test."

Mars clenched his jaw. "You're a fine one to cast stones—" The words were hardly out of his mouth before a hand came down, slapping his face with enough force to bring tears to his eyes.

"Careful, Mars," Venus said. "Or I may rethink my visit."

The god of war bowed his head. "Apologies, goddess."

Venus ran a hand through his hair, the same hand that had just left its red imprint across his cheek.

"Poor Mars. Everyone thinks you're so fearsome and strong. But I know better, don't I?" She fisted her hand in his hair, forcing his head back. "Don't I?" Mars swallowed, and Venus watched, tracing the way the muscles of his throat rippled. "Don't I?" she repeated.

"Yes," Mars managed.

"Yes?"

"Yes...goddess." Eyes heavy with need, begging her with every blink, Mars drew an unsteady breath. "Please, Venus," he said. "Please."

Venus nodded. "Better." She let go of his hair, the sudden loss of tension causing him to sway. Brushing past him, Venus snapped her fingers. "Go," she ordered.

Venus continued across the room, gazing out the window as she listened to Mars scramble to his feet, then hurry down the hall. She could feel herself calming; visiting Mars always had such an effect unless he was freshly from the field of battle, but she had long since learned to leave that particular lust to be sated by whatever unfortunate mortals happened to be nearby. With the calm, though, came a cold sharpening of her fury. Her hand flexed at her side. She heard a heavy tread behind her and knew Mars had returned. She waited until she heard the soft thud that confirmed he was on his knees, then turned and looked down on him once more.

In his hands, lifted to her like an offering, was the leather whip she had given him so many centuries ago. She picked it up.

"Over the table," she said, a small smile breaking as the great warrior god rushed to do her bidding. Venus eyed the thickly muscled back stretched before her, appreciating the grooves and contours and scars etched from millennia of battle and, well, this. Who dared question her power, when she brought such a god to his knees?

Approaching with a casual stride, relishing the lazy power that had entered her limbs, Venus drew back her arm, and began.

WHEN THEY HAD FINISHED, most of the maps and notes and careful markers Mars had been studying littered the floor. Venus lounged, shaking her hair out from its confines, as she watched Mars move about the room, restoring the items to their original positions. The expressions he tossed her way as he worked stoked the warm flame at her center. Adoration. Gratitude. Supplication. This was her right, what she had risen out of the ocean to receive from the world. The world seemed confused as of late but here, in this room, things were exactly as they should be.

Mars placed the last marker with care upon its spot on a map, then crossed to her, stretching himself alongside her with his head in her lap. She sank her fingers into his hair, stroking.

"Thank you," he said.

Venus waved a hand. "You need not thank me," she responded, *just keep worshipping me.*

"Will you stay for a meal?" he asked, and Venus did not miss the careful casualness of the question.

Venus considered. "No, I cannot. I must find Mercury, and Jupiter knows that can take forever." Mars stiffened at the mention of the messenger god. Venus tapped his nose in reprimand. "Are you about to be unpleasant?" she asked. She felt Mars force his body to relax.

They lay like that, finding rest with one another, for several minutes. It was Venus who broke the silence. "My son has betrayed me," she said.

"How is that?"

"He has taken as a lover the one person I asked him to rid me of, and what's more, he kept it a secret from me."

"He is old enough both to make his own choices about his lovers and to own his behavior; it sounds childishly done," Mars said, half into her leg. Venus nodded, fingers still scratching his scalp.

"Yes, very childish. He came to me after their first spat, seeking comfort, though he still has not himself revealed the circumstances of his distress. I must decide what to do about it."

"This is why you're going to find Mercury?"

"Indeed."

Mars pushed himself to a seat then and raised a large hand to cup her cheek. "Make this person pay, love, both for their earlier transgressions and for taking your son from you in this way. Through their suffering, Cupid, too, may learn to see the error of his ways. You are Venus, and woe to those who forget it."

CHAPTER 19

Cidippe went into labor nine days after Psyche had arrived. The sisters were sitting in the garden, watching as Agneta and Aindreas toddled about, waiting on their little sister, Ianthe.

"They remind me of us," Cidippe said, groaning as she shifted her position. "Like Aglaura and I hovering over your cradle."

Psyche smiled, remembering the small box under her childhood bed that still held the tokens left by her besotted siblings.

Even at almost three years old, Agneta and Aindreas made her think of the immortal twins Diana and Apollo. She had still not confessed to her encounter with the sun god, but the buoyant magnetism of his presence appeared to be a trait her nephew shared. Smiling and affectionate, the occasional jabs and disagreements with his sisters seemed to roll off him with ease. Psyche marveled that he was the son of Marinos; had her brother-in-law once been so? Of course he had been a child, but had he been born with the darkness he now possessed, or had he once shined as brightly as Aindreas did? The thought unsettled her, and she rubbed a hand over her own belly, fingering the amulet at her neck. Cidippe noticed.

"Are you feeling alright? We can move inside, if you wish."

"No, no," Psyche said, "I was only thinking about the twins, how they seem to embody all the goodness in the world."

"Well, and a fair amount of the frustration," Cidippe responded. "You should have seen them yesterday when Aindreas took the blanket Agneta wanted."

Psyche laughed. "Oh, I think I heard the fallout of that."

Cidippe shifted again, breathing deeply. "But I do take your point. They are lights for me in this home."

"Do you think Marinos was once like them?" The question was out before Psyche could consider how it might affect her sister. Cidippe appeared startled, then cautious as she responded,

"Elaborate, please." At that moment, Agneta came barreling into her mother.

"Ianthe bite me," the little girl said, thrusting out her arm for inspection. Cidippe peered at the offered limb, rubbing a light finger over what were indisputably teeth marks.

"You're alright," she said, leaning to place a kiss on the mark. "If Ianthe is biting, then go play elsewhere in the garden." Agneta frowned, clearly about to argue the point, then was distracted by a call from Aindreas that he had found a bug, and bounded off to examine the insect with him.

"I just…" Psyche sighed, tracing an absent finger up and down the marked pad of her palm. "I don't know what to do, Cid. My child has an immortal as a father; will I be able to relate to it at all? But then I think, Marinos is what he is, and yet look at them." She gestured a hand at the three children, two crouched over a frozen cricket, the other spluttering after attempting to eat a flower. "If his seed can create things so pure, perhaps he too was once so; perhaps he was corrupted somewhere along the way."

Cidippe was quiet as she considered Psyche's words. Then, "I have to believe, Psy, that we make a difference. If I didn't believe that, I'd go mad." Her eyes on Psyche were steady. "However—removing their exposure to Marinos would be the best and surest way to counteract his influence."

It was the first time she had made a direct reference to her request since it was first posed it over a week before. Psyche squirmed. It wasn't that she didn't want the future Cidippe imagined—she did!— but she felt so unmoored, so at a loss as to where to begin sorting the pieces of her own life that making such a commitment felt impossible. An awkwardness fell over the garden. Finally, Psyche opened her mouth to respond but was cut off by a sudden sharp cry from her sister.

"Cidippe?" Psyche rushed to put her arm around her. "Are you alright?"

Cidippe's eyes were shut tight, her breathing deep. "I think the babe is coming," she said through gritted teeth. "I've been having contractions since this morning, but this is the first that feels real."

"The first that feels real?" Psyche said in disbelief. "Why did you not tell me? I would have brought the children down on my own; you could have stayed in bed."

Cidippe opened one eye, her face still tight with pain. "That's why I didn't tell you," she said. "Hold on." Psyche watched her sister for several frantic moments; eventually, both Cidippe's face and body relaxed again. "We should move inside now, though. And call for the midwife."

WITHIN THE HOUR, the children had been secured with their nurse, the midwife had arrived from the village, and Cidippe had taken up residence in her room. Psyche hovered around her with anxious attention.

"What can I do, Cid?" she begged, hating herself for not intuiting it but unable to watch her sister's pain a moment longer without a task that might relieve some of it.

"Fetch clean linens," the midwife said, bustling into the room. "And tell the kitchen to send up hot water and keep it coming."

Psyche drew a nervous, comforting hand down Cidippe's arm, then rushed to comply.

When she returned, it was clear something was wrong. Cidippe was bent over, arm braced on a table, screaming through gritted teeth as her body shook with a contraction. The midwife, despite the firm hand she held pressed to the small of Cidippe's back, looked worried. She shot Psyche a warning glance.

"Here, love," the midwife said to Cidippe, "try your hands and knees." She led Cidippe to the bed, helping her clamber on top of it. Another contraction racked her, and Cidippe howled. "There, you've got it, you've got it." The midwife was moving the base of her palm in firm circles. "When the pain sits in the back like that, this position can help. Move your body as you need to; I'll be right back with a hot cloth." She hurried toward Psyche, frozen in the doorway. "Don't just stand there," the midwife snapped, taking a cloth from Psyche's hand and pulling the girl into the room to allow the kitchen staff through with the ordered water. "Go, press on her back as I was, hold her hand, talk to her. You know her better than I. She's going to need strength for this one; she's already in far more pain than she was with the other two births and I'm going to need to turn the babe."

Psyche rushed to Cidippe's side, pressing her hand where the midwife had indicated and murmuring jumbled nonsense. Later, she would be unable to remember a single word that left her mouth at this time, her mind filled instead with images of her sister.

Cidippe, back arched and belly hanging low, howling through streaks of tears.

Cidippe, face turned and buried in her own shoulder, muttering over and over, "Please, Diana, please, Juno, please, *please.*"

Cidippe, gripping Psyche's hand so tightly, red became white.

Cidippe, ripping at her own clothes because she needed them to be off, off, off, the only item left on her body her own aetites amulet, dangling between her breasts.

When the midwife began to demand that she push, Cidippe bit her lip so hard Psyche saw blood. The pushing felt like it went on for hours. At one point, Cidippe tried to climb off the bed, managing enough words to convey that she wished to move about the room, but the moment the next contraction hit, she screamed with the pain, crawling her way up onto the bed.

It was horrific.

Psyche had heard, of course, that birth was painful, had been told that even by her sisters. But never had she imagined the scene before her. The midwife had said this was worse than Cidippe's earlier births, but all Psyche could think was that if those three had held even a fraction of this agony, why would a woman ever do this, even once?

The clean linens had been exhausted, and the stream of hot water had slowed, staff having to now venture out of the home to retrieve water to heat. Cidippe was still on the bed, face pressed into the mattress, knees splayed wide over a red-brown pool of blood, hands clutching at the blankets as she muttered, words nonsensical. Psyche ran a useless hand down her sister's arm, over and over, and looked up to meet the eyes of the midwife.

Psyche saw death for the first time that day. Not death in its form as a body robbed of a soul, but as a hovering specter, waiting with agonizing patience for its moment. Psyche saw that specter in the midwife's eyes, knew it for what it was in an instant.

"No!" she said, her arms coming around her sister to hold her tight. "Come on, Cid, push, you're so close, you must, you must!"

"I can't..." Cidippe's voice, always so sharp, was soft, far away.

"You must, you can, I need you to, Cid, I need you." Tears fell, mixing with the sweat already soaking Cidippe's hair.

"I... I'm sorry Psy," Cidippe said, not opening her eyes. "Tell Aglaura I'm sorry."

"I won't; you tell her, you tell her you're sorry you ever doubted yourself, push, Cid, push!"

But Cidippe had pushed her way through the last bit of pain she could stand in one life and was already drifting into the next.

PSYCHE REFUSED to leave the body for hours. She lay curled around Cidippe, the kicking in her belly between them a perverse taunt of the stillness that now lay in her sister's. The midwife didn't try to argue with her, channeling her own emotions instead into cleaning the rest of the room. It wasn't until Marinos burst in, when the sun had nearly disappeared from the sky, that Psyche even began to register herself as a separate body and still alive.

"She's gone, then?" There was grief in his voice, which startled Psyche. She sat up, pushed her hair away from her face. She remained curled around Cidippe, though, protecting her now in the way she had been unable to during life. Looking at this man, whose fists and words had so weakened her sister's body and spirit long before his seed killed her, Psyche felt hot hatred kindle on her numbness.

"You did this," she said, words low. Marinos started, eyes averted both from her and from Cidippe's body.

"I didn't," he said, sputtering. "I wasn't even here; I just returned. I didn't know—"

"You hurt her." Psyche's fists clenched. "You hurt her, and you hurt her, and you hurt her, and you had three children already but insisted on laying with her, and now your lust has killed her." Marinos gaped. An uneasy awareness was clawing its way into Psyche's consciousness; she had only ever seen Marinos wearing his public face, heard the stories of his temper and its effects. She had never witnessed such vulnerability as she saw now, like a bear laying on its back, exposing its belly. She felt sick.

"I didn't," he said again. "I mean, I hadn't, I—never when she was with child."

His words hovered in the air, failing to fully sink in for a moment. When they did, Psyche found herself lost for any responding words of her own. Instead, she screamed at him. She screamed and screamed and screamed until he fled the room and she was alone with her sister again.

CIDIPPE'S FUNERAL was held two days later, far too little time for any other family to make it. Psyche supposed she should be angry with Marinos for this, but mostly, she felt a selfish relief. She would certainly lose what little control she had over her emotions in Aglaura's presence, and there was no world in which she was at all prepared to face her parents.

By the time she stood before her sister's body burning on a pyre, Psyche's tears had run themselves dry. She stared into the flames, eyes unseeing through the sting of smoke. Her nieces and nephew were huddled around their nurse. Marinos stood on Psyche's other side, his mask in place once more. He had not said a word to her since the day Cidippe had died. She didn't know what to think of any of it, and what was more, she didn't want to. She didn't want to think, to feel, to

160

engage with anything, for to let anything in would be to let everything in, and she wasn't sure she could survive that.

The day after the funeral, Marinos summoned her for an audience. She stood before him, staring unseeing past his shoulder, her hate dulled by her grief. He spoke with firm condescension, the vulnerability of that night gone.

"You must leave."

Psyche nodded. She agreed with that. This seemed to take Marinos by surprise. He continued, severe.

"I'll have the staff pack you what provisions you need, and you may have one of the older horses."

Psyche nodded again. Of course he would offer only what was next to worthless to him. She moved to leave, stopped when she heard him clear his throat.

"I did care for Cidippe."

Yet another nod. She had seen that; it turned her stomach.

"Well, then. That's all."

Psyche turned and left.

PSYCHE DIDN'T HAVE much to take with her. A couple dresses, sandals, the amulet Cidippe had bought her. She stared at the brown stone for a long time—considered hurling it out the window, for all the good such a charm had done for her sister—but ended up fastening it around her throat once more, the heavy weight of it against her collarbones both a prayer and a penance.

After packing her things, Psyche made her way to the stables to claim the horse that had been promised her. She hadn't bothered to inquire into the provisions Marinos had mentioned, so was surprised to find them waiting, neatly packed within the stable door. There was a sour taste in her mouth when she looked at them, so she didn't let her gaze linger long. Instead, she stepped inside, looking about for a groom.

"Hello?" she called.

From a stall near the end of the stables emerged a figure, long and wiry, more limbs than trunk. The figure stumbled toward

Psyche, and she saw that it was a man, his face streaked with still-wet tears.

"You're Psyche," he stated, not a question.

She nodded. "Marinos promised me a horse for my journey."

The man's head bobbed. "Yes, of course, I've prepared Elpis for you. She was—that is—" He swallowed, hard. "Your sister loved to ride her."

Psyche stared at this man, at the pain in his voice. Her sister was not unkind to staff by any measure, but Psyche had also not witnessed any of them mourning her death with such acute grief. This man must have something else going on, for such brokenness could not have been brought about by—

"I loved her," he said, barely over a whisper. "I want you to know she was loved here."

Then again, perhaps it could. Psyche struggled to find words and failed, taking in this man who, in a single sentence, had rearranged everything she thought she knew about her sister's life. She shook her head, eyes everywhere but on him, tears threatening once again to spill over.

"I have to go," she said.

"I know," he said.

CHAPTER 20

When Psyche departed Marinos's estate, she had no destination in mind. Her body was still numb with shock, and she had a strong, irrational sense that she could not now seek shelter with Aglaura.

Though she had been witness to Cidippe's death, had seen first-hand the way nature had reclaimed the life it had once granted, Psyche could not shake the sense that her own actions had somehow decided her sister's fate. Cupid's vitriolic reaction to the topic of her sisters, his anger and desertion when she had discovered his identity now seemed to sit heavy with foreshadowing.

It was horrific to consider, but who was she to say there had been no immortal hand at work in the room that day? She knew only a man who said he loved her when she existed within the parameters he set; even as she ached for his embrace, she knew nothing of the choices he might make now she had ventured outside those parameters. She had no context for how far he might go to force her back within them.

And so a visit to Aglaura was out of the question. Returning to her childhood home and her parents was inconceivable. They had offered her to be wed to a serpent on the word of prophecy; there was no predicting what their fear might compel them to in these circumstances, only that it would not be in Psyche's favor. So she rode and rode until her seat was numb and her joints ached and her eyes blurred.

Her pregnant body was hardly one shaped for extended time on horseback, but an unexpected benefit was that the constant motion seemed to lull the babe growing within her to sleep. The subsequent stillness meant that for stretches of time as she rode, Psyche could almost forget she was with child, could pretend that she alone was venturing out to explore the world.

Where might she go if it was only her? Athens? Thebes? Perhaps she would journey to Troy, walk in the space of another woman whose life had been undone by the gods. And yet, thinking of Helen made her realize—setting up residence in any town would be risky; there was no place Psyche could go where her face would not be a problem. Perhaps she would search for the legendary Amazons, discover if the female warriors of myth existed. The notion of independence excited her, and yet she also shrank from a life that required so much internal conviction. What Amazons would ever take seriously a woman who walked so meekly to her own doom?

If she had been different, better able to accept the facts of her situation and turn them to her advantage, perhaps she could have used Cupid sooner to help get her sister out of Marinos's house and bed. Perhaps she could have had more to offer Cidippe in those agonizing last moments. Perhaps if she had been less absorbed with herself, her sister would have trusted her with whatever had existed with the groom. Instead, Psyche had remained blind within the world of her own discomfort, using her energy to beg boons for herself, leaning on her sisters instead of becoming an equal they could lean on in turn.

The disgust Psyche felt became so overwhelming she brought the horse to a stop, sliding down and leaning over as she vomited. When she finished, she spat the last remnants, then wiped tears from her eyes as she leaned against the horse's side. What was the name of her mount again? She couldn't even remember. How could she ever care for a baby when she could not even remember the name of her horse?

"I'm sorry, girl," she said, stroking the rough, dark mane. "I'm sorry, I'm so, so sorry." The tears fell in earnest then, Psyche's arms coming around the mare's neck, the great animal shifting from hoof to hoof, but nonetheless seeming to lean into Psyche, sensing her need, which only made the girl cry harder.

"Do let me know when you've finished."

The call startled Psyche, her tears stopping with abrupt tension. Sniffing and wiping her eyes, she turned toward the voice, her legs wobbly from long riding. She saw no one.

"Who is there?" She sounded shaky within her head; she hoped she sounded less so outside of it. Her eyes scanned the treeline. From a copse higher up on the gentle hill leading down to the road emerged a figure, tall and lithe. Psyche had the rather absurd thought that if a bow, with its strong, flexible curves and reserved power, took living form this would be the result.

"Well, you are not as I imagined." The goddess—for it was very clear this being was a goddess—looked hard at Psyche, giving a small shake of her head. "For Venus to be in the state she's in, well, I admit I expected more."

Psyche gritted her teeth. "You and everyone," she said, at her limit of respect for immortals. "My inability to live up to my great myth is what landed me here, so if you have no more to offer, I beg privacy to mourn alone." Despite her words, Psyche scanned the goddess for hints to her identity. She had greater presence than Cupid, compelling in the way Apollo had been. She was dressed for hunting in garments typically donned by men, and her single adornment was a silver crescent hanging between her breasts. The goddess made no response, simply stood, hands on hips, considering Psyche in return. "Diana," Psyche said, anger bursting in a quiet flame low in her belly.

Diana inclined her head. "Indeed. And I shall grant you your privacy, for I highly value my own, but I will be waiting for you just beyond the hill." She indicated where she had come from. "Join me once you are through with your tears, and we will talk." The words were light enough, but the tone in which they were delivered brooked no argument. Diana departed without waiting for assent from Psyche.

Psyche knew little about the moon goddess, sister to Apollo, huntress who scorned men—most of what she knew was from Cidippe. Wiping her face and eyes with the hem of her dress, Psyche grimaced at the pain that shot through her stomach when she bent over too fast. Her body was now grown enough that it was starting to affect actions that before had been executed without thought. Pulling on clothes, crouching to lace a sandal, lying down for the night—all now provoked an immediate awareness of her physical condition that still surprised Psyche. Taking a deep breath to steady her nerves, Psyche limped toward the copse where Diana had disappeared, leading the horse as best she could.

Beyond the trees, Psyche found the moon goddess perched on a wide, flat rock, arms resting on her knees, hands clasped loose before her.

"Goddess." Psyche inclined her head, eyes fixed to the ground. Diana's lips curved upward.

"Now you show respect? Diminish yourself not on my account, Psyche of Crete. If you have one thing in your favor, it is the flickers of conviction you've shown over the past months. Abandon it, and I assure you, you are doomed."

Psyche bit her lip, then met Diana's eyes, leaning on her horse for support. "As you say, goddess," she responded. "Why have you sought me?"

Diana's smile widened further. "What makes you suppose I sought you? Perhaps I simply came upon you; perhaps you, in fact, stumbled onto my land. Perhaps you are the one seeking me."

Psyche's response was flat. "I seek—and have only ever sought—a single god, and that is the one whose child I carry." She indicated her swollen belly. "And if I've learned nothing else, it is that humans behold gods only when immortals themselves grant the audience."

Diana laughed, and her eyes roved Psyche with a fondness the girl found confusing. "Orion had just as little patience for games." Though she looked off into the landscape, it was apparent that Diana's gaze had turned inward. "For other things, he had all the patience in the world."

"He clearly meant something to you," Psyche said.

"He was the only man in whom I've ever seen worth," the moon goddess said, still lost in memory.

"Isn't the lord Apollo your brother?"

166

Diana's gaze snapped to Psyche. "Careful," she said. "I enjoy boldness but I'll not hear disrespect."

Psyche swallowed. "Yes, my lady."

Diana came to stand before Psyche. She extended a hand, offering to lead the horse. "Come, walk with me."

Psyche stood, accepting the offered aid, and the two walked nearly a quarter mile before Diana spoke again, Psyche chastened enough that she dared not ask where they were going.

"You're in a bad position, you know," the huntress said. "It is not only that Cupid disobeyed his mother; it is that he loves you when before he only ever loved her. She doted on that boy, and every god on Olympus knows it. To lose his love to one who has proven a threat to her godhood—well, that is not a dispute in which you will find many allies."

"So I've heard." Psyche's voice was weary.

Diana shot her a sideways look. "You do not defend yourself? Argue that you've taken nothing from Venus? That Cupid owns his own actions?"

"I do not see the advantage in that," Psyche said, careful. "I do not seek a quarrel with Venus; I seek only her son."

"So you say. But suppose he won't have you? Why not disappear, raise your child in anonymity and peace?"

Psyche choked on a humorless laugh. "How, precisely, would I do that? My face is what began this madness; I can't live life in a hood and cloak. Cupid has abandoned me; my parents left me to be claimed by a monster. I sought refuge with my sister, who is now with Pluto, along with the babe she carried, and I dare not visit my remaining sister." She took a steadying breath. "Is it Venus enacting her retribution? Or does despair follow me like a hungry dog begging for scraps? I cannot say. I begged your brother for protection, to no avail. And now you seek me out. Lady Diana, I've encountered more gods in the past year of my life than, honestly, I ever even prayed to in all the years I lived prior. To suggest, at this point, as known as I am to Olympus, that anonymity is an option—well, I may not live up to legend, but I'm not that naive."

Diana stopped, turning to study Psyche again. "You're going about it all wrong," she said, beginning to walk once more and offering a hand as they reached a rocky patch. Psyche realized that the road they were following was about to take an upward trajectory, and her body ached in preemptive response. Diana flashed her a sympathetic smile, seeming to read her thoughts. "It will hurt," she acknowledged. Taking a deep breath, Psyche started up the hill with the goddess, Diana still leading the mare with an expert hand.

"You said I am doing it wrong," she said between breaths.

Diana, unwinded, nodded. "Yes. You are. You are begging like a human instead of demanding, as befits the consort of a god."

"I am a human and no longer a consort." Admitting that felt like a hole in her chest.

"Ah, but I have it on good intelligence that he loves you still. Venus's wrath is proof enough of that. And whenever we love, we cede power—gods perhaps even more than humans. If you have any hope of achieving the peace you long for, you must claim that power."

Psyche considered. "I would not know how to do that; going around yelling at gods does not seem like it would yield helpful results."

Diana laughed, holding a branch out of Psyche's way. "Oh, that would be entertaining, but you are correct, the results would not be what you desire. No, the power you must claim is a simpler thing: you need to name Cupid's actions." Psyche's face betrayed her confusion, and Diana sighed. "Would that we lived in a world not so wholly shaped by the desires of men; I see I must spell this out. Tell me how you and Cupid came to be together."

Psyche frowned. "The Oracle at Delphi. The Pythia decreed I was to be sacrificed in marriage to a great serpent; only, when the time came for the sacrifice, the West Wind carried me to Cupid's estate, though, of course, I did not know then who he was."

"And?" Diana prompted, "There must be more to the story, considering you now carry his child."

"Yes, of course." Frustration was creeping into Psyche's tone; she willed herself calmer. "He came to me that first night and nearly every night after and lay with me. He was always gone before morning, so I did not know with whom I slept until my sisters convinced me to hide a lamp in order that I might know the father of my child."

"Did your father, Psyche, ever agree that you should be carried off by the West Wind?"

"No—"

"Is Cupid a serpent?"

"Of course not, but—"

"And when the arrogant, overgrown child came to you, did he confirm your desire to lay with him as well, or did he proceed as if that was assumed?"

"The latter, I suppose—"

"You suppose, or you are sure?"

"I'm sure."

Diana's face flashed with something like triumph, then settled into a satisfied smile. "Then you have him." She shrugged. "If, that is, you decide that you want him."

Psyche's mind raced, turning over Diana's words. What did it matter, her wants at any given time? "Forgive me, Lady Diana, but I fail to see your point."

"Rape," Diana said, not slowing her pace. And suddenly, all the pieces fell into place, even as Psyche recoiled from the word. She had been carried off, defiled, and never married. Had Cupid been human, he would have been subject to punishment by the law. But he was immortal, and surely the gods were not held to the same standard? Psyche knew enough stories to know that gods had raped humans with impunity for centuries. She said as much to Diana, who nodded in acknowledgment.

"That is true and one of the many, many reasons I prefer to live alone with my dogs, but the critical piece you are not considering is Cupid's continued love. Jupiter raped Leda because he wanted her, and she then bore Helen and Polydeuces. Then he wanted Danae, and the world got Perseus. But wanting is not the same as loving—once Jupiter had spilled his seed he was done, ready for the next conquest. And so the stories go. In all the long millennia we have existed, there have been but a handful of great love stories between gods and humans: Dionysus and Ariadne, Eos and Tithonus, myself and Orion.

And love stories, Psyche, do not involve rape. If Cupid has raped you, then he has betrayed the very tenets of the love he professes to feel for you. He has made himself an oathbreaker."

Psyche thought about that, and while she was pretty sure the tale she had heard about Ariadne involved the girl being carried off much as Psyche had been, she was starting to grasp Diana's point. "It's the story," Psyche said, slow. "That's why Venus was angry with me at the very beginning—the story being told of my beauty was beginning to eclipse her own."

Diana nodded, pleased. "Exactly. Stories are important to humans, but they are the most powerful armor the gods possess. And at the moment, Psyche, you have control of this story. For good or ill, a god must be trusted to be worshiped, and oathbreakers are scorned by gods and mortals alike. You want the power to influence your own fate? Name his actions, declare them rape, and you threaten the very foundations on which his godhood is built. You will bring him to his knees."

Psyche pressed her lips into a line. "You would have me wield my pain like a blade."

The moon goddess gave a short laugh. "I would have you claim the only advantage you possess."

"But I—" Psyche broke off, uncertain how to say it. "You say he still loves me? Could I not seek reconciliation? I don't—that is to say…" She drew a deep breath; her hand ached. "I've been scratched by one of his arrows."

Diana didn't stop, didn't even slow. "Then you have even more reason to hold him to account," she said.

The rest of the walk passed in silence. When they reached the top of the hill, Psyche turned to Diana.

"Why are you helping me?" she asked. The goddess reached out, tucking an errant strand of hair behind Psyche's ear.

"Who can say?" she said, eyebrows arching. "In the end, the why is unknowable. It is only the story that matters."

Psyche considered this. "In that case, what story would you tell, of you offering me aid?"

Diana's smile was wicked. "I? I'd go with a classic: one jealous goddess attempting to bring down another. That one stands the test of time." She took Psyche's shoulders, turning her to look beyond the hilltop where they stood. "Now, focus. Beyond that next hill, do you see?" She extended a long arm, pointing, and Psyche squinted, nodding as she caught sight of the structure Diana was indicating. "You will find aid in that home for as long as you need."

Before Psyche could thank the huntress, Diana was striding away. Psyche opened her mouth to say something, anything, then closed it again, watching as the moon goddess drew further and further away. The flame of anger she'd suppressed since the goddess's appearance sparked once more.

"Wait! Lady Diana!" The goddess stopped, turned. Psyche ran toward her, then came to an abrupt stop as pain shot down her leg. Hand at the base of her spine, she panted, "My sister. Cidippe. She was devoted to you. She called for you in her last moments. Why—" Psyche stopped herself; the why was unknowable. She stared hard at Diana while her mind raced. Finally, she said, "You didn't help her." Her voice was small, but strong for it, the grief and fury an echo of Cidippe's in those last moments. Diana's chin raised, and for a moment, Psyche thought she would not respond. But then,

"I've heard that story before. Go, tell a new one."

CHAPTER 21

P syche made her way down the hill, mind churning with Diana's conversation.

The proposition laid before her was daunting; to accuse Cupid of rape seemed the highest of follies—loving him aside, she was human, and he was immortal. Humans did not get to make accusations of an immortal and live to tell the tale. Besides, if she could find Cupid, and if his anger toward her had cooled, then perhaps she could negotiate support for herself and her child without any public campaign. Perhaps, in time, she could achieve reconciliation.

And yet. Yet.

Diana's point about storytelling was a compelling one. Psyche's future, now, rested on the knife edge of Cupid's goodwill—and his mother's, it seemed. Venus reportedly hated her, and despite Cupid's apparent well-known love for her, he had abandoned her at the first true test. Perhaps it would be foolish of Psyche not to claim the narrative advantage where she could.

When Psyche reached the path that led to the door, she brought her mare to a halt as she looked around, taking in the area. The road she traveled had been deserted, with few human structures interrupting her journey, but here she saw a modest-sized home, well-kept and tended, with a garden beyond large enough that

Psyche could see cultivated rows of vegetables and flowers spilling out from the sides of the house. Just as Psyche was about to turn back, to take cover again and consider her options, the front door opened.

A woman about the age of Psyche's mother approached, gray-streaked hair twisted into a practical bun that made her appear taller than she was. Her smile was warm.

"Psyche," she said, extending her hands. Psyche blinked.

"Um—"

"Here, let me take your mare." The woman reached for the horse's reins, which Psyche surrendered without protest. She watched as the woman stroked the mare's nose, leaning her head into the animal's neck and murmuring words of praise. She felt a another kick of guilt for how far she had pushed her horse.

Psyche cleared her throat. "Thank you," she said, "The lady Diana told me I would find shelter here, but I do not wish to impose. If I could beg water for my horse and a bit to eat for myself, I will take a few moments to rest and then be on my way."

Her face still pressed against the mare's, the woman considered Psyche, her expression mild. "Be on your way to where, child?"

"To—" Psyche stopped. She didn't know where. Now that she had put some distance between herself and her sister's grave, Psyche realized she never had settled on a destination. She closed her mouth, feeling a sudden urge to cry again. The woman reached out, taking Psyche's hand in her own.

"Forgive me, but you seem in no state to continue further at this time, nor does your horse appear to have much energy left. Sit a moment in the garden while I fetch wine and bread; then we can discuss what comes next."

Psyche could not muster the energy to be suspicious of such kindness, so she said, "Yes, thank you," and followed the woman and mare to the edge of the garden, where she collapsed onto a bench. The woman walked the horse to a trough filled with rainwater, disappeared inside, then emerged with the offered wine and bread. Psyche accepted with gratitude.

The woman sat by Psyche on the bench, far enough away not to crowd. A breeze, cool for autumn and carrying on it the faint sound of rustling leaves, brushed their faces.

"I want to love this time of year," the woman said, "and yet it always reminds me of what is about to be lost."

"It will forever remind me of what has been lost," Psyche responded. The silence that fell was question enough. "My sister died five days ago."

"Ah," said the woman, "a wound still raw. You have my sympathies."

"Thank you."

They sat, the weight of their words between them. Psyche wasn't sure what compelled her to begin speaking again.

"She died in childbirth; the child died also. A boy, it was a boy. She said it would be a girl, that the pregnancy had been too easy to be a boy, but she was wrong, and it killed her in the end. The baby killed her, and I'm so angry with it, but who can be angry with a baby, especially one who never even lived?"

"I've found," said the woman, "it is possible to be angry with just about anything, given the right circumstances."

"Well, I'm so angry. And I'm angry with her husband for hurting her, and with her for dying, and with the groom who I now think was her lover and may have been the father of this baby for all I know. I'm angry she didn't tell me anything, and I'm angry with myself for never asking." Psyche's voice broke on the last word, and she bent at the waist, clutching her belly as she began to sob again.

A hand came to rest on her shoulder. "Anger with oneself is the hardest sort," the woman said. "You are carrying a heavy load."

Psyche didn't respond, remaining instead hunched over, feeling her baby kick within her. After several long moments, the woman spoke again.

"You do not know me, and you have no reason to trust me, but I can offer you food and shelter while you determine the next step in your journey. I ask only that you help in keeping the house clean and tidy, and perhaps commit a small amount of time to helping weed my poor flowers." Psyche glanced over at the garden indicated; it did appear behind in its maintenance. "For what it's worth, I, too, have felt the pain of losing the person dearest to me, and it is a hurt that never fully heals. Let me give you a safe place to mourn, at least."

Psyche looked up at the woman. "Are you an immortal?" she asked.

The woman tilted her head. "Does it matter?"

Psyche let out a breath. "I suppose not."

PSYCHE STAYED WITH THE WOMAN, who told Psyche she could call her Deme, for nearly two full turnings of the moon. Her days were slow and filled with the sundry tasks of maintaining a home, a rhythm that was new to Psyche. As the daughter of a royal house, Psyche had never needed to perform most of the tasks for which she was now responsible, and at Cupid's estate, she had done only what appealed to her. But Deme was patient and generous with her time and teaching, and soon enough, Psyche was caring for things at the house on her own while her host tended to the fields and embarked on day trips from which she returned with provisions for the home. Psyche was surprised by how much comfort she found in her new routine. There was so much that was out of her control, but now she could wash linen and hang it to dry. She could weed a garden, sweep the floor, brew a medicinal tea. She even tried her hand at making bread, and while her results were dense and chewy when compared to Deme's loaves, they were nonetheless nourishing, and there was a deep satisfaction that came with that.

Throughout all of it, though, her body called for Cupid and her mind churned with what Diana had proposed. Could she really accuse a god of rape? A part of her shrunk from the suggestion, wanted to protect both him and herself, but then she would think again of Cidippe and Marinos, and her anger would stoke hot. She might as well say publicly that she had been abducted and raped by Cupid; keeping her head down had gotten her nothing but a dead sister.

Beyond giving her space to grieve and think, Psyche's time with Deme was bonding her more and more to the child in her belly. With nothing else to distract her, Psyche became aware of the babe's movements and preferences, the way it seemed to turn somersaults as soon as she lay down for the night, appeared to kick with joy when she spent time among the flowers. The tea Deme had taught her to brew soothed the burning in her chest and the pain in her joints, and for the first time, Psyche imagined what a life with this child could be like.

She thought of her loom, of the half-finished blanket that waited at Cupid's estate. She pictured her child wrapped in the finished product and sleeping in the shade by the garden as she tended to the weeds. She imagined it toddling, unsteady on its feet as Ianthe, reaching up with grubby fingers for a piece of warm bread. And she thought about how nice it would be to curl around that small, precious body at night, her arms keeping it safe and warm the way her sisters used to do for her. The way she had been unable to do for Cidippe.

And so Psyche was unsure. One night, as they sat by the fire sipping their tea, Psyche raised the issue with Deme.

"The father of my child is not a mortal," she said into the comfortable silence. The other woman nodded but waited for Psyche to continue. Never overly chatty, Deme nonetheless seemed to have fewer and fewer words the farther into winter they drew. "He has abandoned me, and I do not know how to find him. I thought to stay with my sisters, but..." Psyche trailed off.

"You have already lost one and now fear for the other's safety," Deme finished.

Psyche nodded. "There is a part of me that wishes to call him to account for what he has done," she said, "but I fear the consequences of making such charges against a god."

"And you love him," Deme said, and there was a curious undercurrent of resignation in her voice.

Psyche didn't try to deny it, noting that, on cue, the still-red line of the arrow cut flared with pain. "I do. Or, a part of me does."

Deme's hands were wrapped around her cup of tea; she stared into its depths. "What do you wish to ask me, Psyche of Crete?"

Psyche swallowed. "Could I— I mean, I don't want to presume, but — is there—" she squared her shoulders. "Is there a world in which I could remain here, with you?" Now she had voiced the request, the words tumbled faster from her mouth. "I could continue tending the responsibilities you've given me, could learn more. Once the child is born, I could be of help to you in the fields." Deme was silent, and

Psyche rushed to continue. "I need time, time to figure this out, time for everything to settle down. I know who you are," she said, wincing as it emerged like an accusation when she had intended it as a reassurance.

Deme looked up. "Do you?"

"Yes, I mean, I have a good idea."

"And who am I, Psyche, princess of Crete, consort to Cupid, mother-to-be of a demigod?"

For the first time since she had arrived, Psyche heard something other than gentle compassion in Deme's address to her.

"I— I believe you to be Ceres, goddess of the harvest, mother to Proserpina and Bacchus."

Deme nodded, slow, curls of silver hair falling from where it was twisted atop her head. "I am all of those things," she said, voice soft but steady. "And if you know this, then you know also that I cannot grant your request."

The small house was silent then, both women deep in their own thoughts. Despair bloomed in Psyche's belly, spreading to her chest and limbs. Did she know why Deme—why *Ceres*—could not allow her to stay? She racked her brain. It had seemed such an obvious solution to her. She and her child would be safe in the care of a god while still serving a god. What was more, she had expected the goddess would be inclined to sympathy, considering the fate of her own daughter.

Details varied, but all the stories agreed on one thing: Ceres absolutely adored her daughter, Proserpina. When Pluto abducted Proserpina to be his bride in the Underworld, Ceres' subsequent depression had threatened the Earth's very survival. And though an arrangement had been reached whereby Proserpina spent spring and summer with her mother, Psyche had watched all through the autumn as Ceres' energies and enthusiasm waned the longer her daughter was gone.

In Psyche's imaginings, she could give birth, and her child could grow, and enough time could pass that humans would forget about her, and perhaps Venus would let go of her grudge, and maybe, just maybe, she could figure things out with Cupid. And Ceres would have help around the farm and a child to love. Psyche didn't see a downside.

Before Psyche could voice this, Ceres began to speak again.

"I have been a waypost on your journey and happy to be one. But I am not, and my home can never be, your destination. You have much to settle with Venus, and while I hope for a solution that suits everyone, it is not my place to interfere more than I already have."

The despair flooding Psyche's body turned with sudden heat to anger. All she wanted was to give birth and raise her child in safety. She opened her mouth, then shut it, not trusting the words climbing her throat. Ceres watched her as though she knew exactly how Psyche felt.

"You are strong," the goddess sighed, "strong enough, I think, to bend with the wind."

Psyche didn't respond. She didn't feel strong. She felt broken and impotent and alone, all the confidence she had built up over the past weeks deserting her. If she could not remain here, then she needed to leave, now, this instant, before she deluded herself again with dreams of a peaceful, pastoral life.

"I'll ready my horse," she said, words stiff. "Thank you for all you've done for me; I will never forget it." And, rising from the table, Psyche collected her things, few as they were, and walked out Ceres' door for the last time.

RIDING AWAY from Ceres hurt more than departing Cidippe's home had. Then, she had been numb and relieved to be putting distance between herself and the memory of Cidippe's last moments; this time she had healed enough that she felt the loss of all her imagined futures like pieces of herself that had been carved away.

Psyche felt the creeping of despair and pushed it down with furious vehemence. She could not afford to fall into that place, not now. She needed to be strong. And so she focused on the most energizing emotion she could access: fury.

Psyche still had the small amount of money Marinos had sent with her. She used it to buy passage on a trade vessel bound for the nearby island of Kythera, site of one of the oldest temples to Venus. She sold her mare to a stable near the dock, wrapping her arms around the animal's head and pressing her face to the muscled neck.

"Thank you," she whispered. "You've served me well. May the Fates continue to care for you." With one last scratch behind the mare's ear, Psyche picked up her bag and walked out of the stables.

The looks she got from the sailors as she boarded would once have made her withdraw further into her cloak; now, she met their eyes with flat challenge until they looked away, whispering among themselves. Welcoming the cold that bit at her cheeks and nose, Psyche settled herself at the bow of the ship and stared out over the churning water as they cut through the waves, fingers playing with the stone at her neck.

CHAPTER 22

Disembarking the ship in Kythera marked the second time Psyche's feet had ever touched non-Cretan soil. Grateful to be leaving the rocking nausea of the ship, she found herself moving more briskly than she had in weeks, hopeful that she had left the worst of her pregnancy symptoms on board.

As she made her way through the port town, she saw things that caused her chest to ache with the memory of Cidippe. She would have been delighted by the street vendors, the smell of fresh seafood, the general hustle and bustle. Remembering what had brought her sister joy sharpened the awareness of her absence, and Psyche blinked several times to hold back tears. She was hungry, tired, and the baby was kicking. She needed to find shelter and a meal before she could trust herself to think anymore on all that had been lost.

About a mile into the city, tucked into the corner of a street lined with private residences, Psyche spotted a sign for an inn. Slipping a hand into her bag, she weighed her pouch of coins in her palm, feeling a grudging gratitude for Ceres' preference for labor as payment. She should have plenty of coin for the night here.

She was greeted with cheer by the innkeeper, who was thrilled at the prospect of a paying guest, and soon enough Psyche was seated at a small table, attempting to spoon stew into her mouth at a pace that didn't completely betray the extent of her hunger.

"Your room is ready." The innkeeper approached, one hand slapping a key onto the table, the other wiping at her face with the hem of her apron. Her hands then went to her hips as she considered her guest, curious eyes lingering on the hood pulled low again over Psyche's face. "Is there anything else I can get for you? Some spotting cloths or a hot stone?" Her eyes indicated her guest's stomach. "I know some women don't bleed at all when they're carrying, but I still did, and it is a hard thing to ask for."

This kindness nearly undid Psyche. "I don't need the cloths, thank you, but a hot stone would be wonderful."

The innkeeper nodded. "Just so, I'll have it waiting in your room when you are ready to head up. My name is Eirini; the three little ones running about are mine. My man is at sea, so it's only us for the night."

"Thank you." Psyche smiled. "I'm... Cidippe." She blinked back tears again. "Thank you for your hospitality and your kindness." Eirini patted her shoulder, giving it a quick squeeze before disappearing into the kitchen. Remembering something Aglaura had once said about it being impossible to drink and cry at the same time, she reached for her wine and took a long gulp. Through the window, she heard the shouts and laughter of the children Eirini had referenced, and she laid an unconscious hand across her stomach.

When her hunger was sated and her wine glass empty, Psyche claimed her key, swung her bag across her shoulder and made her way up the tidy stairs to her room. Once she had let herself in, she found the stone Eirini had promised waiting on her narrow bed, wrapped in several layers of muslin. Psyche shifted it so it was propped on the side of the bed, against the wall, then stretched out on her left side until the small of her back was pressed against the warmth of the stone.

She exhaled with the relief of it. She had adjusted to this aspect of pregnancy, slowing her pace and watching her path for anything that could twist her foot the wrong way, but even with the reduction of the sharp, debilitating pain, the ache was always there.

Outside, Psyche heard the patter of raindrops and felt a surge of relief that she was under shelter. Tucking her hands under her cheek, Psyche thought about what she needed to do. The temple of Venus in Kythera was famed for its close connection to the goddess; islanders claimed it was where Venus first emerged from the sea. Though she wanted nothing more than to go that night and demand Venus show herself, she knew she would have a better chance if she took the time to acquire an offering—and inquiring with the locals would help determine what would be most suitable. Tomorrow, then, she would ask around and go shopping. Tomorrow, she would ready herself to confront a goddess. Tomorrow...

Without planning further, without changing from her travel-worn clothes or removing her shoes, Psyche fell asleep to the steady drumming of rain on stone.

WHEN PSYCHE WOKE the next morning, her body ached and felt sticky with the sweats that had woken her through the night. Groaning as she pushed herself to a seat, she yawned, rubbing sleep from her eyes. The sun poured through the small window of her room with the bright clearness of a world scrubbed clean, and she could smell fish cooking downstairs. There was a knock on the door, and without thinking, Psyche called out for the person to enter. The door creaked open slowly, a small, serious head popping in.

"Mother told me to bring you these, but Father says never barge in on a person in the morning." A boy, around five or six, edged his way into the room, the tip of his tongue visible in the corner of his mouth as he frowned in concentration. He carried a full vessel of water with a fresh cloth draped across the top. Psyche moved to relieve him of his burden. As she did so, his eyes rose to hers, and if Psyche's hands had not already been carrying most of the weight of the vessel, it would have crashed to the floor.

Cursing herself for forgetting her face, Psyche shook her head, allowing hair to fall forward, blanketing her profile. "Thank you," she said, using as calm and gentle a tone as possible. The boy continued to stare until Psyche straightened again, and then, as if jolted from a dream, he turned and scampered down the stairs. Psyche watched him until his small form disappeared around the corner, then shut the door, sighing.

Psyche stripped off the dress she had been wearing for days, draping it over a chair to air out. Soaking the cloth in water, she gave herself a grateful rinse, the chill of the air hitting her damp body almost more refreshing than the night's sleep had been. Retrieving her only other garment, she pulled the light dress over her head, smiling when she felt the baby kick.

"Were you tired of those old clothes, too, little one?" she asked as she reached up to undo and plait her hair. Winding the braid at the base of her neck, she pinned it in place as best she could. Once she was dressed, she tied her coin purse about her waist and pulled on her cloak before making a slow, careful descent down the stairs. The dining room was busier than it had been the night before, several men who appeared to be sailors chatting as they ate their breakfast.

"There's food ready," Eirini greeted her, and Psyche didn't think she imagined the note of heightened interest in the innkeeper's voice. "Sit down, and I'll have my daughter Alkmini bring it to you." Psyche thanked her, choosing the same chair and table she'd used the night before, keeping her head down and eyes low. As she waited for her food, she eyed the other guests, then watched the little boy who had brought her the water. He was tugging at the skirts of an older girl bearing an earthen dish and cup and pointing in Psyche's direction. After a minute, the girl shook him off, making her way to Psyche. This was Alkmini, then.

As the girl approached, Psyche saw that she was with child. Psyche herself was not long past the threshold for womanhood; the innkeeper's daughter looked younger. Murmuring her thanks when the food was set before her, Psyche's eyes followed Alkimini as she made her rounds about the room. To still be living in her parents' house in such a state did not inspire confidence in the girl's treatment.

It would have, perhaps, been one of these men or one like them. A sailor, a transient, claiming the comforts of land while ashore. A man who left again, who perhaps never knew the legacy he left behind.

The anger that simmered ever on the edge of Psyche's consciousness flared to life.

The fish was fresh and warm and the wine cool. When Alkmini appeared again, offering a refill of wine, Psyche accepted, biting her tongue to keep from saying something to the girl. The last thing she needed to do was get another innocent life caught up with her own.

As Psyche sat sipping her wine, lost in memory, the chair across from her scraped over stone, and a sun-bronzed, lanky body sank down, tossing an easy smile Psyche's way.

"Do you mind?"

Psyche started, not meeting the curious gaze. "Oh, no," she replied, even as she glanced around the room. Were there truly no other places for this man to sit?

While there were other available chairs, she observed no empty tables and resigned herself to company for as long as it took her to finish her wine. The man inclined his head in thanks, swinging a lyre from his back and setting it down with care.

"I find sailors communicate with a great deal of gesticulation," he said, answering her unvoiced query. "Which is a dangerous state of affairs for my friend here." He patted the lyre like it was a living thing. "You appear to have reasonable control of your limbs, so I thank you for sharing your space."

It was Psyche's turn to incline her head in acknowledgment, and she did so with a small, dismissive smile, keeping her head low and hoping he would turn his attention to his own food and thoughts.

Instead, the man leaned forward, resting his elbows on the table, head tilting to peer beneath her hood. "My name is Nomios," he said. "With whom do I have the pleasure of dining?"

Psyche sighed. "I'm Cidippe, of Crete."

"Ah, Crete! And then, what are you doing in Kythera, Cidippe of Crete? Forgive my saying it, but you do not look the type to have come here for labor." Psyche considered not responding, but she did still need to determine the best offering for Venus. If this man was so determined to chat, perhaps he could at least be of help.

"No, no," she agreed, taking another sip of wine. "I'm here to visit the temple of Venus."

Nomios scratched his chin. "It is a magnificent temple, to be sure, but do you not have adequate temples to the goddess on Crete? Why journey here?"

Psyche's gaze sharpened. "You ask a great deal of questions for a stranger. I could also ask after your business in Kythera, Nomios."

The man nodded, easy. "You could, and I'd tell you I just disembarked from months aboard a ship that promised ripe material for the next great epic and yet yielded about as much excitement as watching sand dry. So, as I put off the inevitable frustration of attempting to turn that experience into income, the plight of a wellborn woman from Crete, apparently alone in an inn frequented mostly by transients and working *very* hard to conceal her face, becomes infinitely more interesting."

At that moment, Alkmini appeared, setting food and drink before Nomios and refilling Psyche's cup again. The smile and thanks Nomios offered the girl, without any trace of condescension or lechery, made Psyche relax a bit. Or maybe that was the wine.

When Alkmini had left, Nomios turned to Psyche, tucking into his fish. "So I ask again, mysterious Cidippe of Crete, why the temple of Venus in Kythera?"

Psyche studied him, then made a decision. He wanted to talk? Well, alright then.

"I need to be in the presence of the goddess," she admitted, "and from what the stories say, the temple here offers the strongest chance of that."

Nomios nodded. "The stories, yes. They are not always to be believed, of course, but in this case, I think you are correct—belief has created reality. I've known of many people who claim to have interacted with the goddess here." He took a bite of his food. "What do you seek from Venus? Reunion with a lover? Release from a bad marriage?" He waggled his eyebrows as if to reassure her he was in jest, but Psyche had not forgotten he had just admitted to being in need of a good story to tell. Her head was warm, her limbs starting to feel languid. She had a good story.

"I do seek reunion with a lover," she said, sipping.

His eyes widened. "Oh, Cidippe, don't stop there! I have half a fish to eat still." He gestured to his food. "Tell me about him. Or her?"

"Him," Psyche confirmed, hesitating only a moment. "He's the son of the goddess."

Looking back, Psyche would remember the sharpening of Nomios's expression when she said this, the way his hand drifted down to stroke the top of his lyre.

"Her son? But that would mean..." His voice trailed off, the corner of his mouth turning up. "Cupid?"

Psyche lifted her glass in acknowledgement. She shouldn't, she really shouldn't, but it felt so good to talk to someone, to share the burden—

"Do you want to know another secret, Nomios, bard of the boring voyage?"

"Desperately," he replied, leaning in, a twinkle in his eye.

"My name is not Cidippe," she whispered. "It's Psyche." She pulled her hood back far enough for him to see her face. He nearly choked, averting his eyes and taking several minutes to cough and clear his throat as Psyche watched him, cup in her hand. Psyche saw the wheels turn, saw the pieces come together.

"Psyche?" he said after an extended moment. "Psyche of Crete was lost, taken by a monster, they say, for threatening worship of Venus."

"Do they say that?" Psyche tilted her head. "I wouldn't know; I've been busy." She let a hand fall to rest on the top of her stomach, pulling the loose fabric of her dress taut and exposing her throat where the aetites pendant lay. Nomios barked out a delighted laugh, even as he regarded her with wonder.

"Oh, but you are my reward for these last months of tedium. Psyche of Crete, not dead, but wed to Cupid—son of the goddess she offended—and pregnant by him to boot, is this the tale you offer me?"

"Oh, not wed." Psyche pulled her hood back into place, took another sip of her wine.

Nomios's eyes shot up. "Not wed? And abducted? But you're with child; is it one of love, or did he..."

"It was not love, not then."

Nomios eyed her, clearly unsure what kind of creature sat before him. Fair enough, Psyche wasn't sure where this side of her had come from, either. When Nomios spoke again, his voice was quiet.

"He raped you, then? The god of love?"

There it was, that word Diana had offered her. The scar on Psyche's hand ached. And yet, here, at this table, with the buzz of wine in her veins and this man looking at her like she was the answer to all his prayers, she remembered the fervor of the crowds that had once made altars at her door. She recalled the fear in her parents' eyes after the prophecy and that in Apollo's when considering the effect the pregnancy would have on Venus. Once before, Psyche had attempted to influence her own fate, but she had withdrawn, had quit when it became too much. Those who had formed a cult around her had not helped Psyche to claim her own marriage, but perhaps now, if Psyche had the strength for it, they could help her reclaim her life. There was no quitting, not this time. She raised her eyes once more to Nomios's.

"Yes," she said, "he did."

CHAPTER 23

Reclining against the stone wall of the bath, Venus watched the steam curling over the slopes of her breasts and shoulders as she listened to the chatter around her. Though this particular bathhouse was usually open to the public, the muses had claimed the space as part of several days of inspirational festivities. Erato had invited Venus, whispering with a smile that any art inspired absent the goddess of love was hardly worth the designation, and Venus had been both receptive to the flattery and aware that guests of the muses tended to be eclectic and diverse.

That was to say, excellent sources of all sorts of gossip.

She was also hoping to run into Mercury to offload the wings she had been carting around. They did actually need some repairs, she reasoned, and besides, Cupid was not suffering, truly, only safely kept while she determined what next to do. As when he had been a toddler, and she would plop him in an empty fountain for safe containment.

"—her son." Venus heard the whisper from behind her and stilled her breath. "Yes, I mean, what else do you do with such a creature, offspring or no?" Venus frowned; the voice continued, "Half bull! I shudder to imagine that birth."

Venus resumed breath, annoyed. While she did not relish the idea that gossip was circulating around Cupid, Psyche and herself, she knew that it was and thus was perversely irritated to encounter people gossiping about anything else.

The water next to her rippled, and Venus glanced over to find the messenger god grinning at her.

"So delightful, how they float," he said, eyes moving downward and head cocking as he considered her breasts. Venus arched one eyebrow, leaning away from him.

"You've been harder to find than usual for a mouthy idiot," she observed. "Though I suspected a gathering of the muses' chosen would prove irresistible."

Mercury settled himself against the stone as well, making no move to come closer. "Ah, well, there have been an abundance of messages to deliver of late. I've had to start escorting souls in groups just to find time to fit it all in." His fingers danced on the surface of the water, playing with ripples. "You know how it is, with all the... What is it, again, that you actually do?"

Venus smiled, let the bait lie. "Delegate. I've brought our son's wings for you to have tuned; I worry about him flying with them in such a state."

"Do you, now?" The messenger god's eyes gleamed. "What an attentive mother you remain, even so far into the boy's adulthood."

This provocation was harder to ignore, but Venus swallowed her anger, giving a gentle shrug instead. "The things we do for those we love," she said, and Mercury gave a nod, conceding for the moment.

"Rumor has it our little bundle of joy has done a fair number of interesting things lately, in the name of love," he said, snapping his fingers to get the attention of a server. A wood nymph drifted over to them. "Wine, please," Mercury directed, "and one for the goddess, here, as well." The nymph nodded, floating away.

"Our son has been keeping secrets," Venus allowed when their wine had been delivered. "I confess to being displeased."

Mercury snorted. "Displeased? Oh, you are achieving admirable self-control. You know the girl has now made it to your island? She's on Kythera now, searching for him; seeks a reunion, apparently."

Venus's head went hot; she had not known that. The last information she had, Psyche was living with a sister. She swirled her wine, waited for Mercury to continue.

"But of course, you knew that, as well-informed as those shrill little fowls keep you." He sipped his wine, then leaned in, looking around to ascertain they would not be overheard. "What troubles me are the suggestions I'm starting to hear of other divine involvement."

Venus's gaze shot up, eyes meeting Mercury's before she could stop them. "Who?" she snapped. "Who dares interfere in my business?" Gossiping was one thing and to be expected. Interference was quite another; interference was a claiming of jurisdiction in what was patently a family matter.

It was Mercury's turn to shrug. "I can't be sure and wouldn't want to expose myself to accusations of slander," he hedged, "but I do get the impression it is a situation more interesting to goddesses than to gods." He took another sip. "Titans, I'd not be paying such attention were it not my son."

"And also, your job," Venus said, voice ice. She pushed to stand. "As ever, it's been a thoroughly irritating time. I shall depart. The wings are in Erato's care, I trust you to retrieve them from her before you leave." And she did; Mercury could be relied upon when it came to things that interested him. She began to push her way through the water to the steps leading out of the pool. Behind her, Mercury laughed.

"Ah, don't be like that, love!" he called. "It's a time for celebration— our first grandchild!"

Venus froze. "What did you say?" Her tongue had trouble forming the sounds, so badly did she want to have imagined Mercury's words.

"You didn't know? Terns unable to recognize such ordinary human conditions? Yes, Psyche is pregnant."

It occurred to Venus, in a distant corner of her mind, that the last time she had felt rage this intense had also been in Mercury's presence and also over an unplanned child. She would not lose her temper this time, though. She would not give him that satisfaction. Gathering her emotions in tight control, Venus turned, slow, matching Mercury's blithe gaze.

"In that case, I appreciate your discharging of your divine duty, in reporting it to me. If you'll excuse me, I have other things to do." And without giving him a chance to respond, Venus turned and left the pool, accepting the sheer linen wrap that was offered to her and pouring every bit of careless sensuality she possessed into her exit.

The moment she was out of Mercury's sight, Venus dropped all affectations of nonchalance, allowing herself to fall fully into her agitation.

Pregnant? Cupid had not only betrayed her by sparing and bedding the girl, but he had been careless enough to leave her with child? Venus was flush with anger, and there was a ringing in her ears as she called for Palaemon, ready to confront her son.

Hearing the urgency in her voice, Palaemon rushed over with the chariot, knocking other vehicles out of the way in the process. Ignoring the cries of outrage rising around her, Venus stepped aboard and was about to order her charioteer to take her home when she paused.

There had been one other time she had been this angry with Cupid; only one, but the confrontation had proven more painful than the inciting event. Adonis's death had been a dagger through the heart, but the fracture in her relationship with her son, well. That was a pain that never left, as if a piece of her was lost. Furious as she was, much as Cupid may deserve it, she had the uneasy thought that if she took her anger to him now, she might lose more than just that piece.

While she was thinking, Palaemon had taken it upon himself to remove them from the party traffic and had stopped along a nearby ridge overlooking the ocean. The winter wind was fierce, and icy spray misted her ankles, but she hardly noticed.

"My lady?" he prompted, hesitant. "Where to?"

Venus's eye twitched. Where to, indeed.

And yet, even as her mind blanked, another image began to form, still of Cupid, but this time, he was not alone. She saw, in her mind's eye, her son bending toward a faceless mortal, saw his hands drawing the mortal close, his mouth kissing her hair, whispering words of love.

She could not take her anger to Cupid, not while it still burned this bright. But there was another who had earned it just as surely.

"Take me back to Kythera."

THE CITY STREETS were dusty and crowded; Venus was reminded why she so rarely ventured further than her home and her temple. Tucked into an alcove, not bothering to hide her face, Venus scanned the bustling throng.

She couldn't be sure the girl was still here; Mercury did, after all, delight in sharing misleading information and half-truths. It could be that Psyche had been in Kythera but would have departed by the time he shared that information or that she had intended to go there but never made it. Venus thought, rather belatedly, that perhaps she should summon a tern or two to track down—

Wait. There.

Venus's eyes caught on a dark figure moving through the market, exceptional only in that the figure was covered almost entirely by a dark brown cloak. Despite the season, few were so bundled up, and the covering spoke of concealment rather than warmth. Venus had moved through crowds in the same way, and—the goddess's eyes darted down, she peered around bodies until she caught sight of her aim. A swollen belly. Not enormous, not yet, but protruding enough that the cloak parted.

Venus's skin tingled with anticipation, and her mind crowed in jubilance. She watched the figure approach a vendor, haggling for several minutes for what appeared to be white candles, before moving on to another stall where she traded her coins for pieces of copper.

She's collecting tribute, Venus realized, mouth curling. *Surely she's not fool enough to—*

But she was. Purchases secured with care in her bag, the cloaked figure was now making her way out of the market and toward a path Venus knew well.

The goddess followed her until she was quite sure of the girl's destination. But it was a long walk—would take the girl an hour at least—and Venus was not in the mood for such exertion.

Circling back to where Palaemon waited with her chariot, Venus found that the elf had fallen asleep.

"Palaemon!" Venus snapped, causing the charioteer to start, tumbling from where he'd been propped against the temple wall.

"Lady!" he said, voice still thick with sleep.

"Take me to the temple," she ordered, "and then fetch the Algea, with as much haste as possible."

Palaemon could not conceal a wince. "The Algea, lady?" he asked. "You did ask me, the last time you saw them, to remind you how unpleasant—"

"And now, Palaemon, I'm telling you to fetch them."

The charioteer argued no further, instead delivering Venus as instructed and then departing once more as Venus watched. When the chariot was out of sight, she turned to the temple, entering through a rear door.

She swept past awe-stricken priestesses without a word, registering with satisfaction the muffled sounds of their knees hitting stone and their whispered prayers. So Psyche had dared to come here, had she? To the very seat of Venus's power? Well, it was only right that the goddess make it worth her while.

Venus used one of the back temple rooms to freshen up, washing her face and repinning her hair as she considered the confrontation to come. She was confident Palaemon would return soon; the Algea were never far. This meant she would have quite the welcome to offer this grasping pretender, and Venus's stomach was aflutter with anticipation.

When at last she heard a commotion from the front of the temple, Venus gave her image in the mirror one last considering look before departing, moving down the hall toward the main altar.

"You've come to beseech the goddess?" Venus heard the voice of a priestess float from around the corner and slowed, listening.

"I'm not here to beseech; I've come to demand an audience with the goddess's son," came another voice. The hairs stood up on Venus's arms. It was her.

"You will want to sweeten your language and tone before you stand before the image of the goddess," the priestess advised, and while Venus was grateful her followers understood her due, she was also irritated Psyche was being offered guidance at all. Leave the wretched girl all the rope; let her hang herself with it.

"I carry Cupid's child"—Psyche's voice again—"yet he has abandoned me. I've come to profess my love and claim my child's birthright." Venus suppressed a snort, a cold smile tugging at her lips. Psyche was rejecting guidance, then. All the better.

"Well," the poor priestess said then, "I wish you the grace of the goddess."

No chance of that. The priestess came scurrying around the corner, falling back several steps when she saw Venus.

"My lady," she murmured, falling immediately to the floor.

Venus laid an indulgent hand atop the girl's head. "Be on your way, I've no complaint about your service." Gulping, the girl scrambled to her feet, disappearing down the hall, her relief at departing palpable.

Venus turned her attention ahead to the sculpture of her she knew lay beyond.

The statue was at once elegant and stately, soft and regal, sexual and romantic. It was also one of the only statues that depicted her armed, bearing a small knife. Venus had seen herself depicted in all shades, but this statue was painted with rich, dark colors, which lent it an intensity of presence that had always pleased her.

"Goddess," Psyche's voice floated around the corner, steady but soft. Venus stayed where she was.

"Venus," the girl's voice came again, and the goddess welcomed the fresh rush of anger such familiarity brought. There was an extended pause, then,

"Mother?"

Venus had thought herself furious already, but this naming—this *claiming*—made her see white. She swept out from behind the corner, taking in the girl standing before a pitiful shrine of candles and copper.

"Psyche."

CHAPTER 24

Psyche stood before Venus. Her feet were raw and blistered, her dress soiled and sticky, clinging to the roundness of her belly. Her cloak had been abandoned early into her walk, left neatly folded for when she returned, but this had left her face exposed, and now it burned with the time she had spent walking beneath the sun. She had never felt less beautiful.

She had never felt more triumphant.

"I've found you, Mother," she said, sinking to the floor in an exhausted heap, propriety and proper reverence be damned. "I've found you," she said again. The two women stared at one another as the candles of Psyche's tribute flickered and waves crashed against the shore outside and gulls called on the wind. Then—

"You presume to call me Mother?"

"I must." Psyche's hand rose to lay gently at the crest of her stomach, visible enough for clarity of the situation.

Venus laughed. "Do you—are you really coming here, to my island, to my temple, with the presumption of claiming familial ties, and yet you sit, an ugly, smelling heap before me, with a paltry tribute but no sacrifice, no prayers even to offer?"

Psyche straightened her spine but otherwise held her position. "I offer my feet in sacrifice"— she gestured to the blistered appendages

195

—"and my naming of you as Mother as my prayer. I only seek to speak once more with your son, Cupid, my lover and the father of my child. We parted on harsh words that I wish to repair."

"Repair?" One fine brow arched. "Repair? Child, you do not repair with a god; you grovel. You beg. You tear yourself apart in remorse. Is this, then, what you seek my help to do?" She held a hard gaze with Psyche until the human woman closed her eyes, mouth tightening.

"No," she said.

Venus smiled. "Then you're just as stupid as I'd imagined." Crossing to Psyche, Venus crouched down until she was nearly level with the girl. She lifted Psyche's chin with two fingers. "Look at me," Venus commanded. After a moment, Psyche did. "You claim me as Mother, and yet, what evidence do you possess that you are or have ever been married to my son? My son, who has known the love of more sirens and nymphs and demigoddesses than you have years on this Earth. That child growing in your belly? What proof is that? Until it is born and grown, it can no more prove its parentage than can a dandelion claim the stalk from which its seed flew. You have no proof. You have no marriage. You have no claim." Venus stood, looking down. "You have *nothing*."

Psyche felt her eyes heat with unshed tears, and she scrambled to her feet. "I have my body," she said, "and I have this child, and if I have to walk this entire, miserable Earth to find your son and hold him to the promises he made me, I will do it. You do not scare me, Venus."

"Do I not?" The amusement in Venus's tone suggested she saw through this bluff. She turned away, pacing before addressing Psyche again. "Do you know where my son is?" There was a new lightness to her words that set Psyche on edge.

"I would not be here if I did."

"Well, I know where he is. And I know his condition. He is languishing, hovering between life and death itself, from injuries inflicted by your hand."

Psyche's stomach dropped before she caught the gleam in Venus's eye. Swallowing, Psyche endeavored to make her own voice as light as that of the goddess. "If a few drops of oil can so vanquish a god, Olympus must be in a state of terror."

Venus clapped her hands. "Oh, well said. No, he is languishing, but I left him more or less comfortable and with plenty of servants to see to his, ah, *every* need. You, interestingly, have not come up as one of those."

Psyche squeezed her eyes shut, filling her lungs, then exhaling slowly before speaking. "Your games are exhausting, Mother. You know I speak the truth. Tell me where to find him or do not, but I am too tired for this." Psyche's body swayed, accentuating the point.

Venus let out a sigh. "And this, Psyche of Crete, is your fatal flaw. You seem to think you have a choice in this game, an option to abstain. You do not." Venus stepped closer to Psyche, her voice lowering and her hand sliding into the girl's hair, first with tenderness, then fisting sharply to force her face upward and hold her in supplication. Psyche cried out in surprise and pain, tears springing to eyes that nonetheless held those of the goddess. "When ever have humans had a choice whether to play the games the gods set? Did Paris choose his fate any more than Hector? The Earth is a board, and you are but a piece on it, raised up beyond your rightful place by the lusty idiocy of my son but still human, still subject to the whims and desires of the immortal. There is no place you can flee to escape me, and even in death will I hunt you to the Underworld and have Pluto deliver you, a quivering shadow, at my feet. You wish to find my son? Well then. Let us play for that prize." Releasing Psyche's hair so suddenly that the human girl fell hard against the stone floor, Venus raised a hand, snapping her fingers, and Psyche heard footsteps from further within the temple.

"I'd like you to meet the Algea, Melancholy and Sorrow," Venus said, her voice warm again, as though introducing Psyche to those she expected to be her closest of friends. From the inner rooms of the temple emerged two of the most beautiful creatures Psyche had ever seen, and yet the closer they drew, the more foreboding she felt.

Melancholy and Sorrow were dressed as handmaidens but despite their unlined faces, Psyche had never seen a human with eyes so dark and deep and aching. Their movements were smoothly automatic, as if their bodies were taking them through the necessary motions of living even as their minds flew far, far away. Appearing at first identical, Psyche could see once they crouched by her that the features of one seemed sharper than the other—Sorrow, she thought.

"They will see to your filthy condition"—Venus's lip turned up slightly—"then outline for you my terms for an audience with Cupid." And so saying, the goddess strode from the temple in a sweep of airy fabric, the scent of roses lingering behind her.

Melancholy raised a slow finger, dragging it down Psyche's cheek as they stared at her. "You had so much," Melancholy murmured, "and you threw it away." They licked a thumb, then scrubbed it against Psyche's forehead, studying with dispassion the dirt that had been removed. "That is disgusting."

For the second time that day, Psyche cried out at the sudden pain of being jerked by her hair, Sorrow having plunged a comb in and yanked so hard that an enormous clump came away with the comb and tears streamed down Psyche's face. Sorrow clicked their tongue. "This will take a while," they said, sinking the comb back in.

Psyche ceased being aware of time as she was subjected to the most painful cleaning of her life. The Algea tore her clothes from her, Psyche resisting only when they ripped the amulet from her neck. Hissing, she snatched it back, holding it tight in her fist, meeting their empty gazes in a challenge they ignored. The cloths Melancholy used to scrub her body seemed embedded with tiny thorns, the water alternating between so hot Psyche thought her skin would peel off and so cold that her nerves screamed with the numbness. After Sorrow had dealt with Psyche's hair, her entire head was submerged in lye as sharp fingernails scratched at her scalp. Once clean, her hair was scraped tight and coiled atop her head, fixed again with pins Psyche was sure were jabbed with deliberate malice. Finally, the Algea turned their attention to the hair of her body, applying rough pumice stones to her legs, vulva, arms, and underarms until she felt little more than a raw nerve exposed to alcohol.

The Algea stood together, heads cocked, examining their work. Psyche curled in on herself on the stone floor, trembling. "She needs a gown, Sorrow," Melancholy murmured, and Sorrow disappeared briefly into the bowels of the temple before remerging with the plainest of gray garments. They dropped it next to Psyche.

198

"Put this on, then follow us," they ordered. The Algea turned, walking out of the temple.

Psyche lay shaking for many long moments before she slowly began to unfold, reaching out to pull on the dress left for her. It was made of the same material as had been used to scrub her body, she realized as she pulled it on, stiff with pain.

"Mortal!" came a sharp demand from outside, and Psyche rose, one hand curled protectively around her stomach, the other pressed to the lightning pain in her back as she limped in the direction of the voice.

When she emerged from the temple, Psyche followed the Algea around the building to a rear entrance and a room that appeared to be the temple's silo. Seven decorated clay pithoi stood, arranged with tidy precision, on a correspondingly decorated table against the far wall, each filled to the brim with various grains. Without a word, Melancholy and Sorrow crossed the room, each lifting one of the pithoi before turning to meet Psyche's eyes as they walked back to the center of the room and dumped the contents, in whole, onto the floor. A strangled noise escaped Psyche at such treatment of precious food stores. The smallest of smiles danced around Melancholy's mouth as they turned to replace the empty pithoi. They then repeated the process until every single container had been emptied, their contents strewn across the granary floor. Psyche watched with muted anger as wheat, barley, millet, poppyseed, chickpeas, lentils, and beans mixed together and rolled across dirty stone.

The Algea came to stand behind Psyche, each with a hand on her shoulder, observing their work. "If you wish to see Cupid," Sorrow said, "every grain will be sorted to its corresponding pithos before Venus returns at dawn."

"If it is not," Melancholy added, "there is no guarantee she will let you walk from this temple with a living child in your womb."

Their words sent Psyche stumbling back, her legs giving out when her shoulders hit the wall of the silo, her body sliding down to collapse heavily on the floor as she stared at the task before her.

"Work quickly, Psyche," Sorrow advised.

"Or not at all"—Melancholy blinked—"for what hope is there?"

. . .

199

IT WAS, as Melancholy had said, hopeless. Hours later, Psyche sat, her legs long numb from the cold, her fingers automatically picking grain from the pile and sorting it according to type. She'd ripped a strip of fabric from the bottom of her dress, using it to string and fasten her pendant back around her neck, and she focused on the weight of it to keep from crying.

As always, when she touched the aetites stone, Psyche thought of Cidippe. She thought she understood her sister better now and why she had never attempted to leave Marinos. Psyche had entered the temple earlier tired but filled nonetheless with righteous anger, ready to speak the truth of Cupid's actions to Venus.

And yet she had not. In the presence of the goddess, faced with the radiant malevolence of the immortal, Psyche had felt herself grow small, her conviction fold in on itself. Diana had said that naming Cupid's actions held power, but Psyche could not imagine any power she possessed great enough to match Venus's.

The sky was still black through the door of the silo, the bright stars mocking Psyche's pain. When her fingers became too stiff and cramped to continue, she paused for a moment, turning to study the stars as she massaged her hands.

"Do you watch me, Juno, through the tiny bright eyes you've tossed into the sky? Do you see where I have fallen? You watched my sister die—a mother, under your protection!—and now you'll stand by and let the Underworld claim my child as well. What are the gods, then? What use are our prayers, our tribute, our labor? What use is any of it?" Psyche's bitter voice had risen, reverberating off the sides of the silo. She listened as the last echoes faded, then turned, resigned, to the pile of grain.

A man now sat across from her.

Psyche screamed.

The man was sitting cross-legged on the opposite side of the grain pile, leaning back on his hands, a broad smile slashing an inhumanly compelling face. At Psyche's scream, his eyebrows rose and he brought a finger to his lips in reprimand.

"Hush, hush, do you wish to summon those miserable puppets?" Wide-eyed, Psyche gave the slightest shake of her head. The man lowered his finger, reclining once more as he studied her. "I must say, this little joke has proven to have longer legs than I ever intended, though I'm certainly not complaining."

Psyche opened her mouth to respond, then closed it once more. What was he talking about? The man continued, chuckling.

"Really, that's got to be what's angering Venus as much as anything —your beauty should be greater to justify all it has wrought. She can't understand it." Psyche stared at him. The man sighed. "That was rude of me. You are, of course, quite fair and, if you will permit me, frankly, blooming in your condition."

"Who are you?" The whisper was laced with fear, suspicion, and anger but also with the tiniest bit of hope.

The man across from her inclined his head. "Ah, Psyche, but you know the answer to that. You've not spent the past several months meeting gods to fail and recognize one now." He lifted a foot, flapping a winged ankle at her.

"Mercury," she said.

"Correct!" He settled back.

"Why are you here?" Psyche's mind was emerging from the shock of his appearance and sharpening to the potential implications of his presence.

Mercury shrugged. "I heard you're growing my grandchild, and frankly, anyone who gets under Venus's skin the way you have absolutely delights me."

"Your grandchild?" Psyche was puzzled. "I thought Cupid was the child of Venus and Mars?"

"Oh, many do," the god said, "but I can report with authority that he is not."

"Oh." Rain began to fall outside, the soft splats against stone the only sound in the silo as Psyche and Mercury considered one another.

"Well," Mercury finally said, "I do have other places to be, so let's get to business. What asinine task has Venus set you here?" A hand swept to indicate the grain pile. "Must you consume this all before daybreak? A cruel edict, uncooked lentils on their own could make you sick enough to end that pregnancy."

Psyche frowned. Outside, the rain came harder. "No, no—I must sort the grain to its original pithos, by type, before dawn. You see my progress." She directed his gaze to the seven small, pitiful piles at her feet.

Mercury guffawed. "Oh, Jupiter's busy cock, she doesn't want you to see the boy. That's impossible."

Psyche's mouth was tight. "Yes."

"Hmm." Mercury sprang to his feet, considering the pile before him, then the hunched girl opposite him. "Fortunately for you there is little I enjoy more than vexing my one-time beloved. Also fortunately for you the rain has brought you aid."

He strode to the door of the silo, crouching down by the frame and smiling at seemingly nothing. "Hello there, little ones. The rain get a bit much?"

Confused, Psyche unfolded her body enough to turn and squint at the god. "Who are you—"

"Ants!" Mercury beamed. He lowered a gentle finger, allowing one tiny black body to crawl onto the tip. Bringing it close to his face, the god then considered the creature with respect. "Greetings, friend," he addressed the ant. "You and your brethren are welcome here as long as you need to wait out the storm."

Psyche could have sworn she saw two fragile antennae dip in acknowledgment of Mercury's words. The god continued.

"While you are here, friend, there is something with which I would beg your aid and the aid of your colony." He walked to the grain pile, bringing the ant with him, then lowering down to a crouch and gently laying his finger along the stone so that the ant could crawl off. "This pile of grain, as you can tell, is dreadfully mingled to the point of utter uselessness. Might you use your time in shelter to help sort it to its original piles? I would consider it a personal favor."

Psyche stared. He was mocking her. Of course he was mocking her. She felt a red fury crawl up her neck.

"How dare you?" she snapped, rising to her feet, her body trembling with cold and hunger and the intensity of her anger. Mercury stood slowly, arms crossed, a smile playing about his lips.

"Oh no, my dear, how dare *you*?" He inclined his head to direct her attention to the floor where, to her stupefaction, a legion of ants had assembled and were already briskly moving about the pile, grain carried high on their backs until they reached the appropriate pile, at which point it was dislodged, and the ant returned for another trip. Mercury clapped his hands together.

"Well. My work, I think, is done here. Good luck, Psyche; you will still need it. Do not think the completion of this task will see the end of your troubles."

THE ANTS DROPPED the last piece of grain into its appropriate pithos just as the sun began to climb the stairs of the granary, peeking in through the open door. The rain had long since stopped, and Psyche watched, still in awe, as the insects marched back outside in a tidy line. Never again would she squash one, she vowed to herself.

Looking at the now full pithoi, Psyche felt hope rise in her chest, despite Mercury's warning. She was still in the process of moving the pithoi onto their table from the floor when a shuffling behind her alerted Psyche to Sorrow and Melancholy's return.

"Oh, she won't like this." Psyche thought the voice belonged to Melancholy, though she didn't bother to turn around, focusing instead on shifting the last pithos into place.

"A bold trick, Princess, but not one that will work." This was Sorrow, who appeared with inhuman speed by Psyche's elbow. "The goddess always checks that the details of her tasks have been—" Sorrow fell silent, staring into the pithos of lentils. "Is it truly only—" Drawing out a long, slender stick, they used it to swirl the lentils around until satisfied it was the only grain within. They then repeated the process with the remaining pithoi. Psyche held her breath, trying not to think for what purpose Sorrow had originally intended that switch. Inspection completed, Sorrow turned, gliding back to Melancholy. The two bent their heads together, whispering. After some time, Melancholy looked up at Psyche.

"A remarkable achievement," they whispered, "that shall be rewarded only in pain."

Sorrow turned their own eyes on Psyche, assessing. "You are

stronger than we believed; know that what will come shall bring us no joy."

Psyche wondered that Sorrow would suppose anyone thought the Algea capable of joy but held her tongue. Instead, she lowered her chin in deference to the handmaidens.

"I merely await Venus's judgment."

As though summoned by her name, the goddess in question swept through the door. She halted, eyeing the bare floor, then raising a glittering gaze to take in the pithoi, returned to their table in a neat line.

"Sorrow?" The name was both a question and a demand. Sorrow drew close to the goddess, whispering words too low for Psyche's ears. She guessed their meaning, however, by Venus's reaction. Where the goddess had entered with the happy flush of wine and pleasure coloring her features, now the same flush morphed into what Psyche read as rage.

"So." The word dripped with acid as Venus stalked to within a hairsbreadth of Psyche, glaring down on her. "So," Venus repeated.

Psyche swallowed, forcing herself to hold the goddess's gaze. *Breathe in, breathe out.* "As you see, Mother, the task you set me is completed."

Venus did not miss the careful wording. "So it is. But what proof do I have it was you that completed it?"

"With respect, Mother"—Psyche was both chilled and charged at the way Venus's eyes flashed every time she used the title—"that was not a requirement of the task, as laid before me."

Without breaking eye contact, Venus shifted ever so slightly toward the Algea. "Melancholy?"

"Sorrow said only that the grain must be sorted, my lady." Melancholy's voice was like an echo on a breeze.

There was a tense moment in which all but Venus held their breath. Then, Venus laughed. "No matter. Follow me."

CHAPTER 25

They flew in Venus's chariot over blue water and bustling cities and green fields until, finally, they landed, Psyche stumbling out past the Algea to vomit even before the carriage came to a halt. Venus did not wait for Psyche to compose herself, leading the group down a steep hill until they reached a grove flanked by a wide, fast-flowing river. Low-lying bushes lined the edge of the water on the opposite side, and dotting the field past the bushes were more small grazing animals than Psyche could count. They had the form of sheep, but the way the sun glinted off their coats made her question her eyes. Venus spoke without looking at her.

"Those sheep are the flock of Helios himself and grow fleeces of pure gold. I've long desired a gown made from their wool but require a sample for my weaver to determine the best method for spinning such a rare substance to cloth. You, Psyche, will obtain that sample for me if you ever hope to see my son again."

The goddess snapped her fingers, not waiting for a reply, and Psyche heard the rumbling of the chariot catching up with them. When her ride had come to a stop, Venus stepped aboard.

"Melancholy! Sorrow!"

Both Algea started, having been staring, slack-jawed, at the animals beyond the river. As they brushed past Psyche, both whispered in her ear.

"To underestimate will be your undoing," said Sorrow.

"So that you do not die on an empty belly," said Melancholy, pressing something into Psyche's hand.

And then the Algea boarded the chariot, and all were gone. Psyche was alone once more. She turned over her hand to see what Melancholy had pressed into it, heart and stomach leaping at the sight of a sizable chunk of bread—a bit stale but free of mold. The fish and wine at the inn seemed lifetimes ago. Moving to the edge of the river, Psyche pulled off her shoes and let her sore feet rest in the water as she forced herself to tear the bread into small pieces to slow her eating of it.

The trickiest part of this task appeared to be crossing the river, the apparent simplicity of which—combined with Sorrow's warning—suggested to Psyche that it would be anything but. Was there a monster lurking in the river's depths? An enchantment of some kind on the water? Psyche studied her feet, toes bobbing at the surface; nothing strange so far. She ate one of the small pieces of bread. Information, that was what she needed before she attempted this task.

The breeze was cool but the sun bright, and the combination of this with the sounds of rushing water and chirruping insects lulled Psyche into a hypnotic state as she stared across the river at the leaves rustling on the bushes beyond. The babe flipped in her womb, and Psyche lifted a hand to her stomach.

To what purpose was she here? To be reunited with a man who, though her body called for him, had used her and then abandoned her when she was pregnant with his child? Were it not for the child, Psyche thought, she might be able to push down the effects of the arrow and run, attempt a life of quiet peace away from the gods.

Psyche felt immediate guilt for this line of thinking, for even as the child tied her irrevocably to the path she now walked, she had become fond of the constant presence within her. But she also had nightmares of Cidippe's death at the hands of a stillborn babe, waking from such nightmares with an aching emptiness in her chest and a righteous fury with not only Marinos but all men. Yet here she was, performing like a dancing pig for scraps of attention from the very man responsible for her impending battle with death.

Psyche's head tilted as she scanned the river before her. Her skin still burned, raw from the treatment it had received, and her stomach turned over, threatening to empty itself once more. What did it matter if there was a monster in the water? If she was unsuccessful, Venus was sure to kill her anyway. If she attempted to swim across and died somehow in the attempt—well, that was one way out, and on her own terms, at least. Information didn't matter, after all. Very little did.

Taking a deep breath, Psyche stood, removing the dress of thorns. She stepped into the water, hissing at the bitter cold. She forced herself to take a step, then another. She was almost waist-deep when a faint voice caused her to pause.

"Psyche..." Her name came floating on the breeze, so delicate that she thought at first she imagined it. But then, again, she heard, *"Psyche..."* and turned in the direction of the sound.

"Who calls me?" she said, wondering if perhaps Melancholy or Sorrow had returned.

"Here..." replied the voice, *"down the bank..."*

Psyche began walking along the shore toward the voice, forgetting her nudity in her focused strain to catch the words that continued to float to her. *"I see you, Princess, and your half-formed negotiation with death. Come, speak with me; do not cast your body into the water and leave your life, and the life of your babe, in the hands of the Fates."*

The voice grew louder the further Psyche walked until she felt she was upon it. Looking around her, however, she saw no source for the words. Reeds swayed at her feet, insects hopped in the grass, and a tall laurel tree stretched above providing shade, but no being capable of speech appeared.

"Who are you?" Psyche asked again. "Show yourself, I beg you."

"Beg no one for anything, Princess; I wish I'd learned that in my own life. But regrets build a cold home; look up and see me, not as I am now but as I once was."

Confused, Psyche glanced up. At first, all she saw was blue sky and clouds peeking through the branches of the laurel, the almond-shaped leaves casting dancing shadows upon the ground. Then, as she continued to stare, the leaves began to take shape in front of her eyes, never actually moving but somehow coming into a kind of focus, revealing a woman's visage, fair, with waving hair of green that seemed to float about her face, then flow down and away, into the trunk of the tree. Psyche blinked; the face was still there. Had she imagined it, or had the leafy mouth turned up, ever so slightly, at the corners?

"*Greetings, Psyche of Crete.*" The mouth didn't form the sounds in the way that a human's would have, but as Psyche watched the face in the tree and listened to the words on the wind, there was no doubt of their origin.

"Greetings, spirit," Psyche said, unsure of the protocol for such a situation but bowing her head slightly in what she hoped read as respect.

An echoey laugh. "*Spirit... I guess that is what I am... Once I had a form like yours, but I, too, negotiated with death, and here I now stand, for eternity, I suppose. The Fates do not play fair.*"

"No, they do not," Psyche agreed, Cidippe's face springing to her mind, sudden tears filling her eyes as she clenched her hand in a fist around the scar left by Cupid's arrow.

The voice hummed with empathy. "*It is children who expect fair treatment from the Fates, and I tell you, Psyche, I died still a child. I would offer what I can to prevent that same fate for you.*"

Psyche nodded. "I welcome any advice you have to offer, with my thanks."

There was a silence, not uncomfortable, where it seemed the spirit was lost in thought. Then—

"*It is not the water you need fear, though you must enter it with a will to live,*" the voice said. "*But look beyond; what do you see?*"

Psyche's gaze followed the line of the branch that seemed to stretch out toward the opposite bank. Again, she noted the shining, sheep-like figures munching calmly on the grasses in their field.

"I see... sheep? The way they shine in the light makes me question my eyes, but they look like sheep. Venus said they were the flock of Helios."

"And Venus did not lie. They are no ordinary animals; from my view here on the bank, I've seen them tear grown men apart, protecting their bounty even at the expense of their own lives. To approach them would be a sure path to the Underworld."

Psyche's stomach felt queasy at these words, not the least because the lengths to which a sheep would have to go to kill a person seemed somehow even more gruesome than, say, those of a lion. Despite her grim musings of before, she realized she did very much wish to live and at once felt a profound gratitude to the spirit.

"I thank you sincerely for the warning," Psyche said, turning her head and shading her eyes to gaze out over the water, at the beasts in question. She took and released a deep breath of despair. "But then, how am I to complete the task Venus has set before me?" She meant it rhetorically, knowing that it must be she who retrieved the fleece; the loophole Mercury had helped her exploit the first time would not work again. So she was surprised when the voice came again in response.

"Oh, that is simple enough." Psyche glanced at the face in the leaves and imagined they appeared amused. *"Look again; what else do you see?"*

Turning her attention once again to Helios's flock, Psyche squinted. She saw water buffeting the far shore. She saw wild grasses chewed low. She saw a high, thick line of bushes that appeared planted with the intention of providing a boundary for the animals. She saw—

"What is that, on the bushes?" Psyche asked, cocking her head and straining her eyes to be sure of what she saw. "They seem to… shimmer." She imagined she heard a satisfied sigh from the tree.

"It's fleece, the very fleece you've been tasked with fetching. The sheep are constantly rubbing up against those bushes, seeking relief from flies and other complaints."

Psyche's heart sped up. "But, if all I need is the fleece, then I need not disturb the sheep to get it." She started sizing up the river and the field beyond, calculating her safest path. A branch brushed her shoulder.

"Wait; Helios himself will aid you here, albeit unwittingly. Ferocious as

209

the sheep are, still they grow tired under the intensity of the midday sun, even in winter, and lie down as a herd, to rest. Make your journey then."

"But—surely it can't be that simple?" Psyche said with a choked laugh. The spirit laughed too, and her voice, when it came, was thick with past sorrow.

"So often we give the gods credit with thinking when the reality is they are nearly always acting on pure emotion."

Psyche turned to the face in the tree, extending a hand and laying it with reverence along the trunk. The tree shuddered at the contact. "Thank you," Psyche said. "I hardly deserve more of your kindness, but may I know the name of the one who has saved me and my child today?"

The tree swayed gently, the face gazing down at her soft. "Once... once, I was called Daphne. Now, I'm just a laurel tree. Go, Psyche, keep your own name and demand the gods say it."

THE TASK WAS ACCOMPLISHED EXACTLY as outlined, with Psyche returned to the shore where Venus had left her even before the sun began to set. Laying the precious fleece between high stalks of grass and reeds to prevent it blowing away, she pulled her abandoned dress over her head, wincing as it scratched but grateful for its dry warmth. Once clothed, Psyche sat, tucking the fleece into the front of her dress and banding her arms around her knees for warmth.

She had no idea when Venus would return. She considered walking down to Daphne to thank her again and confirm her success, but instinct told her that the spirit had shared as much as she cared to already, and besides, she was cold, and Psyche's whole being balked at the idea of uncurling and being once more at the mercy of the wind.

So Psyche sat, alone, and closed her eyes.

WHEN SHE OPENED THEM, Venus stood before her, triumphant. Behind the goddess, a few feet behind, hovered her handmaidens.

"I know humans to be weak, but to not even attempt the task? Truly, I thought my son had better taste."

Psyche didn't answer, only looked up at the goddess, marveling at her beauty. One expected Venus to be beautiful, of course, but even her previous encounters with immortals had not prepared Psyche for the dizzying effect of Venus's presence. To this point, she had managed to place her fascination to the side, but exhausted as she was, she found she had not the energy left to marshal her thoughts. And so she stared.

There was a quality of Venus at once compelling and terrifying, as though she would provoke the most primal of emotions in equal measure and without discretion. For all she had set Psyche a task ostensibly designed to kill her, Psyche felt nonetheless that the goddess was disappointed in what she perceived as Psyche's failure. Yet also she knew, with confidence, that Venus would have been pleased if she had died. It was this in-between that seemed to vex her; prove her love or die, but do not exist between those two.

Psyche retrieved the generous sample of golden wool she had gathered. She extended her hand upward to Venus, unspeaking and unblinking. The goddess seemed flooded at once with both fury and delight. Melancholy and Sorrow drew twin inhales of surprise.

"Well, well, well," Venus said, letting Psyche's hand hang in the air. "And so you have greater support than I realized." After studying the girl a moment longer, Venus swung toward her chariot, ordering Sorrow to retrieve the wool. "Climb on," she said to Psyche.

Psyche scrambled to her feet, stepping aboard the chariot just as Palaemon flicked the reins. One hand reached out to grasp the edge of the carriage, her body flying backwards with the sudden acceleration, and she would likely have fallen off altogether had Melancholy's hand not wrapped around her upper arm.

"Thank you," Psyche said.

Melancholy stared at her, unblinking, hand remaining where it was. "Don't," they said, and the word was so soft, it was almost lost in the rush of wind as the chariot flew.

When they finally came to a stop, Melancholy and Sorrow hurried off of the chariot so Psyche could step down herself and vomit with less spectacle. Once done, Psyche wiped her mouth and looked up at her surroundings.

They were at the base of what could either be considered a very large hill or a very small mountain. It was craggy and sharp-edged, green growth cropping up in wild explosions along the surface that brought to Psyche's mind the image of an old man, who looked at his reflection only to find hair erupting from every orifice imaginable—nose, ears, the indent of his clavicle—while simultaneously realizing that it has disappeared in patchy consistency from his head and chin.

Venus, who had retained her position on the carriage and the additional height it offered her, smiled.

"From the highest peak of this mountain flows a spring, which waters the marshes of the Styx and feeds the streams of the Cocytus. I desire to drink from this spring, but the water must be retrieved from the highest point, where it gushes out from within the mountain itself." Reaching into her gown, she retrieved a small crystal jug, which she indicated for Melancholy to hand to Psyche. "Fill this for me and return with it still cold. I shall remain here, awaiting your return, for it should not take you long if you are fixed on your task."

Psyche studied the shining vessel in her hands, the light glinting off the crystal in ways that seemed to reflect the goddess herself—as inclined to cut you as bathe you in light. Sighing, Psyche nodded her assent, turned, and began to make her way up the mountain.

CHAPTER 26

C upid was quite sure he had never been alone this long in his entire life, and the solitude did not suit him. His burns long since healed, he had drunk half his mother's wine, made an attempt to leave the house, been prevented by Venus's loyal guard, then gone to consume the rest of the wine.

Venus had ordered her entire staff on holiday, save the guard and a single chamber servant, leaving Cupid in the uncomfortable position of having to cook for himself if he desired anything more complex than cheese and bread and fruit. Having no experience, he attempted it for a couple of days, hopeful it would prove a diversion for his mind as well, but after charring some fine meat and burning himself in the process, he decided he could tolerate being bored in his diet.

Tolerating boredom, though, was not a strength of Cupid's. The chamber servant was a distraction for a bit, but after the initial glow of a new lover wore off, Cupid found himself gazing at the servant, comparing him with the perfection of his lost love. Soon enough, even the lad's most eager and practiced of advances failed to rouse any response in Cupid, and it was after one such encounter that Cupid sent him away as well.

Psyche. How he yearned for her, burned for her, would prostrate himself before her if only he could. The intensity and single-minded-ness of his devotion had long since led him to the conclusion that his state must be the result of one of his own arrows, but even so knowing, he could not bring himself to reverse the effect with one of his leaden ones. The lead arrows incited hate, after all, and wasn't it more pleasant to love her than to hate her? Why would he wish to be free of his love for her when it was the only bright spot in his whole boring existence? He must find a way to escape this house, and that was that.

It was into this state of affairs that the tern responsible for Cupid's current situation flew one day, several weeks into the house arrest. Having overheard Venus order Cupid's captivity and still bitter over Venus's treatment of him, the tern had since observed events that would—in his estimation—be entertaining to share with his mistress's son.

And so he had returned for the express purpose of dropping the proverbial match into the proverbial tinderbox.

"I did not know my lord was staying with his mother," dissembled the tern, ruffling its feathers as it settled onto a perch by Cupid's head. The god lay sprawled across the same chaise on which he'd lain when his mother left him, one arm flung over his eyes, the other dangling over the edge.

"What you do not know, tern," Cupid said, not bothering to remove his arm from his eyes or adjust his position in any way, "would fill the Aegean Sea thrice over."

Tutting, the tern hopped from one foot to the other. "Rude, so rude, and I was going to share with you news of your beloved."

Cupid's body went still, his breath even stalling in his chest for a beat. Then, with caution, he uncovered his eyes, blinking at the sudden flooding of light to his pupils, and turned his head until he could see the tern.

"Tell me," he ordered.

The tern blinked a beady eye at him, "But what I do not know would fill the Aegean Sea thrice over."

Cupid exhaled in irritation, swinging his legs around and standing up to cross the room with sudden, nervous energy. "Yes, yes, I'm in a foul mood, and I spoke accordingly. Let us skip ahead to where you cannot bear to depart without relieving yourself of gossip."

In all his centuries of living, Cupid had never heard a bird laugh. He did now. It was unsettling.

"I don't know that I shall reach that part," the tern said, prim. "Gossip is, you know, usually conducted as an exchange, and you have, thus far, offered me only a lack of hospitality."

Cupid dropped his face to his palms, pressing the heels of his hands hard into his forehead. Birds. Breathing deeply, he dropped his arms again, then extended them wide, indicating the whole of the room and its contents.

"You want some gossip? Here's what I offer: my mother has me under house arrest. I've not been outside these walls in over a moon, for she's taken my wings, and I'm about to perish from the tedium of my current existence and my longing for Psyche." He named her deliberately, knowing well that the tern already possessed the information but would be keen for the confirmation from his own lips. The tern flew closer, perching on the branch of a lime tree by the window.

"The goddess of love has her son under lock and key? That certainly explains your absence in the trials of your adored."

The hairs rose on Cupid's arms. "Trials?"

"Oh yes, Venus has been setting her the most impossible tasks, all seemingly designed to break the girl's spirit and, if I'm being honest, her body as well."

Cupid's face went white. "Tell me," he said.

And so the tern did, leaving out the details of how Psyche had been accomplishing the tasks and ending with a description of the spring from which the girl had been ordered to fetch water. Cupid paced the room in agitation.

"I must help her," he said. "She cannot accomplish this; no mortal could!" The tern remained silent, watching Cupid. The god of love turned to the bird, hands clasped in supplication. "I beg you to help me, to help her."

The tern was not used to such sincerity in its dealings and was quite overcome by the request. All irritation and wounded pride from its reception was swept away by the sense of importance it felt, being begged by a god.

215

"I'm not large or strong enough to carry the jug myself," the tern said. "But I am owed a favor by one who is."

"Use it," Cupid said, "and possess instead such a debt from me. And once the task is complete and she is safe, please alert my father to my situation."

The tern puffed up and gave a sharp nod of its beak.

"I'll do what I can," it said. "But I cannot promise the outcome. I'll bear no responsibility for this if things go sideways."

Cupid, whose hands had been raking through his hair, now froze, frowning, then leaned forward to fix the tern in his gaze.

"Be careful you don't overstep, bird," he said. "Fly now, and see that you do everything in your power to protect Psyche's life, for if I ever learn otherwise, you can trust I'll pluck you feather by feather until you're little more than a grounded rat with a beak."

The tern squawked in distress. "Rude!" it said, alighting.

Cupid watched the tern soar from the window, wondering if he had mucked it all up. Heaving a great sigh, he flopped onto the chaise, closing his eyes again, this time to nightmares of his future if Psyche were to die.

CHAPTER 27

P syche trudged upwards, keeping a careful eye on her footing as the terrain could change in moments from soft earth to unforgiving rock. Once again, the task before her seemed simple enough, which made Psyche sure that it was not—at least not without additional information.

She knew, however, that Venus remained below in order to ensure she received no such aid this time. Slipping as her foot came down wrong on a concealed stone, Psyche cursed when she realized the tie of her sandal had snapped. Worn thin as it was already and considering the path ahead, Psyche decided she would be better served barefoot. The pain in her back was already beginning to bloom; if she suffered another similar misstep, she was likely to become immobile. Frowning as she thought, Psyche then reached down and, retrieving the laces from her sandals, tied them together to form one long cord, which she then laced through the handles of the crystal jug and secured above the bump of her stomach, below her breasts. This left both hands free for support.

Slowing her pace and placing one hand at the base of her spine, Psyche used the other, outstretched, to grasp any steadying hold she could find. Trees, at the beginning, but as she drew higher and higher, Psyche found herself grasping on to sheer rock, the repetition and force required scratching her palm until it bled. Nearing the peak, she reached to steady herself and her hand left smears of blood on the stone. As Psyche's hand left one cold rock in search of another, she saw, in the corner of her eye, a flash of movement.

Rearing back on instinct, Psyche turned, stifling a scream when she saw a massive serpent, eyes staring at her as its tongue shot out, as though licking its lips. Scrambling away, she eyed the creature. The snake did not seem inclined to venture further from its hole, but as Psyche eyed the remaining path before her, her stomach sank with the sure knowledge that more such serpents lay concealed in the rocks ahead.

Fisting her hands to slow the flow of blood from them, Psyche took a few careful steps forward, then cried out as her foot slipped, bright red blooming from a gash on the sole. Psyche let out a cry of frustration as she scrambled to a seated position, eyes darting about, searching for more serpents. At first, she seemed alone, but after turning her attention to her foot and bandaging it as best she could with a strip of fabric torn from the dress she wore, she looked up to see countless bright eyes shining in the dark crevices of the rock, watching her with unblinking attention. She gave a choked cry, glancing up the hill. So close, she was *so close*, and yet Psyche knew as surely as she knew her name that the moment she began moving again, so too would the serpents.

Her throat grew thick, and her eyes stung with tears. She shifted ever so slightly to provide relief to her aching joints, only to bump into something loose that then clattered down the way she had come. As Psyche watched the object tumble away from her, she realized it was a human skull. A cry catching in her throat and eyes flying wide, Psyche stared again at the rock face above her and the bright eyes there.

In the same way that Daphne's face formed when Psyche focused on the swaying branches of the laurel tree, so too did the cliff face now reveal itself. The serpents were not just peering out from crevices in the rock; the cliff was embedded with thousands of bones, the snakes curled inside empty skulls, their triangular heads emerging from the gaping eye sockets.

"You won't make it..."

The disembodied voice was somehow both on the breeze and within Psyche's mind, her chest clenching with the despair in it.

"You were never enough..."

"Who are you to think you could survive where we died..."

"Go away, run, run, run while you still can..."

The voices were multiplying so rapidly that within moments Psyche's senses were overwhelmed, and she pressed hard hands to her ears, screwing her eyes shut, only for the words to grow louder within her mind, one tumbling over the next like water over rocks.

"Run, run, run..."

Psyche screamed then, her eyes flying open, and she had the slight gratification of seeing the serpent heads withdraw at the sound. The voices were still there, mixing with the sounds of the burbling stream, and Psyche was about to push herself up to press forward, even if she was met with death, anything to be once again in action, when a heavy weight settled on her shoulder, sharp talons pricking her skin and pressing her back down.

"Be brave and dead or wise and still," a voice at her ear ordered. Psyche froze. The weight lifted from her shoulder, and with a flapping of wings, an eagle came to rest on her knees. The great bird swiveled its head, considering Psyche with a stern eye. "Those skulls are not all human; many are those of ancient Titans, trapped in this mountain in the early wars between immortals, their flesh decaying over time as belief in them eroded. These waters are not even visited by the gods themselves; you have no hope of completing this task on your own."

Psyche stared at the bird, tears beginning to spill over. "Then what am I to do?" she asked.

The eagle considered. "In other circumstances, I would advise you to take your chances with Venus. However, a debt I owe has been called in. Hand me that jug, and I will fetch the water for you."

It took a moment for the words to sink in, but when they did, Psyche scrambled at the knot under her breasts. Once she had freed the jug, she extended it toward the bird, her hand trembling.

"Thank you," she whispered. The eagle seemed to frown, but that also could just have been the set of its beak. Grasping the handles of the jug in its talons, the bird alighted, flying down the very center of the stream, wings careful to skirt the serpents' jaws that shot out as soon as it drew near the water. Several times as the eagle made its way to the mouth of the stream, Psyche thought one of the darting forked tongues had penetrated the smooth feathers, but the eagle continued forward until it hovered above the place the water emerged from a crack in the rock.

Pausing for a moment to gather its strength, the eagle then darted down until the mouth of the jug fell beneath the stream. It took only seconds before the bird was in the air again, wobbling a bit with the added weight of the water but flying back toward Psyche, careful to keep the vessel's contents from sloshing.

As soon as the eagle drew close enough, Psyche raised her hands to receive the jug.

"Thank you," she said again, the words coming from her very core. "Thank you, thank you, thank you."

The eagle settled on her knees once more, its chest heaving with the exertion of the task.

"Yes," said the bird. "You are welcome. And I am no longer in debt. I owe you nothing further, but I will offer one piece of advice: do not try to walk down, but slide for a ways. The serpents are lazy creatures who dislike leaving their homes, but they are angry now at being bested, and it would take but a single misstep to induce them to descend upon you."

So saying, the bird departed, Psyche watching until it was no more than a speck against the horizon. She drew a deep breath, clutched the crystal jug to her chest, and began the careful and painstaking slide down the mountain.

CHAPTER 28

Venus saw the moment Psyche came into view, a tiny dot against the green-gray of the mountain, moving at a slow but steady pace toward the place Venus had left her.

Damn this girl, it seemed she had a preternatural skill for survival. The thought held less rancor than it would have a fortnight earlier. Venus felt a grudging respect for the human princess. Psyche would not, it seemed, take abuse lying down, and while this irritated the hunger Venus felt for revenge, it also spoke to a different, deeper part of herself.

A flutter at her shoulder drew her attention; Venus did not have to look to know a tern now perched by her ear.

"Greetings, tern," she said. She felt the bird bob its head.

"Mistress! A pleasure to have found you; there is much to relay."

"Well then, do it quickly." Venus had little patience today for the bird's natural state of agitation. The little creature stiffened at her tone.

"I did think you would be more grateful, flying as I have for hours now to find you, bringing you information about gossip circulating that concerns your family, but I find you nearly as rude as your son."

"You spoke to Cupid?" Venus could not control the sharp irritation in her voice. "He is under strict orders to receive no visitors during his recuperation."

"Well, and how was I to know that, goddess?" The tern trilled in offense. "I flew in as I ever do, and there he was."

"Fine, fine." Venus waved a hand, knowing full well that Cupid was now, one way or another, on his way to escaping her house arrest. The tern was an excellent gossip precisely because it had such flexible loyalty. "Say what you have come here to say."

"Ah, but I repeat only what every human mouth is saying in the village below, as well as what is starting to be whispered among even the immortals." The tern paused for effect. Venus waited. "Psyche," the tern said, with dramatic emphasis, "has accused Cupid of rape."

Whatever Venus might have predicted the tern would say, it was not that.

"Excuse me?" she said.

The tern preened. "Rape," it repeated. "That is what a new song is saying about Psyche's time with Cupid and the origin of her current condition. There were already rumors she'd been seen alive, so this little ditty is spreading like wildfire; if it hasn't yet reached Crete and the mainland, it will as soon as the next trade vessels land."

Venus was, for once, silenced.

KNOWING NOW that Psyche had not died on the mountain and confident that the girl's return meant she had somehow—somehow!—completed the impossible task set to her, Venus ordered Melancholy and Sorrow to wait at the mountain's base for the princess, then return her to the temple. Shouting for Palaemon, Venus alighted her chariot and departed.

Venus's mind was fixed on a single thought: it was impossible that her son would have raped anyone, much less someone he professed to love. Any other god and Venus would have shrugged, unsurprised, but her son—*her son*—did not treat the act of love with such disrespect.

Cupid had been barely out of diapers when she first spoke to him about the sacred nature of love and the acts of love. Having overheard one of the early terns reporting on Jupiter's most recent conquest,

Cupid had giggled at the idea of the great king of the gods transforming into a bull. Venus had cut her eyes at him.

"Do not laugh, Cupid. Our king makes mockery of what should be sacrosanct."

Cupid had stopped giggling, though less from the instruction than from a curiosity about her meaning. "What is sacrosanct?" he asked.

"Sacrosanct is... too important, too special, to make a jest of," Venus said, dismissing the tern and gathering her son into her lap. He was just past the age where he fit comfortably. "And love, more than anything else, should be sacrosanct."

Cupid's brow wrinkled. "But when Mars was last here, I heard the two of you laughing; were you not being sacrosanct?"

Venus thought for a moment about how to explain. "Love is a connection," she said, eventually, "whether of the mind, soul, body, or some combination of the three. Where there is no connection, there is no love, and where a connection is forced—as Jupiter did by deceiving Europa—there is mockery of the very principle."

Cupid did not reply, considering her words, and Venus had let it lie.

Several years later, when Cupid did begin to take lovers, Venus had sat him down and issued a long lecture on how the body as a source of identity and pleasure was one of the most sacred truths she held. As the son of the goddess of love, his actions reflected on her, and he had a duty to embody the ideal of what a sexual connection could be.

So it was impossible Cupid could be guilty of the accusation leveled at him, which meant Psyche must be lying. Before observing Psyche in the tasks she had set, Venus would have assumed the girl was lashing out, lying for the attention of it. However, that reading didn't sit neatly with Venus's experience of the Cretan princess. Psyche must have reason to think her story would be taken seriously, and Venus had a strong suspicion as to who exactly would have given her that impression.

When she arrived at her destination, Venus dismissed Palaemon and the chariot, then sat down on a bench to wait.

She did not have to wait long.

From her seat on the bench outside a simple but exquisitely

constructed home shaded by towering trees, Venus watched as Diana strode uphill toward her, the body of a deer slung across one shoulder. When she drew close enough to see Venus, Diana stopped, lifting a hand to shade her eyes.

"This is a surprise," she said.

"For me as well," Venus responded.

Diana crossed the remaining distance to her courtyard, swinging the deer down to lie on the stone floor, a slight sheen across her forehead the only evidence of exertion. Venus noted the animal was a buck.

Diana crossed her arms. "I've a kill to dress, Venus," she said. "Why are you here?"

Venus wasn't sure where the animosity between them had originated, but it was two-sided. Everything about the goddess before her offended her sensibilities—the sweat on her brow, the dirt under her nails, the heavy garment that did absolutely nothing to accentuate her shape. The way she rejected men—men were useful for so many things! The killing, for example—Venus wasn't averse to bloodshed, but she so preferred Mars do it for her. The power she felt, knowing not only that lives lay in her hands but that she could inspire others to do violence for her, well, that was an aphrodisiac like no other. Not one she sought often but, when she did, profound in the satisfaction it brought. This business of Diana killing things mystified her, felt like a relinquishing of power. Venus remembered when she first heard of the business with Niobe of Tantalus, how Diana and Apollo had—to avenge the honor of their mother—slaughtered Niobe's fourteen children. Venus shuddered; the lack of coercive delegation was, she felt, a clear sign Diana lacked either the imagination or the intellect to spare herself the unpleasant parts of life. Venus saw little to respect in the huntress.

Which was fine, as the huntress had made clear several times over how little she respected Venus.

"Oddly enough, I've come seeking your perspective." Venus could not quite conceal her wince at uttering such words.

Diana's entire body jolted. "I am, I admit, speechless," the moon goddess said. "But curious as well. You may speak as I dress the buck."

Diana retrieved a long knife from her belt then, and crouched down, shifting the carcass until the animal lay on its back, a position she secured by placing rocks retrieved from her garden beneath the shoulders and hips. Venus watched, disgusted but also fascinated, as Diana then sharpened her knife.

"Is this some sort of test?" the goddess of love asked. "To see how desperate I am for your thoughts?"

Diana flashed her a wolfish smile. "Something like that," she said, her knife moving in swift confidence as it removed the buck's sexual organs. Venus felt for a moment like she might vomit; she fixed her eyes on the horizon beyond Diana.

"I know you spoke with Psyche before she made her way to my temple," Venus said. She felt, rather than saw, Diana's nod.

"I helped her on her journey," she agreed.

"The girl has completed and survived every outrageous task I have set her."

"I've heard gossip to that effect."

"I'm considering allowing her to live."

"Generous of you."

"Perhaps."

A silence fell between them, cut only by the smooth, wet sounds of Diana's knife slicing through flesh and the occasional dull thud when it hit bone. Venus rubbed her arms at the chill that came over her.

"You told her to say my son raped her. Why?" The laugh Diana gave held a sharpness that suggested she was surprised the question needed to be asked. Venus felt her own anger rising, and pinched herself to keep it in check.

"Could be because that's what your son did," Diana said. "Could be that I'm tired of watching him play with people's feelings—especially those of women—with impunity." Venus wanted to shoot back that her son had done no such thing but was uneasy in the awareness that the latter claim Diana had made was, in fact, correct.

"But Psyche is a mortal; what value does a mortal life hold to you?"

Shrugging, Diana wiped her knife on the hem of her shirt. "A mortal who provokes such uncharacteristic behavior from a god, as

Psyche has with Cupid, is interesting. As is watching the fallout of her naming his actions."

Venus stood, unable to bear further the sharp smell of iron floating on the breeze from where Diana was tending to the buck. She crossed upwind to the steps of Diana's home, eyeing the structure as she did.

"For a woman who presents herself with as little care as you do, you have an eye for design," she said. Diana did not deign to reply, so Venus continued. "It should be mine to decide Psyche's fate, and yet your interference means that now, all Olympus will have an opinion on the matter." Still, Diana did not reply. "Most, as you must know, will want her punished for her presumption—likely with death. There is no room, these days, for anything that could threaten tribute. So why encourage her? You're not typically the chaos agent Mercury is. What is your stake in this?" At this point, Venus was speaking aloud to herself, Diana merely a sentient sounding board. Venus glanced over again at the other goddess.

Diana was on her knees, separating meat from bone with sure, smooth cuts, then laying the meat in a neat pile upon a wax-treated linen sheet laid next to her. Her long hair was twisted high on her head, the aspect of feminine expression she and Venus shared, despite its inconvenience in many of her favorite pursuits. Absently, Venus recalled Diana seemed to have a preference for long-haired lovers as well—Orion's hair had been past his shoulders, and Daphne's hair...

Daphne.

"You want Psyche to die," Venus said.

Diana did not deny it. "I want Cupid to lose someone he loves, yes."

"And as it won't be you handing down the sentence—indeed since you encouraged her to advocate for herself from the beginning—the story won't be of your hypocrisy but of the way gods use and abuse women at their whim."

"As it should be." Diana's voice was fierce. "What is one human girl's life beside the countless your son has ruined for his own petty games? With the bow I, in my own foolishness, fashioned for him? Beside those Jupiter and Neptune have shattered with their lust, those my own brother has destroyed in his never-ending quest for admiration? I'd sacrifice a hundred human lives if it meant Cupid was seen for what he is, if his legacy is not one of youthful folly but of deepest betrayal."

Venus closed her eyes, her mind racing. Diana's talk of story and legacy was clarifying something that had been hovering at the edges of her own thoughts ever since she had felt an unexpected wave of relief seeing Psyche descending earlier.

She had wanted Psyche to suffer, had even wanted her to die, to satisfy her own feelings, and she didn't regret her pursuit of that desire. However, now that she had cooled off, and now that Psyche had survived so many of the ordeals set her, it was becoming clear that the girl's death could do Venus more damage than good.

Venus was the goddess of love, of desire and passion. No one would begrudge her righteous anger at Psyche, but the girl's perseverance was now shaping its own story. Oh, Venus didn't believe for a moment the love that drove Psyche was for Cupid, but what did that matter to those who would tell the story? Cupid had made his devotion known. And if Venus allowed such passion to go unrewarded—indeed, if she was herself part of cutting it down...

Well, it wasn't good for her image, and that was that.

Venus uttered an abrupt goodbye, departing before Diana could reply. As she walked away, Venus considered that perhaps all this time, she had underestimated Diana.

WHEN VENUS ARRIVED BACK at her temple, she found Psyche sitting within, leaning against the marble base of the altar, one hand resting atop her swollen stomach. Her eyes were closed and her breath deep, but her other hand was wrapped tightly around the neck of the crystal jug.

"I can see you are awake, Princess of Crete," Venus said. "Perform no more on my account."

Psyche did not open her eyes. "I'm not performing, Mother, simply resting." With her eyes still closed, she pushed the vessel forward. "Your water."

"Yes, well done," Venus said. Now that she was considering the idea that Psyche might survive these trials, she appreciated things about the girl she hadn't before. Despite being near the end of her pregnancy, her body and will were strong and capable—an asset if Venus chose to champion her in front of council. She was also, Venus could now admit, quite beautiful and would shine even more brightly with a wash and some sleep. This, too, would be an asset. Far easier to change minds on behalf of a beautiful girl than a plain one. The thought of beauty gave Venus an idea. One last test, perhaps. If the girl failed, well, good riddance. If, somehow, she passed then maybe she had the strength needed to face what would come.

"You've done much better than I expected," she said to Psyche, who cracked an eye at that.

"Which is to say, I'm still alive."

"Careful, child, I've not yet decided whether you shall carry on that way."

Psyche closed her eyes again. "Do let me know when you have."

Despite the outrageous impertinence of this, Venus found the corner of her mouth twitching. "There is one final task you must complete," she said. "Should you carry it out successfully, I give you my word that I shall take you to my son."

Psyche's words had been bold, but at this announcement, Venus thought she saw the girl's lip quiver. The goddess felt a deep satisfaction at this, which disposed her to magnanimity as she continued. "I require you to journey to the Underworld to retrieve from Proserpina a box of her beauty ointment. I shall not send you in unprepared; Melancholy and Sorrow will see to it that you have coins for the ferryman and cakes for the beast at the gate." Psyche's eyes had opened and her spine straightened as she listened, and Venus felt the warm glow of generosity. "Though it is certainly possible you will die completing this task, that is not, this time, my aim. Prove yourself worthy in this, and I will believe you worthy of my son."

CHAPTER 29

Mercury landed with a light foot in the courtyard of Venus's estate, frowning at the silence around him. Typically humming with music and gentle activity at all times—gardens being tended, marble polished, foods prepared—the home was still in a way that was disconcerting. Hiking the bag that held his son's wings further up on his shoulder, Mercury strode toward the main entrance, which was manned by a single guard.

"Greetings, and thank you sincerely for your commitment to duty," said Mercury, indicating with a waved hand that the guard should step aside. The guard frowned.

"My lady has ordered me to allow no one in and no one out," he said, an apologetic note to his voice.

Mercury rolled his eyes. "Of course she did, for she was in high temper and seeking to regain some control of the situation. Time has passed now, however; she is busy with other things, and I am here to see my son. Now. I approve of your loyalty but would remind you of whose orders I take, for they outrank those of your mistress."

After an agonized moment, the guard stepped aside, and Mercury clapped a hand on the man's shoulder as he passed. "Much obliged," the god said, then began scanning the room for Cupid.

He was not hard to find.

"Father!" The call came from a chaise on the far side, beneath the window. Mercury swung the bag on his shoulder to lay on a table by the entrance and crossed to his son, standing with hands at his hips as he gazed down at the tormented soul.

"You look terrible," Mercury said, reaching out to ruffle the limp curls.

"I feel terrible," Cupid said, eyes gloomy. "Mother's locked me up to keep me from Psyche, and now I've learned from that cursed tern that she's out there torturing her, and there's been not a thing I could do without my wings."

"Psyche is torturing Venus?" Mercury asked.

Cupid huffed. "Do not deliberately misunderstand me; you know well that Mother is the one doing the torturing. You've likely delivered the news several times over by this point."

Mercury laughed, taking a seat on a stool to Cupid's left and leaning back and resting his head on interlaced fingers. "In point of fact, I've actually visited your beloved in her trials. Lovely girl, that one."

Cupid sat upright with such speed he pressed the heel of his hand to his forehead to stop the room spinning. "You saw her? How is she? Do you think Mother has killed her yet?"

"Oh Venus won't kill her," Mercury said, dismissive. "Doesn't have a taste for bloodshed, your mother. Which is not to say she won't let her die. She does have the occasional taste for pain, and Psyche offended her deeply, even before you, ah, *fell in love* with her. However, the girl was well enough when I saw her—exceedingly pregnant." The final words were said with pointed implication, and Cupid, for the first time in his existence, looked sheepish.

"Ah, yes, well. She's growing my child."

"Clearly."

Cupid stood then, agitated, raking fingers through his hair and then shaking his hands as he paced, as though his anxiety could be flung from his fingertips.

"We were in such a good place, Father; everything was perfect, and Mother didn't know, and Psyche was going to have our baby, and I imagined having a little boy to teach to fly and shoot, and then I allowed her blasted sisters to visit, and they made her discontented, and she disobeyed me, and I got angry because everything was ruined, and besides that I was injured, and so I came here for Mother's aid and, well, perhaps that was a mistake."

Mercury's eyebrow twitched. "You don't say?"

"Alright fine, it was a mistake," Cupid said, "but one I now wish to address. Did you bring my wings? I must fly to her."

"Who, your mother or Psyche?"

"Psyche, Father, cease being so tiresome."

"Hm, yes. As it happens, I did bring your wings. All tuned up, as well."

Cupid's gaze focused for the first time on the entrance. Spotting the leather bag, he exhaled in noisy relief, rushing to retrieve it.

"What exactly do you plan to do when you find her?" Mercury called after him, leaning forward to rest his elbows on his knees. Cupid was already shrugging into his wings, and his shoulders gave a couple extra bobs in answer.

"Save her, of course, from Mother."

"Of course. But after that, I mean."

"After that?" Cupid paused, his face drawing in confusion. "Why, we will be together, of course. As we were. Only this time Mother will know, which will be annoying for a while, but I suppose I will get used to it."

Mercury nodded, slow. "You know she's claiming you raped her?"

Cupid shook his head. "No, what an absurd thing to suggest; she would never say that. I made sure she found her pleasure as well. Mother'd have my head if I did otherwise."

It was Mercury's turn to shrug. "Nonetheless, it is what is being said, likely in every house in Kythera by this point."

The two gods stared at each other until Cupid realized his father was not joking. He returned to sit once more on the chaise, his mind spinning.

"Well, does it matter?" he asked, the wound evident in his voice. "Jupiter, Apollo, Neptune—they rape humans all the time."

Mercury considered his son. "They do, and sometimes they even have children by such affairs, but they do not profess to love them the way you speak of Psyche. They do not attempt to live with them."

Cupid sputtered. "But—Pluto! He abducted Proserpina, probably raped her."

"The keyword there, my boy, is probably. Proserpina has never made such an accusation; in fact, she publicly returns Pluto's love."

Cupid began to rock in agitation. "Well, so what? I may have abducted her, but I didn't rape her; I gave her pleasure! We gave each other pleasure! Even if she's a bit confused about that right now, what does it matter?"

Sighing, Mercury moved to sit by Cupid, placing a steadying hand on his son's knee. "It may not matter, but I raise it because if Psyche holds to her claim, and if you remain determined to be with her, it could set a thorny precedent. If a human can accuse an immortal of such a violation so publicly and yet retain that immortal's devotion and the benefit of the connection—well, then there is an issue of power at play. We are gods precisely because we answer to our own laws, not those of men."

"Exactly!" Cupid said. "So her claim is meaningless, for our union is not bound by human morality."

"Eh, maybe," Mercury said, "maybe not. It's not your call to make, and our worship is not as secure as it once was. All the gods have felt the pinch of less tribute, are having to work harder to maintain our relevancy. I've raised all this to warn you that if the situation remains unchanged, the issue shall go before council, and you must be ready to accept whatever ruling is handed down."

Cupid stilled then. "But they might order her killed," he said, pale.

Mercury nodded, mournful. "They might."

Cupid turned on his father. "You say 'they' as if you are not one of them—you are on council, you are Jupiter's son! Surely, you can argue my case. Convince them to let me marry her."

"Marry her?" The high note in Mercury's voice betrayed his shock. "This is the first you've said anything of marrying her."

"I love her; of course I wish to marry her! I wish to be with her forever, to live my immortal life with her by my side."

"So, then, you wish not only to marry her but to have her made immortal herself?" Mercury was incredulous.

Cupid looked surprised for a moment, then nodded. "Yes. I hadn't gotten that far, but I suppose that is the natural conclusion of my feelings."

It was now Mercury's turn to stand and pace. He glanced over at Cupid, standing like a shamed but eager puppy by the door, waiting for his father's approval to leave. Mercury sighed.

"Go, then," he said. "She was on her way to Avernus, I believe. Retrieving some trinket or another for Venus. I'll see what good I can do on this end."

What color had been left in Cupid's face drained from it. "Avernus? Mother truly is trying to get her killed!" He was out the door without so much as a farewell or a thank you.

Mercury watched him go, shaking his head. The wheels in his mind were spinning; this was a different game altogether.

Time; his son needed time.

CHAPTER 30

Avernus, the entrance to the Underworld, was less dramatic than Psyche had always imagined it. The art on temple walls portrayed fire and demons and a sky so dark that shadows danced in the flames. Melancholy and Sorrow led her, however, to a cool cleft in a rock face, smooth and worn but unassuming for all its apparent use. Psyche eyed the opening and wrapped her hands around her bare arms for warmth as chill air spilled out to surround the small party.

"It is here we must leave you," said Melancholy.

"It is here every human is left, eventually," said Sorrow.

"The dead don't feel the cold," said Melancholy.

"But you will shiver in your bones," said Sorrow.

Psyche was surprised to feel a soft touch on her shoulder. Sorrow had removed the shawl draped across their hair and now handed it to Psyche.

"It will not warm you," said Sorrow, "but it will give you something to hold."

"Thank you." Psyche accepted the offered garment with gratitude, pulling it about her shoulders and clasping the ends together at her breasts. Her palms still stung with the cuts from the task before, and she felt blood seep into the soft fabric.

Melancholy held out a small bag, which Psyche took.

"The coins for the ferryman and the cakes for Cerberus," Melancholy said. "There is one each for your entrance and your departure. Place the coins beneath your tongue and allow the ferryman to take them from your mouth himself, and you will have a more pleasant journey."

Psyche nodded, committing this all to memory. "Any other advice?"

Melancholy tilted their head. "Speak not to the dead. The souls of the Underworld crave more than anything another taste of life; give them your attention, and they will suck yours away until you are left too little to depart."

Psyche gave a tight-lipped smile of appreciation, drew in a deep breath, and stepped into the opening in the rock.

The chill she'd felt outside the entrance was nothing compared to the bitter cold that confronted her once she was within. Sorrow had been correct—it entered Psyche's bones and sat, freezing her from the inside out. Before she could dwell on her discomfort, Psyche forced herself to take a step, then another. The darkness yawned before her, a sleek, dark ribbon of despair. Psyche pressed a hand to her stomach, feeling her baby kick.

"Today is not the day we die," she said, and the whispered oath brought to the surface of her mind a tiny flame of hope she had, until this moment, managed to suppress.

Melancholy had told her not to speak to the dead, but Psyche had no intention of heeding that advice. Since Venus had outlined this task, since the moment Psyche had realized where she was going, she had poured all her energy into not betraying the flare of excitement it provoked.

For the Underworld was the realm of the dead, and Psyche had so much to say to Cidippe.

Keeping the shawl wrapped tight about her shoulders, Psyche walked deeper and deeper into the darkness. The silence sat heavy, Psyche's footsteps violent transgressions in the stillness she traveled. She walked for what felt like hours, but it could as easily have been minutes or days. There was no sense of time in this place. There was nothing except Psyche herself and the child in her belly, the babe's increasingly weak kicks the only thing tying Psyche to her own existence.

"Today is not the day we die," she muttered again, her voice less sure than it had been, even as she cradled her stomach. The endless monotony was dulling her senses, tricking her mind. Where was she? Was this truly the path to the Underworld or one last trick by Venus, one final cruel humiliation? Psyche's heart began to pound in panic and she almost turned back.

But then there was a shift. Psyche felt the water before she saw it, the chill dampness warning her that she had reached the Styx. Her body sagged in relief, and she hurried forward until she beheld the great river of the Underworld.

The only light came from a half dozen torches lit by the water's edge, and the reflection of the flames on the water's inky surface gleamed like the coins jingling at Psyche's waist. By the water's edge sat a single figure by a rickety boat.

"Greetings," Psyche called, and her voice was high and thin. The figure did not turn.

"Do you have the toll?"

Psyche pulled a coin from the bag, slipping it into her mouth to let it rest under her tongue. She approached the ferryman, mouth open to her offering.

When she was just behind him, the ferryman turned, looking up.

"Hmph," he grunted, pushing himself to his feet. "You've been well advised." His fingers reached into her mouth and lingered longer than necessary as he rooted to retrieve the coin. Psyche shuddered, snapping her jaw shut as soon as he claimed his prize. Her lips and tongue felt numb where they had touched his skin.

"Will you now take me across?" she asked.

He didn't answer but pushed the boat to the water and took up his oar, indicating she should step in. Taking a deep breath, Psyche did.

As the ferryman moved the boat through the water, Psyche became aware of a discomfort at her chest. Reaching up, she shifted the aetites stone, surprised to find it warm to the touch. Adjusting it to provide relief to the skin against which it had sat, she raised her other hand to her belly, feeling her baby kick. "Keep that strength, little one," she whispered.

The journey across was tense, Psyche holding her breath against the musty, rotting stench from the algae floating on the still water and her heart lurching every time the boat seemed to tip too far in one direction. When they had reached the other side, Psyche hurried out of the boat as the ferryman sat himself down on the shore, exactly as he had on the other side.

"I await your coin on your return," he said, and Psyche found this small vote of confidence in her ability to not be trapped by the Underworld encouraging. She set off down the new path that stretched before her.

When Psyche reached tall, wrought-iron gates, she found the great, three-headed hound Cerberus sleeping a few meters in front. The dog's heads were each larger than Psyche's entire body and the musty smell of wet animal clung to his matted fur, permeating the air about him.

Swallowing, Psyche reached into the bag and retrieved a cake. Holding it extended before her on her palm, she approached the hound with caution. When she was nearly upon him, one great eye opened on the head nearest her. Psyche froze. Cerberus studied her, then looked at the cake in her hand. Lifting that one head only enough to lick the cake from her palm with a single swipe, he then settled back down to sleep.

Shocked and still expecting him to turn on her at any moment, Psyche crept around the massive body until she stood in front of the gates. Raising her hand to the place where the gates met in the middle, she was distracted by what appeared to be gauze at the tips of her fingers. Bringing her hand close to study it, Psyche gasped. The edges of her fingers were blurred, grayed, insubstantial. When she touched them to her face, they felt like wet bread. Psyche swallowed. She needed to hurry.

At that moment, the gates began to swing open of their own accord. Stepping back to allow them room, Psyche tucked her fingers beneath her shawl as though warming them would help and slipped within as soon as the opening was wide enough. She stopped, taking in the landscape before her.

Where the path she just traveled had been empty, what she encountered now was disconcertingly full. It was like a mirror of the world above, only—everything was dead. Trees stood, withered and broken, white-boned birds perched on their blackened branches. The ground beneath her feet was dry, cracked, and scattered with the carcasses of tiny bugs. Animals drifted across the expanse, from one angle appearing skeletal, from another little more than amorphous wisps. It was jarring and yet also possessed an odd comfort; Psyche found dead fullness to be a great deal more heartening than empty nothingness. She moved forward with renewed determination, her sister's name on her lips.

It was some while before she saw any human souls, but when she did, Psyche found Melancholy had not been exaggerating. The souls drew to her like moths to a flame, pressing around her, dogging her footsteps, speaking in echoey, unformed words that Psyche pressed from her mind by digging the soft ends of the fingers holding her shawl into her palm, her other hand coming to rest, protective, on her stomach.

"Cidippe, Cidippe, Cidippe," she whispered, the name both a summons and a shield against the souls that now flowed behind her like a great cloak. "Cidippe, Cidippe, Cidippe."

And then, all of a sudden, she was there. Before Psyche, formless and hovering but recognizable for all that, was her sister. Psyche felt her heart leap to her throat, the hand at her breasts reaching out, the shawl falling away, forgotten.

"Cid!" she said, but then she stopped. Squinted. Something was wrong.

"Psyyyyyyyyy..." Her name was little more than a sigh from the soul before her, heard more in her head than her ears, but it was the wrong voice. This wasn't Cidippe. This was—

"Aglaura?" As she whispered the name, Psyche knew she was right. The soul hovered, and the longer Psyche stared at it, the more into focus her sister came.

"Psycheeee..." The voice was stronger now, and a cry caught in Psyche's throat, her vision suddenly blurry.

This was wrong; it was all wrong. Aglaura wasn't here; she was in Gortyna, with her daughter, tending to her husband's farm. It was Cidippe, it had to be Cidippe, it couldn't be Aglaura.

But it was.

"Psyche." Aglaura's form was recognizably human now, her voice a shadow of what it had been in life, but clear, for all that. There was pain in the pale gray eyes that now met Psyche's. "Psyche, why are you here?"

"Why am I here?" Psyche's response was barely above a whisper. "How can you be here? Where is Cidippe?"

Another soul started to come into focus beyond Aglaura's shoulder. "Here..."

Psyche looked, and it was Cidippe, and held close in her arms was a tightly wrapped infant. Now both of her sisters stood before her, increasingly clear and very dead. Psyche opened her mouth, closed it, then collapsed to the dry ground. Her head fell to her hands as tears raced down her cheeks and then flowed down her arms.

When Psyche was small, about four or five, she got in trouble with the kitchen staff for taking sweet cakes from where they had been laid out to cool. As the daughter of the house, the cooks could not chastise her too harshly but had promised they would take the matter to her parents. Hearing Psyche's cries, Aglaura and Cidippe had rushed in, the former from her regular place before the loom, the latter from outdoors, leaves in her hair and dirt on her fingers. When they grasped the situation, both sisters claimed their own cakes without hesitation, chewing on them with deliberate vigor while staring down the staff. Though they later gave her their own lecture about strategy and careful timing, they also wiped her nose and her tears and made faces to cheer her up and when the three of them were called to stand before their parents and answer for their actions, Psyche kept her little hands curled in theirs. Until her sisters' marriages, there had never been a moment in Psyche's life when she had felt alone.

Now, in the Underworld, eyes shut tight against the truth before her, she let her mind examine the dream that had been forming at the edges of her consciousness over the past several weeks. That she would survive Venus's tasks, earn an audience with Cupid, reconcile, and extract from him a promise that her family be left in peace. That she would then travel to Aglaura, where they would live and raise their children together. With this final task had come the possibility of being able to see Cidippe, as well, to beg her forgiveness, to promise that she and Aglaura would care for their nieces and nephew.

It had been too precious a dream to face until now when she saw how impossible it had always been.

CHAPTER 31

When Juno first received the news of Psyche's pregnancy, she was not concerned. There were innumerable mortals who had been impregnated by gods throughout the ages, and there were established ways with which to deal with such mortals and their offspring. She was a bit more perturbed when she learned that Cupid still professed to be in love with the girl. Love between a god and a mortal was messy, and it was rare that such affairs ended well.

It wasn't until Mercury visited Juno with the news of Psyche's characterization of the relationship and Cupid's dreams of matrimony that she realized the situation would require her attention.

"She's saying he raped her?" Juno was mystified. "And he wants to marry her? Why?" She was in her circular receiving room, taking a moment to herself to water the plants there, when her husband's son appeared seemingly out of nowhere, his dusty sandals leaving dull footprints on the freshly cleaned tile floor.

Mercury's shrug was ambiguous. "Who knows? Perhaps that's his kink? Perhaps he's trying to get back at his mother for some insult? Regardless, you understand now why I've brought this to you, oh patroness of the holy sacrament of marriage and childbirth." He swept low in a mocking bow.

"Oh, get up." One hand went to her forehead, kneading. "This is simply not acceptable," she said to herself, splashing a small amount of water on the moss at the base of an orchid. "What an asinine desire." The last time a god had married a mortal was Bacchus to Ariadne, and it had been allowed mainly because Ariadne was, at that point, living alone on an island, with no connection to the mortal world, and because Bacchus was, well, Bacchus. He got away with things others did not.

Cupid, however, was not Bacchus.

"Don't you have any influence over your own son?" Juno said, irritated.

Mercury crossed to lean against the central table, picking up and cradling the bowl of fruit there. He popped a grape into his mouth and spoke through his chewing. "Forgive me, my queen, but do you? Last I heard, Mars was busy fucking and slaughtering his way through Mesopotamia, with Vulcan crafting and handing out weapons like party favors." Juno scowled but inclined her head in acknowledgment. "Face it," Mercury said, "you're going to have to talk to *him*."

"Do not presume to tell me what I must do," Juno snapped, yanking the bowl away from the wing-footed god. "You've delivered your message, now off with you. Go shore up the reputation of Olympus instead of gleefully shoving a wedge into its cracks."

Mercury met her eyes, brows raised in merry mischief, then slapped his thighs and straightened. "As you will it, Stepmother." With a quick kiss to her stony cheek, he moved to leave, then stopped, looking over his shoulder. "There is, ah, one more relevant piece of information."

Juno waited. Mercury knelt, adjusting the ties on his sandals.

"Mercury," Juno ground out.

The messenger god looked up at her, smiling. "As you likely already are aware, Venus has taken the news of Cupid's affair poorly."

"Indeed."

"Quite. I'm not even sure if she knows about the allegations yet, but she's spent the past several days torturing the poor girl with tasks designed to humiliate and kill."

"And yet you speak of Psyche still in the present tense; pray arrive at your point." Juno prized directness, efficiency, clear communication—all things her husband's bastard with Maia delighted in obscuring.

"An excellent observation, highness. Yes, Psyche has survived thus far, albeit with aid."

After several beats of silence, Juno sighed. "Whose aid, Mercury?"

"Delighted you asked. Mine, actually, for the first task. Then that of a nymph-turned-tree. Most recently, she was helped by an eagle of quite distinctive size and stature."

There it was. Jupiter was already wrapped up in this mess, then, if his bird was providing aid to the girl.

"Thank you for your attention to this matter," Juno said, indicating with a wave of her hand that she was done with Mercury. With one last grin, the messenger god alighted and was gone.

Juno let out a sigh of frustration. The worst thing was Mercury was right. She was going to have to talk to her husband.

She found him lounging in the bath, a chill air blowing in from balcony doors flung wide. A beautiful attendant was working his hands through the lighting god's hair, Jupiter groaning with the pleasure of it. Juno paused a moment to control her face, then raised her chin and approached.

"Jupiter," she said, waiting to continue until his eyes opened and found hers. "You"—she indicated the attendant—"depart." Bowing, the servant did so, leaving the two monarchs assessing one another.

Jupiter's stillness had Juno steeling herself for a bolt of divine fury. Ultimately, however, the god-king merely heaved a great sigh as he stood, reaching for his robe. "What is it, oh wife? Another demigod, about whom you wish to harass me?"

Juno swallowed the provocation. "Not your mistake, this time. It's Cupid."

"Cupid? What's the shit done now? You know his arrows were responsible for that incident with Leda—that's one you need to take up with him."

Juno's hand itched to slap him. "His arrows didn't force you to take the shape of a swan in order to fuck a human," she snapped, then caught herself, pinching the bridge of her nose. "Never mind that; as I said, this isn't about you for once. Cupid's created his own mess, and it's spreading enough that we need to discuss how to clean it up."

Jupiter appeared interested for the first time. "Oh excellent, an opportunity for a bit of payback, then. Come now, tell me what has occurred." He crossed to the balcony, discarding his robe as he went, and sat on a chair in the sun, his body bared despite the cold. More massive than either of their sons, Jupiter's form was what every story imagined him to be: broad, strong, and hard. Once, when she was no more than a girl who idolized the brother who had rescued her, it had made her feel safe.

That was before, of course, she saw to what lengths he would go to hold on to such power. That was before, well, a lot of things.

Juno realized her fists were clenched and released them. Taking several deep and measured breaths, she joined her brother-husband on the balcony, sitting across from him.

"You know Psyche of Crete, of course."

Jupiter appeared genuinely perplexed. "Do I?"

Juno narrowed her eyes. "Well, your eagle was spotted aiding her recently, so I assumed so."

Face relaxing in understanding, Jupiter shook his head. "Aetos has been experiencing a bit of a crisis of identity, of late. I've not seen him for weeks."

Juno felt a wave of relief. The situation was the tiniest bit simpler, then. "Well," the queen of the gods continued, "she's a princess whose beauty so excited the mortals on that island that they began to neglect the temples of Venus. Apparently, Venus had asked Cupid to dispatch the girl in some way, but instead, the boy abducted and laid with her, and now she's pregnant."

Idly, Jupiter scratched his chest. "Who, Venus? By Cupid?"

"No, Psyche of Crete. Cupid abducted and then impregnated Psyche, the mortal his mother asked him to get rid of. I'm here because we need to have a conversation about it, not because I enjoy interrupting your baths."

"There's very little you seem to enjoy doing with me anymore," Jupiter said, rolling his neck. Behind the insouciant posture and delivery was a trace of hurt accusation for which Juno had no patience.

"Jupiter."

"Fine, fine, I hear you. What is the problem with Cupid's impending issue? Besides the fact that it humiliates Venus, which I would have expected to please you."

Juno glared at him, though she could not dispute his words. It did, when she thought about it in isolation, bring her a small spark of delight to imagine Venus at odds with Cupid. The goddess of love had always been so close to her son and had—Juno felt—flaunted that closeness. Despite being the goddess of birth and motherhood, Juno had never quite gotten the hang of it the way, say, Ceres seemed to take so naturally to the task. Juno had certainly never shared with her boys the intimacy Venus had appeared to have with Cupid, and so, Jupiter was not wrong—there was something delicious about Cupid finally doing something to disrupt that relationship.

"It's not the issue of his progeny but rather the narrative surrounding it," she responded. Jupiter raised his eyebrows. She continued. "Cupid professes to love the girl and wishes to marry her, but Psyche has publicly accused him of rape."

It took a moment for Jupiter to process her words. When he did, the sky darkened.

"Of course he can't marry her," he thundered. "What kind of precedent would that set, if humans saw gods condescending to marry mortals? Much less—mortals spouting blasphemy! I don't care how the boy feels; I won't have it."

Juno kept her tone level. "Yes, I expected you'd feel this way."

"And what's more"—Jupiter was up, pacing to the railing, leaning on it as he spoke to the gathering storm clouds beyond—"such an accusation demands a response. Who does this girl think she is to so charge a god?"

"I think she must be very confident in his affection," Juno said, rising to stand beside him, brushing a single drop of rain from her nose. "Regardless, they are clearly making a mess of it, and Venus is busy torturing the girl, so she's not exactly helping the situation."

Jupiter cut his eyes at her; the storm was not breaking but neither had it receded. "Oh, Venus is involved? I don't see why you say that's not a help—sounds like she's punishing the girl."

"Ah, but do you think she will deny him, truly, once her anger is sated? She's devoted to that boy, and if he wants to marry a human girl accusing him of rape, I have little doubt Venus will deliver him just that—albeit a bit worse for the wear."

"Hmm." Jupiter's hands gripped the railing. "You're probably right."

"My point is," Juno said, "that we need to control this narrative, and we need to do it now before it spirals further out of control. We can't afford another Troy."

Jupiter's brow wrinkled at that. "Crete is hardly Troy, and Psyche is no Helen."

"Helen was no Helen until Venus promised her to Paris."

Scoffing, Jupiter shook his head. "That judgment was the result of Eris feeling cranky, not a human lacking such appropriate reverence that she attempts to bring a god to account."

"And you think Cupid won't be cranky if he's denied the woman he loves? You have countless bastards that stand in testament to Cupid's influence when he's in a good mood."

This appeared to strike home for the god-king, who stared at his wife for a long moment before turning back to the landscape and his looming tempest.

"This is bigger than a private conversation with Cupid, isn't it?"

"Based on Mercury's information, yes," Juno acknowledged.

Jupiter made a noise of disgust. "Titans, but they're all children," he muttered. With one last clench of his great hands on the stone of the railing, Jupiter spun, storm clouds dissipating as the king strode to the door. Jupiter threw his next words over his shoulder. "Call a Great Council, then. I'm going to take a nap."

Juno inclined her head. "I'll send the summons."

CHAPTER 32

Gentle, cold hands were at Psyche's shoulders; she felt the shawl wrap around her once more. She let her hands fall to her lap, head still bowed. She stared at her bloodied palms; the gray softness had crept past her first finger joint, and yet she felt no urgency, only emptiness. She could not bear to look up at her sisters.

"Psyche." Now that she knew they were both here, it was clear this voice was Cidippe's. "Why are you here? Did Marinos—"

"No." Psyche cut her off, quiet. A moment, then Aglaura's voice.

"Did Cupid... but you're still alive, aren't you?"

Psyche laughed, a hollow, barking sound. What were they going on about? What did it matter why she was here? *They* were here, that was the only thing that signified. She looked up, abrupt.

"How did you die, Aglaura?"

Her sister's soul swayed. "Sickness," Aglaura said, "right after the harvest. Many in the house were falling ill; I sent Eleni to stay with Georgios's eldest, thank goodness. Georgios remained untouched, somehow, so she still has her father, at least." There was an emotionless affect to her voice, but Psyche imagined she heard a trace of bitterness.

"After the harvest?" she said. "Then you died before—"

"Ag was here when I arrived," Cidippe confirmed. Psyche looked down at her lap.

"Pointless. It's all ever been pointless."

The hovering souls of her sisters settled themselves on either side of her, not sitting but seeming almost to melt into the ground until their faces were level with hers once more. It was disconcerting. Psyche felt Aglaura's wispy hand come up to stroke her hair, touch light as a moth's wing.

"Tell us, Psy," she said. "Tell us."

The whole story came pouring out. Cupid's desertion, Apollo's warning, Marinos turning her out after Cidippe's death. Cidippe hissed, an inhuman sound that caused Psyche to glance in concern at her sister. Then she told of meeting Diana, of finding Venus, of the tasks she had been set to earn an audience with Cupid. And then, with hesitation, she shared the dream she had only just dared face and how seeing Aglaura had shattered what last bit of hope she held.

The three of them were silent when she had concluded, then Aglaura said,

"We must get you to Proserpina."

Cidippe voiced her agreement.

"What?" Psyche was confused; she didn't want to see Proserpina, she wanted to stay here, with her sisters, forever. Cidippe floated so her face was before Psyche's, the expression fierce. She gestured to Psyche's hand, which was now gray almost to her knuckles.

"You wished to beg my forgiveness? Well, little sister, there was nothing to beg. But if you do not complete this task, return to the land of the living, and extract from this god of yours protection for all of our children, then I don't know if I will ever be able to look at you again. Hope is not lost to you, it is merely taking a form different than you expected. Stand up, wipe your eyes, and follow us before you linger too long to be able to leave."

Startled, Psyche blinked several times. It was of no use; the tears streamed down her cheeks and chin, pooling at the base of her neck.

"She's right, Psyche," said Aglaura, gentler. "You must complete this task, and you must leave. But we will be with you until you do."

Taking a deep, shaky breath, Psyche stared at her feet. In her belly, her baby flipped, and at her throat, the aetites stone burned hot enough that she shoved a piece of her wrap beneath it to absorb the heat. A short, broken laugh escaped her, making an abrupt shift to a hiccup at the end.

"Alright, then," she said. "Take me to Proserpina."

Psyche could not have said what she expected from Proserpina's receiving hall, but it was not the elegant, light-filled room in which she now stood. Cut glass and crystal lined the walls and ceiling so that the light from mounted candles reflected and refracted until the whole ceiling seemed lit from within. Smooth, colored marble had been laid into an intricate mosaic on the floor, depicting a great tree at springtime, leaves swaying in the wind and bright flowers blossoming on the branches. Shelves of scrolls and books lined the far wall, before which Proserpina herself lay, reclined on a chaise, head propped on one hand as she considered the women approaching her.

"I did wonder when I'd meet you, Psyche of Crete," she said, and her voice was musical, lilting, like a breeze on the brightest day. "We have much in common, you and I. Mother has written to me of you."

"Ceres was very kind to me," Psyche said.

"*Ceres,*" Aglaura whispered.

Proserpina smiled. She gestured to Cidippe and Aglaura. "I presume one of you is the sister who died in childbirth?" She eyed the bundle in Cidippe's arms. "Ah, you, then."

The sisters stood before the goddess, unsure how to proceed. Proserpina met their gazes with calm consideration, content to wait. Psyche cleared her throat.

"Goddess, if you know my story, then you may have some inkling why I am here. I have been sent on behalf of Venus, who begs of you a box of your beautifying ointment."

Proserpina's expression betrayed nothing. "Yes, of course, I shall send a box with you; I send a box every moon for Venus."

Psyche opened her mouth to respond, but Proserpina held up a silencing finger. She swung her legs to the floor, placing her hands in her lap and tilting her head as she studied Psyche.

"Mother is very curious how this drama will play out, as am I."

Under Proserpina's gaze, Psyche felt the presence of her sisters and was at once grateful for their support and sick at the idea that she must abandon them once more. Proserpina was still watching her, waiting for a response.

"I seek only to complete these tasks and be reunited with the father of my child," Psyche said, unsure what Proserpina wanted from her.

"Do you?" Proserpina was calm. "But have you not accused him of rape?"

Beside her, Psyche felt the souls of her sisters tremble with shock.

"Rape?" Aglaura whispered. At her sides, Psyche's hands gripped her dress tightly.

"I simply shared a drink and a story," she said.

The smile had fallen from Proserpina's face as she continued to study Psyche. "You knew what that man was, how he would use your tale. Do not try now to equivocate. What I want to know is what advantage you hoped to gain from it."

"I—" Psyche paused, regrouped. She was unprepared for this inter-rogation. "I was hurting, and it felt good to have someone listen, and I was tired of feeling abandoned by the gods. It felt like maybe telling the truth would force them to listen."

"Well, they're listening," Proserpina allowed. "Now, what is it you hope to achieve?"

"Hope?" Psyche burned with sudden anger. "What hope? Your mother dashed the last I held of that currency. You immortals speak to me as though I'm playing some game poorly, but what you fail to acknowledge is that not one of you truly considers me a player to begin with."

Proserpina shook her head, lilting voice cold. "You speak as a child. So Cupid raped you. Three of the four women in this room have had men take them without consent." The goddess studied Psyche, and the girl saw herself reflected in the wide, bottomless pools of Proserpina's eyes. "Do you think I welcomed Pluto after he seized me from my life in the sun to be his bride in these shadowed halls? Do you suppose I invited him to my bed with fair words and touches? But there was a bigger truth at play than my feelings, and because I recognized that, now at least I spend half the year above. Now, at least, I remain myself." Proserpina's voice had risen, and she broke off, closing her eyes to compose herself before meeting Psyche's gaze once more.

"I don't care, Psyche of Crete, what the god of love has done to you. What I would like to know is how you intend to use it."

Psyche's stomach dropped and her eyes burned. Use it? She had only recently found the strength to name what had been done to her, the effects of which her body was still enduring. Was that not enough? Had she not endured enough, lost enough, without this additional burden? All she had ever wanted had been ripped from her minutes before, and Psyche ached to set down the pain she carried. She could spend eternity as a shade, clutching the soul of her unborn child as her sister did. At least she would be with those who loved her.

But Cidippe's gaze was hot on her back, and Aglaura's airy fingers were brushing her own, and Psyche knew that such an escape was not an option. She looked up at the goddess of spring, who had been taken from her own family all those millennia ago.

"As would I," she whispered.

Proserpina stood for several long moments watching the sisters; Psyche couldn't tell what the goddess thought of her answer. Finally, Proserpina nodded, slow. She tipped back the remainder of her drink and turned away, waving a hand in dismissal and calling over her shoulder as she departed, "The box is by the door already; you passed it when you came in. See yourselves out and with haste."

When Psyche glanced down at her arm, it was gray to her elbow.

THE SISTERS WERE silent as they hurried out of Proserpina's hall. Psyche was aware these were her final moments with them, until she herself died, and yet she could think of nothing to say. With the small box contained safely in the bag at her waist, she reached out to take her sisters' hands. They were cold and insubstantial, like holding airy clay that would flow through her fingers if she squeezed it too hard.

When the three of them reached the gate, Aglaura threw her arms around Psyche. For all it felt like being wrapped in a damp towel, Psyche never wanted her to let go. Beyond Aglaura's shoulder, Cidippe stood, eyes locked with Psyche's, clutching her babe tight to her chest.

"You can do it, Psyche," she said, voice soft but intent. Pulling partly away from Aglaura, Psyche held Cidippe's gaze, swallowing. Aglaura looked from one to the other.

"Do what?" she asked.

Cidippe's eyes stayed trained on Psyche. "Psyche is in a position to protect our children in ways we could never have dreamed, provided she doesn't die over this foolish accusation."

"It's not foolish, it's true." Psyche's protest lacked heat.

"But you will never wield power enough to hold him to account for that!" Cidippe's voice was pleading. "Please, Psyche. I love you, and for the love you bear me, think not of your pain but of your babe, of mine, of Aglaura's. For your child, and for ours, walk this path with care."

Psyche nodded, tight, and felt the arms of both sisters encircle her.

"Go, Psyche," Cidippe said, "before it's too late."

"You've become so strong," Aglaura said, a hand to Psyche's cheek. "We may not have lived to see our gray hairs, but we are luckier than most, for we have you."

The tears Psyche had been holding fell then, her throat choking with the finality of the moment.

"I'll— I'll try," she promised. "I love you."And then she turned and pushed through the gates before she could succumb to the aching desire she had to throw herself back into their arms.

CERBERUS WAS as docile upon Psyche's exit as he'd been on her entrance, barely lifting his heads from where they rested on his paws, one great tongue lolling out for the remaining cake. As Psyche placed it with a gentle hand, she wondered—was this the fierce beast of the stories? Did that beast even exist?

Psyche's eyes dropped to her extended arm, now fully gray, and she gave one of Cerberus's heads one quick scratch before rushing away toward the river. Once more, the ferryman took a coin from her mouth and rowed her with silent solemnity to the other side. And then it was time for the journey through the stone.

Psyche's body was so acclimated to the bone-deep cold that every slight increase in the temperature as she drew nearer the entrance felt like a wave of heat, and the stone on her chest felt like a living flame. Her body, which started strong and sure, began to feel heavy and sluggish. Cradling her stomach and fixing in her mind an image of her nieces and nephew, Psyche dragged one foot after the other until, finally, she glimpsed a sliver of light ahead. The exit was there within reach, and she was so, so close...

But Psyche's body, which had to this point taken orders from her mind even against its better judgment, had reached its breaking point. She had spent too long in the realm of the dead, had spent too much time with her sisters' souls and their aching desire for life. Even as the sliver of light grew wider and brighter, Psyche felt her legs failing her, saw her feet gray, her mind succumbing to a peaceful sort of numbness.

She was tired, so tired. And her sisters were here; surely staying couldn't be bad if she was still with them. The children would join them in time. They would all be together anyway; she didn't need to make it out for that to happen. But her sisters had wanted her to—Cidippe had said she would never be able to look at her again if she didn't return to the living world.

This thought cut through the fog of Psyche's mind, and she raised her head to find she had collapsed to her knees and was leaning against the wall for support, shoving more of her shawl beneath the aetites stone, crying out when it brushed the burned skin beneath. She squinted at the light in the distance. She must make it, then, she must. But first... first, she needed to rest. Yes. That was it. She would close her eyes for a brief rest, regain her strength, and then push through the final stretch. That was what she'd do. And so, content with her plan, Psyche closed her eyes and fell asleep.

CHAPTER 33

Cupid flew as he had never flown in his life, as though there was a whip at his back and fire at his heels. His mind was filled with images of Psyche: drowned in the River Styx, pulled into the dark depths by the souls within; ripped open by Cerberus, the beast's multiple heads each gnawing at one of her limbs. He could not conceive of a scenario in which she had survived, and so his grisly imaginings played on repeat the entire journey, and with each replay his anger mounted. Who was his mother to play so free with the life of the woman who meant everything to him?

As he approached Avernus, he slowed, as a man fearing and yet compelled to approach his doom. He landed with a heavy step, all of his usual grace deserting him, and leapt to the crack in the stone.

He stumbled on something just beyond the entrance. Looking down, he cried out when he realized it was Psyche's crumpled form.

Scooping her into his arms, he retreated from the stone, stopping only once they were beneath sunlight. Sinking to his knees, Cupid cradled Psyche in his lap, a hand smoothing her hair away from her face over and over as he whispered her name.

She was not the translucent shade he had feared, but neither was there much life to be found in her. Blood had abandoned her skin, except for a red, blistering burn at her throat, and her body was cold and half-gray from her time spent too long in the Underworld. When he pressed his lips to the pulse beneath her ear, however, there was the faintest flutter, and Cupid's mind leapt with hope.

Gathering her closer still, touching as much of her body to his as he could in order to share his warmth, Cupid scanned his surroundings in desperation. Something, there must be something he could use to help. Wild parsley or sideritis or—a buzzing by his ear tore Cupid from his racing mind. The thought forming even as he raised a gentle finger for the bee to land, Cupid's gaze landed on a hive not a hundred meters away. Honey.

He sprang to his feet, Psyche still clutched tight to his chest, the bee departing. When he reached the hive, Cupid shifted so he could withdraw a small knife from his belt, then reached up with a single awkward arm to the hive.

"I thank you, bees, from the bottom of my heart, for your gift," he said and, with as gentle a touch as he could, sliced away one of the hanging combs.

Cupid sat again with care, leaning against the tree trunk. Lifting the arm on which Psyche's head rested so she was propped at a more advantageous angle, he pressed open her jaw and squeezed a large chunk of honeycomb on her tongue, watching with anxious eyes as the honey slowly dripped down her throat. Nothing happened. He pressed his fingers once more to the spot beneath her ear; the flutter was still there. Cupid repeated this process with the honey until the entire comb had been squeezed dry.

And yet Psyche lay, unresponsive, across his lap. Cursing, Cupid was about to retrieve a second comb when a small noise froze him. He looked down at the pale face in his arms.

"Psyche? Love? Was that you?" What felt like the longest moment of his existence passed, and then—the tiniest of honey-fragrant exhales. Cupid's entire body went limp with relief; he gathered her close, burying his face in her neck, feeling that precious pulse start to beat stronger and stronger. "Psyche, Psyche, Psyche," he said into her shoulder. "Love, I'm so sorry, I'm here, you're safe."

How long they sat like that neither could ever say, but it took some time before Psyche was strong enough to even be aware of her position, much less to seek a different one. Once she was, however, she found herself disinclined to move away from the god of love, who was weeping—weeping!—into her hair, and so instead shifted only to adjust her head to a less painful position on his thigh.

Breathe in, breathe out. She was alive. He was here. Even as her body relaxed into his, even as her senses sang with his closeness, her mind tumbled over what it all meant.

"Psyche." Cupid's voice was at her ear, his hands urging her up so that she was curled in his lap, head on one warm shoulder. "I thought I'd lost you," he said, breath against her hair.

"You left me," she said, voice faint. His own, when he replied, was wet with the tears that still flowed.

"And I despise myself for it; I swear it will never happen again." He moved his hand to thread his fingers through her own. "My mother has held me captive all this time; I came to you as soon as I could," he said. "You must believe me."

"Oh, I do," Psyche said, too tired to pull her hand away. A part of her wanted to argue further, to scream and shout and accuse. But a greater part of her was relishing the reunion, and besides, her body was a long way from recovered. There would be time to hold him to account when she was stronger.

That thought triggered a panic in her, and she ripped her hand from his to wrap both of hers around her belly, pressing with frantic fingers. It took what felt like an age, during which Psyche's recently revived mind went black again, but then, finally, came a small but fierce response. Psyche exhaled more air than she'd realized her lungs could hold, clutching her now-cool pendant.

Her child was alive.

She was alive.

Now there were promises to keep.

PART FOUR

CHAPTER 34

Council was held every turning of the moon, but a Great Council was called only in times of utmost need. A Great Council had been called when the Greeks set sail for Troy; a Great Council had been called when the wolf mother first sniffed Romulus and Remus; and a Great Council had been called when rumors spread that a human girl named Psyche had accused Cupid, the god of love, of raping her.

It was rare that the twelve Olympians gathered in their entirety. On any given moon, it could be expected that at least one or two would be otherwise occupied, one or two would get distracted along the way, and one or two would forget entirely. Thus the most reliable council members were: Juno, the queen of the gods; Ceres, goddess of the harvest; Minerva, goddess of wisdom; and Vulcan, god of the forge. Jupiter was always there as well, his presence as king a requirement for any official council meeting, but he could not in truth be called a reliable member since he was as likely to sleep through the monthly gatherings as participate.

On the occasion of the Great Council called to address the matter of Psyche vs. Cupid, the four reliables had a difficult time concealing their annoyance at the sudden interest of their colleagues in council matters.

"Neptune was beaching his chariot as I arrived," Vulcan announced, lowering himself to the edge of his lounger with his hands on his knees, tense as always. From her position leaning against a column, Minerva snorted.

"Of course he's early," she said. "The notion of mortals objecting to their use by the gods is a terrifying one for him."

Ceres glanced up from where she was setting out flasks of wine and ambrosia on the central table.

"It is not only mortals for whom this bears implications," she said, gazing out over the cloudy winter landscape with a far away look.

At that moment, the subject of their discourse swept into the room, cloak spraying seawater as he swung it from his shoulders to drape it across his chair. Minerva frowned, brushing wet droplets from her arm. Noticing the movement, Neptune chuckled as he settled himself into his seat.

"Apologies, niece, I know how uncomfortable you are with getting wet."

Putting distance between them, Minerva thought not for the first time, of how grateful she was not to be a resident of Neptune's ocean realm.

As the immortals began to fill the room, chatter began about the issue at hand.

"What's the fool's rebuttal?" Diana asked Minerva, hands propped on her hips as she came to stand by the goddess of wisdom, who had positioned herself as far from the sea god as possible.

Minerva glanced over at her. "That he loves her, of course. That's the whole problem. He wants to marry the damn girl."

"And she's standing by her claim?"

Minerva shrugged. "That's my understanding; she'd have a case in a mortal court. They consider rape an insult against a woman's guardian—the abduction piece, Cupid cannot argue, and he certainly didn't obtain permission from her father. Mortal law would convict him."

Diana shook her head as she scanned the room. "Of course, of no importance is the fact that she didn't want him in the first place." An arm came down suddenly about her shoulders, and she stiffened.

"But she's pregnant," Apollo said, too close to Diana's ear. He bit into an apple, the sound causing the moon goddess to lean away, face drawn in displeasure. "Everyone knows that a healthy pregnancy is evidence the womb wanted the seed."

"The innumerable half siblings we have scattered around the world would seem to be evidence to the contrary," Diana countered, shrugging him off.

Apollo raised his brows, shaking his head. "I don't know, Di; I've not yet met a human who didn't ultimately want to spend a night with a god."

"That would be because you favor sycophants." Minerva's voice was even, but her eyes flashed.

Apollo laughed, an edge to it. "And you, tedious, emotionally dead academics." He tossed his apple core into the bushes lining the open chamber. "Anyway, it doesn't matter what Cupid did or didn't do; the point is that this girl doesn't get to drive the narrative."

Across the room, Mars sat by Pluto, who turned his head to fix an impassive gaze on his nephew.

"Not that I like to complain about business, but do you plan to leave any of the Germanic tribes alive?"

Mars gave a short laugh. "I've considered shifting to aid them, to tell the truth. They're far more interesting of late than some of the new Roman generals."

Inclining his head, Pluto leaned back, stretching his legs before him. "Well, Proserpina asked me to relay that she would appreciate a slowing of new souls." There was a silence between them. "Which means *I* would appreciate a slowing of new souls."

"My brother does not find women relevant to his decision-making." Vulcan's voice was rough and betrayed the strain his walk to the chamber had taken. He took a seat on the other side of Mars, who cast an unimpressed gaze his brother's way.

"Are you near finished with my order?"

"Actually, I've asked him to withhold it," Pluto said, cold. "Until my home is a pleasant place again."

Mars's mouth tightened with anger, but he did not challenge the older god, acknowledging his receipt of the message with a curt nod.

Venus entered then, settling herself beside Vulcan, the scent of roses trailing after her. She ignored the eyes of both brothers, turning instead to Mercury, seated on her left.

"Have you seen him yet?"

"Since returning his wings? No." Mercury's fingers were laced behind his head, his foot tapping with anticipation.

"I know you helped the girl."

"Well, it would hardly have been fun if she never made it past the first task."

"*Fun* wasn't my aim."

Mercury's hands parted at that, arms spreading in an exaggerated shrug. "And that, my former beloved, is why we didn't work out."

The room fell quiet when Jupiter appeared, adjusting his seat and fiddling with the pillows provided with the casual ease of someone always the center of attention.

"Thank you all for coming today on such short notice!" Somehow, despite the open design and lack of ceiling, Jupiter's booming voice managed to resonate about the room like a plucked string. "We have quite the case, so I hope you're all prepared for a long day. You all know the past century has been a hard one; mortals are not worshipping the way they once were, and I daresay every god in this room has felt the pinch of diminished tribute and standing. The charges here today and the way in which we respond to them could shape the very future of the relationship between gods and humans. I ask for your commitment, focus, and thoughtful debate as we proceed. Mercury!" The messenger god snapped to attention.

"My lord!"

"We are all present; fetch your son and the mortal girl so that we can begin."

When Mercury returned, he was trailed by Cupid, absent his trademark wings and bow, and a human girl large with child whose weary appearance prompted Neptune to mutter, "Really, this is the chit causing all the trouble?" which, echoing throughout the chamber, provoked an icy stare from the god at her side.

"This is Psyche," Cupid said, sliding an arm around the woman's shoulders. "Speak of and to her with the same respect you do me."

"None, then!" Apollo called.

A bolt of lightning shot from the sky, striking the very center of the room and shattering one of Ceres' pitchers so that the faces of the gods seated nearest were misted with a wet burst of ambrosia. "Silence!"

Using the corner of his chiton to wipe ambrosia from his eyes, Apollo muttered an unintelligible acknowledgment, and Jupiter settled back, satisfied. He gestured to the couple. "Cupid, you and Psyche may sit here, between me and Juno—yes, there, a step below, excellent. Mercury!"

"My lord!"

"Pray share with council the information you've gathered. To the rest of you—there will be time at the end to submit addendums and commentary and engage in debate. Until that point, I ask you pay Mercury the respect of your silence and attention."

Mercury clapped his hands. "Excellent, thank you. Well then. Let us begin."

WHEN MERCURY HAD FINISHED the telling, there was a silence in the hall that felt almost more full of words for their absence. Psyche kept her gaze forward, fixed beyond the edge of the room, to the gray-blue sky and the sun peeking from behind clouds. Nonetheless, she was aware of every god there.

Mercury, gulping water after recounting the story for nearly two hours and winking at his son.

Venus, impassive and regal, sipping her wine.

Vulcan, grunting in pain as he shifted his position, brows drawn in conflict.

Pluto, shaking his head, radiating irritation.

Mars, fidgeting, head rocking.

Juno, placid but alert, indicating with a gracious nod that Mercury should take his seat.

Jupiter, deep in thought.

Minerva, unreadable.

Apollo, asleep.

Diana, the faintest smile about her lips, extending a long leg to kick her twin awake.

Neptune, swollen with indignation.

And Ceres. Ceres, whom Psyche had met as Deme and whose eyes were fixed on Psyche. Whose eyes Psyche would not, could not meet, lest the fear within her trigger a flood of tears that would never stop.

Agneta, Aindreas, Ianthe, Eleni. Psyche chanted their names in her head, reminders of why she must endure this. Must survive this.

It was Ceres who broke the silence, standing to address Jupiter and the council.

"Brother," she began, "may I offer comments?" Receiving an affirming nod, she continued. "This story seems to me rooted in the relationship between a mother and her son. Had Cupid not felt it necessary to hide the identity of his love from Venus, neither would he have needed to withhold his identity from Psyche, which would have eliminated the issues we find ourselves now facing. I therefore suggest that it is not for this council to decide the fate of Cupid and Psyche but is instead a family matter to be resolved between Venus and Cupid."

Ceres looked again at Psyche, who still could not meet her eyes. The expression the goddess wore was one both compassionate and resigned. "The actions this girl has taken, the choices she has made, have been in direct response to the conflict between Venus and Cupid —not an attempt to challenge Olympus. I move we dismiss council immediately and let her negotiate her own fate with the ones bound up in it." Ceres sat, and Psyche dared glance around the room. Vulcan was nodding, as was Mercury.

"Whether she intended it or not, she has challenged us all," Neptune said, voice thick with disgust. "If a human girl can spout such accusations with impunity—more, while retaining the apparent devotion of the god she has accused"—he cast a disparaging look Cupid's way—"then what message does that send about our power? What reason to fear if insolence is not only accepted but met with reward?"

"What strictures would it place on your ability to take lovers at your whim, you mean," Minerva said, mild but pointed. Neptune glowered at her, but before he could respond, Mars cut in.

"I am confused over the fuss. I'd kill the girl, were it me, nip the problem in the bud. But if Cupid wants to keep her, I don't see that the issue has such lasting significance—if future mortals take it in their heads to behave similarly, they die until the message has been received."

"The careful consideration you've put into your response is, as ever, inspiring." Diana stood, plaited hair heavy down her back, flinty eyes taking in every person there. "This is an issue of the gods' violence against women of every type. Ceres says to leave it to the family; I say leaving it to families is how this violence perpetuates. The abduction, rape, and ruination of female life by men is propped up and, indeed, validated by the behavior of gods in this very room. As a mortal, Psyche was foolish to voice such an accusation against Cupid, but she was not lying."

Startled, Psyche's gaze snapped to the goddess, who looked at her with cool appraisal as she continued. "Cupid saw a woman he wanted, abducted that woman, and then laid with and impregnated her all without ever revealing his identity. And he didn't think twice about this—argues even now that the orgasms he eventually coaxed from her translate into consent!—because of the example set for him by you." The vicious slash of Diana's voice fell like a whip across the room. Psyche felt herself panicking—drawing other gods into Cupid's culpability seemed the surest way to align them against her. What was Diana doing?

The goddess turned to Neptune, seated beside her. "You set the example, Uncle, when you raped Medusa." The sea god raised his chin but didn't respond. Diana looked at Mercury. "You set the example, Mercury, when you raped Lara on her journey to the Underworld and when you tricked Venus herself into carrying your child." Her gaze moved on, even as Mercury sputtered. "You set the example, Pluto, when you abducted Proserpina, and you, Mars, rape women as an afterthought."

Diana had now reached Jupiter, who had straightened in his throne and wore what all knew to be a dangerous expression. Diana locked eyes with her father for several moments before pressing her lips into a line and turning to her twin.

265

Apollo gazed up at his sister with an expression of curious annoyance. "Come now, don't spare me because we shared a womb. Say what you began all of this nonsense to say."

Diana's eyes were bright now with held tears. The goddess of the moon spoke in a voice laced with pain and disgust. "You set the example, Apollo, when your violent pursuit and attempted rape of Daphne rendered existence as a tree preferable to one borne under your attentions."

Beside Psyche, Cupid let out a long, slow exhale. "So she's still on about *that*," he said, too soft for any others to hear.

Once, I was called Daphne. Now, I'm just a laurel tree. Psyche jolted as she made the connection, and Cupid shot her a look both curious and cautioning.

When Diana spoke again, her voice was smaller, as close to pleading as Psyche imagined the goddess capable. "How does it stop?" she asked. "How does it ever end if those in this room continue to use their power in such a way?"

The room was quiet until Vulcan cleared his throat.

"I would speak," he said, turning a considering eye to where Diana still stood, gaze locked with Apollo's. "As the only man in the room not accused, I feel it incumbent on me to highlight the gaps in your argument."

Diana now turned to look at Vulcan, and Psyche thought that if such an expression were leveled her way, she would explode on the spot. Vulcan continued, slow and measured.

"I cannot help but notice that for someone so worked up over issues of consent, you have failed to mention any male victims of the act, which I expect you would argue is because it is less prevalent, but when claiming the gods in this room have made the issue of rape one of negligible concern, it does seem odd not to highlight the indiscriminate way in which the crime is committed." He held up a hand when Diana opened her mouth to speak, "No, you've had the floor; let me finish. I find it interesting, as well, that the trials of this mortal woman spark such anger in you on her behalf, while those of the princess Merope at the hands of Orion were so easily overlooked."

At this, Diana paled, hands fisted so tightly at her side that Psyche saw her knuckles blanch. Vulcan continued, his words thrown with vicious precision.

"Finally, even assuming your good faith in raising these accusations in pursuit of a more punitive treatment of the crime, you have failed to offer any suggestions as to how this all should apply to the case of Cupid and Psyche. Are we to punish Cupid? Let Psyche live? She's a mortal, and that has different implications, whether you like it or not. And what about calling for justice for the actions of a god—she cries rape, and you argue passionately that she is justified, but what would have happened if Niobe had come to hold you to account for the slaughter of her children?"

"I hardly think that's the same—" Diana cut in, but Vulcan interrupted her.

"Perhaps, perhaps not. An issue for another council. Nonetheless, that brings me to my conclusion—that this is wholly personally motivated. We all know of your love for Daphne and of Cupid and Apollo's roles in her transformation. Apollo's raped a lot of beings over the years, of every persuasion. For you to raise one instance where he actually failed to commit the crime—well. Your emotions have run away with you, is all I'm saying."

"Maybe they have," Diana said, "but haven't theirs as well?" Despite the pain on her face, there was satisfaction in her voice. When Psyche looked around the room, she saw why.

The gods accused, excepting only Mercury, were red and tense with anger, their fear stoked by Diana's words. Psyche's heart sank.

Juno observed the shifting tone of the room and acted with decision. "Enough for today, I think," she said, laying a hand along Jupiter's arm as she did. The lightning god looked up, taking in the faces of the Olympian council. He nodded.

"Let us break. Tonight, we will feast, and there is to be no talk of the case. Tomorrow, we will reconvene to decide Psyche's fate."

CHAPTER 35

The gods filed out of the great hall, muttering among themselves, Cupid keeping a protective arm about Psyche's shoulders. As they stepped into the shade of a tree in the courtyard, Venus appeared before them.

"I must speak with Psyche," she said, the words a command.

Cupid frowned. "Mother, if you think that after the way you have treated her, I trust you to—"

"It is fine," Psyche cut him off, placing a hand on his arm. She looked at Venus. "Your mother and I have much to discuss."

Cupid started at being so dismissed, looking from one woman to the other. "Well, then, I suppose I shall wait here. But play nice, Mother." Venus arched her brows, and Cupid added, "Please."

Watching his beloved walk away and disappear with his mother, Cupid felt a flicker of unease. He shook it off, attention drawn to a presence that had appeared at his side.

"A fine mess you've made, Nephew," Apollo said, studying his nails. "And I don't just mean Psyche—you've got my sister in a state I've not seen her in since the death of that insipid long-haired hunter."

Cupid's brows drew together. "Let's not pretend, *Uncle*, that you're blameless here. I was not, in fact, the one pursuing the woman she loved."

"No," Apollo admitted, "that was me. But the technicalities don't matter to Diana; she seeks to punish us both."

"Us both?" Cupid's voice went high. "I am the one who may lose the love of my life; in what way do you suffer here?"

"Oh make no mistake, Cupid, should your lady's accusations stand, Diana will take the opportunity to provoke public criticism of my behavior at every turn. Come to think of it, even if Psyche dies for her transgression, I imagine Diana will hold the hypocrisy over our heads for a millennium." He grimaced. "Titan's teeth, but she's difficult."

Cupid considered this. "And if she dies, there is a double hypocrisy for which to hold you accountable."

Apollo squinted at him. "Eh?"

"Yes," Cupid said, realizing the truth as he said it. "You aided me through your oracle at Delphi. What validity will your oracle hold, moving forward, if it emerges that it was used as a tool to fulfill a god's pleasure? You need our tale to be one of destined love."

Apollo stared at him, swore, stalked several meters away, stared into the distance, then stalked back.

"I truly despise when you are correct," he said. Cupid shrugged. Apollo exhaled, then paused, the corner of his mouth turning up. "You know she was nearly mine? Psyche?"

"Do not bait me, Uncle; I'll not rise to it," Cupid said, but a faint flush had appeared on his neck.

The sun god straightened. "Oh, but it's true; I saw her in the market shortly before the hysteria set in, and had Aetos not found me at that moment with a summons from Jupiter... Well, it's interesting the games the Fates play, is it not?"

Cupid's fists were curled tight, his body vibrating with anger. "You'll not touch, her or I swear—"

"Oh, calm down," Apollo cut him off. "I don't want her; I'm honestly sick of hearing about her, though it does seem I need her to live." Cupid relaxed a degree. "But her accusations simply cannot stand. Can you convince her to recant them, do you think?"

Cupid took several deep breaths before replying. "I can try," he said, tone less confident. "Perhaps Diana's performance in council has caused her to reconsider." He ran a hand through his hair, staring at the spot where his mother had disappeared with Psyche. "I can't lose her, Apollo," he said.

"Well," Apollo said, "the person you really need is Jupiter. Even Diana stopped short at accusing him to his face; cut a deal with him, and you may just squeak through this."

VENUS LED Psyche to a private room, where she took a seat before a mirror and began freshening her appearance, arranging her hair into careful disarray.

"And so you refuse to die, would-be daughter," she said.

Psyche leaned on a table by the door, watching the goddess. Her body still felt weak.

"A known fault, I think."

Venus laughed. Psyche reached into the bag knotted above her stomach and then walked with slow steps until she could reach out and set the box from Proserpina on the table before Venus. Then she turned and lowered herself carefully until she was lying, propped on her side on a nearby chaise. She watched as the goddess finished her beautification rituals.

"What in the world could Proserpina have provided to enhance your beauty?" Psyche asked, voice tired. "How could you even begin to possess more?"

"Seek not to flatter me, human princess," Venus said, dabbing a rich purple into the crease of her eyelids, "it shall only inflame me against you further."

Psyche closed her eyes. "It all feels like such a waste," she said, quiet, more to the empty space in the room than to the goddess.

"Ah, but it would not have been a waste, now would it, had you ended up dead. Then this council would be a very simple thing." Venus laid down her brushes and turned at last to face the mortal woman. "How did you do it, by the way?"

Psyche did not open her eyes. "I asked nicely."

Venus snorted. "Oh, Proserpina's eager to share anything that connects her to the world of the living. No, I meant, how did you make it out alive, when I have it on good authority you spent significant time with the souls of your sisters?"

Psyche sat up as a chill washed over her. It took her several moments to find her words. When she did, they came out as a whisper. "You knew about Aglaura and Cidippe?"

Venus sounded amused when she responded. "Of course. I certainly needed none of Proserpina's beauty secrets."

Psyche opened her mouth. Closed it again. Her body shook, hands fisted in the skirt of her gown.

"Did you— Were you—" She gulped, blinking back tears. "Did they die because of me?"

It was not the way she had intended to ask the question; she'd meant to ask what part, if any, the goddess had played in their deaths. But in that moment, in the shock of Venus's reveal, she could utter only the rawest of her fears.

Venus looked bemused. "And this is why I was so surprised you made it out of there; that guilt alone should have bound you to the dead. But I suppose I underestimated you." She shook her head at Psyche, reaching out a finger to brush away an escaped tear, almost motherly. "Your sisters were mortals, their deaths written the moment they were born. You, however, find yourself with the opportunity to gainsay the Fates, so pull yourself out of this pitiful self-flagellation and negotiate."

It did not escape Psyche's notice that her unsaid question remained unanswered. She thought she should feel angry, that the ice in her veins should grow so cold it transformed into a burning flame. But she was at her capacity for emotion, it seemed, and instead of bursting into flame, the coldness she felt subsided into a kind of empty numbness.

"You do your work well, goddess," she said, wiping her eyes. She heard the smile in Venus's response.

"I do. But you have not answered my question. You should not have been able to make it to the entrance alive; how did you?"

Psyche felt the ghost of former pain in the red mark on her chest where the aetites stone had burned. "Love," she said.

Venus's face folded in a deep frown. She rose, her gown swirling and the scent of roses floating off of her to fill the air of the room. She crossed to the table, poured herself a glass of wine, then eyed Psyche. "Let us speak openly. We are at an impasse."

"Are we? A wise woman once informed me I was ever at the mercy of the gods."

"And still you are," Venus snapped, "so I instruct you once more—tuck away your tongue and your pride and speak to me instead as the woman who has suffered much for the sake of that tiny mortal life growing within." Psyche did not respond, but her shoulders softened and her spine seemed suddenly more elastic. "That's better. Now, tell me what it is you need."

Agneta, Aindreas, Ianthe, Eleni. Psyche thought about how much truth to tell. Venus was better informed than she had realized, but stating her desire too plainly could backfire if she wasn't careful. She settled on starting with the broadest honesty.

"To live my life free from the gods," Psyche said.

"Impossible. Try again." Venus' tone was dismissive. Psyche shook her head.

"No—that is what I need. A place to live with my child free from the rules of men and gods and the arbitrary and unceasing pain of existence."

Venus considered this. "I could argue that 'to live' is, by definition, to endure such pain, but I am above such semantics. I take your meaning. What I need is to be the one to offer Jupiter an acceptable resolution to this mess before Diana does. One that, ideally, does not leave my son heartbroken or diminish my position in the process." Psyche waited for her to continue, but Venus seemed to have slipped into deep thought, sipping her wine and considering the dirty, bruised, exhausted woman before her. "You think me cruel, but I have empathy for your situation. I, too, found myself with a child I did not seek, absent the father. Your very existence offends me, and yet, your fortitude through the tasks I have set must be recognized. I cannot—as you must already be aware—grant your wish, but perhaps we can come to an understanding."

Psyche blinked. "An understanding?"

Venus smiled. "Indeed." The goddess crossed and sat beside Psyche on the chaise, folding one of the girl's hands between both of her own. "You wish to escape? I can give you that. There is an island, unknown to all but me, where I could build you such an estate that you would never need to leave if that remained your wish. I would staff it with the most trusted of my servants and you would be free to raise your child as you wish, apart from the cares of both gods and men."

There was a long silence while Psyche absorbed these words. "Yet still I would exist at your mercy, your word my only promise of safety. You'll understand why that is not a comforting thought."

Venus' turned Psyche's hand over in her own, tracing a single delicate nail down the lines of the girl's palm. "It is, however, the only offer you have and that you are likely to get. I am willing to be quite generous."

"At what cost?" Psyche was relieved to hear her voice emerge without a wobble.

Venus cocked her head. "Come again?"

Psyche pulled her hand away and straightened her spine, not without effort. She met the goddess's eyes. "Do not pretend to benevolence, *Mother*. What is the cost of such a life?"

Venus sighed. "I have told you what I need—that is the price. Your need for mine."

"Pray elaborate on the specifics of your need," Psyche said, keeping her voice level. Venus shifted her weight, and Psyche got the sense that whatever the goddess was about to say was the true purpose of the conversation.

Venus's voice, when it came, was iron. "My son did not rape you," she said. "Such a claim, in light of his demonstrated love for you, would be most disruptive to our position. If you accept this deal, you will recant all claims of violation, citing pregnancy madness or whatever else you deem believable. Further, you will attest not only to his love for you but to the increasing strength of your love for him, as demonstrated through the tasks you endured for the sake of reunion."

The space behind Psyche's eyes ached. "Do tell, Mother, how I am to achieve such a reversal from a remote island?"

Venus waved a dismissive hand. "Oh, a few public statements

before you leave should do. The muses can do the rest." The women stared at each other for what felt to Psyche like an eternity.

"Fine," Psyche said. "I accept."

Venus wagged a finger. "Ah, ah, not yet. I've not finished with my conditions. In addition to the public statement, you and Cupid will wed, after which you will drink from a cup of ambrosia."

"But that— that would make me immortal." Psyche's mind stuttered over the implications of this. Bound to Cupid not only for the rest of her mortal life but for all of time. Forever separated from her sisters.

"Just so." Venus beamed.

"And my child?"

"Also immortal," the goddess confirmed.

Psyche was silenced. She had not, in any imaginings of her future, conceived of this possibility. Cupid wanted her, she knew that, and she believed that he loved her as much as he was able—at least as much as she'd loved him since being scratched by his arrow. But ultimately, Psyche had always considered Olympus and its residents a trial to be survived, not a final destination. This had to be yet another test. She spoke slowly.

"Why? After you've gone to such lengths to kill me, why now offer me not only a way out but immortality?"

Venus did not bother to dissemble. "Because he wants you."

"Excuse me?" Psyche stared.

Venus raised her chin. "He wants you. And however much my son may have embarrassed me, he is still my son, and his happiness is my own."

Psyche learned two things from this statement. One, no matter what promises Venus offered her in this room, she would be swayed by Cupid's wishes when the time came to deliver on them. Psyche would not be getting a private island, and immortality was a nonnegotiable.

And two, she had more leverage than she had thought.

"I see," Psyche said, pushing away the sudden realization that under these conditions she would watch her nieces and nephew grow old even as she remained unchanged. "But what about me?"

Venus looked baffled, a rare expression on her face. "What about you? You're getting what you want, I'm getting what I want, and Cupid gets what he wants."

Psyche did not bother to challenge Venus on whether she would actually deliver on the promise of the island. "You upped the stakes. I have lost already the two people dearest to me; your terms ensure I would eventually watch the rest die as well. I want more for the price you have set."

"Ahhh." The confusion cleared and Venus looked at Psyche, eyes glittering. "Your flashes of boldness continue to surprise me. What is it, then?"

Psyche swallowed, very aware that what she was about to say was as likely to damn her nieces and nephews as save them. "I wish to claim my sisters' children, to raise alongside my child. They are in bad positions, having lost their mothers, and I would do all in my power to care for them as my sisters would have." Psyche took a breath, then continued. "I ask for your support in this and protection of them, both while they are in my care and once they leave it." She held her breath as Venus considered, staring at her as though she were some fascinating new specimen.

"You know that the only immortals Pluto allows to enter his halls are Mercury and Proserpina? If even Ceres cannot visit her daughter, then you certainly will not be able to consult with or save your sisters or whatever other silly notion you might have? That these children would be your responsibility alone?"

Psyche's throat tightened. "I do now."

The goddess tilted her head. "This is truly what you would ask of me?"

"It is." Psyche's head was hot with the anxiety of what Venus would next say, whether she could trust it, even if the goddess did agree.

"Very well. Your family for mine. A fair deal." Venus rose, looking down on Psyche. "I think," she said, "that I am glad you did not die."

JUPITER NARROWED his eyes as Venus finished, considering her words. Beside him, Juno's face was unreadable.

"It is a poor precedent to set, to condone the marriage of a human to the god she has accused of rape."

Venus nodded her agreement. "That is well observed, my lord, but in light of my son's continued professions of devotion, it is, I think, the most advantageous way forward. The girl has agreed to withdraw her accusations, and with time, the tale will be one of a great love for the ages. Cupid and Psyche, who so moved the mighty Jupiter with the strength of their feelings that he personally blessed their union."

"I see." The god-king stood and paced to the window, fingers combing his beard as he thought. Juno remained seated, watching her husband. Just as Venus began to consider pressing her case further, Jupiter spoke again.

"You are wise to flatter me, for I do not like what else you say. There is logic to it, but I dislike the idea of your son bringing such discord to Olympus only to be rewarded with what he most desires." He stopped, frowning. "And what of your part in all of this? You've hardly played the role of supportive mother."

Venus shrugged. "True, but all I have done has been in protection of my son. Surely, it can be understood that once Psyche's love was proven as strong as Cupid's, I embraced the union and accepted her as a daughter." Venus had never used her charms on Jupiter, had always felt a mild offense that he'd never pursued her, but she poured every bit of her appeal into her next words, aware the outcome of the meeting may depend on Jupiter's response. "If my lord will allow—and I know his behavior has earned him nothing, but I must beg on his behalf, in the name of love—my son greatly desires an audience with you to apologize and offer whatever services he can in recompense."

Juno locked eyes with Venus. The goddesses shared a long, word-less exchange in which Venus, for the first time in her life, lowered her gaze in respect, and Juno's chin raised, considering. The queen contemplated for a moment, then directed her focus to Jupiter. "The boy does have great skill," she observed. "Imagine the power of it, properly directed."

Jupiter's expression, heretofore irritated and skeptical, morphed into something altogether brighter and more calculating. Venus could practically see the wheels turning in his head, the affairs already half begun.

Jupiter waved a hand. "I can't imagine what the boy thinks he can do to make this right, but it would entertain me to hear him try. Bring him in."

CUPID FOUND Jupiter lounging in one of the private gardens adjacent the council hall, with Juno sipping tea beside him.

"My lord," Cupid said, dropping to a knee. Jupiter eyed him.

"Child, never have you addressed me with such respect. It is strange; please stand."

Cupid did so, pushing down his embarrassment. "I wish to beg a boon," he started, then paused, unsure how to continue. Jupiter sighed, shifting his body to stretch cramped muscles.

"Yes, that was evident enough when Venus requested this audience. Pray get to the point."

Cupid could not hide his surprise. "Mother asked for an audience?"

"Of course; why do you think you were allowed entrance to the garden?" Jupiter was becoming irritated. "Boy, for someone who has caused a great deal of trouble for everyone here today and who is at risk of losing the person he professes to love, you are taking a remarkably long time to make your case."

"Yes, yes, of course," Cupid said, trying to organize his thoughts. "My lord," he began again. Jupiter inclined his head. "My behavior has, I know, created great consternation for the council, which has only been exacerbated by Psyche's public accusations. But I appeal to my lord's great capacity for love—Psyche is not a passing fancy. She is my soul's anchor, and even the painful charges she has leveled at me weigh little in the balance of my devotion to her."

"Your extended recuperation from a few drops of oil speaks to such devotion," Juno said, dry.

"Mother locked me in," Cupid snapped, then took a deep breath. "Apologies, my lady." Juno did not respond, merely waited for him to continue. "I wish to marry her, to have her drink from a cup of ambrosia, and be with her forever."

He had succeeded in surprising them, it appeared. Juno was the first to speak.

"I knew of your desire to marry," she said, "and was prepared to lecture you on the sanctity of such a union and the mockery you've made already of it with your fake oracles and abduction and hidden identity and rape, but I find myself forced instead to focus on the second of your requests—immortality? You are truly requesting she be made immortal?"

Cupid nodded, swallowing. Jupiter sat up, leaning forward, intrigued.

"Surely you know that is rarely granted? And when it has been, it has not gone well—Endymion lives and yet does not wake, and Tithonus didn't ask for youth and so aged until Eos finally put him out of his misery. This is not a casual thing you ask."

"I know," Cupid said. Jupiter sat back, considering.

"Venus has argued that the optics on this will be better if we can sell it as a love story," the lightning god said, as much to Juno as to Cupid. "That 'Cupid and Psyche: Greatest Love of an Age' will ring better through time than 'Cupid and Psyche: Mortal Raped and then Struck Down for Accusing the Gods.'"

"She has a point," Juno said, "and I've ever been inclined to let the girl live, but our brothers are calling for her blood."

Jupiter waved a hand. "Ah, sometimes Neptune and Pluto need reminding of their place. But even if we pursue the love story angle, barriers remain." The god leaned forward again, arms on his knees as he studied Cupid. "She must renounce her story—it is problematic, to be sure, but if she recants now, it will be forgotten in a generation."

Blowing out an unsteady breath, Cupid nodded. "I can try... I can convince her of that, I think."

"You think?" Jupiter's tone was the distant roll before thunder.

"No, I can!" Cupid rushed to correct. "She will renounce it, I swear it."

All joviality once more, Jupiter nodded. "Excellent. Assuming she cooperates, I think we can have the muses spin a very convincing love story from the events recounted, which would certainly remove the need for public consequences."

"And you will have to marry her, as you profess you wish to," Juno added.

"Yes, thank you, my lord, my lady, thank you." Cupid's head bobbed in eager appreciation.

Jupiter frowned once more. "Again, I find your courtesy disconcerting. Your mischief has caused me all manner of grief over the years, inspired me with those cursed darts of yours to become a swan, a snake, my own damned daughter, in pursuit of my pleasure. The number of offspring I've been required to attend to in some way has increased by at least a third since you reached maturity. In fact, I find my own moderation in this matter remarkable in light of your history of behavior." Cupid opened his mouth to apologize but was interrupted by Juno clearing her throat. She shook her head, barely perceptible. Cupid shut his mouth again. Jupiter waited. Finally, Cupid said,

"I am good at what I do, my lord. In recompense for past crimes and in gratitude for your support in this matter, I not only promise to refrain from making my lord the object of my amusement but offer what skills I possess in whatever way my lord requires, for however long my lord requires."

Jupiter's face split then into a wide smile, teeth gleaming.

CHAPTER 36

The feast that evening was a feral, riotous affair dressed as a state dinner. Rain had pushed everyone under cover and the atmosphere was thick with the weight of long histories and deep resentments, even as the musicians in the corner struck a lively tune and all manner of nymph and fawn and lesser gods milled about with oblivious cheer.

Apollo lounged with Mercury, several glasses deep and eyes heavy with the passion of his convictions.

"—the last time I aid your son, Mercury, I swear it."

Mercury popped a grape in his mouth, signaling to the musicians to increase their tempo. "Ah, but this has been such fun, don't you think? How often do we get to watch Neptune squirm?"

Apollo gave a vigorous shake of his head, "No, no, no. Not worth it. Nothing is worth that glint in my sister's eye and the threat to my oracular practice. I'm done with it; I wash my hands of the whole affair. Why, I sent a whole host of doves to keep watch over Hyacinth, so nervous does Diana's current mood make me. The tasks Venus set Psyche? Child's play compared to what I've seen my sister do."

"Well, Psyche didn't exactly complete those tasks on her own. There were, ah, interested parties assisting her."

"Hmph. Yes, well, I am Hyacinth's only interested party, and

Hyacinth's the only being on this whole wretched Earth who loves me, so as I said, I wash my hands of this whole thing." A wide gesticulation of his arms sent his goblet flying, wine splashing onto the couch on which he lay, then dripping into tiny red pools on the tiled floor. Apollo blinked at the mess, tears visible at the corners of his eyes, as several nymphs appeared to clean it up.

"I need more wine," he said, stumbling to his feet.

Across the room, Minerva observed his intoxication.

"Your brother is in rare form tonight," she said to Diana, who stood beside her, long braid now wrapped like a crown about her head.

Diana's smile was predatory. "He's terrified I'm going to come for his lover," she said, "and well he should be."

Minerva cut her eyes at the moon goddess. "Out of character of you to be playing the game with such artifice," she commented, raising her voice to be heard above the music.

Diana inclined her head. "Direct would have been easier for them to ignore; already, the words I spoke today slip from their mind. But the fear of being called to account? Of losing privileges on which they have shaped their godhood? That haunts them. I can only hope it will haunt them well after this affair is wrapped."

Minerva reached up to stroke the head of an owl that fluttered down to her shoulder, talons gripping hard enough to pierce the linen garment she wore. "I dislike it. Justice is not a shadow business but a reckoning laid down in the cold, clear light of day. Either Cupid is guilty, or he is not. Either Psyche is guilty, or she is not. Each will suffer the consequences of their own actions, accordingly."

Diana studied her half sister, taking a small step forward so that she could speak quietly. "Is it because you sprung from our father's head fully formed that you truly cannot see? No one contested Cupid's guilt, did you notice? Psyche was not even questioned, and yet every person there believed her claim. But her crime in speaking of it, still, is greater than his in committing it."

Minerva huffed. "Well, that's not because he's a man but because he's a god and she's a mortal. There is an order to the world that her story disrupted; you are trying to make this something it isn't."

Diana looked away before she responded, voice thick with frustration. "These gods do not suffer consequences, ever. Goddesses bear the weight of the gods' follies; I don't know how to change this, I don't know if it can ever be changed, but I saw an opportunity to make them feel something, to make them face for even a second the truth of what they do, and I seized it." She paused, sipped her water. "I shall not apologize for it."

"Nor should you," came a new voice. Minerva and Diana turned to find Venus, all elegant sensuality as ever, lifting a goblet of wine in a toast. "To being unapologetic."

Narrowing her eyes, Diana raised her cup in response. Minerva remained unmoved, arms crossed. The bird on her shoulder ruffled its feathers.

"You should know," Venus said, lowering her glass and running a finger around the rim, "that Psyche has agreed to retract her accusation. She and my son will be granted their eternity together."

Diana gave a sharp laugh. "Of course she did," she said. "What choice does she have at this point?"

Venus gave a shrug. "Little," she agreed. "But I did not seek you to gloat in my victory."

"Did you not?"

Venus smiled. "Perhaps a bit. But primarily, I wanted to say that I agree with you."

The silence that dropped between the three lingered for several moments, the chatter and laughing around them forming an encompassing wall of sound, until Diana said,

"Pray elaborate."

Venus cleared her throat, a rare openness in her expression. "You and I have never agreed on much, nor have we been kind to one another. We pursue our desires in different ways, and I confess to never having much interest in understanding your motivations. But I see now that we are often responding to the same struggle—to claim an identity, to be heard, in a world built by and for gods. I think the same could be said for you as well, Minerva."

The goddess of wisdom and rationality stiffened. "I reject such an analysis," she said. "The world is as it is, and each of us finds our place in it, gods and goddesses alike."

Pressing her lips together, Venus shook her head. "I don't think that's too far off from the point I was making, but no matter." She waved a hand decorated with delicate rings of gold. "I've felt little camaraderie or friendship from either of you over the centuries, and I don't expect that to change. But I have found, through this, a respect for you and your position, Diana, that was unexpected to me. That is all I wished to say." Venus turned as if to leave, then paused. She looked back over her shoulder at Diana. "You were right, you know."

Diana tilted her head. "Oh?"

"Yes." For a moment, it seemed Venus had thought better of what she had intended to say, but then she continued quietly. "About Mercury and what it meant for him to use me the way he did the night Cupid was conceived. I just wanted to say—you were right." And then the goddess of love turned and departed.

Diana and Minerva watched Venus walk away, steps light and hips swaying as she approached Mars, running her hand up the base of his spine to his neck as she circled around to slide into his lap. Minerva was frowning.

"That was uncomfortable," she said. "I must speak with Vulcan." As she departed, the owl's head swiveled around to lock its gaze with Diana's, who remained in place, turning over what Venus had said.

VULCAN WAS SITTING along the room's edge, propped on a stool with one weak leg outstretched. His gaze was on his wife when he glanced up to find four steady eyes fixed on him.

"Greetings, goddess," he said, spine straightening and shifting his body so he was better angled toward her.

Minerva stared at him until he said, a note of irritation entering his voice, "Did you need something?"

"It was hypocritical of you to speak as you did today, and you know it." The owl on Minerva's shoulder gave an accompanying hoot.

Vulcan's eye twitched. "I said I was the only male in the room not accused; that was accurate."

"Father was not accused."

"A technicality; Diana lost her nerve. Everyone knows Jupiter would not be the appropriate voice to respond to claims of rape as a systemic issue."

"Well, neither were you."

Vulcan took a hearty gulp of wine, then and pushed himself to stand. He stared up at his half sister and her pet. "Say what you mean to say, Minerva, and have done."

The goddess of wisdom pressed her lips together and looked away for a moment. Her face betrayed nothing when she turned back to Vulcan. "I only wish to remind you—failure to complete the act and a new name does not leave you among the blameless. Do not presume again to speak from a supposedly unbiased position."

Vulcan shook his head, returning with care to his seat, refusing to meet her eyes. He stretched out his leg once more. "I'm not debating this with you tonight. You are raising a centuries-old grievance; do not take out on me your frustration with the emotional vulnerability of the council."

Minerva glared, then kicked the stool from beneath him and stalked from the room, one hand coming up to stroke her owl's head as Vulcan roared in outrage behind them.

PSYCHE FOUND Ceres tidying the table and calling for fresh platters of food.

"It is good to see you," Psyche said, head bowed in respect. Ceres paused, bowl in hand, and turned to look at the human girl. She smiled, though the expression did not quite reach her eyes.

"How are you feeling?" the goddess asked, placing a gentle hand on Psyche's stomach. Anyone else touching her belly in that way would have caused Psyche to tense with revulsion, but she found herself wishing she could lean into Ceres' touch, to lay her head on the goddess's shoulder and cry like a child. She blinked several times.

"It hurts to exist," she said, honest.

284

Ceres nodded. "It does," she agreed.

"I wanted to thank you"—Psyche's words tripped over themselves as she continued—"for the time I spent, the time you gave me, in your home. You were generous and direct, and I did not then appreciate these qualities as much as I do now."

The goddess studied her, and Psyche thought she looked sad. "You owe me no thanks, but I appreciate the words. I, too, have interest in the way this plays out."

Proserpina's face flashed in Psyche's mind.

"I have—" Psyche paused, started again. "I would seek your insight on another matter if you are willing." Ceres inclined her head, waiting. Psyche swallowed. "I scratched myself with one of Cupid's arrows before he departed that night. It was an accident, but—"

"But now you don't know what thoughts and feelings are your own," Ceres finished. Psyche nodded, relieved. The goddess of the harvest was gentle when she asked, "So what is your question, Psyche?"

What was her question? Psyche found that putting words to it was difficult. Finally, she said, "How do I know what is real? What is right for me and my babe?"

Ceres sighed. "Oh child, I say to you now what I said to my own daughter so many centuries ago: it's all real, now, in that you have to live with it. You must choose, through the pain and the disappointment and the longing, what you will hold up as your truth. No one, not I, not Venus, certainly not Cupid, can do that for you." Ceres set down the bowl she held, then, and took Psyche's shoulders in both her hands. "You were raped. You were scratched by a magical arrow. Would that you lived in a world that cared, but you do not, and so you must build your own. These are things that have happened to you, and they have had their effects. It is up to you, now, what you make of those effects." The goddess leaned forward, pressing a kiss to the girl's forehead. "Trust your own voice, and you will be fine." She let go of Psyche, then, reclaiming her bowl. "I'm going to take this to the kitchen now and then take myself to bed. I will see you tomorrow, Psyche of Crete."

.   .   .

WHEN CUPID WENT to look for Psyche, she was nowhere to be found. Before he could depart for their room, a smooth hand appeared on his forearm, halting him.

"Come, walk with me," Venus said. With one last forlorn look around the room for Psyche, Cupid complied, following his mother to sit outside by a fountain, stars reflecting in both the rippling water of the pool and in the stones gleaming with fallen rain.

Mother and son sat for a while in silence, then Cupid pointed at the sky.

"There's Orion," he said. "Do you think if he was still around, Diana would have been such a pain today?"

Venus's voice was mild. "Gods and humans alike behave in strange ways for the sake of love. If these events have proven nothing else, they have demonstrated that."

Cupid shifted on his seat, uncomfortable with his mother's calm. "I heard Mars speaking of you to Apollo," he said with a sidelong glance at Venus. "Apollo is worried you will seek vengeance on him for his part by hurting Hyacinth; Mars claimed you would never use love as a means of punishment, that it was too sacred to you."

Venus was silent, so Cupid continued.

"Only you did, didn't you? Or, you wanted me to, on your behalf. Since I was a child, you've lectured me on treating love with reverence, have expressed your disapproval for my intrigues, and yet when faced with the possibility of irrelevance, you threatened the very same."

Venus shrugged. "Mars sees the best in me, but I, too, am but a vessel for love."

Cupid flushed at that. "A vessel for love, are you? It was love, then, that had you set my beloved tasks designed to kill her, to send her into the very seat of death itself?"

Venus sighed. "After a fashion, yes. Love for myself, love for you, love for the life I am able to maintain with proper worship."

Shaking his head, Cupid drew with a wet finger on the stone edge of the fountain. "No," he said, "that was pride, ego, fear. Not love." He started when Venus gave a quiet laugh. "Do you deny that?"

"No," she said, standing, crossing to examine a bush of roses in

286

bloom. "But all of those stem from desire, which is a form of love. Tell me, darling boy, when you took this girl without her consent—first from a cliff face, then in a bedroom—was that love?"

This silenced Cupid, whose finger froze where it had been tracing wet spirals. When he did speak, his voice shook.

"I love her, Mother."

"Of course you do."

"I loved her then as well."

"I'm sure you did." Venus skimmed her fingers over delicate petals on the verge of opening. "Does loving her preclude that you hurt her?"

The fountain burbled, and in the distance they heard a barn owl screech.

Venus spoke again, thoughtful. "When I first emerged on the beach so long ago, the one right outside my home now, I knew nothing except that there was a profound pleasure in the sensation of soft sand beneath me, cool water lapping my toes, warm sun on my skin. Where I had been, what I had been before, I could not have said, but the body I found myself in—well, that was a means for sensation I'd never known. I did not make myself the goddess of love, Cupid; it is simply what I have always been." The goddess walked to sit by her son, taking one of his hands in hers.

"I have spent my existence working to sort out what it is to be love embodied, first as Aphrodite and now as Venus. Love takes so many forms, few truly gentle. Of all the forms I've encountered, however, my love for you has been both the purest and the hardest."

"Okay," Cupid said, cautious. "So, are you still angry with me? For I tell you that my love for Psyche was as inevitable as you describe your calling."

Venus snorted. "And if you scratched yourself now with one of your leaden arrows? Would that love feel quite so inevitable then?"

Cupid started at that, meeting her eyes for the first time. Venus smiled, releasing his hand. "I think you will get what you are seeking tomorrow; Diana has ruffled feathers, but ultimately, the balance is weighted against her. Which means you will be tied for eternity to this girl, your image entwined with hers." Venus gazed into the distance, looking into memory. "Many have questioned my relationship with Mars, you know, as well as with Vulcan. How can I love both? How can love take the form of pain? The thing is, Cupid, I don't answer to anyone. I have been named the goddess of love, and thus, all I do must stem from such. I am the definition, you see?"

Cupid did not see. "If you are the definition of love, what does that make me?"

"Oh, my boy, you've been a crueler, more childish version of love," Venus said, laying one hand alongside his cheek. "And, for the most part, I have delighted in it. But now is your chance to become something more than what you have been."

"Are you saying I did no wrong, then, acted only as was my nature?"

"I'm saying that you're a god, and if she is to become a goddess, then the two of you will be linked forever, Cupid and Psyche, heart and soul. Jupiter will have the muses shape your story, and mortals will interpret it for generations to come, but it is you, and Psyche, who will have to exist within it. Will have to grow within it." Venus sighed, ran a hand through her boy's hair. "Go, talk to your beloved. She's survived much to be able to speak to you. And as you talk, know you are laying the foundations on which the two of you will have to live for ages to come—you say you wish her to be immortal; well, start treating her as such."

And so saying, Venus pressed a hard kiss to Cupid's forehead and then departed for her own quarters.

When Cupid returned to his own room, Psyche was already asleep, curled on her side with one arm tucked under her face, the other thrust under her belly and between her knees. She was, Cupid thought, so beautiful.

He sat on the edge of the bed, lifting a hand to brush hair behind her ear. Tomorrow, they'd speak. Tomorrow, when she was finally his.

CHAPTER 37

Council opened with Jupiter inviting every member to state their position, in brief, and the action they recommended be taken. He asked Minerva to begin.

"I fully expect you to ignore all of this, but for the record I observe two transgressions: Psyche's challenging of the gods in her public charge against Cupid, and Cupid's own oathbreaking, by raping and then abandoning one he professed to love."

Cupid stood in outrage but was silenced by a stern glance from Jupiter. Sitting back down by Psyche, Cupid pulled her close, pressing a kiss to her temple that was as much for show as for comfort. Psyche tried to school her own face into one of bland deference.

Minerva continued. "For the former, I recommend Psyche be executed after the birth of her child; for the latter, that Cupid raise said child and have his bow, arrows, and wings stripped from him until such time as that child is grown." Reclaiming her seat without looking at the couple, the goddess of wisdom gestured for Apollo to say his piece.

"Ah," said Apollo, rising with deliberate slowness. He clasped his hands beneath his chin. "When this council began, I felt similarly to Minerva, but I confess that the telling of the tale has quite affected me, and I could not bear for Cupid to endure the same pain of loss I have so recently endured." Beside him, Diana's foot tapped the ground. Apollo rushed to finish. "Yes, yes, so I recommend that Psyche be spared, and I guess it's up to Venus and Cupid what happens from here." No sooner had he sat than Diana began to speak, her voice carrying even as she remained seated.

"You've heard my position; what a travesty it would be to slaughter an innocent woman for the crime of stating baldly the violence done to her, and to so many others, by the men in this room."

Neptune was next.

"Much as you may wish it, Diana, this is not an issue of gender but of natural order, and a mortal leveling such an accusation against a god cannot be tolerated. I say Psyche should be executed today. As far as Cupid goes, I suggest he consider keeping his mouth shut about his feelings for any future conquests."

Then Ceres.

"I maintain it is a family issue; return the girl to Venus and Cupid and have done."

Mercury.

"I want my boy happy, of course; we can sort out the rest later. Let the girl live."

Venus.

"A rare occurrence, but I agree with Mercury."

Vulcan.

"Psyche should be held to account in some way, as should Cupid, but I find death too harsh a sentence. Perhaps the child must be given to Venus to raise and Cupid denied the marriage he seeks."

Pluto.

"Let her join her sisters."

Mars.

"I'd execute her, but I don't begrudge Cupid his toy."

And last, Juno.

"I do not wish her dead, but nor do I wish the institution of marriage so mocked by having her wed Cupid under the weight of her current accusations. Should she desire to recant, then perhaps there is a path by which we reshape this story into one of mutual love and devotion. Husband, I am eager to hear your thoughts now that we have all claimed our positions."

Jupiter steepled his fingers as if considering all he had heard. The votes had come out in favor of Psyche's survival, but every person in the room knew that should Jupiter disagree, the vote was pointless. One did not become the king of the gods by bowing to democracy.

Psyche's hand was in Cupid's, held tight enough to cut off the blood flow to her fingers, and it was on this spreading sensation of tingling numbness that Psyche focused in order to keep herself from going mad with the tension. They had a deal; she should be safe, and yet she had trusted Diana, too.

"It is a rare case we heard today," Jupiter began, his words echoing through the silence in the hall, "one that forces us to consider the very nature of our own position and immortality. What is life without love? Without pleasure? A cold, barren thing, I'll tell you that. And yet what is a god without respect, without worship? Little more than a cliff face, observing the world but with no real impact. Twice has this human girl threatened the respect due to a god—first when her face drew worshippers away from the temple of Venus and again when she publicly accused Cupid of raping her. Either of these crimes could warrant—and have warranted, in past councils—immediate execution." Psyche forced her features to relax, desperate not to reveal the anxiety screaming beneath. She rested a hand on the underside of her stomach, feeling her child move and counting the kicks. One, two, three. *Breathe in. Breathe out.*

Jupiter dropped his hands to his knees, pushed himself to stand. "And yet, Cupid loves her still. And Venus herself desires the girl live. And so we must ask ourselves—shall we condemn one of our own to a life without love?"

"Too many in this room have lost love to Cupid's arrows," Diana said, rising. "What consideration does he deserve from us?"

"Sit down, daughter," Jupiter thundered. "You have said your piece." Diana obeyed, her eyes remaining trained on her father in challenge. Jupiter continued, calmer, turning to direct his words now to Cupid. "She is right, though. You, boy, have played recklessly with the affections and impulses of those in this room, myself included.

Too often have you blackened my reputation with lust, transforming me into all manner of beast in the pursuit of its satiation. I am not above feeling some satisfaction for your current plight, and I hope it shall kindle in you even the smallest flame of awareness when next you pick up your bow."

Cupid hung his head, a show of contrition. "It shall, my lord. It has already."

Jupiter placed a benevolent palm atop Cupid's shining curls. A small snort came from the other side of Jupiter's throne.

"Once again, we observe a farce performed in a court of feelings, far from any notions of logic or justice," Minerva said, low enough to be missed by most of the council. Jupiter had heard, however, and Psyche watched him shoot the goddess of wisdom a warning glance. The god-king continued.

"I have heard the council's recommendations, and they are inclined toward leniency. I confess I am as well. Let us now hear from you, Cupid. In the event that we spare Psyche, how do you recommend we proceed?"

Cupid rose, not letting go of Psyche's hand. Psyche pushed herself to stand, Cupid using their interlaced fingers to tug her close to his side.

"Psyche and I apologize to this council for the inconvenience and embarrassment we have caused," Cupid said, and Psyche hoped the solemn line of her lips read as agreement. "We wish only to spend our lives together in love, raising our child—he placed a palm on Psyche's belly—"with all the joy in which the group of you raised me." Venus's eyebrows rose at this, but she remained silent. Cupid took a breath. "And so, Psyche and I ask permission to marry, and that she drink from a cup of ambrosia, be granted eternal life and youth, and that our futures and that of our child might be secured for all time." Most in the room had heard, by that point, of Cupid's wishes, so there was little surprise expressed. Faces turned to Jupiter, who was nodding, slow, apparently deep in thought.

"It is a tremendous thing you ask and not lightly granted. Were I to even consider it, we would first need to lay to rest the matter of this accusation." The lightning god's gaze swung to Psyche, piercing. "Are you prepared to recant your statements, to claim the madness of pregnancy and proclaim instead your undying love and devotion to my grandson?"

Psyche raised her chin, eyes suddenly bright with unshed tears.

She thought about the future she once believed would be hers; marriage to a kind-enough man, children, visits with her sisters and parents. She thought about the darkness into which she had fallen in Cupid's home, before she knew his name. She thought about the way her world had shifted on its axis when she realized she was pregnant, responsible for the life of another. She thought of the way it had shifted once again when she brushed against the arrow. She thought of sitting with Cidippe and her children in the garden and then of watching a life more precious to her than her own blink out in the most painfully ordinary of ways. She thought of the tasks she had completed for Venus, of her moments in despair. She thought of her sisters and what they had asked of her in the Underworld.

Keep your own name, and demand they say it, Daphne had said. Psyche swallowed. What was her name if she disavowed her truth? But what was her truth if it doomed those she loved?

"I'm ready," she heard herself say. For a moment, time itself seemed to stand still. Then Jupiter clapped his hands together, jolting the room back to the present.

"Wonderful!" he said. He turned to Cupid. "Your beloved has made her promise; now you must make yours." Psyche felt Cupid's hand twitch in her own— did she imagine his hesitation before responding? Nonetheless, his voice was steady when he spoke.

"You have my word, mighty Jupiter, on my worship and the lives of those I love, that my bow and arrows shall henceforth be yours to direct as you desire, and never again shall they cause you embarrassment or pain."

As the weight of Cupid's oath settled on the room, Psyche had to work hard to keep herself from dissolving into a fit of hysterical laughter. This? This was the price of her life and the life of her child? The unfettered access to and use of any being that caught Jupiter's eye moving forward? She had just promised to withdraw her accusation of rape, and it appeared that her very withdrawal had ensured future instances of the same crime. Her eyes found Diana's across the room, and for the first time since the goddess's betrayal of her had been revealed, Psyche felt she understood Diana's game. The goddess had, of course, lost, but was it ever possible to win against the gods? Psyche was beginning to think not.

Agneta, Aindreas, Ianthe, Eleni. Psyche chanted their names in her head, reminding herself why she was here, why she could not scream with the absurdity of it all. The immortals in this room may never experience real consequences, but she had, and this was her one chance, her last chance, to do something for her sisters. *Agneta, Aindreas, Ianthe, Eleni.* They needed her, and so she needed to keep hold of her emotions. She started when she heard her own name.

"Psyche?" Jupiter was frowning at her, his tone suggesting this was not the first time he had tried to get her attention. Psyche sank with awkward care to her knees.

"My lord," she said, keeping her still-agitated gaze fixed to the stone floor. The god-king stepped forward, two fingers coming beneath her chin to tilt her face until she was looking up at him. He took in the gleam of her eyes, and Psyche felt sure he could feel wild energy vibrating beneath her skin. Jupiter smiled.

"You've come far, lovely one. There is now only forever to go." Removing his hand from her face, Jupiter helped Psyche to her feet, extending his other arm to receive the goblet Mercury held ready. Jupiter pressed the goblet into Psyche's hands, wrapping her fingers around the cup.

"Drink, Princess of Crete," he said, raising his voice for the benefit of the council, "drink and let both your life and youth become immortal. Let Cupid never part from your embrace, and let me declare you husband and wife in a marriage made for eternity." There was a mocking in his voice that surprised Psyche, and in that moment, she realized that Jupiter knew. For all he played the bored monarch, he saw the situation as clearly as she did, and he knew he was coming out on top. His words were a dare, testing Psyche one last time.

Straightening, Psyche kept her eyes locked with the god-king's, lifted the goblet to her lips, and drank.

CHAPTER 38

"How do you feel?" Cupid's hand rested on the small of Psyche's back, his head bent to her in concern. Despite her disgust over the bargain that she herself had just sealed, Psyche found herself relaxing into his touch. The physical relief provided by Cupid's presence was truly unsettling—her hand hurt now only when she imagined parting from him.

"Brand new," she said, and it was true. A single cup of ambrosia and, while she was still very aware of being pregnant, the aches and daily pains that had been with her for the past several months had all but disappeared. Psyche was not ready to think too hard about all the implications involved in her new status as an immortal, but this perk, she welcomed.

Council had dispersed with little pomp following Psyche's transformation and their exchange of vows. Once business concluded, it seemed, the gods had little interest in each others' company.

The newlyweds entered their shared room, and Cupid led her to the bed, helping her to sit before settling beside her, hand now on her knee as though not touching her was an impossibility. Psyche closed her eyes, folding her own hands over her stomach. She felt warm lips brush her forehead.

"I feel like half of me was missing and is now restored," Cupid said against her hair. He stood, stretching. "That, however," he said, "is not something I wish ever to do again."

Psyche lay back, staring at the painted ceiling. "What?" she asked. "Get married or stand and justify yourself before all of Olympus?"

"Either," Cupid said. "The former because I'm content and the latter because it was awful."

"Mmm."

Cupid collapsed next to her, sprawled so he covered over half the bed. Now that the urgency of their situation had been put to rest, the weight of that last night at Cupid's estate settled between them. Cupid cleared his throat.

"Leaving you as I did was poorly done," he offered, voice sincere. "It will not happen again."

Psyche nodded as she turned on her side, not yet trusting her voice. She did not doubt him—he now had everything he wanted. Her mind protested it was merely the product of his arrow, but there was a significant part of her that was content as well, ready to accept his unsaid apology and move on. Even now, in her late pregnancy and exhaustion, her body craved him, as if her nervous system was truly calm only when they touched. And yet the easier he made her body feel, the exponentially greater her struggle was, for though her mind may have been soothed, it had not forgotten.

She had not forgotten the powerlessness she had felt on that cliff face, nor the empty despair that built following the first night he claimed her—the first night he raped her. She had not forgotten his distrust and irritation over her need for her sisters or the way he had dismissed her concerns for their child. She had not forgotten the way he looked at her that night when he told her that she was no more than a mortal, doomed to time.

Well, she was no longer a mortal. No longer doomed to time.

"Why did you not use an arrow on me?" She asked the question that had been gnawing at her ever since she realized who he was. "That first night, or on any after, you could have compelled my consent, likely avoided all that has transpired. But you didn't. Why?"

Cupid's response came sooner than she expected. "I don't know," he said. "Would you believe me if I said it never occurred to me?"

Psyche eyed him. "No."

His mouth pulled up in a half grin. "Ah, well. It occurred to me, but not that first night. Not until later, when you were begging for those cursed sisters of yours." He did not seem to notice the way she tensed at his language around her sisters, continuing, "Certainly Apollo was playing on my pride, that I might need an arrow to keep a lover content, but I also think I wanted you to love me without it." He paused, considering his next words. "It is— it can get, well, lonely."

Psyche shook her head. "But you abandoned none of the other advantages of godhood in that supposed pursuit; you used Apollo's oracle and Zephyr to abduct me, kept me in a home maintained by invisible spirits, used your wings to visit me only in the dark. You told me love cannot live without trust—well, arrow or not, true affection can never grow under such unequal circumstances."

This seemed to get under Cupid's skin, and he sat up, agitated. "Can it not? I saved you from my mother's intentions, then attempted to protect you from her retaliation. I gave you every luxury, every indulgence you asked for."

"Except the truth," Psyche said, quiet. "Except any real pieces of yourself."

"Every word I told you was true! Every piece I gave real!"

"Nothing could be real without the truth of your identity, can't you understand that? Nothing! I was scared and sad and more than a little bit broken by what my parents had done—what *you* orchestrated— and then you swept in, not to free me from that, but to place me in a prettier cage. And you were successful, Cupid, you won. I carry your child, I've drunk ambrosia, I am bound to you for eternity. But I need you to see—I'm *begging* you to see—that what you did was for yourself, not for me."

Cupid stared at her for several long moments, hands white knuckled on his knees, and Psyche saw the strain on his face as he struggled not to respond immediately. Eventually, he took a deep breath before speaking again. "I understand I have hurt you," he said, "but that is in the past. We have a whole eternity before us, why begin it with such ugly debate?"

Psyche's heart ached at his words, at the realization that no matter how much she now loved him, there were things he may never understand or take accountability for. Still, she wasn't finished.

"We just left a council called, in part, because I told a bard my story and that you raped me. I don't know how we can ignore the ugliness."

"I did not rape you, Psyche, we both know that."

"Do we?"

Cupid paced to the balcony, then turned back to her as he reached the threshold. His eyes blazed. He pointed a finger at her. "You felt pleasure," he said. "I know you did."

Psyche held his gaze as she considered how to respond. While hurling all her pain at him now might be cathartic, it would not help her win his support for her immediate goals.

"If your concern was for my pleasure," she began, "I ask you to consider how much more my pleasure would have been had I consented, with full knowledge of your identity and the security of a marriage blessed by my family." Her words fell like stones in a stream; she could almost see the ripples they made in her husband's mind as he considered them. His brows drew together, stubborn.

"But then Mother would have found out, and she would have been angry. Mother is quite brutal when she is angry."

"I am aware," Psyche said.

The tension in Cupid's face lessened a bit. The corner of his mouth quirked up. "Ah, you are, aren't you?" He crossed to the bed then, sitting next to Psyche and taking her hand in his. "I take your meaning," he said. "I do not know that I agree with your conclusions, but what is past is past, and I regret any pain you felt. As I see it, now we have nothing but a happy future before us. You know who I am, have consented both to our marriage and to retracting your accusations, and have been granted the unheard-of gift of immortal life and youth. Let us start fresh with our love; mine for you is brighter than it has ever been."

Psyche thought that was about as close to an apology as she would ever get. She allowed him to hold her hands.

"I have love for you, too," she said, watching his eyes brighten. She continued, "But the wounds of our past have not fully healed; I can promise only that I will try my best to close them. To that end, though, I beg your help."

His expression dimmed, but his spine straightened.

"Anything, my love," Cupid said.

CHAPTER 39

The sun was brilliant and the wind fair the morning Mercury found Nomios the bard propped against a tree, his lyre tucked under his arm. Though his eyes were closed in apparent sleep, his mouth tightened at the sound of grass shifting under the god's feet.

"Who have they sent for me, then?"

Mercury swept a mocking bow. "Greetings, musician."

Nomios opened his eyes, taking in the being standing before him.

"You are like a song come to life," he said, fingers twitching on his lyre. "A punchy major chord."

Settling next to the bard, Mercury propped his arms on his knees. "Do indulge me, then." He gestured to the instrument. "Play me." Nomios met the god's eyes. Swinging the lyre onto rest against his thigh, he turned his focus inward, eyes closing again.

The first few notes he played were slow, their bright sound hovering in the air as the strings vibrated. Settling into the piece, he began to pluck faster, the rhythm jaunty and cheerful but with a minor chord running beneath. When he finished, the two sat in silence, listening to the notes fade away on the wind.

"You are not a fool, bard," Mercury observed.

"My lord Mercury flatters me," Nomios returned, tone tired but not yet resigned. "I am but a humble servant of the muses; what they reveal, my fingers play."

Mercury's lips turned in a bemused smile. "Ah, but you cannot lay this visit at the feet of the muses."

"Can I not? I was hungry, nearly broke, with months wasted chasing an epic that never happened. And then, like a gift, the muses sent me a tale to tell, a song to sing."

"Still, you chose to sing it."

Nomios hesitated, weighing the risk of pushing further. "If you'll indulge me, Lord Mercury, what is choice, absent power? A calculation in survival, usually. Psyche chose to tell me her story, in full knowledge of my profession and position. Did a muse lead me to her table that day? Did the Fates? Because I tell you, it felt in that moment like she needed my skills as surely as I needed her story. To question such a meeting would have felt, well, blasphemous."

Mercury eyed the mortal man. "And the light in which you cast my son—that did not strike you as blasphemy?"

"*Your* son?" Nomios shrugged. "I've heard convincing tales otherwise. Who am I to mediate the truth? As I said, I but play what the muses reveal."

The messenger god was silent for a long time then, absently plucking blades of grass and throwing them away as he thought. Finally, he said,

"It was bold of you, and I admire a risk taken. But that risk has caught up with you, as you must know."

Nomios inclined his head, though the white fingers clutching his lyre betrayed his tension. "As my lord says."

Mercury considered the bard further. "I've been sent to kill you," he remarked, "but now I am not sure that is the most helpful way forward."

Nomios dropped his gaze, subservient. "My lord, of course, knows best."

Mercury's dimples emerged. "Well, perhaps we can come to an agreement, then."

"Anything," Nomios promised.

Mercury nodded, satisfied. "You will, of course, no longer speak, sing, or play in any way the tale you've been spreading about Cupid."

"My song was about Psyche." Nomios regretted the words as soon as they were out.

Mercury's gaze cooled. "Watch yourself, bard." When Nomios swallowed, remaining silent, Mercury settled back and continued. "You will, in fact, play nothing at all until such time as you receive a visit from the muses—in flesh, not revelation—who will deliver to you the version of the tale you are to share from that point forward. I offer you this because you amused me and because I enjoy a well-played lyre, but know that if ever I hear even a whisper of you doing other than I have instructed, we shall have another chat, one in which I will be less amused."

An involuntary twang rang from the lyre. "Yes, as you say, lord. Thank you lord."

Mercury brushed off his legs, pushing to stand. "You are welcome," he said, "but I cannot leave without punishing you in some way, you understand." He winked. "I, too, answer to higher powers, on occasion." Striding out from under the shelter of the tree, the messenger god took to the air, gazing down at the bard. "Farewell, mortal, remember our agreement." And with a twist and a flash he was gone.

Nomios exhaled a breath he hadn't realized he had been holding, heart pounding in his chest and mind stuttering over the fact that he was still alive. While he hadn't known such a visit was coming, the way in which his song had taken hold and spread in only a short time had raised the hairs on his arms, and he had been waiting for the other shoe to drop for some time now.

And yet it seemed, somehow, he had cheated the Fates yet again. Nomios sent a silent prayer of thanks to the muses.

When he went to stand, however, Nomios found his legs weren't responding the way he expected. Looking down at his body for the first time since Mercury had departed, the bard let out a cry. Where before his legs had emerged from his tunic, sun darkened and strong, now were the sharply jointed and furred rear legs of a goat. The straps of his sandals were burst and as Nomios followed their path down to his feet, he saw the soles now hung on sharp hooves.

Nomios shoved a fist in his mouth to keep from crying out again. Eyes darting to the sky, he searched the horizon for the messenger god, but Mercury was well and truly gone. Looking down at what was now the lower half of his body, Nomios took several moments to get his breathing under control. So he was a satyr now. Mercury had said he still needed to be punished, and even in his despair, Nomios could see the advantage the god had claimed here—songs by a human were well enough, but those of a creature of myth carried an extra weight of authenticity.

Pushing to stand with awkward movements, the weight distribution required for balance completely changed, Nomios used one hand to brace himself against the tree while retrieving his instrument with the other. He might have been spared by the gods, but if he wanted to retain that mercy, he needed to put more distance between himself and human habitation. Hobbling from under the shade, Nomios set out, no direction in mind, to find a safe place to live while he waited for the muses.

CHAPTER 40

The first project Psyche embarked upon when she and Cupid had returned to the estate was to construct a means of travel to and from the house that required neither wings nor an amenable wind spirit. Cupid was wary of the prospect of unintended guests, but Psyche insisted that if she was to retrieve and raise her sisters' children, she must have a reliable means of travel.

And so a path was hewn into the cliffside, long and winding in order to achieve the safest angles possible but wide enough for a horse and cart to navigate with confidence.

The first trip Psyche hazarded on her new road was to go home.

Standing in the great room, where she had spent hours as a child playing with her sisters, Psyche met the stunned gazes of her parents.

She thought she had moved beyond the hurt of their abandonment, that all she had suffered and lost had thrown their betrayal into a category of lesser pains. And yet, as she looked at the two people who had brought her into the world and then been all too easily persuaded to see her leave it, she found she had only a single word.

"Why?" Psyche asked.

Her father looked confused, but her mother's face lit with instant understanding. Her hands clutched together so tight that the knuckles shone pale as bone.

"Psyche, we did what we thought we had to do to protect us all from the gods' wrath."

"I would say you sent me into that wrath to spare yourselves," Psyche said. "Though maybe if you'd realized you would lose Aglaura and Cidippe you would have considered a bit longer before sacrificing me on a cliffside." The anguish evident from both of them when she uttered her sisters' names was another cut—they should be able to mourn their loss as a family, to be there for one another, and yet she was forever now on the outside.

"We've heard rumors," her father said, stiff. "It seems you've defied fate after all."

Psyche focused on him. "Fate?" she asked. "Is that what we call a bored immortal playing with smoke and mirrors and the eager faith of a priestess?"

Something like anger flashed in her mother's eyes. "Do not mock the gods, Psyche," she said.

Psyche blinked, stifling a laugh. "I'll mock them all I wish, Mother. I am one now, after all."

Her mother took an involuntary step forward at these words. She stopped herself, gaze still consuming her youngest child.

"We had heard this rumor," she whispered, "but I hardly dared believe it." Her eyes dropped to Psyche's stomach. "And your child...?"

Psyche nodded confirmation. Her father gave her a small, sad smile.

"It may be no comfort to you, and I imagine there is no world in which you find forgiveness for us, but I confess that seeing you well and hearing that your future is secured is a much needed balm to my heart."

Fury rose in Psyche's chest. "Well, I'm glad I could soothe your broken conscience," she snapped, then took several deep breaths to regain her composure. "I came not for you but for Aglaura and Cidippe, whom I have spoken with in the Underworld." Her parents' eyes widened. "They are together, along with Cidippe's infant son." Tears spilled down her mother's cheeks now, and even her father's eyes were looking glassy. The fight went out of Psyche as suddenly as it had come. She sighed. "I came also because I am going, now, at their

305

behest, to retrieve their children. Your grandchildren will be raised together, in safety, with every advantage I am able to offer them. The knowledge of this is the only kindness I have to offer you at this point." At her sides, Psyche clenched then unclenched her hands, considering whether to say more. The words wouldn't come. "Goodbye, then," she said, turning to go.

"Wait." Her mother's voice carried across the hall.

Psyche stopped, but did not turn around. "What?" she asked. When her mother responded, wiping her eyes, there was wonder in her voice.

"You are a goddess now; your child will be an immortal as well, and your sisters' children will be raised in the protection of the gods. As much as you may hate what we did, can you not acknowledge the blessings borne of the outcome?"

And that was all it took for the lid to finally fly off of Psyche's fury. She rounded on her parents, body trembling with outrage.

"Don't you dare, even for a second, congratulate yourself or take a single ounce of credit for anything but the pain and suffering every one of your daughters endured." Psyche's voice rose.

"Psyche, darling, we did the best we could." Her father's voice was weak.

Psyche glared at him, eyes shining with unshed tears. "It wasn't enough. So while I offer you the knowledge of my fate and the fate of your grandchildren as a kindness, do not presume to claim the light I have coaxed from the ashes as your own." And, unable to bear looking at them a moment longer, Psyche fled her childhood home, her body emptier than it had been when she arrived.

PSYCHE ARRIVED at Marinos's estate the day after the visit with her parents. She arrived as a goddess, flown by the god who was now her husband, in the chariot of the goddess who was now her mother-in-law, and she reminded herself of all that as she stepped into the main hall.

Cupid was at her shoulder.

"Marinos!" Psyche said, her voice echoing. Nearby servants shrank from the pair, even as their eyes stayed fixed in fascination. "Marinos!" Psyche called again.

From within, footsteps approached. Marinos emerged into the hall, his face twisted with irritation.

"What—" He stopped when he saw Psyche. His eyes widened, darted away, then narrowed. "Psyche?"

"You will address my wife as befits a goddess—on your knees," Cupid said, and after a quick glance at the god's face, Marinos dropped to the floor.

"Apologies, goddess," he said, his voice betraying his confusion.

Psyche shot Cupid a frustrated glance over her shoulder. "This is mine to handle. If you cannot allow me that, then I ask that you wait outside." Cupid rolled his eyes, then his shoulders, but did not say anything further. Psyche turned to Marinos.

"I will be taking the children with me," she said, raising a hand when he began to sputter. "No, I'm not interested in your protests. I have spoken with my sister, and this is her wish. Should you try in any way to prevent me from carrying out Cidippe's wishes or to deny her children their birthright when they are of age, know that I will bring down on you every pain you ever caused her, tenfold." She locked eyes with her brother-in-law, noting the anger and fear that seemed at war within his and feeling a surge of discomfort despite herself. Had Cidippe looked at him like that when he hit her? The thought returned steel to her spine. Marinos opened his mouth as though to speak, then glanced at Cupid and shut it once more. Psyche was suddenly furious.

"Don't look at him; look at me," she said. "He is not doing this to you; I am." She stepped closer to him and crouched down. "I know that to treat Cidippe as you did, you must carry a great deal of pain. I remind myself of that to keep myself from killing you." Marinos started, his eyes burning into her. "But I will not allow you to harm my sister's children in the same way; this hurt stops with you. I hope you find a better way to bear it, for if I ever again hear that you have laid hands on a woman, I will personally oversee the removal of those hands."

She stood and swept past him, not sparing him another glance.

When she reached the nursery, she paused in the doorway. Agneta and Aindreas sat stacking wooden blocks, each with one arm thrown out in protection, to keep Ianthe from getting close enough to topple the structure. The memory of when she had last seen them swept over her, tears filling her eyes. Taking a deep breath, she crossed to the children, slowly lowering herself until she was cross-legged beside them.

"Hello, sweet ones," she said. The twins didn't spare her a glance, so focused were they on their task, but Ianthe looked up and her face split into a wide smile. She toddled around Aindreas and threw herself at Psyche, soft arms tight around her neck. Startled, Psyche hugged the little girl back, pulling away only when she felt slime on her collarbone. Ianthe giggled at the snot left on Psyche's chest, reaching a finger out to poke at it.

"Ewww!" she said, delighted. Psyche used the collar of her dress to wipe the spot, smiling at her niece.

"Ewww!" she echoed.

When Psyche departed, she took with her not only the children but their nurse as well. It was a tight fit in Venus's chariot, and Psyche kept her arms wrapped around all three children for the duration of the trip, but when they all landed at last at the estate, tumbling out of the carriage in relief, Psyche felt something strung tight within her release. They were here. They were safe—or as safe as it was within her power to make them.

Leaving Cupid to manage the chariot, Psyche showed them to their quarters, which had been constructed with supernatural haste in preparation for their arrival. Once they had settled in, Psyche collapsed onto her own bed, her swollen body exhausted.

"I did it, Cid," she whispered to the ceiling, aetites stone in her fist. "I've got them, and I will love them and keep them safe for you. I promise." And while Psyche had no notion how the Underworld worked, whether souls could hear the messages of the living, she felt the first warm, gentle breeze of spring, and it felt like a blessing.

. . .

RETRIEVING Eleni was a far less dramatic affair. Georgios had older children from a prior marriage, so inheritance was not an issue, and his own maladies had taken a turn for the worse since Aglaura's death. Though clearly fond of his youngest daughter, he was also a pragmatic man and knew well she would receive better care with Psyche than she would on his estate.

"Will you bring her to visit me while I still live?" Georgios coughed as he spoke, the linen he held revealing red spots against the bright white. Psyche nodded, feeling an odd affection. Georgios was not an exciting man, but he was steady, and he was kind, and he had been both of those things to her sister. She reached out to cover his hand with her own.

"I will, I promise," she said. "Eleni will know of both her parents, I swear it."

Georgios nodded. "Such a tragedy, to lose Aglaura as we did," he said, again between coughs. "She was so strong. For her to go before me, well, the world is rarely fair, but that was especially offensive."

Psyche squeezed his hand, her face wet with tears again, as it seemed always to be lately.

"Yes, it was," she agreed.

Eleni had never met her Aunt Psyche and was wary of the stranger who came to tell her she was going to live with her cousins. But when her father assured her it was for the best, and when she realized her nurse would come as well, the little girl squared her shoulders and walked on her own to the chariot with such determined confidence that Psyche felt for a moment she was watching a young Aglaura.

When the cousins met for the first time, there was a natural hesitation and skepticism. Soon enough, however, the four of them were running wild in the garden, chasing the unseen but uncommonly cheerful voices of the Lares, and Psyche's heart felt at peace for the first time since before Aglaura's marriage all those many years ago. She had lost her sisters, her parents, and her mortal life but perhaps, in pouring her love into these children, she could yet preserve something of her humanity.

Cupid came up behind her, where she sat before her loom, finishing the blanket she had started so many months ago. Through the window the children could be seen playing in the garden. A hand came around to rest on her stomach.

"Just one more to go," he said in her ear, and Psyche did not lean into him, but neither did she pull away as she adjusted the line of the weft. Cupid had been eager and attentive since the trial, confused still at Psyche's grievances but nonetheless resolved to prove his love.

She had not yet invited Cupid into her bed, and this had been the source of numerous arguments between them. He could not understand how, if she loved him, she could keep him at such arm's length, and she could not find the right words to make him understand.

Now that she was immortal as well, the parameters had changed, along with the balance of power. She was still figuring out what that meant in terms of her own independence; thus far, all her energy and influence had gone into retrieving her nieces and nephew. Now, her focus needed to shift to the life within her, ready to enter the world any day.

Once her baby was born, then perhaps she could sort out her relationship with Cupid. Sort out everything that had happened to her. Been done to her.

Until then, she'd keep weaving, and keep not pulling away.

"I think the babe's eager to join us," she replied. "The head now sits so low in my pelvis that I worry I'll give birth as I walk."

Cupid looked alarmed. "Is that possible?" he asked. "Could that happen?"

Psyche shrugged. "I don't think so?"

When Psyche's contractions began to increase in speed and severity a couple of days later, she retreated to her room without telling anyone, claiming as many moments alone in her labor as possible. It was only when she finally cried out that Cupid and the Lares realized what was happening, the former dashing off to tell Juno while the latter scolded Psyche for not allowing them to help her earlier.

Fresh linen and hot water began to appear around her, and Psyche had a flash of that day with Cidippe, that last day. She had come to believe that there were things in the world wholly the province of the Fates, and it lent Psyche a strange calm to imagine that birth was one of them. That Diana could not have helped even if she'd wanted—that no one could have—that some things were outside the control of both mortals and gods.

As a girl, Psyche had thought she knew her fate, that it was already written. She saw now that it was not but that it was far more complicated than simple acceptance or action. There was a price to be weighed, always, and it was rarely the one expected. Perhaps all anyone could do was choose the love they kept close and hold it tight as long as they could.

"Alright, little one," Psyche panted softly at the end of a contraction. "Let's do this together."

CHAPTER 41

Despite her parentage and the excitement surrounding her conception, Volupta was born of Psyche in the same way millions of babies had been born before her, red and squalling as she emerged, dragging behind her the bloody afterbirth. Her mother nursed her, milk shot with ambrosia, in the same way babies had nursed for millennia.

Unlike her father, Volupta had experienced actual mortality for eight months in the womb, though she would never be able to recall the time. Unlike her mother, Volupta would never understand the fragile, transcendent beauty mortality lent to that which was fated to die.

Volupta entered the world through her mother's body and landed in her father's hands. As those hands placed her with care into the waiting cradle of her mother's arms, Volupta's cries lessened, then ceased, the child soothed by warmth and the imminent promise of food.

Psyche looked down at the soft weight in her arms and burst into tears. She was alive. Her baby was alive. Even knowing she had drunk ambrosia and feeling the changes it wrought in her body, there was a part of Psyche that had not expected to survive this ordeal. That had been sure this was the time, finally, that she would be reunited with her sisters. The absence of such a reunion was bitter, and yet, looking into her daughter's red, squashed newborn face, Psyche felt something sweet course through her. Volupta meant pleasure—a name Cupid had suggested—but now, in spite of the birth and all the pain that had led up to it, Psyche saw that the child may be just that. This child, who had until this moment still felt abstract and more a product of Cupid than herself, was hers. Hers to protect, hers to keep safe.

Hers to love.

Venus was by her side, stroking the infant's head, hardly a minute after the babe had been laid in Psyche's arms.

"The most worthwhile pursuit in all creation," she murmured, her eyes wide and warm. "You are going to be a beauty, aren't you, my Volupta?"

Psyche held her baby tighter, her jaw clenching. She looked over to where Cupid sat, leaning forward, arms on his knees, expression one of cautious eagerness. Beyond him, by the birthing chair, Juno's hand-maidens were busy cleaning up the blood and afterbirth, Juno herself having departed as soon as Volupta was safely delivered. Psyche sighed.

"Might we have a moment alone, Mother?" she asked, willing her voice gentle as she draped the blanket she had woven around her daughter's tiny body. Keeping Volupta tucked securely in one arm, she stretched the other toward Cupid while keeping her eyes on Venus. "As a family, I mean?"

Psyche watched the awareness flood Venus's features, the emotions flit across her face with such swiftness it would have been easy to think they were never there at all. But Psyche saw them— confusion, jealousy, anger, and then—only then—respect.

"Of course, daughter." Venus' voice was as sweet as Psyche's had been. "Celebrate this precious time together. And know I'll be waiting just beyond."

As Venus departed, Cupid came forward, but Psyche dropped his hand as soon as Venus was out of the room. Cupid looked hurt.

"You said you were going to try," he said. Psyche did not look up at him, focused on the tiny body squirming its way up her own, mouth opening and closing like a fish as the infant searched for food. Acting on instinct, Psyche took her breast in hand, guiding the nipple to Volupta's mouth. The child fumbled for a moment, then latched and sucked. Psyche relaxed at first, then gave a sharp gasp as the nursing child provoked a stab of sheer, blinding pain from her womb. One of Juno's handmaidens looked up from where she was cleaning.

"That is normal," she said, eyes nonetheless sympathetic. "Your body is continuing to expel and retract; the more she nurses, the quicker the pain will lessen."

Psyche managed a tight nod, her whole body still clenched in agony.

Cupid cleared his throat.

"Psyche?"

"Mm?" The sound was pitched with pain.

"You said you were going to try," Cupid repeated. "But between shunning my bed and dropping my hand, it really feels like you are not. This should be a joyous moment for both of us."

The pain began to retreat, and Psyche breathed deeply. Sated, Volupta let go of Psyche's nipple, her head lolling into the crook of her mother's arm. Psyche stroked one tiny foot with her thumb, her eyes drifting to the clumsy weave of the blanket covering them.

Aglaura would have made a much finer piece, she thought, more colorful, the design more intricate. And yet, Psyche was proud of this blanket, this thing she had made that would, whatever else it lacked, keep her child warm.

It settled on her then what she must do, but still, her eyes burned. She wasn't sure she had the strength for it. Psyche did not look up at her husband.

"I wish for you to live elsewhere," she said, wincing as the scar on her hand screamed. There was a stillness, and the remainder of Juno's handmaidens scurried out of the room as Psyche silently counted her breaths.

"Excuse me?" Cupid said.

"I wish for you to live elsewhere," Psyche repeated, clenching her protesting hand into a fist, her resolve hardening even as her heart broke. "With your mother, with Apollo, in your own place. I don't care. We have eternity together; perhaps somewhere in all that time, I will find a way to forgive you, but for now I must focus all my energy into Volupta and my nieces and nephew, and I do not wish to live with you while I do that."

Cupid's mouth opened and closed, in comical similarity to his infant daughter's. "But— she's my daughter as well," he protested.

Psyche did look at him now, eyebrows raised. "And you wish to care for her? To wash her and change her linens and soothe her when she cries?"

Cupid reared back. "Well— no. But I wish to be near you—to support you!—while you do those things."

"And I don't wish for you to be near me. So. Please, Cupid, relocate."

Cupid's jaw worked, his anger and hurt palpable. "I love you," he said, stubborn.

Psyche watched him with a steady gaze. "Then, this is your chance to show it. If you love me, leave me alone."

And after a long, hard look and a single crooked finger brushed against her cheek, finally, Cupid did.

Late 2nd Century AD

Since she was utterly alone, she trembled and shuddered in fear for her virginity, and she dreaded the unknown presence more than any other menace. But now her unknown bridegroom arrived and climbed into the bed. He made Psyche his wife and swiftly departed before dawn broke. At once the voices in attendance at her bed-chamber tended the new bride's violated virginity.

— APULEIUS, THE GOLDEN ASS

Mid-20th Century AD

When she felt him beside her and heard his voice softly murmuring in her ear, all her fears left her. She knew without seeing him that here was no monster or shape of terror, but the lover and husband she had longed and waited for.

— EDITH HAMILTON, MYTHOLOGY

Bibliography

Apuleius. *The Golden Ass.* Translated by P.G. Walsh, Oxford University Press, 1994, pp. 81-82

Hamilton, Edith. *Mythology.* Little, Brown and Company, 1942, p. 124.

ACKNOWLEDGMENTS

This book has been in the making since I first read Edith Hamilton in middle school, but it really swung into gear when I finally encountered Apuleius's original version in The Golden Ass (also known as Metamorphoses, but that's far less fun). It struck me as fascinating that such an obvious (to me) work of satire had survived throughout history as a supposed ideal romance and three years and over 100,000 words later, here we are.

Even doing this on my own (and perhaps even more because of it) there are an outrageous number of people I am lucky to have in my life or to have met along the way, and without any one of them *Psyche* would be the weaker. So without further chat, here are my thank yous.

To my parents, sisters, and other early beta readers: Ann Gladstone, Mike Gladstone, Lilian Gladstone, Emma Rogers, Maggie Gladstone, Erin Gregory, Jim Skehan, Lauren Manson, Lauren Axselle, Erin Fifer, Madison Peters-Hagemann, Julia Bankert, Maggie Roberts, April Lambert, and Deborah Roberts. You all saw this story in some of its most raw forms and you each gave me feedback that made it stronger. I cannot adequately express my gratitude.

To my later beta readers: Frossi Pitsalidou, Sarah Boyd, and Caryn Pine. Sometimes the internet is a great place. You each brought perspective and insight unique from any I'd gotten so far and it was absolutely invaluable. Sarah also did my proofread and thank goodness she did.

The stunning cover art is the work of artist Charlie Wall; I could not be more thrilled with the result. Thank you, Deborah, for connecting me with Charlie and for being such an incredible support and cheerleader as I figured out the publishing process. On that note, additional thank yous to Alex McGlothlin and Samantha Callaghan for their intros into this complex world.

The cover design is the work of my sister Lilian, whose attention to detail and passion for font absolutely inspires me. Thank you for gifting me precious hours of your professional skill and eye; I love your work and I love working with you.

Finally, a massive thank you to my husband, John. You have been cheerleader, editor, brainstormer, patient listener— basically whatever I needed at any given moment. From the day we met you have supported my dreams and ambitions with an "of course you should do that" attitude. So proud to report- I did it! Thank you, I love you.

About the Author

Forrest Gladstone lives with her husband, kids, and cats in Richmond, Virginia. She earned her BA in Religious Studies and Anthropology from the University of Virginia, and her masters degree in Education from the College of William and Mary. She has taught language Arts, theatre, and writing. Psyche is her first novel.